T0368106

Seven Days of Destiny

PETER A. LAPORTA

authorHOUSE

AuthorHouse™
1663 Liberty Drive
Bloomington, IN 47403
www.authorhouse.com
Phone: 833-262-8899

Published by AuthorHouse 12/03/2024

ISBN: 979-8-8230-3893-5 (sc)
ISBN: 979-8-8230-3892-8 (e)

Library of Congress Control Number: 2024925465

Print information available on the last page.

Any people depicted in stock imagery provided by Getty Images are models, and such images are being used for illustrative purposes only. Certain stock imagery © Getty Images.

This book is printed on acid-free paper.

Also Available by Peter A. LaPorta

Ignite the Passion, A Guide to Motivational Leadership (2003 Edition)

Who Hired These People?

A Quote for Every Day

Adventures in Autism

Adventures in Leadership

Normandy Nights

The Card

Turtle Master-A Passage Through Time

The Widow's Box- A Test of Time

**Ignite the Passion, A Guide to Motivational Leadership-
20th Anniversary Collector Edition (2023)**

Sanctuary

To Schedule a Speaker Event, Book Signing or Seminar, please access

https://www.laportaenterprises.com

For

all the loves of my life; past, present, and future.

Seven Days of Destiny

Sunday Services

Mondays at the Mall

Tolerant Tuesdays

Wednesday-Spaghetti Day

Thursday Walks in the Garden

Friday Night Musical Revue

Saturday at the Shadowland Ranch

Sunday

SERVICES

1

"Good morning Father."

The Priest turned around to see the elderly woman enter the parish office.

"Well good morning, Mary. What brings you to the church at such an early hour? The sun is barely up on the horizon and I just finished my morning prayers."

The woman made her way to the coffee pot in the office and began the ritual of changing out the coffee filter and adding water. Once the new grounds had been added, she pressed the brew button. She turned slowly back to the Priest who had not waited for a response and had gone on to read his mass homily.

"I had hoped to find you here in the office Father Derek."

"Is there something you wanted to speak about, Mary? We could go to the confessional. There is still time."

"Oh no, Father. Nothing like that. Besides, at 80 years old, there's not much to confess these days. I may try to sneak an expired coupon through at the grocery store but I'm fairly certain that doesn't break any of the commandments."

The Father simply shook his head and chuckled. "There may be a case to be made for the essence of such activities, young lady."

"Father Derek. You are old enough to be my grandchild. I haven't been a young lady since the Korean War."

The Father tried not to laugh but broke out in the end so he could return to his review of the morning service.

"Well, if you are not here for confession, Mary, why are you here so early?"

The elderly woman made her way over to the coffee pot and poured two cups of coffee from the freshly brewed liquid love. Handing the Priest a cup, she sat down next to him.

"If I told you I was here to make you a cup of coffee, Father, would you believe me?"

The Priest took a sip of his coffee and put the mug down on the table.

"I would hope that at your age even little white lies were beyond your actions."

"That is true, Father. I try to never lie. Besides, the truth is often dismissed by the youth of today very easily."

"Indeed Mary. Sad but true. So you really came in this early just to make me coffee?"

The woman placed the coffee cup on the table and reached into her purse to remove a handkerchief. Slowly, she removed her glasses and wiped away the small tears that had formed in the corners of her eyes.

"Mary? Are you ok?"

"Yes, Father. Don't mind me. I'm just being a silly old woman. My family is all gone now and living their own lives. The kids and grandchildren all live in different states and have their own lives. Sure, they come visit now and then but it is not the same as caring for someone. Now that my Joe has passed on, I've got no one to make coffee for. I used to get up every morning at 5am and make him coffee before he went off to the factory. Now, I know some women leave their men to fend for themselves at that hour, but not me. I made Joe coffee every morning for the last 60 years, ever since he came home from Korea. Now that he's gone, I only make coffee for myself and then it just goes to waste."

"You know you can always just get a Keurig. Then you can make one cup at a time."

Mary took another sip of her coffee and licked her lips. "Never trusted those contraptions, Father. No matter how you dress it up, it's still just instant coffee to me. I like the smell as much as the taste of a fresh brewed cup of Joe. There's no wonder my late husband and this delicious treat shared the same name."

The two shared the peaceful moment as they drank their coffees and smiled. Mary was reminiscing about her late husband and the Father found humor in her response. Besides needing to return to his homily, the Father continued the conversation.

"Mary, would you mind if I gave you some advice?"

"That kind of goes with the territory I would think Father. You are kind of in the advice business aren't you Father?"

"Well, among other things Mary."

"Of course, Father. You serve the Lord. So what in God's service do you have to say that can guide me on my remaining days?"

"You are still quite sharp for your age, Mary."

"There is still plenty of spring in my step, Father and the cobwebs haven't gathered too much in the attic."

She accented the last part by pointing to her head full of grey hair. The Father chuckled and patted her hand.

"Mary, I'm sure there is plenty of spring left in your step. That is why my advice is so pertinent. I think you are lonely."

The elderly woman chuckled with her coffee mug in her hands. For a moment, the young Priest thought she might drop the mug on the table.

"No offense, Father, but I don't need a Priest to point that out to me. Like I said, there's no one around to make coffee for, clean up after or do anything for. My days of caring for others is in the past."

"But they don't have to be, Mary."

"You're not going to tell me to go out a buy a cat, are you Father? I refused to be an old cat lady a long time ago."

"Not at all Mary. My point is you don't have to be lonely. Your husband has passed on but I am certain he would want you to move on. In fact, Joe told me so in his final days. He wanted you to be happy Mary, not lonely."

Mary once again wiped her tears away from her wet eyes.

"Joe told you that?"

"Yes he did. He knew you had many years left before you could join him so he wanted you to be happy. It's been six months, Mary. You have mourned long enough."

"Oh, Father. It's only been six months."

"Not to be transparent, Mary, but you are not in grade school anymore. Six months at your station in life is quite a long time."

Mary chuckled. It was her turn to pat the Priest's hand.

"Delicately put, Padre. I understand my *station in life.* I truly do. I'm just not sure I could share my bed with another man in my late years."

The Priest threw his hands up in jest. "Whoa, young lady. No one said anything about your bedroom. I was just suggesting that there may be other men in our town that would enjoy a cup of fresh brewed coffee from your kitchen."

"Well, I must admit. I miss cooking for someone. Spending a day in the kitchen after the coffee has gotten cooled is a wonderful blessing."

"If I'm not mistaken, you spend plenty of hours in the Social Hall making coffee and serving donuts to our parishioners."

"That's not cooking, Father. That's just opening up boxes of donuts from the Donut King and putting them out on trays. I'm talking about cooking good food from scratch, like I've done all my life."

"...and I'm talking about the social aspect of the Social Hall. During all of those hours serving coffee and donuts have there not been any elderly gentlemen that have caught your eye?"

"Why do they have to be elderly, Father? Like you said I have plenty of spring left in my step. Maybe I have an eye on a younger man or two."

Father Derek broke out in laughter. Finishing off his coffee he placed the mug in the sink, gathered up his papers and patted the woman on her shoulder.

"You are definitely full of life, Mary. Wherever your wings may take you I hope that you fly again soon."

The Priest walked out of the office smiling while he left Mary to finish her coffee in solitude. It took only moments for the loneliness to creep back in. Drinking the last few drops she wished she had someone to clean up after the morning coffee cups were cleared.

2

Samuel Barnes parked his large sedan in the handicap space of St. Patrick's Cathedral as he did every Sunday and every other Wednesday. At the age of 82, he was still able to drive and get around but his knees were a different story altogether. He had spent the majority of his life delivering letters and packages to people and his legs were feeling their miles as the years ticked off.

A soldier in the Military Postal Service, Samuel served his country well from 1950-1954. His one tour of duty during the Korean War was enough for any man. He was initially relieved when assigned to Postal duty, but soon realized that mail went to the front line as well as the tanks and soldiers. Far too often, the mail and packages intended for the soldiers to brighten their days arrived too late to matter. The mail was returned along with the coffins stateside.

Returning home after the war, the mail carrier bug had gotten him. The idea of delivering mail without having to dodge bullets was appealing. In their hay day, mail carriers were revered as civil servants and welcomed on every doorstep. He enjoyed the warmth of the community and the continued routine of rising each morning and putting on a uniform. The stripes on his arms may have been different but he was serving his country none the less.

Retiring at age 62 with a full pension, the years hitting the pavement and sidewalks had taken their toll. Samuel had spent the last 20 years hobbling along, rubbing ointment on his aching limbs continuously. His post war bride, Katrice, stayed with him through all the years in his postal duty but passed on soon after his retirement. She had developed Stage 4 Kidney Cancer and died six months into his leisure life. Samuel Barnes was widowed moments after his duty was done.

The past two decades passed much like his four years in the military. He followed a daily regimen of rising at 5am whether he had a job to go to or not. He ate the same things on the same days at the same times, just as the mess halls in Korea had engrained in him. He drank his coffee black as he did out of his field canteen in many a foxhole. The fact that he did not have a woman to come home to or press his uniforms only mattered briefly. Like an internal instinct, he reverted back to his military days as if someone had called him to attention.

"Good morning Samuel."

"Hello Father."

"There is no need to race inside Samuel. There are plenty of seats in the house of the Lord."

"Always a prophet you are, Father."

"It is my calling just as you were the deliverer."

"I was simply a mail carrier, Father Derek. There was nothing profound in delivering monthly bills and overdue notices to people."

Samuel was leaning on his cane more, trying to stand steady as he talked to the Priest. The non-verbal behavior was clearly noticed.

"My apologies, Samuel. Do you need to go sit down?"

"Bah. All I do is sit these days. When a man has lost his purpose he loses his spirit as well."

The Priest stepped forward to assist Samuel maneuver the sidewalk. Waving him off, the two men simply walked slowly towards the church.

"Can I shed some light, Samuel?"

"You are the lighthouse, Father. What say you?"

"It troubles me that you believe you have lost your purpose. While your days of walking the streets of our beautiful town to deliver your mail are behind you, the joy you brought to people will last for many years."

Samuel broke into laughter that was often reserved for the chosen few.

"I highly doubt my efforts to bring mail to people ever brought them joy, Father. Perhaps the young men who intercepted their mother's lingerie catalogs could offer an argument but I don't believe anyone else would."

"All comedy aside, Samuel, do you think you brought joy to all those men fighting in the war when you delivered the letters from their loved ones?"

Samuel slowed his stride long enough to look directly at the Priest.

"I suppose that's true, Father, but that type of mail was a long time ago."

"True, Samuel. Very true. Let me phrase it a different way. In a more recent parameter that I can speak more intelligently about."

"Ok, Father."

"You say that in your mail carrying duties you simply brought bills and overdue notices. Do you think I received many of those in all the years you brought mail to the church?"

"Everyone has to pay the piper at some point Father."

"While that may be true, the bills that came and continue to come are paid by the parish office. As a Priest, do you think I handled many of those?"

"Probably not, Father Derek."

"And yet, I saw you pretty much every day delivering mail to me throughout the years. What do you think were in all of those letters?"

"I would think that's Priest business and none of mine."

It was the Father's turn to laugh at this comment.

"You are correct. But in that same flavor, I received hundreds, if not thousands of letters from people seeking my prayers and the comfort of the church. Had you not delivered those letters to me, I would never have known. I would never be able to share those blessings with people that could not come to the church. You brought them to me. You delivered those people to me one by one, in sealed envelopes, with the stamp of the day on top. As I said, you were and still are, the deliverer. Without their prayers and resolutions, every one of those people may have gone down a different path. Because you delivered to me, I delivered to them. Years later, I am certain their lives are better because of you."

Looking over to the aging man in front of him, Father Derek noticed Samuel pull out a handkerchief from his back pocket to wipe his eyes. The Priest waited patiently with empathy until the proud man was resolved.

"That was beautiful Father. I never thought of it that way."

"Samuel, it is never too late to teach an old dog new tricks."

"Then I better get inside so you can teach me something new about the Lord that I didn't know before. I'll see you from the cheap seats, Father."

The Priest waved to Samuel and watched him walk slowly through the doors of the church.

3

"In the name of the Father, The Son and The Holy Spirit..."

"AMEN"

"Everyone please be seated for this week's announcements."

The congregation collectively took their seats in the pews. Samuel slowly descended leaning on his cane so he did not fall.

"Thank you. The Knights of Columbus is holding their Annual Tootsie Roll fund drive after each of the masses today. You will see many of the Knights in yellow vests holding donation canisters along with buckets of candy. When you make a donation today, you will get a nice piece of candy to take home with you."

The people simply nodded. There was not a member of the church that was not aware of the annual drive. There was no need for explanations.

"On Tuesday evening, there will be a rosary prayer group meeting here in the chapel for all those wishing to attend."

Samuel patted his jacket pocket feeling comfort from knowing that his rosary beads were close by. This particular set he had kept his whole life and had ventured half the world and back. He remembered like it was yesterday, sitting in a foxhole, praying the rosary in hopes that he would make it home alive.

"On Wednesday night, in the Social Hall, there will be a meeting of the bereavement support group. Those people going through the stages of grief due to loss of a loved one are encouraged to attend."

Mary simply nodded. She had been going to those meetings for months and there were simply no more tears to shed. At her age, she was looking forward to how she could live rather than looking back to what she had lost.

"On Saturday morning, the youth group will be hosting a pancake breakfast. Your donation of $5 will get you a plate of pancakes along with bacon or sausage. Beverages will also be available for purchase. Pre-sale tickets are available in the lobby after the mass or on our website. You can also stop by the Parrish office and purchase your tickets there."

All the talk about food had Samuel's stomach growling. It was time for the Father to wrap things up.

"...I am sure all this talk about food has you hungry. Following the mass this morning our Women's group will be serving coffee and donuts in the Social Hall. Stop on by and have a donut while you meet a new friend. That's all the announcements for today, all rise for the Prayer of St. Michael."

"ST. MICHAEL, THE ARCHANGEL, defend us in battle..."

As the prayer continued, Mary gathered her belongings and exited her pew. She was one of the volunteers this morning that would be serving the donuts and coffee so she thought she had better get there before the crowd.

"The Mass has ended. Go in peace. In the name of The Father, The Son and the Holy Spirit."

The music began to play as Samuel lowered himself into the pew. He had learned that there was no honor in trying to rush when he moved as slowly as he did these days. He knew there would still be plenty of coffee by the time he arrived in the Social Hall. He was also certain that there would only be plain donuts left at that point because the colorful ones would all be taken. That also suited him just fine. He was a simple man with simple tastes and a plain donut would be just as filling as one of those fancy ones.

With most of the congregation already exited, Samuel started his slow pace towards the door of the church. In the lobby, ticket sales for the pancake breakfast seemed to be going well so there was no sense in stopping now. He could always pay at the door on Saturday if he decided to come. Sundays and Wednesdays had him coming to the church and adding a third day might be taxing to his aching joints.

Samuel made his way past the crowd that had gathered around Father Derek. It was the usual occurrence for people to stop, pay their well wishes while seeking some additional prayers for one thing or another. He shared a silent smile with the Father as he passed him on his way across into the Social Hall. Stopping by the front door, a young lady who seemed not a day older than ten, was holding the door for him.

"Are you going in to get a donut mister?"

"I'm going to try young lady. Do you think there are any left?"

"I hope so. My mama said I can have another one if I hold the door open for people like you. She said it was the Cathy way which I didn't understand because my name is Sandy."

Samuel chuckled even though his knees were burning standing at the door talking to the young girl.

"I think your mother meant the Catholic way. I don't know anyone named Cathy either."

The young lady seemed to think on this for a moment before pressing on.

"Well, I guess that makes more sense seeing that we are all Catholics and stuff. Anyway, are you going in to get a donut?"

"I am. Thank you for holding the door open for me. Just give me a minute to get through it before you close it."

"I will mister. I'm pretty good at this. Enjoy your donut."

Samuel was more concerned about a nice strong cup of coffee at this point but he didn't want to dawdle with the child any further.

Entering the Social Hall, the elderly man was surprised not to see more people. It was generally a good turn out when things were offered for free but there did not seem to be many people inside. There were several small groups sitting at the cafeteria tables that had been set up, sipping their coffees and enjoying their sweet treats. He had the passing thought that maybe the tootsie rolls and the donuts on the same morning might have been a bit much for some of the people. He slowly made his way over to the counter to see the women who were in charge of dispensing the goods.

"Good morning, what can we get for you?"

"Coffee, please."

"Would you like cream and sugar as well?"

"Nope. Just the coffee."

The woman looked over at the other ladies behind the counter and rolled her eyes. *Here goes another grumpy Gus.* Chuckling to herself, the woman poured out a cup of coffee from the percolator pot.

"Here you go young man." Mary placed the coffee cup on the counter in front of him.

"I don't know who you think is young but I hope this coffee is as strong as your perfume and your sharp tongue."

Mary ignored the comment.

"The Father doesn't let us spike the coffee anymore so all you get is regular perk, sorry to say."

Samuel chuckled to himself as he took a sip of the hot coffee. "Well, it's not strong but it will do. Never turn down free coffee, even if it's bad coffee. That's the way I figure it."

Again, Mary ignored the comment about the bad coffee.

"Well, if that's the way you figure it than why don't you have a free donut as well."

Samuel limped over to the open boxes of donuts. Looking over the choices, he removed a plain donut. No glaze. No sprinkles. No flavor.

"There's still a few good ones left in there. Besides, I think you might need a little sweetening up."

Samuel gave Mary a scorn before turning away. Balancing his donut along with his cane, he took the coffee cup with his free hand and made his way over to an empty table to sit by himself. Turning to the other ladies in the group, Mary asked quietly about him.

"Ok, who's the stiff?"

The other ladies laughed hard enough to make several conversations in the room stop and to look towards the cackling hens. Samuel went right on drinking his coffee and picking at his plain donut unbothered.

"That's Samuel. I'm surprised you don't know him."

"Like I know all the dried up old prunes that walk through those doors?"

"No, not at all. Just that, you've both been around the church a lot over the years so I thought you might have seen him before."

"Well, I probably did. He's not that memorable."

"He's a widower just like you. Longer though. Been a long time. Never re-married. Unlike you, he never went to any of the grief meetings."

"I guess we know why he's so ornery, then."

"Loneliness gets to you. At first it's unbearable but then you learn to live with the silence. I think Samuel is just so used to it he doesn't have any need to be around people. He was the mailman in town for years."

"That's right. I do know him. He's the mailman that chases dogs just to bite them."

"Oh, Mary. He's not that bad. Why don't you bring him a cup of coffee and see if he warms up to you?"

Mary shrugged her shoulders. Why not? The crowd had died down and now there was just a bunch of people milling around talking anyway. She poured a fresh cup of coffee into a Styrofoam cup and exited the kitchen area. Samuel didn't even look up when he felt her approach.

"Here you go, Sam. I brought you another cup of coffee."

"I beg your pardon?"

"Coffee. I brought you another cup of coffee. Thought you would like to enjoy it."

"What I would enjoy is you not butchering my name."

"How can I screw up Sam. It's a pretty easy name to say"

"It would be if that was my name."

"Oh my goodness. I am so sorry. They told me your name was Samuel."

Samuel simply shook his head. "That exactly the point. My name is Samuel. It's not Sam or Sammy or anything of the sorts. You can call me Samuel or Sir."

Mary shook her head with a smile. "Well, then, Samuel. I brought you a fresh cup of coffee to refresh the one that you have. You seem like a gentleman that enjoys more than one cup."

Samuel looked her over with scrutiny but reached out his hand cautiously. He took the cup of coffee and placed it on the table in front of him.

"Thank you, ma'am. That was nice of you."

"Well, Samuel. You can call me Mary instead of ma'am. Even in my advanced years I haven't gotten used to that term."

"Very well, Mary. Is there something else I can do for you besides drink your coffee?"

Mary seemed to be thrown back by the comment.

"Um, no. I simply thought you would enjoy the company and conversation since you were sitting all alone."

"There is a reason I am sitting alone, *ma'am*. I live alone, I eat alone and I definitely drink my coffee in peace and all alone. So if there is not anything else...."

"Of course. *Sam*. You just go on sitting *by yourself* and drinking your coffee *by yourself*. I'll make sure no one bothers talking to you any further."

Mary walked away in a huff and resumed her place in the kitchen counter area with her face clearly flushed. The other women knew enough to leave her alone to cool off.

Samuel continued to drink his coffee in peace as the world seemed to evolve around him. Since he had seen enough people in the war and all his years as a postal carrier, there was no need or desire to people watch. He minded his own business and expected people to have the same courtesy to him. His own cup of coffee was just fine without having to deal with the candy striper wanna be that had interrupted his peace.

4

"Your cholesterol is a little high Samuel. Have you been eating the oatmeal every day like I suggested?"

The doctor was reviewing the test results on his laptop as Samuel sat on the examining table with his legs swinging like a ten-year-old in a barber chair.

"I may be old, Doctor, but I don't need to eat mush. I can still chew my food fine. I eat my eggs every morning as I have for most of my adult life."

The doctor simply shook his head. He knew better than to argue with his aging patients but he had an obligation to guide them on healthier paths.

"Your daily regimen of eggs may be the cause of your cholesterol spike as we have discussed before. Have you at least switched to egg alternatives."

"That fake egg crap is disgusting. I ate enough powdered eggs in the war to last a lifetime. It's real eggs or nothing for me."

"Samuel. It's been 60 years or so since you got out of the military. It's quite possible the *fake eggs* as you call them, taste a little better than they used to."

"Trust me, Doc. Once you taste shit you don't need to try it again to know it tastes like shit."

The doctor broke out into laughter. Samuel may be a gruff but he was a funny gruff at times like this.

"Please tell me you are not making it worse by eating bacon everyday with your eggs, Samuel."

The elderly man simply shook his head. "No, sir. I have never been a bacon man myself. A couple of sausage links and some rye toast with butter and it is a complete breakfast. I wash it down with my black coffee and it all works."

The doctor scrolled down the page on his laptop searching for results that were simply not there.

"It has been some time since we checked your heart. I think it is time for a stress test young man."

Samuel shook his head in defiance. "My heart works just fine, Doc. Besides, I am retired. I try to have as little stress as possible."

The doctor simply stared back at his patient trying to find the right angle to approach the argument.

"I'll tell you what. I'm going to write down on this paper the number of cups of coffee you should have in a day. If you are drinking any more than that you agree to go and get a stress test. Is it a deal?"

"I'm not a gambling man, Doc. Never have been."

"Then let's just call it a gentleman's agreement. You are a gentleman aren't you, Samuel? Can we at least agree on that?"

"You think you are a clever wordsmith, young man, but you are not. I can see your game coming a mile away."

The doctor ignored Samuel's comment and wrote down the number on a piece of paper and folded the paper. He laid it on the examination table next to his patient.

"So, let's have it. Last time we talked you would not admit to the number of cups of black coffee you drink a day. I'm assuming you start the day with a cup at breakfast as you just indicated."

"Yup."

"Ok. There's one. Assuming you are like most coffee drinkers, you need a cup in the afternoon to get you over the hump. Shall we just call that one 5 O'clock coffee?"

"That's a little late for me Doc but I'll agree to the sentiment."

"So a cup in the morning and one in the afternoon. That's two cups of coffee. Miraculously that's exactly what I wrote on the piece of paper."

"Figured as such."

The doctor looked over his aging patient and decided it was time to go all in. it was no sense bluffing at this stage in the game.

"So, Samuel. We have established that you enjoy two cups of coffee a day. Do you have yourself a Keurig or drink instant coffee."

Samuel simply shook his head.

"All that is like the fake egg crap. I'm a real man and I drink real coffee. Brewed in a pot like any self-respecting coffee drinker."

The doctor smiled as he knew he had snared the elderly man in his trap.

"Since you brew your own coffee in a pot, how many scoops of coffee do you put in the filter."

"I like my coffee strong like I had it in the war, Doc. Eight scoops in a filter and a full pot of water go into the machine before I hit the button."

The doctor smiled once more. "So, it's a full pot of coffee twice a day is that we are saying Samuel?"

"Ayuh. That's what we said. Two cups a day. One in the morning and one in the afternoon. I thought we already established that."

"No Samuel, we said two *cups* not two *pots*. With eight cups of coffee in each pot, that makes 16 cups in a day and I still think you are shortchanging me."

Samuel just stared at his doctor in disgust. "Just give me the damn prescription. I'll get the test done next week."

The doctor smiled as he went back to his laptop to key in the heart stress test for his sly but not as sharp aging patient.

5

The Wednesday night bereavement group was never a happy gathering. Mary had been attending for months now and she could only remember a few instances of laughter being shared along the way. People were kind most of the time. They wanted to share their stories of pain and suffering and reminisce about brighter days when the people they loved were still in their daily lives. There was never a shortage of tears and the tissues were always close at hand.

On a few occasions, the pain got the best of individuals and they lashed out to the others in the group. They were angry their loved ones were taken. They were angry that they had to wake up every day in beds by themselves. They were angry they had to pay their bills and go to functions without the support of others. They were angry there was no one there at the end of the day to ask them how their day was and sit down to dinner with. They were angry to be alone.

On those rare instances when the voices were raised in frustration, the others simply bowed their heads in prayer. They knew how it felt. They knew the fire that burned inside them and they knew that longing to bring their loved ones back. They understand when voices were loud and took comfort knowing that it was not their day to lash out in pain.

Mary had never taken her turn at being vocal. She was content to sit with others that understand why she missed Joe so much. He was her lobster, her partner for life. They had one of those post war romances that never subsided. They formed the family unit, took care of the family house, and went through all of the family checkpoints spelled out in the Saturday Evening Post. They were brave as they stood and sent their son off to fight in the Vietnam War. They watched with warm smiles of wonder as Neil Armstrong took the first step on the moon. They comforted each other with tears, holding hands as news of Kennedy being shot came across the television. They were together at every milestone in their shared life until Joe became his own footnote in history and added an end date to his tombstone.

It is said that misery loves company and the adage proved true on every other

16

Wednesday evening in the Social Hall. They sipped their coffee together and someone usually brought sandwiches or some kind of cake. Mary often thought that the concept of comfort food didn't hold ground when it came to those in deep grief. A plate of homemade mashed potatoes with gravy or a scoop of macaroni and cheese never compared to coffee and cake. There was coffee and cake at the town hall when Kennedy was shot. There was coffee and cake when that nice young man Martin Luther King Jr was killed. She even recalled having coffee and cake when Elvis stopped moving his pelvis. Mashed potatoes tasted great going down but it was coffee and cake that provided padding to the hearts that were broken.

Mary plated up the banana bread and moved on to slicing up the lemon crème cake that someone had brought. She moved about in the silence of the kitchen as she listened to the latest mourner pouring their heart out to the group. The poor woman had lost her son in a car accident just weeks before and had moved past her shock to fall into the deep whole of grief. She felt it in her soul and was not eating or sleeping. She was a wreck. Mary knew that she would bring the first plate of cake to the woman and place it in her hands. She was doubtful that the snack would make it to the woman's stomach but she thought that the simple act of kindness might carry some weight.

"I just can't believe he is gone…So young… So full of life…"

The woman was blurting out words almost incoherently as the warmth of the group tried to envelop her.

"Carmen, we understand your pain." The Father had stepped into add comfort.

"How could you understand Father? You are married to God. You have no wife, no children, and no one to love. How can you possibly understand the pain that I feel?"

The Father did not take the woman's comments to heart. He had been the brunt of such outbursts before. He simply bowed his head and asked for strength in his short prayer.

"My dear Carmen. Every soul in our congregation is my child and my family. When a member crosses over I feel pain and loss. When we lose someone we love, we must learn not to live without them but to the love they left us with."

The woman pressed her crying face into her hands and sobbed. She wept as the Priest came up and placed his hands on her shoulders and silently prayed to heal her pain. After a few minutes, the tears subsided and she raised her face to meet Father Derek's.

"Father. I am so sorry. I didn't…"

"Now, now. It's ok. Every member of this group has felt pain and anger at some point. I just happened to be there in your moment of weakness."

Carmen resumed her sobs at hearing this. Later, she would wonder whether she was happy or sad that her harsh response to her Priest were met with understanding. She was angry that her son was taken from her and she wanted someone to take up the fight against her so she could fuel her rage.

The moment passed as the conversation continued with others. They went around the room and each shared their moment and tried to focus on the positive things that happened in their lives since their last meeting. The group tried to end their meetings by focusing on the fact that life goes on. It may move forward without the love of your life by your side but the clock is a machine that never stops. You could focus on the lights of the horizon or drown in the darkness of grief. Father Derek was always trying to change their focus to the light.

"If I am not mistaken, I believe Mary has once again taken care of the coffee and cake tonight. I think we all could benefit from the blessed combination."

Mary chuckled at the Father's remark. As she was just thinking, coffee and cake were the magical serum for the grieving masses but now they had received the official term of being a *blessed combination*.

"Mary are you all set for us?"

Mary smiled and nodded in her usual pleasant demeanor as she walked out of the kitchen with a small prepared plate for the grieving mother.

"You betcha, Father. Everyone come on up and help yourself. The coffee is ho..."

The words trailed off and the group turned towards the elderly woman just in time to see her drop to the ground. The plate of cake she was carrying tumbled to the ground as her eyes rolled back in her head. Luckily, there were no sharp objects for her to impale herself on as she fell but her head struck the tile hard as she collapsed. By the time Father Derek reached her, the blood was already beading up on her forehead.

"She is having a stroke. Someone please call 911."

At least three members of the group reached for their cell phones as they collectively dialed the emergency services number. In the end, the call was only needed by one of them but the resulting action occurred. Within minutes, they could hear the wail of the sirens approaching. The Father continued to give directions to the others as he held Mary on his lap.

"In the back closet of the kitchen there are some blankets on the top shelf. Can someone get a couple for me? I want to cover her up to keep her warm. She is feeling cold."

The group members looked at each other with silent pain. They knew what a cold body in their arms felt like and had no desire to be sitting where the Father was in case Mary did not make it. One of them broke away and retrieved the blankets from the kitchen area. By the time they had gotten back, they could hear the ambulance pulling up outside. Moments later, the doors to the Social Hall flew open as the paramedics made their way inside. The group leader approached Father Derek as he continued to hold Mary.

"Can you tell me what happened Father?"

18

The other paramedics were busy taking out their various packs to administer first aid. One was busy wrapping an arm cuff on Mary's arm to take her blood pressure while the other took out a gauze bandage and alcohol wipe to tend to Mary's head wound.

"She was walking out of the kitchen and talking when she stopped in mid-sentence and then just dropped to the ground."

"So did she trip over something or did she just fall on her own accord?"

"No, there was nothing in her path that I could see. I think she just fell down and fainted."

"You are close, Father. Let us slowly lower her down so that she is flat on the ground."

The pair carefully lowered her and the Priest removed himself from the area so that the men could attend to their patient. He could see the paramedic lead speak into his communicator but could not make out all the details of the conversation. Moments later, the doors to the Social Hall opened again as a stretcher was rolled in. The immediate concern by the group was palpable.

"Is she going to be ok?"

The paramedics were trained to be diplomatic even in the face of extreme circumstances. They remained silent as the lead replied to everyone collectively.

"We are doing our best to make her comfortable. We are transporting her to the hospital so we can get a better idea of what's happening to her. Does anyone know if she has someone we can contact to be with her at the hospital?"

Father Derek was the first to respond.

"Mary is a widow that lives alone. Her children don't live in the state but I'm sure we can find their contact information."

"That's unfortunate Father that she is alone but I am sure you will come to visit her."

"Of course, Thomas. I will follow along with my car."

Moments later, Mary was loaded onto the stretcher, secured by straps, and rolled out of the Social Hall. The group of grieving parishioners looked at each other in silence. They hoped they would not have another soul to pray for at their next meeting.

6

"Do you have any of that sugar-free syrup back there or do we just have to go dry if we don't want the sweet stuff?"

"Good morning, Samuel. How odd to see you here on a Saturday? I didn't know you were a fan of pancakes?"

The Youth Group Pancake breakfast was in full bloom as the flapjacks were coming out of the kitchen with great speed. The Social Hall smelled to Samuel like an old Howard Johnson's on a Sunday morning. He remembered going there with his late wife, Katrice, every week after mass. He would always get the pigs in a blanket and she would opt for the early Sunday lunch and get a plate of fried clams. He often thought that in those moments, his wife loved those clams more than she loved him. She would savor each and every one of them; getting side after side of tartar sauce before she would sit back in her chair with her britches about to pop. After another cup of coffee and possibly a trip to the head for each of them, they would sit in silence and split a strawberry shortcake. If he closed his eyes he could still taste the sweet strawberry on his lips that would linger long after their drive home.

"Are you ok, Samuel? You seem lost in thought."

Samuel shook off his trip down memory lane and focused on the task at hand.

"I'm perfectly fine, Father. I was just thinking that the strawberry sauce down at the House of Pancakes would be a fright tastier than any syrup. Do you think those young'uns have any strawberry sauce laying around?"

The Priest laughed heartily in the brevity of the moment.

"Samuel, my friend. I don't believe they have anything remotely close to that here. These are just a group of young people led by other young people and they barely know how to flip a pancake without burning it. I might be able to find you some sugar-free pancake syrup that you asked about but the strawberry sauce would be worth a king's ransom."

The elderly man simply nodded his head. "I suppose you are right, Father, but it was worth the ask. I hanker for some good strawberries now and again."

"Nothing ventured, nothing gained, Samuel. Now, would you care for bacon or sausage with your pancakes?"

He looked back and forth between the two choices and smiled. "There are always perfect pairings young man. Peanut butter goes with jelly, fried clams go with tartar sauce and pancakes go best with sausage. I never heard of any bacon in a blanket but those piggies always had a home there."

Laughter filled the Social Hall as Father Derek burst out exuberantly. The fellow servers in the food line joined the young Priest and soon there was contagious laughter everywhere.

"Then pigs in a blanket are yours to enjoy, Samuel. See the young man at the end of the counter to settle your tab."

"Not until I pair it all with a finely brewed cup of coffee."

"Of course, Samuel, of course. Heaven have mercy on any man or woman that stands in the way of your mighty cup of joe."

It was the older man's turn to smile this time. "You are learning, young man. Indeed, you are learning."

Samuel moved his breakfast tray to the end where a pimply faced young man was ringing up the breakfast crowd and seemed to cower with each passing sale.

"Did you pre-pay at the parish office, Sir?"

"Since it would be bad taste to lie in church I would have to say I did not."

The teenage boy looked at Samuel with confusion. The older man decided to let him off the hook.

"No, I did not pre-pay, young man."

The boy keyed in the breakfast purchase carefully. "That will be $5, Sir."

"A fin for a couple of flapjacks and some links? That seems a bit steep."

The boy once again cowered in embarrassment. "I'm sorry Sir but…"

"It's all ok, young man. I was just having a moment with you. Add in a coffee for me, will ya? Is it per cup of can I get refills?"

The teenager reached behind him and gave Samuel a coffee mug. "It will be $1 more for the coffee, Sir. $6 total."

"That is perfectly fine. Here is seven. Keep the change. I plan to fill my coffee a few times before leaving."

The cashier looked at the extra dollar with incredulity. He seemed confused at what he should do with it. Father Derek, who had watched the whole transaction came over and helped the young man put the extra dollar into the register.

Samuel used his cane with his right hand while balancing the tray with his left. He thought that is was good that his mug was empty as the tray seemed to resemble a balancing act on a tight rope.

"Do you need some help sir?"

Samuel turned just enough to see a young lady approach him on his flank.

"You startled me, young lady."

"I'm sorry. Do you need help with your tray?"

Samuel turned and sat down at the nearest empty table and placed the tray on top gently. Picking up his mug, he handed it to the girl.

"I'm good with the tray but you could help me out by filling up my coffee mug. Can you do that or do I need to get back up?"

"No, Sir. I'll get it for you. Would you like cream and sugar with your coffee?"

Samuel chuckled. "Not at all, young lady. Men like their coffee black. Cream and sugar are for the ladies and the children. If you fill up the mug with just coffee, I would be pleased as punch."

The girl scuttled away towards the coffee urns and waited behind three people that were busy filling their mugs and adding their sweeteners. Samuel looked on and peered at the girl through the whole process. He was more than capable of getting his own coffee but he thought he might as well let the young lady feel useful. He watched her take every step and would send her back if she spilled even a drop. When she returned, she placed the coffee with both hands onto the tray in front of him.

"Thank you, ma'am. That was kind of you. Now run along and help someone who needs the help."

As the girl turned, Samuel thought silently of his encounter the Sunday before with the ornery woman who didn't like to be called ma'am.

"Say, young lady…"

The young girl turned around, slightly afraid of what the elderly man was going to ask of her now.

"Yes, Sir?"

"There was an old lady here last Sunday. She got my coffee for me too. I don't see her around today. Do you know who I am talking about?"

"Was she a really old lady, like you?"

"Do you think I'm an old lady?"

The girl blushed. "No Sir. Not at all. I just meant…"

"I know what you meant. So do you know who I am talking about?"

The young girl looked around the room to make sure she wasn't spreading any gossip that she wasn't supposed to.

"I think you are talking about Mary."

"Yes, that's it. Mary was her name. I real firecracker with a smart mouth. Is she around today? I feel up to sparring with her a little more."

"I'm not sure I'm supposed to say."

Samuel looked at the girl oddly. "What do you mean?"

Spying the Priest, she saw her way out of the situation.

"Hold on one moment. Let me get Father Derek."

The girl hurried off and approached the Priest quietly. She whispered to him and pointed over to Samuel as he was now starting to drink his coffee. Father Derek patted the young lady's shoulder as she went off in the other direction. The Priest made his way over to the table and sat down next to Samuel.

"How's the coffee?"

Samuel looked at the Priest without emotion. "No need for small talk, Padre. What happened to the gal, Mary? I may be a little old but I know when something is up."

Father Derek looked down at the table for a moment as if to say a quick blessing. "Do you know Mary very well Samuel?"

"Not at all. I just met her last Sunday. She was a little bit of a firecracker and gave it right back to me as I gave her some grief. I like a woman with a backbone. Did she run out of people to give a hard time to?"

"Not exactly Samuel. She had a little accident the other night. Right here in the Social Hall. I would have thought the rumor mill would have filled you in."

"I have no time for rumor or chit chat for that matter. People think older people have all the time in the world but the truth is we are just selective as to whom we spend it with."

"Well, that being said...maybe you could find some time to visit Mary in the hospital. I understand that not many have been up to visit her."

"Hospital? What happened to her?"

"I would rather not tell her business. What I can tell you, Samuel is that she is sick, she is in the hospital and that she is all alone. As a good Catholic that should be enough to make you want to go and visit her."

Samuel took a sip of his coffee and smiled. "You talk a good game, Father. Are you a poker player?"

The Priest simply smiled and said nothing.

"Well, I can tell when I have been played. In fact, my doctor played me the other day and now I have to go to the hospital for a test. Maybe I will stop and see your lady Mary while I am there."

"I'm sure she would appreciate it."

Samuel went back to pouring his sugar-free syrup on his pancakes. "I'm not sure if she will appreciate seeing me, of all people, but I'll stop by and see her while I am there since it won't take me out of my way."

Father Derek rose with a smile on his face and patted Samuel on his back as he walked away. The older man went back to his pigs in a blanket and retuned to memory lane as he reminisced about a time when he had a gal to share his meal with.

7

The outpatient and testing facility at St. Vincent's Hospital was located in the newly renovated West Wing. Samuel had the very vocal opinion that the renovation was hogwash. A hospital didn't need a facelift just to cure sick people. If they were going to spend that much money on a fresh coat of paint and some new plants, they could sure as heck do something about the cost of healthcare inside the hospital.

His complaining always started in the parking lot, as there were never enough handicap spaces there to park his large sedan. He often wondered how a hospital, which by definition, housed nothing but sick people, could only have a few handicap spots and the rest were for regular parking. He would often bicker with the hospital staff stating that there should be more handicap spots than regular. The daring young ones usually quipped something in retort, stating that the spaces would no longer be special if that was the case.

After parking and making his way inside, he was already stressed out. If they couldn't let him park any closer than the least they could do would be to bring the stress test closer to him. He was huffing and puffing already and he had only made it to the lobby. If they hooked up a monitor to him at this point he was sure to fail and they would certainly make him cease and desist all coffee enjoyment.

Checking in with the security desk, Samuel was reminded of the comical checkpoints he would encounter while delivering mail in Korea. He would bring his Army jeep up to a make shift barrier in the middle of nowhere as they would check his credentials and let him pass towards the next checkpoint. He often thought it was a scene out of the funny pages when he encountered them. He could just as easily drive his jeep to the left or right and avoid the checkpoint altogether. Sometimes the military never made sense. In fact, the times it made sense during war time was few and far between.

Samuel made his way down the hallway to the next checkpoint which happened to be the reception desk at the cardiology unit. He gave the young child his name and wondered if she even knew how to spell Samuel. She asked him to repeat his name three times as if she had never heard it before and told him to have a seat while she continued to scroll through her computer screen. Samuel figured she was looking through all the names that started with the letter S that were scheduled around the same time as check in.

As he waited for his name to be called, he patiently sat with his hands folded neatly on his lap. Samuel had never caught the cell phone bug and often laughed as he observed people withering their lives away stuck in an electronic machine. He was not one to scroll through the pile of magazines as his back ached just looking at them. If you had to lug a satchel full of Sears catalogues or the latest edition of Teen Beat, you would be less likely to pick them up to dawdle away your time.

"Samuel Barnes? Is there a Samuel Barnes here?"

"You just checked me in five minutes ago. I'm sitting right in front of you."

"Come this way Mr. Barnes."

Samuel simply shook his head and wobbled to find his footing. Once balanced, he followed the young girl down the hallway towards the testing room. Once inside, he was introduced to a young man who instructed him to have a seat. Before he could place himself down in the chair, the young lady left the room and closed the door.

"Good morning, Samuel. Would you prefer Mr. Barnes or is Samuel ok?"

"Seeing that you already went with Samuel, let's stick with that."

The technician ignored the sarcasm and moved on.

"Ok. Samuel. Have you been through a stress test before?"

"I was in the Korean war before your father was in diapers young man. I've seen more stress than you can even imagine."

"Let me rephrase that. Have you even been through a medical stress test before?"

"Yes. For some reason they like to give it to the elderly."

The technician again ignored the elderly man's response.

"Then you know the routine, Samuel. Take off your shirt and so we can begin. I will be hooking up small wires to your chest that will measure..."

"I know damn well what it will measure. Let's get on with it. The sooner we get this started the sooner I can get out of here."

The technician knew better than to get into it with the old man. His whole day was full of grumpy people just like him that could not wait to be done with the ugly chore ahead of them and get on with their day. He moved about the room gathering everything he needed to get Mr. Barnes set up for his test. As he began hooking up the electrodes, he looked over and eyed the man's cane.

"Samuel? Do you need the cane to walk?"

"No, young man. I just enjoy looking like Kris Kringle as I go about my day. Of course I need the cane. Do you think it is just decoration?"

"You seemed to walk in on your own accord. Do you think it will be an issue on the treadmill?"

"I think as long as you let me hold onto those railings and take things slow, we will be just fine. As I've said before. It's not my first rodeo. I've been through this test before."

"Ok. I understand. Is there a reason why your doctor ordered the test this time? Did you have a heart episode?"

Samuel looked at the young man with wonder and skepticism. "A heart episode? Is that the best you could come up with? No, there was no *heart episode* as you call it. My doctor is trying to prove a point and I can be just as stubborn as he is. Let's get this done."

The technician had a passing moment when he thought about inquiring further but then decided against it. He proceeded with hooking the elderly man up to the monitor and instructed him to get on the tread mill.

"Do you need help getting up there Samuel?"

"Not that I would admit to a young'un like you, but I have no problem getting it up."

The young man was flustered. "I only meant…"

Samuel chuckled. "I know what you meant. I just wanted to see you get a little red in the cheeks."

Samuel moved forward and got himself up on the treadmill with a little wobble. The technician stood close by in case he started to fall.

"If you move much closer, you are going to get a lot more stress in your life, young man. I didn't sleep next to men in foxholes and I'm not about to start now with an orderly."

"Sir, I…I only…"

"Oh just get on with it already. You are much too easy of a target."

The technician started the treadmill at a very slow pace and let Samuel get acclimated. After putting one foot in front of the other, the test had begun. For the next 15 minutes, Samuel limped along holding the handrails as the various machines beeped and picked up his vital signs as his heartbeat increased. When the test came to a stop, Samuel felt as if he had run a marathon.

"I hope you got what you needed young man because I am done."

The technician started to remove the wires and assured Samuel that he had. "We captured all the data we needed. Your doctor will review the results and get back to you with a recommended course of action."

Samuel was still huffing and puffing and felt like there was an elephant sitting on his chest. He took out his handkerchief from his back pocket and wiped his brow. Slowly he slipped his arms into his shirt and began buttoning up to go. He knew damn well what the recommended course of action would be. The Doc would tell him to cut back, way back, on his caffeine intake. In other words, be miserable. He had survived the war in Korea and worked his feet to the bone delivering everyone else's love letters and happy correspondence. By the time he could settle down and enjoy life, his wife was gone too quickly. He was never a smoker and very rarely took a drink. Every year, on July 27th, he had a shot of whiskey and toasted to his brothers in arms that died in the war; but that was the extent of his indulgence. He didn't even have anything special on his birthday. They could call up the funeral home and give the undertaker a heads up. This old man wasn't giving up his coffee for anyone.

The impatient technician was anxious to get Samuel out of the room.

"If you need a few extra minutes before you head out, we can have you lie down in the room next door if that makes you comfortable."

Samuel simply looked at the young man with scorn.

"I don't need a nap junior. I just move a little slower than the next patient. If you are in a hurry, maybe you should relax a little. I hear cutting back on those energy drinks I see on your table might do the trick."

The technician just shook his head and moved to the door. When it was obvious Samuel was not following him, he took it upon himself to go to the restroom. Maybe when he returned the old man would be gone.

After gathering himself together, Samuel rose slowly and exited the room. Looking out into the hallway he didn't see the technician anywhere. In fact, the other people working in the Cardiology unit didn't pay him any attention at all. Perhaps they were too buy admiring the new paint job and wall coverings to give the patients a second thought. With a shake of his head, Samuel walked down the hallway and out into the main lobby. He was halfway across the main entranceway to the security guard station when he remembered telling Father Derek he would check in on the coffee woman. He changed his trajectory and walked over to the security guard he had checked in with earlier.

"I'm looking for a woman…"

"Ain't we all buddy…"

"Not that kind of woman. I'm looking for a woman that was brought in the other day from St. Thomas. Her name is Mary something or other."

The security guard looked up at Samuel with a perturbed look.

"Mary *something or other*? Really, Mack? That's the best you got? Is that with one S or two? Have you noticed we are a hospital here? We get quite a few women named Mary coming through the doors."

"Listen, *Mack*. I delivered mail for this town for most of my life. I can count the number of women named Mary on one hand. I'm pretty sure if you looked up the name Mary you wouldn't find too many laying in a bed somewhere upstairs."

The guard thought a moment about arguing with the man but thought otherwise. Like the technician, he figured the argument would be senseless. Old people always thought they were right. On second thought, what he said probably made sense. He typed the name *Mary* into the database.

"We got two Mary's here. One is in the Maternity ward popping out some kid and the other is in ICU. So, which one is gonna be?"

"Well the Mary I am looking for had a stroke. Since she is around my age I doubt she is pushing out any more pups so I figure we better go with the one in ICU."

"The problem with that old-timer is that only relatives are allowed in ICU. Since you didn't even know her name I'm guessing you are not related."

"Nope, not related. Not even friends. I'm here on behalf of the church so..."

"That's all you had to say. Fill out this name tag and you can head up to the third floor. See the nurses at the ICU station and they will let you right in."

"Now wasn't that easy?"

The guard didn't bother with an answer. While Samuel filled out his nametag, the guard went on to help the next person in line. He didn't pay the older gentleman any attention as he walked towards the bank of elevators behind the guard station. *Great security in this hospital*, Samuel thought humorously. Maybe the guard should have been trained in Korea.

8

The elevator stopped at the third floor and Samuel was the only rider to be getting out. ICU always seemed to live up to its anagram of Intensive Care Unit. The atmosphere was eerily intense. Compared to the rest of the hustle and bustle of the hospital, Samuel found the silence a welcomed change. Finding his way across the small lobby, he arrived at the ICU nurses station.

"Good morning. Can we help you?"

"I'm looking for Mary."

The charge nurse looked down at the patient files in front of her and then up at the man standing before her.

"Do you mean Mary Stables?"

"Is that her last name? That's rather interesting."

"...and you are?"

"My name is Samuel Barnes. I am visiting Mary on behalf of Father Derek at St. Thomas."

"Of course. Father Derek has been Mary's only visitor so far. Up to now anyway. Did you say your last name was Barnes?"

Samuel nodded in silence. He saw where this was headed.

"Well, isn't that a coincidence. You are the Barnes and she is the Stables. All we need are some horses and we have ourselves a hoedown."

Samuel stared back at the woman without emotion. He wondered why everything about Mary put a strain on his name.

"Well, I think it's funny anyway. Come along with me, Mr. Barnes. I'll take you down to her room."

Samuel followed the nurse down the hallway until he came to the glass walled room. He had seen enough people in hospitals to know that there wasn't much privacy in the ICU. They wanted to be able to see the patients at a moment's notice.

"Here is Mary's room. She is pretty sedated but you are welcome to sit and visit with her. Being from the church and all, you probably want to pray for her too."

Samuel looked over at the women with disdain. "I am sure I will find something to occupy my time. Is there a chair in the room or do I have to stand?"

"There is a chair right next to her bedside. You can stay as long as you like but I'm not sure how long she will be under with the sedation."

Samuel ignored the comment and walked slowly into the room. The rubber tip on his cane seemed to stick a little to the smooth tile in the room and made a small popping sound each time he raised it. Looking over at the patient, she seemed unfazed by the noise and continued sleeping amid the many beeps and sounds of the medical equipment. Looking over at her, Samuel felt something akin to compassion in his old grumpy heart. She may have been curt about his name in the Social Hall, but no one should be alone in a room like this going through whatever she was going through.

Looking over at the dry erase board on the wall, Samuel could see all the info he had not known before. Name-Mary Stables. Age-80. Diagnosis-Stroke. Emergency contact- Father Derek. The Father had been right. She had no one. Samuel took a seat next to her bed and gently lowered himself into it. Resting his cane against the side of the bed, he took a closer look at the younger woman. He chuckled at the term but two years was two years. Depending on how you measured it, she may have been born in a different decade.

Samuel thought to himself that Mary's bark was worse than her features allowed. She seemed like a kind soul as she lay there sleeping. She wasn't giving an old man a hard time about his coffee or his name. She was breathing peacefully without the assistance of a respirator and her cheeks were a little flush from the cold air in the room. Reaching over to the foot of the bed, Samuel grasped the blanket that was draped across her legs and pulled it higher to cover her up. He thought for a second that he noticed a response from her but the moment was fleeting and she resumed her breathing pattern without skipping a beat.

Sitting back in the chair, Samuel continued to take in the surroundings of the room. There were no flowers from friends or family but a single sunflower placed in a cup by the window. The flower was most likely placed there by the hospital staff and could have been real or fake. In the end, he decided that it made no difference either way.

Looking up, he was surprised to see that the television was on without any sound playing. Since Mary was sedated, he failed to see the purpose unless it was the other way around. If they didn't want her to feel lonely in her sleep, they should have turned up the sound so she could hear it even with her eyes closed. He chuckled at the fact that he fell asleep that way most days in his living room chair. Since he had nowhere to go and all day to get there, Samuel found the television remote and turned the station to something more of his liking. Turning up the sound until he could make out the words clearly, he sat back and settled in for an afternoon siesta.

9

Daybreak in a hospital room is a far greater disappointment than watching the sun rise over the horizon in any other corner of the Earth. The nurses come and go with the obligatory rounds of testing. They poke here, they prod there, all the while assuring that they are not trying to disturb you. Before the morning tray of food brings even the faintest odor of coffee, the doctor enters to do their rounds. Some days they arrive by themselves while others they enter with an entourage in tow. Mary Stables was pleased to see the doctor arrive by herself.

"Good morning Miss Stables."

"Good morning."

"How are you feeling this morning?"

"I am tired and a little irritable. I'm tired of being here in the hospital. When can I go home?"

The doctor looked at the patient's chart and examined the latest test results that were captured within. She purposely was ignoring Mary's question as she weighed the impact of the numbers as if she was formulating her response.

"Tell me Mary. Who is the President of the Unites States?"

"Who cares. They are all crooks and liars."

The doctor laughed.

"I suppose that is a perfectly valid response. Do you know what happened to bring you here?"

"You asked me that question yesterday."

"I did. I want to make sure you did not forget since then."

"I may have plenty of years on the wheels but they are still turning." When the doctor did not take the bait, she kept going. "I was serving refreshments at St. Thomas. We were in the Social Hall and there was a meeting of those who have suffered a loss. The Father asked me to serve refreshments and I came out of the kitchen carrying them. Before I could get to the table, I felt light headed and must have fallen down. When I woke up I was already at the hospital and your fellow white coats were having their way with me."

The doctor laughed once again. "Well, that is very sharp, Mary. Pretty much exactly what happened, all the way up to my *fellow white coats* running their tests on you. I've never heard them referred to in that way but I kind of like it."

Mary sat up slightly in her bed. "Do you like it enough to let me out of this *hoosgow*? I would like to get home to my plants. I am sure they need some watering by now if they are not dead already."

"Isn't there someone at home that can be watering them for you?"

Mary closed her eyes as a small tear appeared in the corner of her eye. "No, I live alone. I have been a widow for some time now. My kids are off living their best life. It's just me and that's ok. I can't imagine I have that long to fuss about it."

The doctor stepped forward and patted the back of Mary's hand. "I'm pretty sure you have plenty of charge left in those batteries, Mary. Besides, I hear you had a gentleman caller yesterday. Is he caring for your plants while you have been here?"

Mary looked over at the doctor with an inquisitive look. "Father Derek was here? When did he come? He usually leaves something for me when he stops by and prays." Mary looked around the room and saw no resemblance of any visitor to her room.

"I can check with the nurse's station but I am fairly certain it was not a Priest. The ladies told me that an older gentleman visited you and actually took a nap next to you."

"We have a picture of him."

Both ladies turned their attention to the door as one of the morning nurses appeared without notice.

"Did you say you have a picture of him?"

"Yes, Mary. My apologies. We don't usually take pictures of patients while they are sleeping it was just that the two of you looked absolutely adorable sleeping next to each other. You were sleeping in the bed and he had dozed off in the chair next to you. It looked like a Hallmark movie scene. How long have the two of you been together?"

"Together? I'm not together with anyone. I am a widow. Who was this man who came in and slept next to me? Is there no security in this hospital?"

The doctor and the nurse looked at each other with growing concern. "I assure you, Mary. You were never in harm's way. We watched from the nurses station the whole time. He literally came in, turned up the television and fell asleep in the chair next to you. Oh, and he covered you up with a blanket because you must have seemed cold to him."

Mary looked at the two of them with wild wonderment. "Can you bring me the picture of this stranger you let into my room? I would like to see who I need to include in my lawsuit."

The doctor simply shrugged her shoulders and nodded towards the door as the nurse turned and exited. A few moments later, she returned with a cell phone in her hand.

"Here he is, Mary. Again, my deepest apologies. We meant no harm. As you can see in the photo, you two were just simply the sweetest couple. We thought it should be a greeting card."

Mary took the phone from the nurse in her hand and looked at the photo. At first she couldn't make out who the man was but when she did recognize him, a slight smile appeared on her face.

"I can tell by your expression, Mary, you know the man. Do you want to share who your gentleman caller was?"

Mary shook her head slightly but kept on smiling. "His name is Samuel. No, *Sammy* Barnes. He goes to my church."

"That's right. Both the security guard downstairs and the nurse who greeted him indicated that the man said he was from your church. He was on some sort of faith mission."

"Well..."

"Well what, Mary? Is that not the case? If it's an issue I will need to file a report."

Mary went on smiling at the photo until she finally handed it back to the nurse. "There is no need. He is who he claimed to be. I am certain Father Derek asked him to come by. That old fool wouldn't go out of his way to see me without being prompted to. I've only got two questions for you."

The two women looked at each other with amusement. "Sure, Mary. What are your questions?"

"Well, again. When can I get out of this hoosgow and did the old man bring a cup of coffee with him?"

With this last question the patient burst out into laughter. Both the nurse and the doctor came to the same conclusion. It was time to send Mary home.

10

Father Derek was wearing non-liturgical clothing as he tended to the garden outside of the church office. He was watering some begonias he had been growing carefully over the last few months and did not hear his visitor arrive.

"You know it's time to transplant those and get them into a greenhouse Father. They are not going to last long when the cooler temps settle in."

Father Derek turned to see Samuel standing behind him holding his cane in one hand and the mail for the office in the other.

"You delivered mail to this office for decades, Samuel. You don't have to do that anymore. I am fairly certain your pension from the post office reminds you of that monthly."

Samuel snickered. "Well, it's not that much of a reminder every month now is it Father."

The young Priest smiled broadly. "The Lord blesses us in many ways, Samuel. Who are we to judge the baskets of fish and bread that are left behind."

"Always the prophet, Padre."

"What brings you here to the office, Samuel? We have no activities planned today."

Samuel stepped forward and put the mail on the steps next to Father Derek.

"I got a call on the volunteer list. I guess it was my lucky number to be called. They asked me to come by the office and pick up some paperwork."

The Priest silently smiled and lowered his head.

"Why do I think it wasn't random that I was called?"

"Before I answer that question truthfully Samuel, perhaps you can answer a question for me."

The elderly man smiled and nodded. "A little quid pro quo, eh? Ok, I'll bite. What's your question for me?"

Father Derek placed the hose down on the ground and removed the gardening gloves he had was wearing.

"Were you able to go by the hospital and pay Mary a visit like I asked Samuel?"

"Oh that? Yes. I stopped by when I was there getting some tests done. I visited Mary like you asked but I don't think she appreciated it much."

"Why do you say that?"

"Because she was sleeping the whole time I was there. If I knew that was going to be the case, I would not have wasted my time."

"I am certain that she felt your presence as she has when I have come by. Did you pray for her Samuel?"

The older gentleman lowered his head sheepishly. "Not exactly, Father."

Father Derek smiled. "There is no need for embarrassment Samuel. I was simply asking if you prayed for her while she was sleeping. What does *not exactly* mean?"

"I had all intents and purposes to pray for her and actually have a conversation with her but she was sleeping. So..."

"So?"

"Well, I turned on the television and took a little nap. I figured we would talk when she woke up but she was still sleeping when I opened my eyes. I simply gathered my things and left. No harm no foul as they say."

"So Mary did not even know you were there?"

"Not unless the nurse told her. Like I said, she was sleeping Father. Why is that important? I thought you just wanted me to check on her. I did. She was fine."

The Father turned back towards his begonias and put his gloves back on. Picking up the hose he began to water the beautiful flowers in front of him.

"Did you forget my question Father? Remember quid pro quo. Why did I get a call on the volunteer list? I didn't think it was my turn again for a while?"

The Priest turned off the hose again and turned back to face his parishioner.

"I believe I told you a little more about Mary before you went to see her. She is alone, Samuel. There has been no one up to visit her while she has been here. I'm just a little disappointed she did not know that someone cared enough to visit her."

Samuel felt like a teenage boy caught doing something wrong by the nuns that taught him in school. He nodded his head in acknowledgement of the situation.

"Not to fret, my friend. All is forgiven. However, you were correct. I asked the office to give you a call."

"Sure Father. Whatever you ask. I will gladly help."

The Father turned away with the slightest smile on his face. He knew that Samuel would not deny his request at this point.

"I am glad to hear that Mr. Barnes. It would seem that our friend Mary is ready to go home. Since she was transported to the hospital in an ambulance, she does not have a ride home. The hospital staff phoned us and asked if we could arrange transportation for her. Would you be so kind as to give her a ride?"

Samuel shifted his feet as he changed his balance on his cane. "Of course,

Father. Of course. Unless she needs a ride when I'm doing something else. In that case, I could find someone else to…"

"I'm so glad to hear that Samuel. Mary is ready to go now. Just drive on over to the hospital and get her. I will give them a call and let them know you are on your way."

Samuel just shook his head. Once again he was outsmarted by one of the young ones. Maybe he was getting too old to know when he was getting conned. Then again…maybe he just needed more coffee.

11

Samuel once again pulled his large sedan into the parking lot at St. Vincent's hospital. He first drove up to the porte-cochere hoping that his passenger was waiting outside but he figured that was too much to ask. He also knew that once he parked somewhere and hobbled inside they would tell him to go back out to his car and pull it up when she was ready. He quipped that sometimes doing nice things for people wasn't worth the effort.

The handicap spaces were all taken once again and Samuel ended up parking a few rows back. Getting out of his car he stumbled for a moment and caught himself using the top of the car door. He wondered how he was supposed to help other people when he could not even help himself. Getting out his cane and wiping his brow with his handkerchief, he proceeded his slow walk into the hospital main entrance. Once in the lobby, he approached the security booth where he was once again greeted curtly by the guard who was too busy looking at his phone to look up.

"Yea?"

"Is that actually what the hospital pays you to do? Maybe you can at least pretend to be working."

The security guard looked up from his phone to see the familiar face in front of him.

"Oh. Hey old timer. You ever find that broad you were looking for the other day? I'm sure an old guy like you doesn't get to find that many women. Am I right?"

Samuel simply ignored the remarks.

"I am here to pick up Mary Stables. The folks at St. Thomas sent me to give her a ride."

The guard put his phone down and moved his hands over to the keyboard. Typing the name into the system, he came up with the desired results.

"Yup. Checks out. Looks like they are getting ready to release her now. Go ahead on up and they will have you sign her out."

"Sign her out? I'm no relation to her. I'm just giving her a ride."

"Listen, Mack. I don't care what kind of ride you are giving the broad. Hospital regs say someone has to sign her out. Just go on up and sign for her and then you will be on your merry way."

Samuel took the visitor pass that the guard handed to him without a word. Even though he had spent decades dealing with people as a postal carrier, he would never understand them. His disdain with the public had hardened since retirement and he relished the time he spent alone away from the world. There were times when the loneliness got to him but he would prefer being more selective on who he had to deal with.

Taking the elevator up to the third floor once again, Samuel made his way over to the nurse's station where he was greeted by a different nurse.

"Hello, can I help you?"

"I'm here to pick up Mary. Is she ready to go?"

"Are you referring to Mary Stables?"

"Yes, how many Mary's do you have in ICU?"

The nurse chuckled at his gruffness. "Actually, at the moment we don't have any. Mary was sent to a regular room yesterday. Let me see what room she is in now."

"Why didn't they tell me that downstairs?"

"I'm sorry sir. I'm not sure why. Maybe they thought you already knew."

"How the heck…"

The nurse interrupted him before he could go any further. "Here she is. They moved her to room 222. That's on the second floor. Do you need someone to show you the way?"

Samuel simply looked at the nurse with a blank stare. "Young lady. I was a postal carrier for most of my life. I could find any address in this town. I'm fairly certain I can find a numbered room in the hospital."

The nurse waved off the remark without acknowledgement. "Ok, well good luck. Have a nice day." She walked away without hesitation and the elderly man translated her response to the vulgarity that he knew she was thinking. Turning around, he made his way back to the elevator and proceeded down to level two.

By the time he reached the correct place, Samuel was winded. He walked right past the nurse's station and proceeded to Mary's room. As he knocked on the door and entered, he found her sitting on the edge of the bed waiting with her pocketbook on her lap. Looking up at the doorway, she rolled her eyes when she saw Samuel.

"Well it took you long enough to get here. I thought Father Derek was sending someone that could help me, not challenge me."

Samuel tried to respond but he was finding it difficult to catch his breath. Seeing his distress, Mary rose from the hospital bed and went over to him.

"You are all out of breath you damn fool. Come sit in the chair for a moment."

Samuel simply nodded and went a few steps into the room until he found the chair and flopped down into it. His breathing was labored as he hunched over to look at his shoes. Concerned, Mary went over to her bedside table and poured him a glass of ice water from her hospital pitcher. Walking back, she rested her hand in his shoulder while giving him the glass of water.

"Drink this Samuel. You'll feel better in a moment."

He nodded his head in agreement and slowly drank the water down. Shortly, his breathing came back to normal and sweat broke upon his forehead. Without hesitation, Mary went into her bathroom and returned with a paper towel that had been ran under cold water. Placing it on his forehead, she paused for a moment before pulling the towel away. She took the glass from Samuel's hand and replaced it with the damp cloth.

"Thank you, but I thought you were the patient here."

"Well, we all need a little bit of care and attention sometimes."

"…and here I thought you only served coffee."

The two chuckled and delighted at the break in the conversation. After a moment, Samuel started to rise from the chair and Mary again placed her hand on his shoulder.

"No need to get up. They are still processing my paperwork. Lord only knows how long it is going to take."

"Hospitals are like that. They take their time until it is time for the bill. Then they send it out express. Trust me, I delivered enough of those envelopes."

"Were you a delivery man before you retired, Samuel?"

The elderly man chuckled. "You might say that. I was a Postal Carrier for most of my life. Delivered mail as well as plenty of packages to pretty much every address in this town. Not really what I think of when you say *delivery man* but I suppose you are right."

Mary looked out at the nurses who seemed oblivious to her desire to be checked out. Not wanting to sit in silence, she kept the conversation going.

"That sounds like a wonderful career. How did you get into that? There weren't many who took to public service back in the day."

"Very true. After the war, most GIs were more interested in making a quick buck or two. For me it was all I knew how to do. They taught me in Korea to deliver the mail no matter what. We found servicemen while they were in foxholes with bombs dropping all around them. We knew that a letter from home would mean more to them than anything else at that moment so we pushed on. Not like these young mailmen today. They get a little bit or rain and they want to stay in their mail trucks."

Mary looked on with a new sense of admiration.

"My late husband went off to fight in Korea. Like the rest of the fellas who went over there, he was a long way from home. Thanks to men like you I guess, we were able to stay in touch somewhat. Not like these new phones with the internet on them that you can talk instantly to your loved ones. We had to wait for a letter to be delivered to them or from there. I have a lot of respect for those mailmen Samuel. You included."

"That's kind of you to say, Mary. Did your late husband pass in the war or did he make it home?"

"My Joe made it home. We had a good, long life together but he passed on last year. My children and grand-children are all scattered around the country. Now, it's just me. A silly old woman locked up in a hospital room waiting to go home."

"Well wait no more Mary."

The conversation stopped as the two of them turned to the doorway of the room. The nurse had entered without hesitation with a clipboard full off discharge papers.

"Is it finally time? I didn't realize it was Christmas already."

"Funny. Funny lady you got here. You wouldn't know she had a stroke a short time ago. Maybe it turned you into a comedienne. What do you think Mary?"

"I think you better get on with it before we get any older."

"Fair enough, Mary. Here are the discharge orders. The doctor wants you to follow up with your own physician within 24 hours. We are releasing you but to their care. You have had a stroke. This is a major health event that needs continued care. Your physician may want to put you on a restricted diet plan along with some physical therapy."

"Oh, here we go…"

"Sir? Did you have something to add?"

"Nope. I'm just the driver but my doctor sings the same tune. Restricted diet is just another term for misery."

It was the nurse's turn to laugh. The reaction was contagious as the three of them shared a happy moment.

"Well, that being said we will let your physician pass on that misery. We only want you to be happy today, Mary. Sign here and also on this page and we will get you out of here."

"Do you need me to sign something too?"

Mary and the nurse exchanged confused looks.

"Why would you need to sign anything?"

"I have no idea. The guard downstairs told me I had to sign her out."

"Well, she is not a child and she definitely can sign for herself. Maybe he thought you were Mary's husband or something."

Samuel and Mary shared concerned glances at each other but the moment was broken when the nurse took the papers from Mary's hand.

"Give me a moment to get you a wheelchair and then your friend can wheel you out of here."

The nurse exited the room quickly and left the two alone once again.

"You don't have to push my wheelchair. I could see you have issues walking."

"I'll be fine. Actually, I'll probably do better leaning against the wheelchair. As long as you hold on to my cane I think we will be fine."

Once the wheelchair arrived, Samuel helped Mary into it and placed her pocketbook on her lap. Taking his cane, she sat back and put her feet up on the footplate. They moved slowly towards the elevator as the nurses in the ward looked on with admiration. Love was special at any age but at their age it was something to be admired.

12

"Why didn't you park in the loading zone?"

"You are only supposed to park there for a few minutes. I didn't know how long I was going to be."

"Why didn't you just use the valet then? The hospital has free valet service so you don't have to walk to your car."

"Then they expect a tip…"

"Not more than a buck or two…"

"A buck here, a buck there. I have a public servant pension. You have to watch what you spend your money on."

"Do you re-use tea bags too?"

"I don't drink tea."

"That's right. Coffee, black. Is that it?"

"Pretty much. Along with some water that's all I drink."

"Where is your car?"

"It's a few rows back."

"Why didn't you park in the handicap spaces? Don't you have a placard?"

"Of course I have a placard. There were no open spaces."

"There's never enough handicap spots. I always have to park somewhere else when I come here. It's a hospital. You would think they would have enough handicap spaces."

At her remark, Samuel stopped the wheelchair and looked down at Mary. His opinion of the woman changed instantly.

"I…well, I completely agree Mary."

"Are we going to stand here on the sidewalk and wait for your car to come to us or are you going to go get it?"

"Do you want to wait here for me?"

"Well if I come with you, we will have to return the wheelchair anyway. Then what are we going to do?"

"Ok, ok. I'll go get the car. Give me my cane."

42

Mary handed Samuel his cane as he started to hobble his way down the sidewalk.

"Don't leave me sitting here all day."

"Why, are you in a hurry to go somewhere?"

"Well, it's almost lunch time. I would like to eat at some point today."

Samuel waved his hand back to her as if to calm her down. After taking a few steps he turned back to Mary and looked at her with fresh eyes.

"Speaking of food, what do you think of pigs in a blanket?"

Mary looked back at him like he was crazy.

"Pigs in a blanket? I haven't had seen those in years. They used to serve them at the Howard Johnson's down on the Post Road. Do you remember the place?"

"I do. Always got them there. Is that what you ate too?"

"No. Not me. Too much pancake for me. I always used to get the clam strips. They were my favorite."

Samuel turned around without another word. The smile that appeared on his face had not been there for years.

13

The dark suit was laid out on the bed with care. All parts were complete along with suit jacket, trousers, button down shirt and matching tie. On the floor next to the bed was a pair of black shoes and black socks. There was no need for a matching hat. Those accessories were never needed where these clothes would be worn.

The aroma coming from the kitchen was familiar. The sausages were sizzling in the pan as the thin pancakes were just starting to bubble up. A sure fire way to tell when to flip them. Once flipped, the sausages were placed on the edge of the pancakes and rolled inward. Together, the three pigs in a blanket were gathered up with the spatula and placed on a plate. It was always his favorite meal and he deserved it on his special day.

The coffee pot had completed its brewing cycle and the aroma joined the others as it traveled throughout the house. A meal bell was not needed to be rung. Breakfast was always served at the same time every day as it had been in all the years he had experienced in the military.

Stepping out of the shower, Samuel dried himself off and entered into his bedroom where his clothes had been laid out. Silently, he put himself together as he had since he was a small boy. After buttoning up his shirt, he tied his necktie with a double Windsor knot as his father had once taught him. The tie he wore at the post office was a clip on but he never forgot how to tie one. He continued to wear one every Sunday as he went to church. This special day was no different. He would wear a tie with his suit until the day he died.

Walking slowly with his cane, he entered the kitchen and sat down at his traditional seat. His coffee was poured into his favorite mug and the pigs in a blanket were placed down on the plate in front of him.

"What's the special occasion, my love?"

"You know damn well what day it is, you old fool."

"I just wanted to hear it from you Mary. After all, it's not every day a man turns 85."

44

Mary leaned over and kissed Samuel on the cheek. "Happy birthday dear husband. Now eat your breakfast. Father Derek has a special birthday greeting for you today at mass."

"Since it's my birthday, do I get an extra cup of coffee with breakfast?"

"Do you want to live until your next birthday?"

Samuel looked up at his bride of nearly three years. He still felt like every day was his honeymoon and his life now complete.

"Only as long as you are by my side my love. I never want to live another day without you."

Mary turned smiling as she returned to her stovetop. Who knew that the man of her dreams would be disguised as a grumpy old man who wanted another cup of coffee.

Mondays at
the Mall

6:30 AM

"Jan? Where the hell is my red tie? I have an important meeting this morning and want to wear it."

Mike Nichols stood in the middle of his walk-in closet and screamed at his wife. The possibility of her hearing one word clearly was highly unlikely. The closet was situated on the second floor of their five bedroom, 4000 square foot house. The plush carpeting in the bedroom had a dampening effect to begin with and the noise canceling insulation that cost a bundle during construction was not helping matters at all. The drawbacks of living in what some would classify as a mansion often outweighed the benefits. Holding the back-up yellow silk tie, he passed through the red mahogany door which swiveled slightly against the brass handles.

"For crying out loud, Jan. Did you hear what I said?"

"Whhhh…"

Her reply was barely audible as he moved closer to the broad spiral staircase overlooking the rotunda by the front door.

"I said…where the hell is my red tie?"

"Hold on a minute."

The sounds emanating from the vast kitchen downstairs indicated that she was on the move. Appearing in the middle of the rotunda, her heels echoed against the marble floor and bounced against the walls of the vast room. Dressed for the day already with her make-up and hair done, Jan was wearing her cooking apron to prevent any unwanted splatters during her meal preparation.

"What are you yelling about now, Michael? I was busy making breakfast."

"I said…where the hell is my red silk tie? I have an important meeting with the Japanese group this morning. You know how those pricks like red clothing."

"You sent it to the dry cleaners last week after you spilled your martini all over it at the country club. Not my fault you can't hold your liquor."

"Screw you, Jan. How long does it take to clean a damn tie?"

"The tie along with the rest of the dry cleaning was ready on Friday. You were too busy playing 18 holes to stop and pick them up before they closed, remember?"

"Fuck!!"

Looking up, Jan ignored his vulgar outburst.

"Why don't you just wear the yellow one? I see it in your hand from here."

"Those Japanese pricks think yellow is for cowards. Where is my other tie rack? I think I have another red one on there."

"Look in the guest bedroom closet. We moved some of your old suits and ties in there after Christmas last year."

"For crying out loud, Jan..."

The rest of his rant was muffled as he walked down the plush carpeted hallway towards the guest bedroom. Jan Nichols was glad she could no longer hear the hysterical rantings of her husband and his stupid tie. At age 52, her tolerance for her husband was waning. He was a few years older than her at age 55 which meant that he would reach retirement before she did. The thought of having such an uptight tyrant around 24/7 made her skin crawl. With any hope, his high stress job coupled with his short temper would provide for a lethal outcome. She could bear the thought of being a rich widow but knew that they would both be miserable if they survived to old age.

Walking back into the kitchen, Jan thought about her training as a Human Resources professional. She was highly educated and respected in her profession but her husband still viewed it as her "little job". Her salary was far from the almost seven figures that her husband brought in but it was important work. Where he played with his computers at his software company, she dealt with people. Real human beings that had real problems and not a series of numbers and symbols on a screen.

The advice she gave to individuals on a daily basis was far from the advice that she followed in her own life. She encouraged people in similar situations to take action. She advised people with children still living at home in their 20s to give them a little push towards the door. She encouraged women in verbally abusive relationships like her own to move on, more forward, and never look back. In reality, Jan Nichols was a hypocrite and she hated herself for it. She wished she had the courage to leave it all behind. She wished she could pack up her Porsche and drive away into the sunset. She could leave the money and the country club living behind. She could even deal with the scorn from her only son who still had a cushy place to live in the in-law apartment off the kitchen even though he was 25. What she couldn't leave behind was the house itself.

They had purchased the house ten years ago when her son, Mitch was just a freshman in high school. He was bullied because of his parent's wealth in an otherwise middle-class area. The move at the time was simply motivated by the desire to be around like-minded families that shared a desire for the finer things in life. For Jan, the house became a mecca of all the things she wanted growing up.

She remembered sitting for hours at a time playing with her doll house. She dreamed of how she would decorate each room and make each scene worthy to be in a magazine. The wall colors, the linen, the carpeting and even the accessories were idealized long before she stepped foot into the real deal. When Michael told her that he could care less about how she decorated the house, she had the open runway. When he told her simply not to embarrass him when he had clients over, she took it as a personal challenge.

The transformation from the previous owner to her own personal vision took almost three years. She had gone room to room and adorned every inch of her palace. Looking outward, she took great care to design and accent even the pool and patio areas. If her husband hadn't been so uptight about the garage and his computer part storage area, she would probably have decorated that filthy hole as well. The house was her monument and it was a testimonial to every moment she put into her fake marriage. It was spotless on the outside and in all the social pages but like the basement, it had dark hidden places as well.

The marriage of Michael and Jan Nichols had been something out of a fairy tale for the past 27 years. Jan grew up in a poor neighborhood with a poor family that struggled to simply put food on the table. Her beauty and sensibilities put her in the right places at the right times to meet the right people and she was able to scrape by. For Michael, his family was somewhat middle-class but his fascination with the budding world of computers and electronics made him an outcast socially. He never met the right people at any time and pretty much kept to himself through all of grade school. When the two of them attended the same college and took the same core math class as freshmen, he found himself finally in the right place to meet the right woman at the right time.

During those college years, they learned to use each other to gain footing. When she was pledging to be part of an elite sorority, Michael hacked into the group's computer voting matrix to make her a top entry. When he needed to impress his fellow IT nerds with not only a female escort to a banquet, he brought a beautiful sorority girl with him. His status among the other computer geeks catapulted him to elite status. Together, they graduated with top honors and had a foothold socially on campus.

The real world endeavors began somewhat like their initial paths. Jan used her degree in Sociology to work with under-privileged families in a public social-worker position. Michael entered a position as a video game software specialist in a booming gaming environment. When one of his games sold like wildfire, his value as a programmer went to the highest bidder. Within just a few years of graduating college, he landed a six figure income and took it upon himself to bring along his social worker girlfriend to his new lifestyle. When discussions about her profession became an embarrassment at work social functions, Michael drew the line. He would marry her and give her his name with newfound wealth but in return she would quit her job dealing with such low life people. She sold her soul to the devil himself and they were married soon thereafter.

When Jan became pregnant with Mitch, her husband flashed her around like a balloon in the Macy's Thanksgiving Day parade. He wanted no part of her morning sickness or aches and pains. He once again just wanted his status to be raised as the husband of a beautiful woman that was soon to give birth to his heir. In the pageantry after the birth, he often forgot to mention his wife and only focused on the fact that he, Mike Nichols, king of the nerds, now had a son. She of course rounded out the family photos as Michael held his son adoringly in his arms.

The years that followed passed by with a blur. Michael was always away on some IT business as Jan stayed at home and cared for their son. When he was home, he insisted on silence. When his child cried out for whatever reason, he was passed along to his mother. His father could not be bothered with such things and found the pains of raising a child a nuisance.

Once Mitch was old enough to go to school, Jan sighed relief. She had free time when she wasn't playing the adoring wife or having to care for their child 24/7. She was finally able to sharpen the skills she learned in college and use them in part time work. Her time away from home was allowed for two reasons. The first being that she was working in the Human Resources department of a prestigious law firm which did not cause her husband any embarrassment. The second and more pertinent matter was that it did not affect Mike Nichols in any way. His wife left for work after he did and was there when he got home. The child was still being cared for, from what he could see, and he did not have to be annoyed by the wife or offspring when he was trying to unwind. As long as she was still there to pose for the occasional photo, he cared less how she spent her time.

The new house balanced well with Jan's part-time work but soon that balance was lost when the house was complete. Three years into the transformation, Mitch went off to college and Jan had no more home projects left to occupy her free time. With her husband out of town more than he was at home, the part-time role at the law firm was not enough. When a full-time position came up that was more of a challenge to her in the same department, she jumped at the chance. Voicing her interest was enough to secure the position but she failed to get the approval from the man of the house. That argument seemed to linger for months into her new role and dampened her excitement for it from the start.

A vast empty house was not an environment for a marriage estranged. With five bedrooms and their son off to college, there was no need for them to share a bed any longer. When Michael returned from one of his many business trips to the orient, he found his clothing moved to the guest bedroom. With his growing distaste for his wife's independence, he happily ventured into his new room on the other side of the house. He finally had the best of all worlds. He shared a house but not a bedroom. He shared photos without the depth of love. He shared marriage without the depth of intimacy.

Jan thought back on those initial days of freedom with anxiety. She kept wondering when her husband's anger would get the best of him and he would strike out. Every day that passed they argued more and more. Peace of mind and spirit were only achieved when they were at work. The pressures of each of their jobs was nothing compared to the internal pressures of the Nichols' household. When the tension in the house had climbed to a fevered pitch, it was their son that provided the cooling effect.

Mitch returned home from college with no aspirations or goals for the future but simply to move back to the house he had left behind. He had grown accustomed to a life full of parties and little responsibility and he did not want to give it up. He returned home to a strange new world where his mother and father worked all the time and slept in separate bedrooms. The two of them challenged each other in attempts to spend time with him alone and he drank it all in like a Saturday night keg party at the fraternity house he just moved from. Like his father, he reveled in the new house arrangements and the three of them found a healthy rhythm in their own private bubbles.

"Is the damn breakfast ready yet? I don't want to be late to this meeting."

Jan was so lost in her memory lane that she almost burnt the eggs and bacon in front of her. Snapping out of her dream-like state, she pulled out a plate from the cupboard and placed her husband's breakfast on it. Taking the rye toast from the toaster, she knew better than to add butter to it. Like his heart, her husband preferred his toast cold. She cut the pieces in half triangles, plated them, and set it down on Michael's place setting.

"Is there coffee or am I just swallowing my spit?"

Jan thought for a moment that she should just pour it over his head and let the French press grounds get caught up in his finely greased hair. Instead, she placed the china cup and saucer in front of Michael and took a seat opposite him. Placing her tea bag in her own cup, she poured hot water over if and let it steep. Turning her attention to the grapefruit in front of her, she buried her spoon in its endocarp. Thankful for the leveling effect, Jan smiled when her son lumbered into the kitchen.

"Morning Mom. Morning Dad. Having a nice breakfast, I see."

"Mitch. Can you for once put on some clothes before coming downstairs? No one wants to see your stained t-shirt."

"That's the whole point, Dad. If I wear this out anywhere, the villagers will stone me."

Jan chuckled silently. She did not want to set Michael off this morning.

"Funny. Very funny, young man. You are 25 years old. Isn't it time you stop dressing and acting like a teenager?"

"For crying out loud, Dad. Let me have some coffee before you start in with me. Besides, don't you have some big meeting this morning?"

Mitch poured himself a cup of coffee and sat down between his parents. His father shoveled his food like it was his last meal and his mother pecked away at her grapefruit lost in her own little world.

"Most mornings I would enjoy the silence the two of you share but I need a favor from one of you."

"Of course. I should have known. You need more money. You know it doesn't grow on trees, Mitch. You can..."

"Woah there, Daddyo. I didn't say anything about money. I was just wondering if I could borrow one of your cars this morning."

"What's wrong with your own car?"

"Nothing, Dad. My Toyota is running fine. It's just that I have a job interview this morning and I wanted to..."

"Wait. You have a job interview? For what? Where? Why is this the first I am hearing of this? Who is it with?"

"Not a big deal, Dad and not officially a job interview."

"Oh." His father immediately lost interest and went back to devouring his breakfast.

"So what is the meeting then, Mitch?"

His mother always had the softer approach.

"I'm having a morning breakfast meeting with an Ad Executive downtown. It's at an outside café and I didn't want to pull up in my car. I was thinking I would give a much better impression if I pulled up in one of your cars."

"So you think a Porsche will seal the deal? Is that it Mitch?"

"Yes, Dad. Something I learned from you. All that matters is what people think. It doesn't matter what you actually drive; if they think you drive a Porsche you gain respect."

"At least you learned something at that college. I was beginning to think it was just a waste of money."

"You always thought it was a waste of money. So, is that it? Can I use your Porsche?"

"Not me." His father wiped his mouth with his napkin and drank down his coffee quickly. "I need mine today for the same reason. I can't have those Japanese clients thinking I drive a kid's car."

"Isn't Toyota a Japanese car?"

"It was at one time and they aren't too happy that it is an American car now. Besides, I have to go. Ask your mother to use hers."

Without waiting for a response, Mike Nichols left the breakfast table as quickly as he had arrived. There were no heartfelt goodbyes; not even a wave of the hand. If not for the front door closing as he exited, his wife and son would not be certain that he left.

"Bye, Dad. Thanks for stopping by."

"It's ok, Mitch. That's just his way."

"Yes. I know. It's always his way. Why do you put up with it Mom?"

Jan picked at her grapefruit before answering.

"Are you happy living here, Mitch?"

"Oh, don't start with me too, Mom."

"That's not what I mean. Isn't this house wonderful? Isn't this neighborhood wonderful? Aren't you happy to be able to borrow a Porsche every now and then? Would you be happy being poor? I grew up poor, Mitch. It stinks."

"So that's why you put up with him? Because you don't want to live anywhere else?"

Jan took a sip of her tea quietly. She ignored her son's question and asked one of her own.

"How long do you need the car for?"

Mitch was happy to move the conversation along. He didn't get up early very often and he definitely did not want to waste the opportunity.

"It's a breakfast meeting Mom. I can bring it back in a couple hours if you need it. Otherwise, you can just take my car this morning. You are ok with that right? You like to drive my car."

His mother chuckled. "We both know which car I prefer to drive but that is fine. Is there at least gas in your car or do I need to fill it up too?"

"Well..."

"No need to answer. Now go get yourself ready for your big breakfast meeting and let me enjoy my breakfast in peace."

Mitch got up and kissed his mother on her cheek. He thought he had gotten the best end of the deal but the smile on her face indicated she had a much better day planned.

7:00 AM

The kitchen door opened abruptly startling the woman and her children. Looking to the door, they broke out in smiles.

"You're home early Frank. Did something happen?"

"Nice to see you too, June."

"Yea. It's nice to see you home early. I just meant...."

"Don't worry. I didn't get fired or anything like that. We just ran out of things to stock. The second shipment never came in yesterday. Something about a trucker strike out west. They were not driving on weekends or something like that. Anyway, we processed everything we had on the line so they let us cut out early."

June Morris turned away towards the children. They both seemed content to eat their breakfast without caring about their parent's squabble. Turning back, she ventured into dangerous territory.

"Did they pay you for the full shift or were you docked because you left early?"

Frank slammed his lunch pail on the counter. The children froze in fear of the upcoming battle.

"Why must it always be about money, June? Don't I work enough? I bartend six nights a week with every uptight cheap drunk sitting at my bar. When I am done there, I stock shelves like a teenager on third shift just to bring home some extra money in a regular paycheck on top of my tips. I'm sorry I have to sleep every once in a while or I would get a third job too. I work until I am ready to drop and you worry when I shorten my shift by an hour or two so I can come home and see my kids when they are both awake. I'm sorry if my check will be short $20 because a truck didn't show up but it's not my damn fault."

June felt the words sting but decided to let them go. Her husband was obviously tired and sparring with him as they passed in the night would not benefit anyone.

"Are you hungry? Do you want me to cook you dinner?"

"Looks like you just finished cooking breakfast. I'll just have some of this. No need to cook something different. Besides, we wouldn't want it to go to waste."

56

"There's biscuits and gravy with some brown and serve sausages. The scrambled eggs might be cold but I can heat them up if you want. You can make a nice bowl out of it."

"The biscuits are real good daddy."

"That's great kiddo. Eat up so you can be big and strong."

"Just like you, Daddy?"

"Just like me. But daddy doesn't feel very strong at the moment. Daddy just feels tired."

The Morris family had two children. Kate was the older daughter and her younger brother was named Billy.

"I have a baseball game tomorrow daddy. Are you gonna come?"

Frank and June exchanges glances. It was yet another bone of contention between them. Working two jobs and sleeping in between meant that there was not much time for anything else. They both knew if Frank came to the game he would have to cut his sleep time considerably.

"I'm gonna try Billy. Let me see how I feel tomorrow."

"Ok."

Billy was truly hopeful but his sister simply rolled her eyes. She knew about her father's empty promises. She had spent far too many moments hoping her father would come to her dance recital, play, or girl scout function. She knew that dad meant well but even if he did show up, he would be too tired and just fall asleep in the middle of it. The children loved their father but would not know for decades the sacrifices he had made to keep a roof over their head and Converse all-stars on their feet.

Frank Morris walked over to the stove and started to make himself a plate. He opened up the cupboard above the stove and pulled out the ceramic canister. With clear awareness that he was being watched, he reached into his pocket and pulled out the cash tips from the night before. He knew that his wife would count the money as soon as she had the chance and then scrutinize the amount that was in there. Placing the cover on the canister, he returned it to its sacred place above the stove. He often wondered how they had fallen into the routine to hide the money there. The children were too young to be picking out a few bills for beer runs and any self-respecting thief would check the kitchen for hidden money first. Frank took a small amount of solace knowing that the money would not be in there for long.

The Morris family was not always strapped for cash and it often confused both Frank and June how they were now. Back in the day, when they were young and starting out, they both smoked like chimneys. They would go thru a few cartons of cigarettes a week. That, combined with their liquor money, was a large chunk of their limited incomes. June stopped smoking when she got pregnant with their first child and never started up again. For Frank the habit ran dry when it became a choice between cigarettes and food. He figured he had no right smoking up his money when his family was living on Ramen noodles and various canned vegetables to choke them down with.

For Frank, it was never about being lazy when it came to jobs. He had held a variety of different careers over the years and could not be proud of any of them. Since he never finished community college, he seemed to be destined to work an endless stream of dead-end jobs. He left one for another in search of higher wages and better hours. Seeing that his current jobs had him working 2nd and 3rd shifts, he figured the road to success was littered with garbage.

His wife was a different matter altogether. June had worked in the same job for the past 13 years of their marriage. As a daytime cook at a convalescent home, she was literally the epitome of a dead end job. She cooked meals for the sick and dying until they could not eat any more. Each day she reviewed the food order charts. When she no longer had to prepare the strained carrots or peas for Mrs. Jones, she knew that Mrs. Jones was no longer among the land of the living.

They met appropriately at a bar. He was throwing darts in a league and she was drinking with a friend. After several shots of tequila, she challenged him to a game. Three corks later, she overcame her point deficit and sealed the deal with a kiss. The rest was history. From that night forward, they were never apart.

The early years were full of fun and excitement but soon enough the married life kicked in and June grew bored. Her rare nights out with her husband transformed to include many nights out with her friends. She soon was having much more fun with them than the occasional date night with Frank. When the inevitable occurred and she became pregnant, her partying days were over and they both slid into misery together.

June worked until the day she gave birth to Kate. To those around her she appeared to be holding on to her old life until the very last minute before entering motherhood. Frank prepared the nursery and stocked it with every possible need without interference from the new mother. She didn't care to be bothered by such things as the child would certainly put a damper on not only her social life but her life overall.

The first year of Kate's life and her impact on the Morris marriage resembled much like the un-mooring of a boat from its marina anchor. There was not a storm surge or even a giant wave that made the boat go about, but simply the gentle current that flowed about. Frank and June naturally grew apart as the responsibilities of parenthood set the water adrift.

With June out of work, Frank picked up a second job to bridge the wage gap in the household. It was necessity at first but then became common place as time ensued. Even when his wife returned to the work place, he was expected to keep the balance of two jobs at all times. When one would inevitably go badly, he would have the other to fall back on. The same rhythm established itself with the marriage.

Frank and June became like two ships that pass in the night. Mother worked the day shift and returned home only to pass the baton off with father that worked second and third shift. The fact the Billy was ever conceived was a miracle in itself. There are certain basics to the human act of child making that require the mother and the father to be in the same bed at the same time. If not for a drunken holiday party with a babysitter in house, tab A may never have found slot B again.

When the voices of two children echoed through the walls of their small home, the silence between the parents became deafening. There were passing conversations of bills and household amenities. There were notes about child feeding schedules and the obligatory bath schedules but never a note about love. Frank never wrote that he missed June and June never told Frank that she loved him. They created a life of family without a family of love.

"I guess you were hungry."

Frank looked down at his bowl and realized he had eaten everything while he was lost in thought about his lonely marriage.

"Yea. I guess I was."

June busied herself with clearing the dishes from the table as the children grew restless and ready to start their school day.

"Can we go now, mom?"

"Go get ready for school. I'll drop you at the bus stop on my way to work."

"That's ok. I can walk them up."

"Are you sure? I drop them off every day. It's not a problem."

Frank looked up at his wife. He knew the jab was intentional but he let it pass. He was looking forward to walking with the kids.

"It's all good. I'm home early so might as well take advantage of it. Besides. I can't remember the last time I walked the kids to their bus stop."

"Neither can I, Frank. Neither can I."

7:20 AM

Jan was still seated at the breakfast table when her son came bounding into the room. He was wearing a polo shirt tucked into his khaki slacks with a pair of Dockers on his feet. Mitch looked more suited for a day out on his yacht than a job interview.

"I thought you had a job interview? Are you sure you are not heading out for a date? I don't want you taking the Porsche if you are being dishonest."

Mitch simply looked at his mother for a second with incredulity.

"Sometimes I think Dad influences you a little too much. He has turned you into skeptic, Mom. I told you, it is an informal breakfast meeting. I don't want to appear too aggressive or needy. I thought this outfit was more along the *business casual* umbrella of things."

Jan looked her son up and down from head to toe and then smiled back at him. "I'm sorry, Mitch. You look terrific. You are probably right. Being married to your father for so long has not had a great effect on me."

Mitch walked over to the refrigerator, opened it and pulled out the orange juice. Taking out a juice glass, he poured himself a drink and turned back to his mother.

"I wouldn't say that, Mom. I think you have done quite well pulling away from the shadow of Dad. He hates that you have a good career and don't need to wait on him hand and foot to be happy. You keep doing you and ignore his negativity and narcissism."

Jan looked up from her tea. "Do you think your father is a narcissist?"

Mitch broke out in laughter. "Of course I do. He is the textbook definition of one. He wants to the world to not see it but we know better. Why? Don't you think so too?"

It was Jan's turn to break out in laughter. "Michael Nichols has been a narcissist his whole life. It is part of his natural charm. If he thinks even for a second that he fools anyone into believing otherwise he must also believe in Santa Clause."

"Mom? Are you saying Santa Clause isn't real? Are you really telling your only child not to believe in Kris Kringle?"

Both mother and son shared the laugh together.

"I love you Mitch. I really do. Maybe I don't tell you enough but I really do."

"I know you do, Mom and it's still better than Dad. He never tells me."

Jan shook her head and felt like crying. At least her son felt her love.

"You better get out of here before I start crying. I put the keys for the Porsche by the door. Be careful with it. That car is my baby."

"I thought I was your only baby, Mom?"

"Well, if you wreck that car neither one of us will have to worry about it. Your father will kill both of us. You for crashing the car and me for letting you drive it. Just take it and be careful."

"Sounds good Mom."

Mitch bent over and kissed his mother on her forehead bringing a smile to her face. Sometimes her son could be so sweet.

"Hey, before you go. Did you forget something?"

Mitch stopped in mid stride and looked back at his mom. "What? Do you want a hug too? I've got to go Mom."

Laughing, Jan simply shook her head. "No, Mitch. Not a hug. But I do need your car keys if we are switching cars."

"Oh. Sorry Mom. I almost forgot."

Reaching into his pocket he brought out the keyring and placed them on the counter.

"Ok. Here you go. I put them right next to your purse. What time did you need to switch back?"

Jan Nichols smiled liked the Cheshire cat. "No hurry. I can find ways to occupy my time today. Just make sure you are home and the car is in the garage before your father gets home."

Walking away shaking his head, Mitch got the last laugh. "No need for concern there, Mom. The way Dad comes and goes these days we may not see him before it is time for bed. Even then, who knows."

Jan sat backed and smiled. Her day was going splendidly already. Father and son off in different directions and she was left to her own devices. Time to plan her own excursion.

8:00 AM

"Dad, can I come to work with you sometime?"

Father, son and daughter walked down the sidewalk from the house toward the bus stop that was two blocks down.

"I'm sorry, Billy. Daddy works at night while you are sleeping. You know that. Besides, it's pretty boring. A truck pulls up to the dock and we offload the boxes."

"Where do you put the boxes when they come off the truck Dad?"

"It depends, Kate. Sometimes we put them right onto these carts with wheels on them called U-boats. Other times we put them on wooden things called pallets."

"Can you go on the water in the U-boats, Daddy?"

Frank started to laugh. "No, kiddo. They are not that kind of boat. They don't float on water. They are on wheels instead."

"Then why do they call them boats?"

Frank had to think for a minute before answering. "I guess it's because they float on the ground kind of like a boat floats on the water."

The two children tried to picture a boat floating on the road instead of the water. The three of them started to chuckle at the thought of it.

"So why are you two so interested in dad's job today?"

The two children looked at each other without really having an answer. They both shrugged as they continued to walk.

"What about the drinking job, Daddy. Can I come to that one?"

Frank burst out laughing. He never thought of his bartending job as the *drinking job* but he guessed that's exactly what it was. Had to love the mind of a child.

"Not that one either, Billy. That one really is just for adults only. Kids aren't allowed to be around there."

"What do they do there?"

Kate had more formulated questions but they were still from a child point of view.

"Well. People come and sit at my bar. They ask for drinks and I make them.

Sometimes they talk to me. Sometimes they talk to each other. Sometimes they just sit there and watch TV. When they finish drinking, they get up and leave."

"Sounds pretty boring, Daddy."

Frank laugh again. "It is most of the time. Sometimes there is a game on TV so the people get loud and yell at the TV."

"Like you do, Daddy?"

"Yes, Kate. Just like me sometimes."

The three of them came to the corner, looked both ways and then crossed the street all holding hands. When they arrived at the other side of the street, the conversation flipped and it was time for Dad to ask the questions.

"Are you excited for your game, Billy?"

"Yes. I always like when we play. I wish you could be there, though."

"I'm sure you will do great. How about you Kate? Anything fun at school this week? Maybe in science class? I always loved that when I was your age."

"We are going to dissect frogs next week. Did you like doing that?"

Frank shrugged. "It was ok. I wasn't thrilled about the smell. I liked mixing things in chemistry class the best, though."

"Maybe you can come to class one day with me, Dad."

"Does Mom go to school with you at all?"

"Sometimes. When there is a meeting or something."

"Oh, yea. I guess she does that."

"You and mom don't get to spend a lot of time together do you? Between your work and her work, it's usually just one of you home. Do you like that, Dad?"

Frank simply looked at his daughter as they approached the bus stop.

"You are pretty smart for your age, Kate. Did you know that?"

"That's what my teachers tell me. Mom doesn't think I'm too smart though. She is always telling me I have to study."

"Me too."

"That's just your mother wanting you both to stay smart. If you stop studying, you get like Dad. You just go to work. Neither one is fun."

"Don't you like to have fun, Daddy?"

"Of course I do, Billy. Of course I do. But for now, your bus is here. Go have fun in school while you still can."

"Are you going to stay home and have fun, Daddy?"

Frank gave both his children a hug and a kiss and before answering them. They both turned to get on the bus as their father smiled broadly.

"I'm sure gonna try. I have all day to have fun."

The children boarded the bus thinking their dad was going to stay at home and play video games or do something fun by himself. The fun he was thinking of was a totally different kind of game altogether.

8:30 AM

Text 1: *I have a delivery for you.*
Text 2: *I have been waiting for my package.*
Text 1: *Delivery pending for 10am.*
Text 2: *10am will be perfect.*
Text 1: *North Entrance?*
Text 2: *Confirmed.*

10:00 AM

The Sandlewood Mall was located on the outskirts of the city. A regional mall whose heyday had come and gone, it was mostly inhabited by independent retailers as opposed to the National names occupying prime real estate in power centers across the country. With traffic on the decline, mall operating hours had been reduced from the typical 9am opening time to opening at 10am during the week. The Monday morning traffic was at the lowest point of the week.

Spread out among the 200-acre parcel, the Sandlewood Mall had five main entrances. One from each point on the compass dial and one directly off the food court in the center of the mall. All mall employees were required to use the food court entrance parking and access the building via the utility corridor during pre-opening hours. That requirement left the North, South, East and West parking areas open for guests. The North area was the most remote and was surrounded by trees that blocked visibility from the main road.

The blue mini-van came around the bend in the perimeter road and entered the deserted parking area via the access point designated by the white lines. Following a loop of the area, the van came to rest in the back row under the shadow of the surrounding trees. Backing into the parking space, the driver had full visibility to any cars approaching the area.

Approaching from the other direction, the white Toyota circled the perimeter road and followed a similar path to ensure they were not being followed. The car circumvented a wider loop in the parking area and pulled up along-side the van. Once parked, the engine idled for several minutes before the driver shut the engine off. Both drivers remained in their vehicles, counting down the ten-minute pre-arranged wait time before exiting. Opening their doors, they both stepped out into the mid-morning air and looked over at each other. The smiles were immediate but their eyes remained cautious. Moving around to the rear of the van by the tree line, the two approached each other.

"Why do you have Mitch's car?"

"He needed to use the Porsche this morning."

"I thought it was someone else, I almost drove away."

"Who did you think it was? This mall is deserted at this hour. It's a miracle they are still in business. I'm sure there are more employee cars than shoppers."

"I don't know. I was pretty sure that it was your son's car but we can't be too careful. What if your husband borrowed his car?"

"What if your wife had your car?"

"I am just trying to be careful. We...."

"Are we going to stand here and play the *what if* game or are you going to kiss me? I have waited all week long just to feel your lips."

Frank Morris smiled broadly and set his fears aside. With great relief, he pulled Jan Nichols into his arms and kissed her passionately under the shade of the oak trees.

10:30 AM

The walking thoughts always came back to the same sequence of events. Over and over, the pair replayed the steps that lead them down this journey for the last two years. It was not always Mondays at the Sandlewood Mall. That evolved as a need for the two of them over time. They needed some continuity in their otherwise whirlwind romance. They had created different rendezvous in locations all over the city. Sometimes they ate lunch in the park. Other times they walked hand in hand at the zoo. They liked to fool themselves into thinking they were a normal couple and the fact of the matter was that they were fugitives of the heart.

Both lovers found it hard to believe they met two years prior. A chance meeting that changed their destiny; at least in the short-term timeline. That day was like any other in the real world of adults. Jan Nichols had a terrible day at work and she was not looking forward to making it worse by going home to her husband. Like many distraught individuals, she sought out a lonely bar stool in a dark, quiet bar, where she could be alone with her thoughts and apply mental salve to her wounds.

Like most changes in the avenues of life, Jan found the Owl's Nest Bar because of a wrong turn. She was not paying attention to her GPS as she was lost in a recap of her day. By the time she thought to take the corrective action on the electronic device, she was more frustrated than ever. As she turned her car around to avoid the illegal U-turn, she found herself right in front of the decorative front entrance. The fact that a large ceramic owl was perched on a nest beside a fake tree was clearly an indication that she was definitely lost in the woods of her mind. Perhaps a wise old owl could get to the center of her issues and not just tell her how to get to the center of a lollipop. Parking her high caliber car at the well-lit curb, she exited and walked right into the next chapter of her life.

The mid-week crowd was light and provided the perfect atmosphere Jan was seeking. The bar was evidently a sports bar but devoid of an active game, the televisions were tuned to a quiet golf event. The sparse patrons who sat around the dark room barely noticed the little white balls traveling the greens on the golf channel. They all seemed engrossed in their own private dilemmas which served Jan just fine. Taking a corner seat in the bar away from the view of the televisions, she had a bird's eye view of all the people coming and going.

Patiently waiting for service, she began to wonder who was tending bar. There was only one cocktail waitress and she was slowly walking from table to table without urgency. After taking a refill order from one couple, she approached the service bar area and waited for the bartender to fill her ticket. Both the waitress and Jan were pleasantly surprised when Frank Morris exited the back storeroom carrying a case of beer.

At first glance, Jan was simply happy to know that she would soon have a glass of wine in her hand. The bartender took care of filling the beer order by grabbing two long necks and handing them to the server as she walked away back into her world. Turning his attention to the few people sitting on stools, he glanced at the new addition in the corner and smiled at his luck. Even if it was a slow night he might have an attractive woman to look at as the clock ticked by.

"Sorry about that. I was in the back getting some beer. What can I get for you this evening?"

Jan watched in a trance as the bartender placed a bar napkin in front of her place setting. She had a noticeable delay in her response which prompted an eyebrow raise from the man behind the bar.

"I'm sorry. It's been a day. You caught me deep in thought. I'll take a glass of Pinot Grigio if you have it."

"Not a problem at all. It will just take a minute while I open a new bottle."

As the bartender walked away, Jan could not help but watch him. He was the antithesis of her husband. Instead of a tight military haircut like Michael wore, the bartender had long wavy, curly hair. Where Michael had a smooth clean shave every minute of the day, this man had a scruffy beard that sent tingles to her as she observed. The clincher were the blue jeans that adorned his back side very well. She could not take her eyes off of the way it hugged his buttocks. Her husband would never be caught dead in anything other than designer slacks.

"Would you like something to snack on?"

Jan came out of her illicit thoughts in a snap.

"Excuse me?"

"I'm sorry. You were off in thought again. I was asking if you wanted some snacks. I have pretzels and popcorn. Would like any?"

"Yea. That sounds great. Popcorn might be a bit too much with the wine so let's go with a bowl of pretzels."

"Sure thing."

Frank Morris turned and walked over to the other side of the bar. Bending over, he scooped a wooden bowl full of pretzels and walked back. Jan never took her eyes off of him.

"Here you go."

"Thank you. Believe it or not, that's exactly the simple meal I need at the moment."

"I wouldn't say a bowl of pretzels are a meal but sure, why not. Sometimes I am good with bowl of popcorn to fill the gap."

"Popcorn is definitely in the comfort food group. I just hate to pick the kernels out of my teeth. They never seem to end."

Frank turned smiling to do a visual check on his other bar patrons but quickly surmised that everyone was set. He was free to relax for a moment. Throwing his bar towel over his shoulder, he turned back to the beauty at the end of the bar.

"My name is Frank, by the way. Welcome to the Owl's Nest. I haven't seen you in here before."

"Hello, Frank. Yes. This is my first time here. Just wanted a glass of wine before I went home and I happened to drive by on a wrong turn."

"Was it that kind of day?"

"You have no idea."

The cocktail waitress cleared her throat in a subtle attempt to get Frank's attention. He excused himself from his conversation and walked back to the service area of the bar. After reading the drink order, he set the process in motion. Scooping ice into the blender, he added the tequila, triple sec and lime juice, placed the cover on the blender and started the ice in motion. As the frozen mixture was churning, he turned to salt the margarita glasses and caught the stare from across the bar. His new bar guest had not taken her eyes off of him. Smiling, he turned with the salted rims and placed the glasses on the counter. Stopping the blender, he poured the mixture into the two glasses and spooned out the remainder. Finishing off the presentation, he added two slices of lime to the rim and set them on the tray. As the drinks were whisked away, he took a second to look around and wipe his hands before turning his attention back to the other side of the bar. Frank walked slowly towards his bar guest as she was picking up a pretzel.

"Should I just call you pretzel lady or do you have an actual name?"

Jan smiled. The flirting had begun. Having been in a loveless marriage for so long she had actually forgotten what it was like. Being a Human Resources manager at a law firm, there were not many people who even looked at her twice let alone were bold enough to flirt. She felt her cheeks go warm and knew that it wasn't due to the small amount of wine she was consuming.

"You can call me Jan."

"Is that short for January or something in a warmer month?"

Jan laughed demurely. Taking a pause for the cause, she brought the pretzel to her mouth and used her tongue to hook the loop of the pretzel into her month. Frank was mesmerized. After what seemed like an eternity, she answered him with a smile on her face.

"Nope. Just Jan. Not Feb, April or June. Just Jan."

The pair shared a comfortable laugh and simply gazed at each other; not knowing where to take the conversation next. Seeking to break the tension, Jan finished off her glass of wine and placed it on top of the bar. Pushing it forward, she looked down at the glass and then back at her bartender. Taking the non-verbal, cue, he picked up the glass and turned to fill it. The pair used the brief moment to step back and regroup. When he returned with the second glass of wine, the flirtation had cooled slightly.

"How was your day so stressful if you don't mind me asking?"

Jan took the glass and slowly took a drink from it. She knew that she was at a fork in the road and needed to proceed carefully. In her professional work, she was well aware of that moment when people crossed the line. Most times it was without intent but it was still a step over the line. She carefully toed the line and smiled back at the handsome man in front of her.

"Are you a therapist as well as a bartender?"

"It kind of comes with the territory. People come to a bar to talk to their bartender because he is less judgmental than their Priest and the session costs a lot less than their psychiatrist. Besides, here at the bar we have pretzels and wine."

Smiling, Frank took a pretzel out of the bowl and placed it in his mouth. They were now in a tennis match of sorts and he had just served the volley to his opponent. It was up to her to return the serve or let it go out of bounds. She picked up the virtual ball and set the game in motion

"Ok fair enough. I'll play. It was a day battling wits with unarmed people. Without going into detail, it was a day filled with good people making bad decisions. Some of them realized their actions were bad a little too late."

Chuckling, Frank responded warmly. "Well, that pretty much sums up most of the people that sit at my bar. Bad decisions are kind of their mantra. Without them, there would be nothing to drink about. Heck, half of the time the liquor is the bad decision in and of itself. Ipso facto; the worst the decision, the better for my business."

"I guess I never thought of it that way. You make a good case. Do you have special training as a lawyer as well?"

"No, just a long history of bad decisions. I'm sort of an expert in that area."

"Order."

The cocktail waitress had returned to the side of the bar and Frank once again excused himself to go make the drinks on her order. Jan looked on at a distance while sipping her wine. Her night had made a turn in a much different direction than she intended when she left work. She had stopped for a quiet drink to forget about the long day she had before encountering a long night evading her husband. Her detour had brought on new possibilities. The bartender finished up the round of drinks and placed them on the server's tray. Without checking on his other guests at the bar, he returned to the conversation at hand.

"Now where were we?"

"You were telling me about your history of bad decisions."

"Oh that's not just a history. That is past, present and future. I'm pretty much on the bad decision express."

Jan smiled coyly. "Are you making any bad decisions tonight?"

Frank returned the smile. "I certainly hope so but it remains to be seen. The night is young and wine is still chilling."

Jan finished her second glass and pushed it forward. "In that case, let's keep pouring and see what bad decisions we can make together."

11:00 AM

"Good morning, Mr. Smith. How are you today?"

"Hello, Henry. Are we having a sale today?"

"Just our usual stuff. Nothing you and the Mrs. haven't seen before."

The couple had been roaming the mall every Monday for the past year. All the people that worked in the shops knew them by name along with their buying preferences. Mrs. Smith was always impeccably dressed and had an eye for the finer things. Mr. Smith was more of a blue collar man and while he entertained his "wife" during their shopping trips, he rarely pulled out his wallet to purchase anything. They were window dressing like the mannequins except the latter were real. Everything this couple portrayed was straight out of a fairy tale.

"Well, as you know, Henry. My wife loves her candles and the finer ones at that. Do you have any of the three wick or the wooden candles on sale? Maybe you could show her those."

"I would be happy to. Right this way Mrs. Smith."

Jan Nichols followed the salesman towards the other side of the store as Frank Morris stood his usual bodyguard stance towards the front of the store. They had been so careful for the past two years and were not about to slip up now. The mall was far away from each of their own neighborhood malls that there was little chance they would be spotted but they were still very much on guard. They took turns *on the lookout* with Jan having more of a keen eye than her make-believe husband. Frank had little notoriety in the city and blended in like any other blue collar worker. It was always possible that someone who once sat at his bar would stumble across his path but his patrons neither knew if he was married or single, living on this side of town or the other. All they knew was that he was a cool guy that poured them drinks when they were thirsty.

Jan, on the other hand, took great lengths not to be recognized. When they were out walking the mall or sitting in the food court, she wore large dark glasses to prevent anyone from noticing her. When they went into the different retail stores, she removed the glasses but turned her hair to the other shoulder and often wore hats. It would be difficult for someone to spot her but given the number of social circles she enjoyed in association with her *real* husband, it was always a possibility.

The pair had a backstory worked out and perfected over the year. If anyone should recognize Jan, she was escorting a client from the firm she worked at. Since it was a highly regarded lawyer's office, no one would dare question and would respect the lawyer-client confidentiality. If it was Frank that would be recognized, Jan would become a distant relative of the owner of the bar he worked at. As a favor to the boss, he offered to drive the relative to the mall. It was more of a risk than Jan's cover story but luckily they never had to use either one. If they had, their time at the Sandlewood Mall would come to an end and they would find a new environment to have their rendezvous.

"What do you think of this scent?"

Jan had returned with the salesperson with several candle jars in tow.

"Your wife has exquisite taste, Mr. Smith. She picked out some of our new scents that have not yet been appreciated by many."

Squeezing Jan's hand with a silent gesture of conversation, Frank smiled.

"You are correct, Henry. My wife has excellent taste and I'm not just referring to the fact that she picked me."

The three shared a light laugh as Jan pulled off the lid to the first jar.

"What do you think this one smells like, honey?"

They always used terms of endearment at the mall. It might be easier to refer to each other by their real first names but the combination of using Mr. and Mrs. Smith with their real first names did not sit well with either one of them. Honey and dear worked just fine.

Frank took a whiff of the candle lid and smiled.

"Smells like a summer rain out by the lake."

Jan picked up the story and ran with it.

"That's exactly what I was thinking. Just like that rain storm we got caught in when we were out in the canoe on the lake."

The two shared a soft fake laugh at the absurdity of them in such a natural family setting.

"Ok. You got that one right. Let's see if you can figure this one out."

Jan put the lid back on the first jar and removed the lid from the second candle as she held it up so Frank could take in the odor.

"Well, that one is easy. That one smells like laundry day. Well, before you changed to that odd smelling detergent for a while. I'm glad you changed back."

The fake married couple smiled broadly at each other. It was a fun game they often played to unsuspecting people. They created every day scenarios full of household memories. They were memories that would never be fulfilled or realized since they lived in an alternate universe. Much like the draw of Cosplay, it was fun to live other lives in another place, if only for one day every week.

"Oh honey. You are too good. That's exactly what I was thinking."

"She is right, Mr. Smith. She was just telling me how it smells like your shirt she likes to put on when she takes it out of the laundry. You are a very lucky man, Mr. Smith."

Taking Jan's hand, he simply smiled. "Indeed I am Henry. Indeed, I am."

Feeling like the third wheel, the salesperson shifted the conversation towards finality.

"So, will it just be the two candles today, Mrs. Smith, or would you like to keep shopping?"

"No, I think that will be fine, Henry. Would you be a doll honey and put these other ones back? I'll settle up with Henry here so we can back to our Monday shopping. There are plenty more stores I would like to hit today."

Frank took the other candles from his pretend wife so she could close out the shopping scene on the Monday fiction. He knew what the hours ahead would include and he was certain that a whole day of shopping was not in the cards.

NOON

"What are you in the mood for today?"

Frank looked over at Jan who was clearly reviewing their food choices in the food court but he had other things in mind.

"I say we skip lunch and move right onto dessert."

"Calm it down lover boy. I need some lunch."

The pair looked around the many choices at the mall food court. They did not need to look at menus as they had been at the same fork in the road every week for the past year. They knew every food choice and had eaten at every eatery multiple times.

"I'm in the mood for Chinese."

"We had Chinese last week. How about Sbarro?"

"Not today. I'm sure it will give me heartburn."

"So why don't you get your Chinese and I'll get a salad. How does that sound?"

Frank looked around the food court at the two locations and then back to the center seating area. "Sounds good. Why don't I meet you over there by the fake fichus after we get our food?"

Jan leaned over and pecked him on the cheek. "Perfect, and Frank?"

"Yes, baby."

"Make sure you use cash."

"I will. I set aside some from my tips last night. Besides, I only screwed up that one time and used the debit card. I know better."

Jan looked over at her lover and gently brushed his face with her hand. "Go get your Chinese Food. I'll meet you back over there in a few."

The two separated and went along their own ways. They did not look back nor did they have to look around. They were for all intents and purposes just another couple getting lunch at the food court in the mall.

As Frank Morris entered the line he pulled out his phone. There were three messages but only one he need to reply to.

What's Up?

There was no response for a minute as the line progressed forward. When he felt the vibration, he looked down at his phone.

Are you sleeping?

Not anymore. What's up?

Sorry, I have a meeting that popped up this afternoon. You need to pick up the kids at the bus stop.

Ok.

You need to set your alarm. They get off the bus at 4pm.

I know what time they get off the bus.

Then don't be late this time.

Frank knew better than to keep sparring with his wife. He waited a minute before replying back to the condescending text.

Fine.

Ill be home around 5. Please make sure they do their homework.

Fine.

The conversation was over. She would work late and he would pick up the kids from the bus. Another day in paradise.

On the other side of the food court, Jan was dealing with a similar conversation with her husband about plans for the evening.

They want to take us to dinner.

Mitch too?

No, not Mitch. Don't be stupid. They are having their wives join us so it will be a couples evening. They are talking about Seasons 52.

Are you asking me or telling me?

I'm telling you. Don't be stupid. Make a reservation for eight of us at seven. Do you think you can handle that or do I need to tell my worthless secretary to do it?

I'll take care of it. I always do.

I figured you would. You are just sitting around your office anyway. I'll be home by 6. Be ready.

Jan knew better than reply. Once her husband was done with her she was cast aside like used garbage. She would simply make that call as directed by her commander. She typed in the information into her search bar and the number popped up quickly. Pressing the call button, the number connected to the hostess station at the restaurant.

Seasons 52, how can I help you?

Hello, I would like to make a reservation for this evening.

How many people?

There will be 8 of us.

Did you have a specific time in mind?

Jan was too busy taking care of the reservation that she didn't see Frank approach the line she was waiting for at Sbarro.

Can we say 7pm?

Of course, can we have a name?

Nichols please.

Ok. Ms. Nichols. We have you down for a party of 8 at 7pm tonight.

Thank you.

As she hung up her phone, she was acutely aware that someone was standing right behind her. Thinking it was just another customer in line, she turned casually to have a look around only to find Frank behind her.

"Dinner plans?"

"Don't ask. Just another notch in the stress meter." Looking down at his hands, she noticed his to go container. "Did you get your Chinese food?"

"Yes, all set. I'll go grab us a table."

Jan watched him walk away and was amazed for the 1000th time how easy life was with Frank. She didn't have to put on airs. She didn't have to make dinner reservations or buy the right dress to wear for clients. There was no one to impress at the country club. It was just take out at the mall. No stress. No mess. No hassle. If only...

Frank meanwhile had gotten a table and made sure his phone was on silent. He didn't need to be reminded again to pick up his children like he was a small child himself. Looking back at Jan, he was not made to feel small and insignificant. With Jan, he was on equal terms. Yes, he started out as her bartender and she was his guest but now they were just two people; two lost souls finding each other in the wilderness.

"Deep in thought?"

"Same old, same old. Did you get your food?"

"Yes, let's eat."

The two lovers sat across from each other in the food court and set up their lunches like an old married couple. They each knew where the other liked their napkin, their plastic ware and their beverages. Within minutes the table was set up as if they had done it a million times before. In unison, they picked up their forks and began the meal.

"So, where are you going for dinner tonight?"

"Do you really want to know or are you just being polite?"

"You know."

"Ok, well, he wants to impress his clients and eat at Seasons 52. Of course he didn't want to trust the reservations to his secretary and since I wasn't doing anything...."

"Of course not. You just have that silly little job at the law firm. Nothing going on there. But, of course you made the reservation for him..."

"What else was I supposed to do?"

"I understand. I do. It's just I hate when he treats you like one of the house servants."

"He treats them better. He knows they see and tell everything. He couldn't risk them telling other servants that he treated them poorly."

"How about you. Did you get your mid-sleep wake up to check on you?"

"Of course."

"What was the excuse this time? She wanted to make sure you mowed the lawn while you were sleeping?"

"No, she needs me to pick up the kids from school."

"So you are supposed to not sleep because she needs to go shopping, or get her nails done? What is the excuse this time?"

"She has to work late."

"Aw, poor baby. Her husband works two jobs and breaks his back. Why does she have to work late, did she say?"

"It doesn't matter. I'll pick up the kids. I just wish she didn't treat me as one. Can we change the subject and eat while I still have an appetite?"

They both ate in silence for a few minutes while they slowly digested their failed marriages in peace. When the tough pills were swallowed, the meal changed for the better.

"You never told me why you had Mitch's car today."

"He had a job interview. Well, sort of."

"How do you sort of have a job interview? I would think that you either have an appointment to meet with someone about a job or you don't."

Jan laughed lightly.

"That's a great way of putting it. Mitch had an appointment to meet someone about a job. They weren't calling it an interview but sort of a meet and greet."

"Well, there you go. I would assume if you are going to meet and greet someone it makes a better impression when you pull up in a Porsche as opposed to a Toyota."

"You would assume correct, kind sir."

"Did I tell you about the conversation on the way to the bus stop this morning?"

"No. I didn't even know you got to see the kids."

"Yes, it was great. Even though I got a few comments for coming home early from work it was worth it because I got to see the kids."

"Were they happy to see dad?"

"Of course. It was kind of funny though. They had all these questions about both my jobs. It was as if they were fishing for information."

"They are kids, Frank. They always ask questions. When they get to be teenagers they stop and for a while you think you went deaf or became a leper. Enjoy the oddball questions while they last. They won't be around forever."

"I know and that's what kills me sometimes. I work so many hours and I don't get to see them enough. I hate when they ask me to go to a game or something and my schedule doesn't allow for it. It's hard to get them to understand."

Frank picked at his food as he thought of missing another one of his son's games. He only stopped jabbing the Chinese food when Jan held his hand.

"Listen to me, my love. You are a fantastic father. You care for those kids like nobody's business. You can't make games and plays because you are so busy working two jobs and providing for your family. You should never be ashamed of that. Most women would love to have a husband that was that committed to taking care of his family."

"Your husband provides for your family. Does that make him a good father too?"

"You know the answer to that one. Half the time he doesn't realize Mitch is even there unless he needs him for a verbal punching bag. There is a difference between providing for your family because you want to and providing for them because they are just there. Mitch and I will always just be tenants in his house until we get evicted. We are definitely not invited guests and we both know that our lease will be up one day."

Frank let the animosity pass before continuing.

"In any case, I don't mind picking them up from school. It will give me another chance to talk to them before I head out to the bar."

"Does that mean you will have to cut our afternoon short, lover?"

Frank reached out and caressed Jan's hand. "Not at all. Eat your lunch and I will give you all the dessert you crave."

She smiled broadly and licked her lips.

"What if I want some whipped cream with my dessert?"

"That could probably be arranged as long as we don't spill any in the van. With such a spotless interior I would hate to leave a stain."

The two broke out in laughter knowing that the best part of their day would be coming soon enough at the quiet edge of the parking lot.

2:00 PM

The best part of parking at the edge of the parking lot is the privacy. Unfortunately, the benefits are challenged when the afternoon rains set in. There were no umbrellas or shade trees to hide under as the couple exited the cover of the mall overhang and sprinted across the parking lot. The first few rows would have simply moistened the skin and the next several rows may have even saved some of the clothing, but the distance traveled to the edge of the parking was daunting. By the time they arrived at the van, they were soaked to the bone. Jumping into the front seats, they closed their doors quickly as the steam started to rise from their drenched clothing.

"Oh my goodness, turn on the heat. I am freezing from the rain."

Frank put the keys into the ignition of the van and fired it up. The engine came to life and he instantly turned the heat indicator towards the red and away from the blue. He did not bother with the defroster as the intention was for the windows to fog up.

"Don't worry about that. Where did you put the windshield cover?"

"It's under your seat. If you can't reach it, I can get it."

"Such the gentleman but I am pretty sure I can handle it."

Jan reached under the van seat and pulled out the accordion looking windshield cover. Unfolding it, she positioned the metallic side outward and placed the cover against the front window. Folding down the visors, the cover was held in place. The van was instantly transformed into a private love nest away from all the rest of the cars in the parking lot. The steamed up side windows provided perfect cover as the two smiled at each other coyly.

"You look pretty wet lady."

"You have no idea. Come with me to the back seat and I will let you find out how wet I really am."

Jan took Frank by the hand and led him between the two front captain chairs as they settled in to the bucket seat in the second row of the van. From their vantage point, they could not be seen by the sliding doors on either side but could still detect movement if someone approached the front doors of the van. The scene was once again set and the rain provided additional comfort to the two lovers.

"I think you would be more comfortable without that wet blouse on."

"More comfortable? You think? I believe we have a rule about being naked in the parking lot of the mall."

"Rule? It's more of a guideline, don't you think?"

"Well, working in the HR department of a law firm I can firmly say that it is a rule that we should follow, rain or shine. For convenience and comfort, I think we can simply unbutton my blouse so we can let it dry off properly."

Jan moved her hands slowly towards her buttons but Frank beat her to the touch. His hands began to unbutton her blouse slowly but methodically with a goal in mind. Feeling the moisture of her skin with the back of his hand, he smiled slowly.

"I think the rain went all the way through your blouse and your bra. I don't think it is safe for you to keep the bra on as well."

Jan returned his smile. "Not safe, huh? What do you think is going to happen to me if I leave my wet bra on?"

"Well I wouldn't want you to catch cold because you had wet clothing against your skin. I would feel terrible if you were sick all week and I wouldn't be there to take care of you. Besides, you might be too chilled to go to dinner tonight."

She looked down at her open blouse and Frank's hand against her skin. Gazing back into his eyes, she whispered. "Then it's a good thing the clasp is in front. All you have to do is set the moisture free."

Frank moved slowly in his actions as he unfastened the front clasp and opened up he bra. Pushing the cups aside with his hands, he brushed her nipples slowly as he felt her shiver underneath his touch. Closing her eyes, Jan leaned back against the bucket seat and took in the moment. Every touch the two of them shared seemed like the first time together. It was always new. It was always exciting. It was always full of life.

"I could say the same for you."

Frank looked over at her with a sarcastic smile. "Me? Oh I don't have dinner plans. I'm just going to work later."

Tugging at his belt, Jan looked up at her lover. "But your pants are so wet. Perhaps you should take them off and let them dry. I'm sure you would be in all sorts of trouble if you had to call in sick to one or both of your jobs."

Frank shook his head. "I can only imagine." Reaching down, he grasped the end of the belt, backed it out of the loop and tugged on it until the clasp was undone. Never taking his eyes off of Jan, he unbuttoned his jeans and slowly unzipped the zipper.

"You are right. I feel so much better now that the air is hitting it. I might have to take them all the way off to feel better."

Raising his bottom off the bucket seat, he tugged at the loose jeans and lowered them past his knees to rest by his shoes. Leaving them still attached was protocol. They were cautious in every step they took. Reaching over, he caressed Jan's leg and ran his fingers up her inner thigh. Coming to a stop before he reached the promise land, he looked up at his lover who was leaning back closing her eyes.

"Are you feeling any warmer now? I'm sure the rain chilled you to the bone."

Jan's breath was sporadic as her heart began to beat faster. She could feel shivers all over her body as Frank touched her. After so many Monday's spent in the same van back seat, she was still rocked to her core.

"Warmer? Yes. Definitely warmer. Getting pretty hot in here."

Frank continued his caress and let his fingers climb her leg until he reached his desired destination. Within moments, Jan let out a moan.

"Don't tease me. Not today. I need you. I've waited all week for this moment. Don't toy with me. I want you."

Frank was not letting up. He continued to caress her with his fingers as he could feel the change in her body escalating.

"Do you want me more than a fancy dinner?"

Panting, she kept her eyes closed but answered in a moan. "Yes…"

Knowing that he was getting her close, he continued his gentle assault on her privates. "Maybe I should just stop. I don't want you to be flush before dinner."

"Stop teasing me…"

"Stop? You want me to stop?"

Grasping the back of his hand, she pulled him in so that she could feel the pressure against her.

"I want you to move your hand so I can put something else in its place."

Frank pushed back against her hand and moved his fingers faster.

"Move my hand? Like this?"

Jan cried out. "I can't take this anymore. I want you now."

"Shhhh…someone will hear you."

"Frank. We are in a closed van at the edge of the parking lot in the pouring rain. Even of someone could hear us, no one would come close enough to know what we are doing. Now stop toying with me. I want you now."

He knew it was time to give in. She was in charge now. He enjoyed when she let herself go like this and took over the situation. He knew that she could never have control in her house, in her regular life. He let her take control as he pulled down his boxers to join his jeans at the bottom of his legs. Lifting her dress up but facing the outer window, she lowered herself down on top of him. She was going to ride her bucking bronco for all he could take.

Frank was unsettled when she took this position because he knew he was helpless. He could not see out the windows so he could not sense any danger approaching. If someone were to knock on the door, he would not be able to answer it. His lover had completely taken over and although she was facing outward towards the parking lot, he knew her eyes were closed. He was at her mercy.

As she began to rock back and forth on his lap, the van began to move. In the back of his mind, he knew she was right. It was pouring rain and the odds of someone noticing the van rocking slightly were small, but it was still a possibility. The small element of danger added to the excitement of the moment as they both reached climax within moments. Jan held on to the roof of the van as Frank clasped desperately to the seat next to him. He knew better than to grab her hips. They could never take the chance of bruising each other. As they both enjoyed their time on cloud nine, they each stifled their inner voices, stopping them from crying out in ecstasy.

Jan lowered her hands to the back of her neck as she rolled her head back. Caressing her spine, Frank showed her the affection he was feeling in the afterglow.

"Oh my...that was amazing."

Frank took a minute to catch his breath before answering.

"Are you ok back there? Did I break you?"

"Is that what you were trying to do cowgirl? Break the bucking horse so he could be put out to pasture?"

Reaching behind her, she caressed his naked thighs, not wanting to move away from the spot that had given her so much pleasure.

"I don't think I'll be sending you out to the pasture any time soon. I like you right where you are at the moment."

"While I wish you could stay there all day..."

"I know, I know. You have to get the kids. Just give me a moment to enjoy this. Close your eyes Frank and close out the world with me. Let there only be us, only for a minute."

He let his lover have her moment. He knew some Mondays were more intense for her than others and today was in that category. He would not take that from her. He loved her and he knew she loved him. It may be for a moment or a lifetime, but he knew she loved him as they completed each other.

3:00 PM

"Do you ever get tired of the secrecy, Frank?"

They were both sitting in the front seats again. They had removed the sun visor and they were watching the rain come down hard. There was not another living soul walking around in the soaked parking lot.

"All the time. Especially on Mondays."

They both smiled quietly as they knew his comment touched too close to home.

"...but every time I think about how much I hate the secrecy and sneaking around I hate the thought of not seeing you even more. I know it sounds strange, but I need you in my life. At times, it is the only thing that keeps me going. Working 16 hour days is worth it as long as I know you will be there for me at the end of a week."

Jan smiled trying to lighten the moment. "Some people say that Monday starts the week, Frank not ends it."

"You know what I mean. All the crap I have to go through to make sure my kids are alright is worth it because you make me happy. Without you, there is just a crappy life, with two crappy jobs and a crappy marriage in a crappy house. I know that doesn't make much sense in your world but it means everything to me."

"It makes total sense to me. More than you know. I get that sometimes you look at my life as entitled and self-indulgent, but just like you I am in a prison of sorts. I have to steal moments like this in my life just to be happy. He may yell at me for different things than she yells at you for, but at the end of the day they still yell. I sleep alone just like you do. I know that you do because you sleep while she works but it's still the same. We both have lonely nights and even more lonely moments when we wake up. I wish things were different but they are not."

"Do you wish he still shared your bed?"

Jan looked down at her hands silently as she twirled her wedding band around. Slowly, she looked over at the driver's seat where Frank was waiting for an answer.

84

"Sometimes I do. But not for the reason you think. I don't want him. I don't want any part of him physically. What I do want is presence. Even when we are both home at the same time, we are not both there. He is doing his thing and I am doing mine. Mitch is doing whatever Mitch wants to do and the three of us are walking around in our own little bubbles. Sometimes I just wish I had someone there to wake up to. I wish that would be you but we both know that is not in the cards. You have your family and I have mine. We call them families on Christmas cards but we both know they are nothing but pictures to the outside world."

Frank let the words sink in. It was nothing new. They had this conversation countless times over their moments together and it always came to the same dead end street. They had each other, but only for a few moments every Monday.

"Well, speaking of families, I need..."

Reaching across the divide, Jan grasped his hand and caressed the back of it. Looking into his eyes she spoke quietly.

"I know you have to go get the kids and I don't want you to be late. But tell me, Frank. Tell me that in a different world, in a different universe we would be together. We would have our own kids and our own family and we would be happy. Am I just dreaming or is that part real for you as it is for me?"

Frank hesitated only to catch his breath. Leaning in, he kissed her softly on the lips and caressed her cheek.

"Of course it is real. I love you Jan. I really do. I know you don't like it when I say that because I am married to someone else and so are you, but I do love you. If life was different, if you and I weren't living in different worlds, I know we would find each other and love passionately. I know that part is real."

Looking into his eyes, Jan responded with all of her heart.

"I love you too, Frank. But like Bogey and Bergman at the airport, it's time to part. You need to go drive back into your life and go get your kids. I need to drive back into my fiction story and get ready for dinner with the clients. We know what we both have to do."

There was silence for the moment as a tear began to roll down her cheek. Frank went to wipe it away but thought best to kiss it instead. As his lips touched her cheek, he could taste the salt of the saline and knew instantly that their time together, at least for the day, had come to a close. Nodding, he sat back in his driver's seat and she gathered her shopping bags.

"Same time next Monday?"

"Let's say eleven. I got out of work early this morning but I don't want to be late in meeting you. If I can do earlier I will let you know."

"You have to be careful about those text messages. I can't always get a delivery on Mondays. If someone were to read it..."

"No one is going to read any messages. We have been careful and will continue to be. I'll tell you what. If there is a change in time for next week, I will text something about some meeting at the legal office. I'm sure that happens all the time."

Smiling, she grasped his hand with her free one and held it momentarily.

"You have no idea. I think those lawyers never have been on time to anything in their lives. It never fails. But that is a story for next Monday. I'll tell you then."

"I look forward to it."

Together they both leaned in for a final Monday kiss that would have to last them 168 hours, or so until the next Monday rolled along. Without another word, Jan opened up the passenger door, jumped out and darted to her car without looking back. Reaching across the seat, Frank closed the passenger door and sat back in his seat as he buckled up. Waiting until Jan was settled in her car with her brake lights pressed, he put the van in gear and exited the parking lot. Like some worm hole in space, he traveled back into a world where he was married with children and had responsibilities for them all. He didn't have to look in his rear view mirror to know that Jan was traveling back to her own universe, light years away.

4:00 PM

"Dad!"

Frank Morris had rolled up in his family van just moments before the school bus arrived. He had just enough time to get out of the van and adjust his clothing as the bus rolled to a stop. As the louver doors opened and his two children stepped out, he was just as happy to see them as they were to see their father.

"Hey Billy."

Father welcomed his son with open arms as he ran up and hugged him joyfully. He was still a few years away from getting the side hug in passing from his son and he thought he should enjoy the moment while it lasted. Kate followed suit but she hugged her dad cautiously.

"Why are you picking us up Dad? Where's Mom?"

"She had to work late but it's ok. I get to spend more time with you."

Kate made a face but started to walk towards the van anyway. She wanted to make sure she got the front passenger seat.

"I got shotgun."

Billy ran after his sister, temporarily forgetting about his father. Kate had the head start so she reached the front door faster than her brother.

"Dad! She always gets the front seat."

"That's because I'm the oldest. I'm big, you're small. I'm smart. You're dumb. Now go eat some worms twerp..."

"Dad! Kate is picking on me."

Frank simply shook his head as he picked up Billy's backpack that fell off as he was chasing his sister. He got back to the van in time to see his daughter jump in the front seat and close the door. Billy stood outside waiting for vindication.

"Looks like she beat you this time, Billy. That's ok. You can try to get her next time."

"But she always beats me to the front seat. Why can't I have a turn."

Frank laughed at the simplicity of life at that age. His son didn't need to worry about working two jobs or providing a roof over the heads of his children. Billy didn't have a wife and a mistress and he definitely didn't have to stay up crazy hours just to see her.

"Just hop in back Billy. It will be ok. We will be home in a few minutes."

The young boy reluctantly got into the back seat of the van and closed the door. Sitting on the bench seat, he could feel that the fabric was wet.

"Dad. It's all wet back here."

Frank had a panicked moment of surprise. It was good that his son caught that and not his wife.

"Yea. I had to run to the store earlier when it was raining so the seat must have gotten wet. Sorry kiddo. Sit on your backpack if you don't want to get wet."

Billy adjusted himself on the seat before securing his seat belt.

"It's ok, Dad. We got rained on at recess too. No big deal."

"Then why are you complaining, twerp?"

"Dad! Kate called me a twerp."

"Do you even know what it means or are you a stupid twerp too?"

"Ok, you too. That's enough. No more fighting. I have to go to work soon and I don't want to listen to it."

The two children sat in silence as their father was lost in thought. What a difference a couple hour makes. A short time ago, there was a much different conversation going on in that back seat. The thought of which left a smile on Frank's face all the way home.

5:00 PM

Jan Nichols pulled up into her driveway driving her son's Toyota only to find him standing outside the Porsche looking down at it with a towel in his hand. Panicked that something had happened to her car and that her husband would be furious, she parked quickly and jumped out.

"Mitch? What's wrong? Did something happen to the car? Oh my God your father is going to be furious…"

"Mom. Calm down."

"How can I be calm. What happened to the car?"

"Nothing happened. I just finished washing it for you. I thought it would be nice since you let me borrow it today."

Jan relaxed and let her cliff-hanging stress subside. After a moment, she chuckled at how ridiculous she reacted.

"I'm sorry Mitch. I should have seen the hose. Thanks for washing the car. It looks nice and shiny."

"That's ok Mom. Hard day at the office?"

Jan thought back to her eventful day and a small smile appeared that did not go unnoticed by her son.

"No, it was fine."

"It must have been more than fine if it made you smile."

Jan, always the quick thinker, had the perfect comeback. "No, I was just thinking about the cake they had. One of the girl's had a birthday and they brought a delicious cake for her. It just made me smile thinking your father would have been furious at how stupid it was to waste time and money that way."

The two broke out laughing because they both knew it to be true.

"How did my car behave?"

Jan simply shook her head. "Fine. It still smells in there like a locker room but the car was fine. Let me get my bags out and you can gladly have it back."

"Bags?"

"Yes. Your car smell bothered me all morning long so I went shopping on my lunch break and bought some candles. Unfortunately, I didn't buy an air freshener while I was there. I'm going to go in and light the candles so I forget that smell ever existed."

Jan walked back to the car and removed the bags from the mall. Turning she looked back at her son and almost forgot the reason he borrowed the car in the first place.

"By the way. How did your meeting go? Did the car impress them?"

Mitch smiled broadly.

"Indeed it did. They invited me to their office for a real interview. I guess I made a good impression."

"That's great, Mitch. Maybe it will get your father off your case. At least a possibility of a job ranks high in his world."

"He just hates to see us enjoying life, Mom. As a matter of fact, I would hide those candles from him when he gets home. If he thinks you bought something frivolous for yourself just to enjoy it, I'm sure he'll start yelling."

You have no idea how much I enjoyed my trip to the mall, Mitch. No idea.

Jan Nichols entered her house wearing a broad smile. She couldn't wait to light her candles, soak in a tub, and think about her wonderful trip to the mall.

6:00 PM

"Ok, I'm out of here"

"What time are you in at the bar?"

"6:30 pm. The day bartender is wrapping up taking their last table now. I should be able to jump right in and get some dinner tables before they taper off to the bar crowd."

Frank Morris grabbed the van keys off the counter and headed towards the door in slow motion.

"You look tired. Didn't you get any sleep?"

"No, June. I didn't. Between you calling me and then having to go to the store and picking up the kids, I didn't get much sleep at all."

"Oh. I'm so sorry you had to spend time with your children. That must have been so hard on you instead of sleeping."

"I didn't mean that at all. I enjoyed picking them up. You said I looked tired. I was just telling you why. Not looking for a fight."

June shook her head. She hated when he would not fight back with her. It was as if he was claiming victory by not fighting in the first place.

"Whatever. Just make sure you work a full shift tonight after the bar. We can't afford for you to have another short shift after having one last night."

"Don't worry June. I'll work all night long. I'll see you tomorrow at some point. If you leave for work before I get home, try not to finish all the coffee."

Frank Morris exited without kissing his wife goodbye. Neither one of them minded and they were both relieved that their Monday was basically over.

7:00 PM

The limousine service pulled up to the entrance of the Seasons 52 restaurant and parked. As the driver exited the car and walked around to the other side, a quick conversation ensued.

"Try not to embarrass me tonight."

"Me? Don't worry. I'm sure you will be too busy paying attention to your potential clients and not spending any time with me."

"What the…"

The limousine door opened before Mike Nichols had a chance to finish his rant. Instead, it was his wife that got the last remark out before they exited.

"Don't kiss too much ass tonight, Mike. I didn't bring any facial wipes for you. Tonight, you are on your own…"

The couple exited the limousine and were immediately greeted by the Japanese entourage. The chief executive approached them as they put on their famous business smiles.

"Mr. Nichols. Punctual as usual. I trust everything has been arranged for our dinner appointment this evening?"

"Of course. I took care of the reservations myself. They should be waiting for us."

The Japanese executive paused and looked at Jan with a broad smile.

"My apologies. I have not made your acquaintance young lady."

Jan smiled demurely as her husband put on his best poker face.

"May I present to you my loving wife, Jan Nichols."

Reaching out to shake the hand of the client, Jan felt the stain of hypocrisy overwhelm her. She had her happy time at the mall and now it was time to pay the piper.

"Pleased to meet you. I can't wait to find out all about your company and how my husband can serve your needs better. Shall we dine?"

Pointing to the front door, the small group made their way inside. To Jan, her continued deal with the devil was once again renewed.

Tolerant

TUESDAY

1

"Is supper ready?"

The large man had no sooner entered his home at 5:05pm and was beckoning for dinner. He hung up his suit jacket and hat on the hat tree by the door over the unused umbrella. The calendar may have indicated that it was the 10th of May in Birmingham, Alabama but there was protocol to follow. Bull Connor made certain that heat or no heat, he was dressed as a man of power. He was the Commissioner of Public Safety and was determined to be respected as the public official he had been for so many terms.

"Almost dear. The roast needs a few more minutes before coming to the table. Go wash up and I'll have your Rheingold waiting for you when you sit down."

"Damn it, Mary. After the day I've had…"

"I heard Theo. It's all over the radio. That's why I made your favorite roast with those little potatoes you like so much. Go wash up and you can relax over a cold beer."

The older man just shook his head and felt defeated. It was certainly a bad day for democracy and he was a part of it.

"Fine. Just make sure there's a glass with it. I'm not drinking out of the bottle like some street criminal. Speaking of low life, where is Charles? I want him seated at the table when I get down."

"I'll call him Theo. He's just out back in the yard. Go wash up and everything will be in place when you get down."

Bull Connor grunted and walked towards the wooden bannister. Each step he took felt like a 1000-pound weight was tied to his ankles. Someone was going to pay for this kind of misery instilled on him. One of those damned colored folks was going to pay.

As she watched her husband climb the stairs slowly towards the bathroom, Mary Connor wiped her hands on her apron and went to the ice box and opened the door. She had wanted one of those new shiny models for years but she also knew that Bull would never let her have one. She had heard it too many times how the world was changing and it was all those colored folks fault. She never understood what a new refrigerator had anything to do with anyone of any color skin, but she left those decisions up to her husband. Removing the brown glass bottle from the top shelf, she closed the ice box door quickly before she let in the May heat. Using the bottle opener on the side of the box, she opened up the bottle and let the cap fall into the basin. Turning, she removed a glass from the cupboard and set it at the place setting at the head of the table. She poured the cold beer carefully into the glass so not to spill a drop. Hearing the screen door open behind her, she knew her son had come back just in time.

"You made it."

"Sure did, Momma. Is he upstairs?"

"Yes. Your father went upstairs to wash up for dinner but he's as ornery as the queen bee on honey day. You best stay clear of him. None of that politics talk at dinner, you hear me Chuck?"

"Yes, Momma."

The teenage boy may have been full of spitfire at 17, but he knew when to stay clear of Bull when he was in a mood. He heard the radio just like his mother did. He knew his father was looking to take it out on someone and he didn't want it to be him. Crossing to the kitchen sink, he washed his hands and dried them with a kitchen towel. Hearing his father trod down the stairs, he quickly moved to his seat at the table and sat down. A few seconds later, Bull Connor rounded the corner and viewed his family scene. His wife was removing dinner from the oven and his son was in his place. In his favorite glass, Bull viewed an ice cold beer with condensation forming on the outside of the glass. America at its finest.

"Did you wash up your grubby hands before sitting at my table, boy?"

"Yes, sir."

"Where? I didn't see you upstairs."

Chuck Connor looked over at his mother for help but he knew he was on his own.

"I washed them in the sink down here, Daddy."

Bull picked up his steak knife and tapped the handle on the table. "How many times have I told you that the kitchen sink is for food and dishes. It's not for your dirt. Do you understand me, boy?"

Chuck knew that his father was simply looking to pick a fight and he was not biting. He knew what his father did to people when he got angry. He turned fire hoses on people in the streets simply for speaking their peace. He was not about to feel the fury of his father tonight.

"Yes, sir."

"Are we clear, boy?"

"Yes, sir."

Slowly, Bull put his knife down and moved his hand over to his glass of beer.

Grasping it tightly, he brought it to his lips, closed his eyes and let the cold liquid quench his thirst.

"Aah. Nothing like a cold beer after a shit day."

"Theo! Must you use that language at the dinner table?"

Although he was a man of power in this city, he was also respectful to his wife and to the Lord, our God.

"I'm sorry, Mary. I told you it was a bad day. I pray for your forgiveness."

Mary turned and smiled coyly. It was her place in her home to keep the peace and no matter what happened, she was able to make the man humble.

"No need. The Lord has already forgiven you with your many good deeds. Could you kindly cut the roast while I get the potatoes?"

"Of course."

It took all matter of restraint for Chuck not to reach out and pick off a crisp edge of the roast. He could smell the garlic and pepper from out in the yard and that was the real reason to come home. His mouth watered as his father slowly cut into the roast as the juicy blood ran down the sides.

"Are you just gonna watch me like some basset hound or are you gonna get me a plate to put this on?"

"Yes, sir."

Chuck reached over and grabbed the serving plate from the other side of the roast as his father sliced off pieces swiftly and placed them in sequence on the plate.

"Thank you Charles."

Chuck shook his head and rolled his eyes as his father finished cutting the meat. When done, he put the plate down in front of the beer knowing who had the first choice of cut.

"Is there a problem, boy?"

"No, Sir."

"Are you sure, boy? It sure seemed like there was a problem when I called you by your name; your God given name."

"I'm pretty sure you gave me that name, not God."

Bull was quick to react as his hand came up in the air and threatened to slap his son in the face.

"Are you back-talkin' me boy?"

"No, Sir."

"Are you disrespecting the name of the Lord, boy?"

"No, Sir."

Bull lowered his hand slowly as he retreated back to his seat, his beer, and his choice of meat. Taking his fork, he stabbed at the top slice and brought it onto his plate. Hesitating only slightly, he brought the fork back to grab a second slice to stake his dominance at the table. Quietly, Mary brought the potatoes over and held the dish as her husband spooned some onto his plate. The scene calmed down as the three of them filled their plates and waited for the man of the house to give the blessing. When he was ready, the three of them formed a triangle with their connected hands and bowed their heads.

"Dear Father. Thank you for this bountiful feast you have bestowed upon us at the end of this troublesome day. May the colored folks who screwed up this day for me be eating the crow they deserve. Amen."

"For crying out loud."

Bull stopped as he had just begun to pick up his knife and fork to stare down his teenage son. If looks could kill, he would be six feet under.

"Is there a problem, boy?"

"Yes. Yes sir there is."

His father slammed down his silverware as his mother recoiled. She knew this was coming from the moment her husband walked into the house.

"Then do enlighten us, hippie. Tell us how the great *Chuck* sees the world as some kind of horrible place that good people like me try to preserve. Tell us what in the Christ is the problem now, boy."

"I'll tell you what the problem is. You claim to be a man of faith but only see people by the color of their skin. You don't care if they pray to the same God you do. If they look different than your uptight friends, you denounce them. Seems to me like you need to do more praying and less judging."

"He will come again in glory to judge the living and the dead and his kingdom will have no end."

"So now you are claiming to be the second coming of Christ? Even that's a stretch for you, dear old dad."

"Do not take the Lord's name in vain, Chuck."

"I'm sorry Momma. I really am. He just passes judgement like he was the highest ruler of the land."

"Think what you want, Charles, but I am the authority in this house and I intend to eat in peace. Now shut your mouth so I can eat this fine meal your mother prepared."

The situation calmed as the three of them settled into silence. They ate looking down at their plates so not to antagonize further fighting. Not suffice to let sleeping dogs lie, it was Bull himself that broke the truce.

"They are calling it the *Birmingham Truce Agreement*. Can you believe that? Like we are smoking the peace pipe with some Indians or something. They want to let them coloreds drink out of the same water fountains and sit next to us regular folks down at the Woolworth counter. Can you believe that? After everything that I have done for this city, they want to let those rabble-rousers out of the jail because the white folks been too mean to them. Is that right? Have I been to mean to those coloreds that caused me so much grief and stress? I don't think so."

Chuck Connor thought twice about opening his mouth but the fire that burned within his teenage bones got the best of him.

"Well you did turn on the fire hoses against them in the street. I would think that some would say that was being mean."

"Is that right young man? And who forced me to turn on those fire hoses? I was doing my duty as the Commissioner of Public Safety. They were causing a riot and a public nuisance. I was simply putting them in their place."

"Was it putting them in their place when you turned the dogs on them too? When those same dogs chewed the little kids who were marching with their parents down the middle of the street? Were those little kids putting anyone in danger?"

Bull Connor tried to eat his food but his face had become as red as the meat in front of him. Mary feared her husband might be giving himself a stroke.

"You know what, boy? I'm gonna let that slide. I'm gonna let that slide because you are a stupid teenage degenerate. You are part of everything that is wrong with society these days. I am part of the solution. Now, if it's not too much to ask. I'd like to finish my meal in peace."

Chuck let his father have the last word in this argument but the war was far from over. Across the table, Bull smiled knowing that war had just begun.

2

Vonda Hart and her younger brother Tyrone walked briskly along the Fourth Avenue sidewalk, trying to get home safely in time for dinner. They were in their part of the city and there was nothing but comfort and heritage with every storefront they passed. In Roy's Barber shop, a group of older men sat in chairs smiling and celebrating the day's victories. There was much to look forward to in their African-American community and the day felt as if there was hope on the horizon.

With desegregation and the promise of economic development in this part of town, the hope was real. Every small store the pair passed on their way home was filled with the same laughter and bright spirits. In Sal's market the shopkeeper was whistling as he swept the wooden floor. Sandy's Wig and Beauty was filled with the ladies of the neighborhood who were seeking the right touch ups for their evening celebrations. Everywhere they passed, the same good vibes were being broadcasted but that did not detract from what their parents warned them about.

A seventeen-year-old female, regardless of skin color, had much to be guarded about in the 1960's. The wholesome days of the 50's were in the rear view mirror. The poodle skirts and bobby socks had been replaced by mini-skirts and flats. Men of any age were turning their heads to see more leg and tighter sweaters, all leaning towards a more cautious environment for young ladies. At her age, Vonda was sure to attract all manner of men and boys and her mother always reminded her of that.

You got the goods girl. Your honey is bringing the bees to the hive and you got to be careful not to get the stinger. Those boys gonna want to stick you but you got to be quicker and smarter than that. You got the brains as well as the goods and you learn to use them both together.

With her mother's wisdom resonating, she always tried to have someone with her, be it one of her brothers or one of their friends. Even though she was only a couple more blocks from her family's apartment, she would not feel fully safe until she got inside the front door.

"Vonda, why we walking so fast?"

"I want to get home before we get in trouble."

"What kind of trouble? Look around, sis. Everybody puttin' on a party. There ain't gonna be no trouble."

"Isn't..."

"What?"

"There isn't going to be any trouble."

"See? Even you say so."

Vonda simply shook her head. Her little brother got her on that one. She needed to be more careful around him. He was getting too old for his britches. Turning the corner, the street in front of their house looked like a street party. There were people standing and drinking and even some of them dancing. She instantly knew that her parents would not be happy.

Sampson and Deidre Hart were simple folks with deep rooted values. They both grew up in the south; he on a tobacco farm in North Carolina and she in the rural area of Scottsboro. They settled in Birmingham to raise their family in peace and lead their congregation in prayer. The Hart family would not be swayed by fire hoses or dogs and they would not be celebrating in the streets with the other heathens. The Hart family would be united in prayer and that is what Vonda expected when she got home. Climbing the stairs to their second floor tenement, she began to smell the aroma of dinner.

"Mmmm, mmm. Smells like cabbage and ham hocks. You think so Vonda?"

"Smells like it, Ty. But don't go grabbin' at the biscuits before we say grace again. You know how mad that makes daddy."

The door at the top of the stairs opened and Deidre looked down at her children dressed in her kitchen apron with a towel slung back over her shoulder.

"It's about time. I was startin' to get worried 'bout you child. Tyrone ain't big enough to hold back nobody."

"I am too, Mama."

"Ok, big man. Go get washed up for dinner."

Deidre tapped the back of her young son as he ran past her to the bathroom. He moved quickly to wash his hands so he could get to the table faster. Vonda moved forward but was pulled aside by her mother.

"Was there trouble down in the street?"

"Not that I saw, Mama. Lots of people are happy down there though. You think there is going to be trouble?"

Deidre Hart just looked down at her feet as she shook her head.

"My dear child. There's always trouble when our people get happy. It's the way of the world. If people learned to keep their heads down and pray for the moment to pass like your father and me, the white folks won't notice us bein' happy. But no. They got to dance and carry on and make fools of themselves so those mean ones like that Bull Connor get a bee in their bonnet. They don't want us happy. They don't want us to get no 'tention. They want us to stay in the dark like our kin done and their kin before them. Mark my words, child. There is trouble brewin' somewhere tonight."

Vonda never knew whether to listen to her mother's rants or excuse them for the older woman that she was. A holy and just woman of the church that everyone looked up to was not the only hat she wore. She was the matriarch of her family and a protective mama bear at that. She would never let harm come to any of her children and would not put her political conviction before church or family.

"Yes, Mama."

"Don't you *Yes Mama* me. There is something big gonna happen. I feel it in my bones. I don't want you goin' out after dinner like you usually do. I don't want you sneakin' off to see your secret boy."

Vonda stopped dead in her tracks. There was no way her mother knew anything about what she was doing behind her back. She knew she was just fishing.

"I don't know what you are talking about, Mama."

"Don't you lie to me, girl. Ain't no need. I know when a girl's in love. I was a young one too. Seems like a long time ago but I still know that glow. I ain't sayin' nothin' to your daddy or your brothers but I know. I may not know who but I'm sure it's one of your brother's friends and that's why you want it to be secret. I ain't stoppin' you. I just don't want you goin' out tonight."

"Ok, Mama. I'll stay right here with you tonight."

"That's a good girl. Now go get washed up for dinner."

Vonda walked off to get clean while the rest of the family made their way to the dinner table. By the time she returned, her brothers were giving her scowls for making them wait for their dinner.

"Nice of you to join us Vonda."

"Sorry, Papa."

"Not to worry. Patience is a virtue dear child."

Vonda took her seat at the dinner table, receiving looks from her siblings as well as her parents. Silently, she joined hands with them as her father lowered his head and began to say grace.

"Bless this house, Oh, Lord. Bless us for the love we share and for the bread we break. Bless us for the food we are about to eat and the new world we are part of. We are blessed, we are hopeful and we are humble, oh Lord. Bless us this night and all the nights to come. Amen."

"Amen"

The words were barely out of Sampson's mouth before the biscuits started flying. Vonda's brothers all dove into the food like it was an island oasis in the dessert. As usual, it was Deidre that put the brakes on the chow line.

"Mind your manners boys and leave something for your sister. There's no reason to act like animals. There's enough of that in the streets tonight."

"They just bein' happy, Mama." Rudy, the oldest brother was the first to chime in. As a working man, he often acted as the third adult in all conversations.

"Is that right, Rudy? You think 'cause you have a job now you can speak for the common man down on the street?"

The boy knew that his father was just trying to get a rise out of him. Since his hunger was greater than his insolence, he subdued himself.

"No, sir. Just makin' an observation."

The six family members chewed their food in silence for a moment while they waited for the tension to pass.

"Your Mama and I were speakin' to the elders at the church. We all fear that there is gonna be some blow back from all this. We would feel better is you all stuck 'round the house tonight instead of goin' out. Same holds true for you too Vonda."

Before she could respond her brothers were putting down their forks to get in their comments.

"Come on, Pops. We were gonna shoot some ball tonight..."

"And we were heading down to the Gaston Motel. The Christian Movement is hosting a vigil for Reverend King, you know to thank him and such..."

"I don't want you anywhere near that motel. You hear me boy?"

"But, Mama. It's not like that. We ain't goin' to the motel for any trouble. It's just to give thanks for..."

"I know what it's for. Don't be a fool."

"Mama?"

"What your mother is tryin' to say is that any fool can see that there's a target on that motel like it was a deer out in the woods. If there's gonna be trouble, it's gonna start there. Those men and their hoses probably standin' out there already waitin' for boys like you to show up. They just waitin' on an excuse to turn their dogs on you. Nope, like I said...tonight all you kids stay inside. Let the dark cloud pass and you can go out tomorrow. It's one night at home. Put your mama and I at peace."

"But Reverend King will be gone in the morning. They say he's movin' on to Atlanta tomorrow so we won't get another chance..."

"All the more reason to stay home tonight. The Reverend is a great man but trouble follows him like a stray dog to scraps. He knows we are all thankful for what he done for us now let him move along to Atlanta. His brother is gonna stay on. Let's see what Wallace gonna do in the morning and we can get back to normal tomorrow. How's that boys?"

The three brothers simply nodded as they continued to eat. They knew there was no use in arguing. Things were not usually up for discussion in the Hart household. When the parents spoke, the children listened. That was the way of things.

"How 'bout you Vonda. You ok with stayin' home with your brothers tonight?"

She sensed that her mother knew more than she was letting on but she also knew that it was probably their little secret. Their little *white* lie that the men folk knew nothing about. Vonda intended to keep it that way.

"Of course, Mama...long as I can have some more of your delicious corn bread."

The tasty treat would have to suffice in the only type of sweetness Vonda was going to have tonight.

3

The noise from the street didn't die down until after midnight. Even though it was a Friday night, there were mixed emotions from the neighborhood. Many were dancing and carrying on because they felt that a battle had been won. It was a crucial battle meant to have repercussions for years to come. Yet, on the wiser more conventional side of the street, there were many who were fearful of the days to come. Like the Hart family, they stayed inside their houses and prayed for the noise to subside, for life to get back to normal, and for the excitement of the day to pass.

Vonda Hart lay in her bed staring out her window at the sky. Since she was the only daughter, she had the privilege of having her own room while her three brothers shared a room down the hall. When she was younger, she had a room with Rudy but as time progressed and they both approached their teenage years, Rudy moved in with his younger brothers and gave his sister her privacy. The decision was not popular in the household at the time, but has since become written in stone. Her brothers wouldn't have it any other way. If they had any choice but to share a bathroom with their sister, they would rather forget she was a girl altogether. They each cringed when they discovered feminine products in the bathroom they held as sacred ground. It was best that Vonda had her own room and all in the family were in agreement.

For her part, Vonda was happy that her room was at the end of the hall by herself. The bathroom, the living room area and her parent's bedroom all separated her from the obnoxious sounds and terrible smells emanating from her brother's room. They were nasty boys. She loved them in every way a sister could love her brothers but they were still nasty boys at the end of the day. It was a miracle that after living her life with them she was still interested in the opposite sex.

The day's events in Birmingham meant more to her and her life than anyone could imagine. Could de-segregation really become a thing? Would there be a day where she could drink from the same water fountain as anyone else? Could she actually shop in the same dress shops as her fellow white teenagers without scorn?

Could there really come a day when she could sit down at the Woolworth lunch counter with her boyfriend and share a shake with him? She could not imagine such a day would ever come to fruition in her lifetime.

Vonda knew that she was a hopeless romantic. She dreamed endlessly of a world where skin color did not matter. She thought that someday, she would be afforded the same opportunities as girls with the same education, intelligence and drive. She felt in her bones that what truly mattered was inside her mind and body and not what the outside world was perpetuating as reality. She dreamed of a world where she and her boyfriend could live happily ever after.

It was not all dreams and fantasy; she had done her research. While the negro libraries were limited by their offerings, she had been to a Freedom Library. The depth of knowledge that was offered to her there made her eternally faithful to the cause and swore never to divulge its location. Rudy had taken her there one Saturday and the two of them had sat for hours reading page after page, in book after book, hungry for the knowledge that had been hidden from them for so long. In those wonderful pages she read about couples like her and her boyfriend, in faraway places, that were able to live in harmony regardless of their skin color. They may have to travel far, but she knew deep in her heart that there was a place in the world for them.

Clink

The noise against her window startled her at first. She was unsure what to make of it as it may simply be a large bug that had smacked against her window pane.

Clink

The second time she heard the noise was enough to get her full attention. She no longer thought it was her imagination or an insect. Someone was throwing something against her window.

Clink

Rolling over to the side of her bed, Vonda raised her head slowly as not to give someone a clear shot at shooting. Her parents often warned to stay away from the windows at night but curiosity was skinning the cat tonight. She could no more stay away from someone throwing pebbles at her window as a moth could stay away from a flame.

Clink

Vonda tried to focus her eyes into the darkness but it was difficult. Her window faced the back alley and not the sidewalk basked with streetlights. In the darkness she could make out a figure; a man with a hooded sweatshirt covering his head. Instantly, she knew who her midnight caller was and she was petrified with fear. Not for her own safety or that of her family, but that of her lover. Throwing open her window, she whispered emphatically into the night air.

"Chuck! What are you doing here? Do you want to get yourself killed?"

"I had to see you Vonda. I just had to."

Looking back into her bedroom and checking to make sure no one was coming to barge through the door, she quickly got up and locked her door. This was a forbidden act in her household but she knew she had to protect herself and her boyfriend the best that she knew how. Coming back to the window, she looked down into the alley where Chuck Connor was still standing. His white face seemed to shine like a lightbulb off the slight moon light that was shining down into the alleyway.

"I miss you too, you damn fool, but you are gonna get yourself killed out there. Why are you on this side of town? Especially this late at night. You better have a damn good reason for risking your life like this."

This time it was Chuck who was checking his surroundings. He had been careful to make sure he was not followed. He parked his motorcycle in the park and walked along the tree line to the other side of the park. When he had eyes on 4th Avenue, he lurked among the shadows, keeping his hood on and his face down. With his hands in his pocket there was not a sole that could tell his skin color, especially at night.

"I'm sorry, Vonda, but I was careful. I wouldn't have come if it wasn't important."

"The important part better not be that I missed our date. You know that happens sometimes. We just can't get away. I thought we…"

"It ain't about us Vonda, baby. It's much more…"

Chuck put his head back down and walked a short way down the alley. Again he was checking to make sure nobody was listening. When he was sure they were still along, he returned to underneath his lover's window.

"Chuck? What's got you so spooked? What couldn't wait until tomorrow? It's Saturday, we could sneak off to the park…"

"There's no time for that baby. I gotta tell you…there's something big happening…something big indeed…I heard my father after dinner. He was talking on the phone. You and your kin gotta protect yourselves. If anything should happen to you, I'll never forgive myself."

Vonda darted around at the mention of her kin. Her mother already suspected that she was dating someone and her whole world would explode if her mama caught her talking to her white boyfriend. With the coast seemingly clear, she returned to face him. She was now scared not only for him but to what he was talking about. Chuck's father was the most feared white public official in Birmingham.

"Chuck. Calm down and tell me. Tell me what you came to say and get yourself out of here before someone sees you."

He took one last look over his shoulder before blurting it out. "It's the Klan baby. They comin'. I heard my dad talkin' to them on the phone. He is callin' every one of them to Birmingham tomorrow."

"What? Where? What else do you know? Tell me, Chuck."

"I don't know much more than that. They comin' though baby. I'm sure they gonna go after that King fellow down at the Gaston Motel. I heard him sayin' something about that. You gotta stay clear of that mess, Vonda. You hear me? You and your brothers got to stay away. There's gonna be trouble..."

Vonda instantly thought back to the conversation at dinner. Trouble was the meaning why they all stayed in on a Friday night. Her mother and father knew there was going to be trouble and this just solidified it.

"Ok, Chuck. I hear you. I believe you. I'll spread the word. Now, you got to get your pale face out of here. You are glowing like a lightbulb on a string. Someone gonna see you. Just get yourself out of here and I'll do the rest."

Tears were flowing down her cheeks by this point. Moments like this made her think they could never be together like a normal couple. He came from white money on the good side of town. She came from black roots on the other side of the tracks. All they could hope for is muddied waters instead of the love they deserved.

"But Vonda..."

She had to be strong for both of them. "You spoke your peace, Chuck. Now go. Get back to your side of town before the Klan catches you and strings you up too."

Chuck knew she was right. He knew he was risking his life with every minute he stayed on this side of town. Of course, his father would come to his rescue but not if he found out what he was really doing over here. He had no choice but to tuck his tail between his legs and get back the way he came.

"Vonda..."

She couldn't hold back her tears. "Go, Chuck. Just go..."

Chuck Connor looked up to the love of his life in a darkened window and whispered the only words that mattered. "I love you, Vonda..."

"I love you too."

He didn't wait another moment and disappeared into the shadows of the alley. Like the whisper of a dream, he was gone like a cloud in the dark night air.

4

The love story of Chuck and Vonda was as foreign as two key ingredients coming together in a chef's kitchen. In their current climate, it was a mix of impossibility. Like every great love story in history, they needed to reach beyond their limitations to find closure. No one had ever thought to add peanut butter to chocolate before 1928 yet they are synonymous with good flavor and decadence today. Like spaghetti and meatballs, Chuck and Vonda were a blend of cultures that worked perfectly if not for the influence of everything else in their word.

The two met coincidentally at a rally that both opposing families were trying to stop. Vonda had marched with her family in solidarity at the way they were being treated. Chuck had attended the rally at the direction of his mother. She was worried about how far her husband was pushing himself in his war against the negroes and asked Chuck to go and keep an eye on his father.

Ironically, his love and empathy was lost as his father turned to a monster before his eyes. When he ordered his men to turn fire hoses, dogs, and battle sticks on innocent people because of the color of their skin, Chuck was lost forever. He could no longer support a man that would do such horrible things to other human beings. His father had been his mentor, a man he looked up to for his undying public service. In short, he believed the rhetoric that his father was doing the best for the community of Birmingham. Seeing the hatred, the prejudice and brutality coming from his father with his own eyes, he was eternally changed for the greater good. The fact that a beautiful young girl lay weeping on a side walk as her family was persecuted led Chuck Connor on a much different path than his father would have intended. Instead of turning the dogs on her while she was down and out, he offered the girl a hand.

The gesture was as simple and fleeting as any moment in life. There was someone that had fallen and Chuck put out his hand to help her up. It did not matter what color his hand was or the color of the hand that he offered his assistance to. He was simply one human offering help to another. In all the chaos, the moment was lost in the background of the day. No one noticed that a white boy was offering assistance to a black girl in a racial protest. She grasped his hand and rose to her feet before she even realized that the help up came from someone as white as the driven snow.

As she got up and regained her balance, she looked into the eyes of her white knight and was instantly captured. Was she dreaming or did she really get assistance from the opposition? Did the redcoats really help the colonials in their attack of the mother land? At the moment, Vonda knew nothing about history and the moment she was a part of. She only knew love at first sight for a nameless, faceless, boy who was looking back at her the same way.

For Chuck Connor, the moment was one of revelation and release. He was raised to believe that people of a different color were his enemy. During the march, he watched his father arm his troops against the enemy, taking fire on defenseless people that were simply marching in the streets. This young, beautiful girl was showing no signs of being an enemy. She was a wounded lamb and he was the silent hero who rescued her.

When she rose to her feet, their eyes were locked. They were both trained not to linger contact with the opposing skin but their gaze remained. Words were not spoken and were not needed. Just moments after the rescue, her brother grabbed her by the arm and whisked her away into the crowd. Chuck wondered for the rest of the day if the interaction actually happened or if it was a figment of his imagination. She would lay awake that night wondering the same thing.

In the days that followed, they both wandered towards the *fringe*. There was a part of the city where an invisible barrier existed. It was simply a street that separated the *white* part of the city from the *darker element* as Bull Connor referred to. In the eyes of those that lived on both sides of the street, the barrier was real. It was like the Berlin wall, separating East from West. For the locals, the *fringe* was an area that divided a city, divided their people, and divided sun from shadow.

Chuck Connor rode his motorcycle along the sunny side of the street very slowly. He looked towards the darkness, hoping to catch a glimpse of the beauty that captured his heart. For Vonda Hart, she walked with her brother along the same street, gazing towards the light in hopes of seeing her white knight. It took only three days for the pair to gaze upon each other once again and the fringe was bridged. He slowed his cycle to a stop and she pretended to look in a store window as their eyes locked. With a nod of his head, Chuck motioned for Vonda to go around the corner. Convincing her brother to go into one of the stores alone, she quickly ventured to the hidden place that would change her destiny. Rounding the corner, she found Chuck waiting for her leaning against his motorcycle.

"Hello."

The sound of his voice made her recoil a step or two. Sensing her justified fear, Chuck tried to put her at ease.

"It's ok. Don't be afraid. I won't hurt you."

"That's what all you boys say."

"Well, I'm not just any boy. My name is Chuck."

"I know who you are. Your father is well known around these parts."

The young Connor boy put his head down in shame at the mention of his father. "I'm sorry. My dad ain't me. I never knew he was capable of such things until I saw it with my own eyes. I'm sorry he done what he did."

Vonda hesitated for a moment before answering. She looked over her shoulder to make sure her brother had not followed her into the alley and then turned back to the boy who had captured her interest.

"My name is Vonda. Vonda Hart. I only have a minute but I wanted to thank you. Most boys wouldn't have stopped and helped me up, Especially a white boy."

"Is that how you see me, Vonda. As a white boy?"

She looked back at him with nothing but love and interest. She knew nothing about his skin color at the moment and thought she never would.

"Surprisingly not. I only see a cute boy who came to my rescue."

"Any time ma'am."

Chuck lowered his head in a gesture that was tipping his hat. His attempt at being a gentleman made Vonda blush.

"I…I gotta go…you know… before my brother comes…then there would be trouble."

Chuck smiled. "No worries, Ms. Vonda. You go right along. I think I'll come round this street most days at this time if you ever want to talk again."

Vonda took a step back before returning the gaze and smile that made her heart melt. "Well, I just may do that Mr. Chuck. I may do that indeed."

The young girl was giddy as she rounded the corner back on her side of the fringe. Luckily, Chuck had exited the other end of the alley since her brother was waiting for her.

"There you are."

"Oh, hey Rudy." His presence startled her.

"Where did you go? I only ducked into that record store for a minute."

Vonda knew her older brother and he would not need much convincing.

"I was chasing a cat. It ran into the alley so I chased after it. It was cute. Really cute. It was small and cuddly…"

"Whatever. Stupid girls chasing after cats. Can we get going now?"

Vonda smiled looking back into the alley. She was happy for the chance encounter with Chuck but knew better than to push her luck.

"Yea. I'm sure that cat run off by now anyway. I'll have to come back tomorrow and see if I can feed it."

"You do whatever you want tomorrow. I'll be workin'. Let Tyrone bring you down here so you can chase a stupid cat."

Chase the cat she did. Some would say that they caught each other in the days and weeks that followed. Their stolen moments in the alley segued to more private rendezvous in the park. Their love blossomed even in the darkness where they were forced to exist. They carried their own sunshine and provided their own nutrients. Soon their flower of love had grown into a deep rooted tree of life that they could never share with the world.

5

Vonda and Deidre were always the first to rise in the Hart household. Weekdays or weekends, they always got up before the boys and made breakfast for everyone. Sampson would always wander in before his sons and pour himself a cup of black coffee. Depending on the day, he would stumble off to get ready for work or church. That Saturday morning, May 11, 1963, started like all the rest of the Saturday free days. With coffee in hand, Sampson mumbled something incoherently as he dragged himself into the living room. Vonda and her mother shared a hearty laugh as they looked on after him.

Deidre was busy whisking the biscuit mix to pour into the pan and get into the oven. Vonda was readying the pancake batter for the griddle and was tossing around in her mind how to broach the subject with her mother. Always sharp as a tack, regardless of the hour, Deidre was the first to coax her daughter into confession.

"Out with it child."

Vonda was startled at first but realized her mother had been staring her down as she was lost in thought churning the pancake batter.

"Mama?"

"Don't you mama me. I can see you got a bee in your bonnet. So out with it child before I start on the sausage gravy."

Vonda had to be careful about how she presented the warning she received from Chuck because her mother couldn't know where it came from. When she didn't come right out with it, her mother kept pushing.

"Nobody getting' breakfast in this house unless you say what you got to say. Those boys are gonna get mighty upset with you child."

"Yes, mama...it's just that...well I heard something last night and it scared me some."

Deidre Hart laughed heartily. "Oh is that it child. Well, your daddy and I were just havin' relations. Ain't nothin' to be scared of. You'll be havin' relations of your own one day with your own husband."

"Mama! That's not it at all. I've heard that…well, let's just say it wasn't what I heard last night. I am talking about something I heard out my window. In the middle of the night."

"What's you heard child that got you carryin' on in a frightful way? Did someone do somethin' bad?"

Vonda hated lying to her parents, especially her mother. She always thought the lies were written all over her face.

"No, mama. But I think they gonna do all sorts of bad."

Deidre put down her whisk and simply stared at her daughter. "Now you got me nervous child. Better start at the beginning."

"Well, I was laying in bed sleeping. It was late, real late when I heard these two men talkin' in the alley. I think they drank a little too much juice and they were runnin' their mouths. They were talkin' about the bad men, mama. The men in the hoods."

"The Klan child? Were they talkin' about the Ku Klux Klan?"

"Yes, ma'am. They were sayin' that the Klan was comin' to Birmingham today. They said they were coming from all over to get on Dr. King. They said somethin' about him stayin' at the Gaston Motel. I'm worried mama. I think you ought to tell the elders at the church. They need to tell people to stay clear of there."

Deidre went back to slowly stirring the biscuit mixture and spooning it out into the pan. Her mind seemed to be running a mile a minute and Vonda didn't want to interrupt her. When she couldn't take it any longer, she put her pancake bowl next to the griddle a little louder than expected. That startled her mother out of her daze.

"You didn't say nothin' to your brothers did you?"

"No, mama. It happened while they were sleeping. While you were all sleeping. I tossed and turned on it all night."

"Are you sure you heard it right child? I need you to be sure? Could it have been a dream that you had that seemed real?"

"No, mama. Not at all. Where would I know any of that stuff anyway? It wasn't a dream mama. I heard what those men were sayin' just as clear as day."

"Ok, Vonda. I believe in you. This is what we gonna do. Don't you be sayin' nothin' about it to your brothers. I don't want to get them riled up. They'll take off like darn fools and do somethin' crazy. No, after breakfast you and I gonna sit down with your daddy. You're gonna tell him what you done just told me. Then he will decide who to tell. He good like that. We are gonna be alright but we gotta be smart girl. We ain't gonna let those white men get us. Nope, not at all. Whitey not gonna win today."

Both women nodded as they went back to their cooking. Vonda was both scared and happy. She was happy that Chuck was so brave to come over to her window and tell her about the danger that was lurking. She was happy to know that he loved her so much that he wanted her and her family to be safe, protected from the Klan. If her mother only knew that it was her white boyfriend that may have saved the day and prevented something terrible from happening to her family she may not have believed him. She might have thought he had different motives and Vonda didn't want her to think that way. Chuck was her knight in white armor as he had been once before. This time he was going to save them all.

6

Breakfast at the Connor household was as regular and precise as a military base filled with young recruits. The first alarm always rang first at 5am so Mary Connor could rise, put on her apron, and get started making coffee. She would boil the water for the oatmeal and gather the milk and eggs from the milk man delivery on the porch, as well as the morning paper to bring them inside. She would add the dairy to the icebox as she removed one egg from the tray to poach for Theo. By the time his alarm went off at 530am, breakfast was well under way.

At 545am, seven days a week, Bull Connor arrived in the kitchen. Sitting down without a word to his wife, he expected to find his black coffee poured into a cup and saucer and awaiting him. Moments after sitting down, his breakfast of a single poached egg, white toast blackened without butter, and a bowl of plain oatmeal, was served to him by his wife. There was no breakfast banter or discussions. The whole meal progressed in peace. By the time Chuck's alarm went off at 6am, the second cup of coffee had been served to his father.

Charles (Chuck) Connor, rose quietly as he knew his father's routine. Whether it was a school day or a weekend, he was expected to sit at the breakfast table with his mother and father. His presence was essential to the family unit but there was no expectation of anything further. He was not expected to take part in any conversations nor was he required to eat. What he was expected of was to come out and sit quietly while his father planned out his daily attacks on the population of Birmingham. Without fanfare, Chuck entered the kitchen with ruffled hair, pulling up his suspenders as he poured himself a cup of coffee.

"Did you bring in the cream, Mom?"

"I did. It's in the icebox with the eggs. Do you want me to get it for you?"

Without looking up from his morning paper, Bull Connor exercised his control.

"Don't you budge from that chair, Mary. If that boy isn't man enough to drink his coffee black, he should get his own cream for his coffee."

"Do I have to drink my coffee black to be a real man, Dad? Is that what you are saying? I'm pretty sure plenty of men take their coffee with cream or even sugar. That doesn't make them any less of a man for what they drink."

Theo gave no thought to the rhetoric spewed by his son. Instead, he flipped the conversation to the offensive.

"No. Real men drink their coffee any way they want it but then again, real men don't gallivant all night long on their motorcycle."

Chuck froze in his tracks. Could his father actually know what he was up to last night? He decided to test the waters before proceeding.

"Not sure what you are saying."

"You know darn well what I am saying. Last night you were out on your motorcycle pretty late. How many times have I told you not to go out late at night? There are elements in the night in this city that I don't want you associating with. Do you understand me boy?"

"Oh, I understand you. What you are saying is that you don't want me going out at night because I might run into some negroes. Heaven help us if we share the same street as the black men."

Mary simply shook her head. "Must you two go at it first thing in the morning. Can't we have five minutes of peace and quiet?"

Both father and son retuned to the tasks at hand. Chuck removed the glass bottle of cream from the ice box, uncapped it and poured some into his cup. Sitting down silently cross the table from his father, the tension was palpable. Mary was the one who finally broke the peace accord.

"Do you want some oatmeal or eggs to go with your coffee, dear?"

"No, mama. It's Saturday. I'm in no hurry to go anywhere. I can eat in a little while."

"Do you think your mother is going to serve you all day long?"

Chuck once again knew that his father was baiting him into an argument. His tired body didn't have the restraint to know better.

"No, I wouldn't want to interrupt her serving you, Dad."

"Charles, don't…"

"It's ok, Mary. The boy is just being insolent. I'm sure a Saturday spent working for the greater good will teach him some respect."

Chuck stopped drinking his coffee and looked across to his father.

"Excuse me?"

"You heard me, boy. I have something for you to do later. You are just 17 years old and as long as you live under my roof, you will do what I tell you."

After what he had heard the night before, Chuck had a pretty good idea what his father wanted him to be involved in.

"How exactly do you want me to spend my Saturday?"

Bull Connor lowered his newspaper to the table and removed his glasses. Wiping the lenses on a napkin, he slowly returned them to the brim of his nose and stared across at his son.

"It is time you take up the cause, young man. I want you to meet some associates of mine as they enter town. They need some local guidance to get them to their destination."

"So you want me to be a tour guide for who exactly?"

"Chuck. If your father needs you to escort some visitors from out of town I'm sure you can do that for him. It doesn't sound like too much to ask."

"But, Mama…"

Bull Connors smiled his sinister smile. "You heard your mother Charles. I need you to meet some men at the train station. You can pick them up with my sedan. I'll let you get ready then you can drive me to the office and drop me off. I have some work to attend to."

"On a Saturday, Theo?"

"Yes, Mary. On a Saturday. The good word doesn't silence depending on the day of the calendar."

Chuck was uneasy about the whole situation. He knew what his father wanted him to be a part of and he would not stand for it.

"What exactly am I supposed to do with these associates of yours once I pick them up at the train station."

Bull drank the rest of his coffee and put it back on the saucer. Without looking at his wife or his son, he rose from the table and placed his napkin on the table. For a moment, Chuck thought his father was just going to ignore him. When Bull spoke, his son wished he had never asked the question in the first place.

"That's just it, boy. You're just gonna pick them up. They need a ride over to a little convention we are putting together."

"…and where is that convention happening?"

"The Gaston Motel. Just bring them there and they will tell you the rest."

Chuck Connor froze as he instantly knew his destiny was sealed.

7

Jake Molina was the sitting resident Pastor at the Southern Baptist Freedom Church in Birmingham, Alabama. A young pastor among the many "elders" of the church, he had been sitting in the leader of the faith chair for 10 years in 1963. When he first took over, the world was in a different place. Fresh out of the Korean War, people were looking to heal and solidify the religion that had gotten them through the rains and pains of the foreign land. Facing the hatred in society just a decade later was a difficult pill for any pastor let alone one that had seen so much.

Jake had received the call from a payphone on 4th Avenue. The understanding around the whole community was that certain phones in town were under wiretap surveillance. Calls coming in and out of the patronage were guarded in nature and the message was clearly identified as an *urgent church matter* that required a pastoral home visit in the Hart residence. Sensing trouble on the horizon, Jake set out on foot to walk the few blocks over to the home he knew so well. The Hart family had taken him in on several occasions where they prayed and broke bread together in the peace of a faithful family. Climbing the stairs to their second story home, he was greeted by the three Hart boys who were leaving together.

"G'morning boys. Where are we off to on this fine Saturday morning?"

"Morning Pastor Jake. We aren't going far. We're just goin' across the way to play some ball. Mama done said that she and Daddy needed to have a chat with you. Don't know why Vonda got to stay and we had to skidaddle but you would know better on that."

"Not at all. I'm walkin' into this field just as blindly as Moses walkin' into the Red Sea. Not sure what's it all about but we sure are gonna find out. Now you boys run along while I talk to your folks."

"Yessir, Pastor Jake."

The three boys hurried down the stairs on their way over to the park. You never knew when the adults would change their mind and find something to mix up a good Saturday but they were certain not to hang around and find out. On the upside, Jake reached the top of the stairs and knocked. A moment later, Deidre appeared in the doorway.

"What you boys forget...oh hello Jake. We didn't expect you to come over so quick. Please come in. Sampson and Vonda are waiting at the table for you."

"It sounded urgent Deidre. I wanted to get here soon as I could."

"Well, could be...but I'll let you decide. Come on in."

Pastor Jake walked into the house that he had been in so many times before. Vonda was sitting next to her father and it was clearly evident that she had been crying.

"Vonda, dear child. What troubles you so on such a beautiful morning?"

"Jake, I think you better sit down. It's not a simple morn' here in our house. Mayhap Deidre can get you some coffee."

"Of course, of course. I didn't mean to set aside the pleasantries. I would love a cup of joe and by the delicious aroma in here, I wouldn't say no to one of your famous biscuits, Deidre."

"Some apricot jam as well?"

"You know me far too well, Mrs. Hart." The pastor pulled back on one of the kitchen chairs and sat down across from Sampson and his daughter. "Now what's all this hullabaloo about? Somethin's got this child all up in a dither. Did someone disrespect you Vonda? Is that what we need to pray on?"

The young lady held back her tears as she wiped her nose with her father's handkerchief.

"No, Pastor Jake. Nothin' like that. I'm just scared is all. I heard something."

Deidre placed the coffee and biscuit in front of the holy man quietly and took a seat on the other side of her daughter.

"Oh, Vonda. We should not be moved by rumor and here say. Such a thing can bring fright to even the strongest of hearts."

"But it wasn't just..."

"That's ok, Vonda. I'll take it from here." Sampson interrupted his daughter before she could disrespect the pastor. Her message was important but the delivery was just as critical.

"Jake. You've been here many a times. You know we wouldn't call on you over some school yard gossip. The girl done heard some men talkin' outside her bedroom window. It was late at night but she could hear them clear as day."

The pastor took a slow sip of his coffee and spread some jam on his biscuit before going on. Placing the knife down, he folded his hands in front of his face before continuing.

"Maybe you should start from the beginning."

"It was late at night and the girl..."

"No. Not you Sampson. With all due respect, I would like to hear what Vonda has to say."

Sampson nodded silently as he knew his place. He was an elder of the church but Jake was the faith leader of their congregation. He looked over at his daughter and gave her the silent approval to go on.

"Like Papa said, I was laying in my bed late at night when..."

Vonda explained to her Pastor everything Chuck had told her. She felt terrible lying to a man of faith, but she balanced it in the belief that it was for the greater good. The message was the most important thing, not on who delivered it. While Pastor Jake would not judge that it was from her boyfriend, he may question the messenger if he knew the color of his skin.

When she was done, Jake had a deep concern across his face. He said nothing at first but simply took a bite of his biscuit and washed it down with some coffee. He was just about to speak out when Tyrone burst through the front door.

"Mama...we just heard..."

"Don't you come bargin' in here child. The adults are talkin' and I told you to go play ball with your brothers. Now, go..."

"But, Mama. Goven'r Wallace just pulled off the troops. He sent the coppers home. He said we don't need no mo' protection."

"Where you hearin' this boy?" Sampson was out of his chair and fired up.

"We saw them. We saw them drivin' by and we stopped one and asked. He said that they had been told to pack up and go home."

Jake and Sampson looked silently at each other and then both turned to look at Deidre. The three of them were in agreement.

"So it's true."

Tyrone was confused. "Of course it be true. We seen it with our own eyes."

"No, not that Ty, shush your face..."

It was Vonda who was struggling the most putting it all together.

"Will someone please explain? How is it that the police leavin' has anythin' to do with what I heard?"

This time, the Pastor deferred to the head of the family instead of the head of the church. He nodded, giving his approval to let the ugliness of the world enter the family's kitchen.

"The puzzle pieces fit Vonda. Don't 'ya see? Wallace pulled out the state troopers because he is letting the Klan come in. With no one to protect us, the Klan is gonna rain down on us with fire and bring Hell to our doorstep."

Vonda began to cry. She wept not only in her fear of what was coming to the city, but knowing that Chuck, the man she loved, was the son of Satan himself.

8

The blue 1961 Cadillac Sedan Deville was the pride and joy of Bull Connor. In the corrupt world where he was a centerpiece, no one dared to question how a public servant, even the Commissioner of Public Safety, could afford such a luxury car. With white leather interior that matched the white wall tires, it was a car to be envied and for Bull, it was a car that commanded respect.

The car itself was a gift for favors rendered. On paper, it was the grand prize of a Christmas raffle that really had no chance of anyone else winning since the only ticket in the winning basket pull belonged to Bull Connor. The car was delivered in style a week later and appeared in his driveway with a large ostentatious red ribbon on it. From the moment he cut the ribbon off the car and climbed into the driver's seat, he revered that car more than his wife or son. He hand-washed the car every Sunday afternoon and applied the Turtle Wax with a hard buff until it shined brighter than the sunlit sky. Nicknamed, "the sedan", the car was his pride and joy.

"You understand the plan for the day, boy?"

Bull Connor had backed the car out of the garage and moments after his son joined him in the passenger seat, the father jumped at him verbally.

"Yes, sir. I do. You told me enough times. It's not that hard."

Bull shook his head at his son's insolence. Perhaps a few hours with some real God-fearing men would put instill some humility in his son.

"If you know it so well, why don't you recite it back to me, boy."

Chuck Connor hated being called *boy* almost as much as he hated the name *Charles* instead of the name Chuck he had grown accustomed to. His father would call him anything that fancied him as long as it knocked his son down a few pegs in the process. *Boy* was his favorite go to as there was no emotion he could possess besides degrading humility.

"Sure Pops. After we share such a warm and joyful ride together to your office, you want me to drop you off while I take the car."

"You are not *taking* the car anywhere. You are simply *borrowing* the sedan to do my bidding. Do you understand?"

"I understand Pops. I understand you have only let me drive your prize possession when you need me to do somethin' for you. Have you ever thought that maybe I might like to take a date out in the sedan one night?"

Bull Connor burst out in laughter. "It will be a cold day in Hell, young man, when I let you take my car out so you can sodomize one of your floozies. You got your damn motorbike. Let them ride on the back of that contraption. The sedan is a work of art and should not be soiled by the likes of them."

It was Chuck's turn to break out in laughter. "So, let me get this straight, Pops. The girls I go out with are floozies, not worth the leather interior for them to sit down upon in their pretty dresses. But you want me to take that same car, and pick up a bunch of red-necked, toothless wonders from the backwoods of Alabama and bring them into town with their White Hoods intact? Is that what you are sayin' daddy? That a bunch of Klansman are worth riding in your car but not a nice young lady I may be datin'?"

Bull let himself calm down a bit before answering. He could feel the heat rise up in his cheeks and before he erupted upon his son, he needed to remember the importance of the day. Chuck was a link, a hinge pin upon which all the rest of the day's events were going to swivel around. If he didn't have him to do his bidding, he would have to switch to less desirable plans of action. As the consummate politician, he knew how to turn a conversation in a different direction.

"Charles. You and I don't see eye to eye on such things. I'm not sure we have for quite a spell now. What I do know is that when you were a young boy, you used to look up to me. You always told people that you wanted to be just like your papa one day. Well, son, that day is here. It's time for you to set aside your foolishness and start acting like a man. I'm not askin' you to man a rifle or take up a hose for the cause, I'm simply askin' you to go out to Gardendale and pick up my guests comin' in from Bessemer. There's no need for you to talk to them or even make chit chat. Just bring them back into town and drop them off. Is that so hard? Why we gotta argue about a simple car ride with some business associates of mine."

"If they are associates of yours then why am I bringin' them to the police station and not your office, daddy? You can call it whatever you want but I think it's dirty. If they comin' in from Bessemer, they in the Klan. You know it and I know it."

"Why? Do you think everyone in Alabama is in the Klan?"

Chuck took a moment before responding to his father. He was dangerously close to tipping his hand but it may be the last conversation he ever had with the man and he wanted to make sure he didn't leave anything on the table.

"Let me tell you somethin' Pops. I'm not the dumb kid you think I am. I hear things. Probably shouldn't hear them, but I do. It's not like you try to hide them around the house. I know you called in the Klan because of what happened yesterday. I know the men you want me to pick up are part of that group. Now, I may not know what you plan to do with those men but it ain't no good business. Not at all. I'll do what you want and bring them to the police station but after that, I'm out. I'll bring the car back and park it in front of your office like you told me too. From there, I'll walk myself home."

Bull Connor smiled. "See that boy? You ain't so dumb after all. I'm glad you know what you doin'. Maybe later in life you'll be proud to know you were a part of history in some way. A man ought to know what he is getting' himself into. For you, it's just a ride in the car with some men. After that, you gone about your way. Go back to ridin' that motorbike or chasin' skirts or whatever you want. For a few hours you are gonna step up and be a man. Then you go back to whatever life you want."

As the sedan pulled up to the Municipal Office building where Bull Connor had his high perch, he put the car in park. Grabbing his briefcase, he got out of the sedan without a word as Chuck slid across to the driver's seat. Looking after his father who didn't care enough to say goodbye, Chuck Connor hoped that those were the last words he would ever have to hear from his father. Putting the car in drive, he pulled away from the curb seeking whatever life he wanted.

9

Vonda knew that if they had no pre-planned meeting place, there was only one place Chuck would look for her. He would be in the alley where it all began, where they first connected and started their journey. Chuck would be in the fray, where dark met light and created a zone of indifference for them both.

They had many hidden rendezvous spots. Sometimes they walked along the river. Sometimes along the tree line of the park. Most of the time, they slithered from one alley to another. Vonda hated when they had to meet in dark alleys. They made her feel dirty and that she was doing something wrong. She knew better and so did Chuck. It was society that had a problem with them loving each other. Not the two of them.

Vonda could never see Chuck in his white skin suit. In her eyes, he was a kind and gentle soul. They began their journey together through his kindness and he proved it any time they were together. He was always the one that was looking over their shoulders. He was not doing it to be ashamed, but rather as the protector, the body guard and the human shield.

For Chuck, his Vonda was not defined by the color of her skin but rather the innocence of her eyes. He fell in love with her the moment he met her simply by gazing into her eyes. She had a gentle touch and saw the world in a different light than he was raised. His parents claimed to be religious but had suck dark thoughts in their dark hearts. Vonda showed him what could be in life if he was brave enough to cast aside all of his foolish upbringing.

Together they were salt and pepper; they blended perfectly to bring flavor to life. They talked for hours about a utopia where they could live in the open. They dreamed of a street that they could walk down the sidewalk and hold hands. They looked forward to a day they could sit together in a restaurant without inciting a riot. That place was not in Birmingham and that day was not today.

On this day, Vonda waited in a dirty alley, sitting on a wooden crate as she watched the rats crawl along the brick wall. She was about to give up and go home when a blue Cadillac Sedan slowly entered the alley off the main road and came to a stop. Without seeing the driver, Vonda stood up and walked towards the vehicle. The driver's door slowly opened and her white knight appeared wearing a goofy smile.

"Hey baby. Watcha doin'?"

"Chuck? Why are you in a car? Whose car is it?"

"This is my Pops car. It's part of the story I was tellin' you last night."

"I don't understand. How? Why?"

"I'll tell you everything but first you got to come here and let me hug you."

"But Chuck, we are too close to the road. Someone might see…"

"Then get in the car and no one will be able to see us."

Vonda walked slowly to the passenger side of the car. The action felt foreign to her but she trusted Chuck with her life. She grasped the door handle and pulled open the passenger door. Once seated, she closed it and they were instantly in a closed room together.

"Ooh Chuck. This is…"

"Right? Now give me a kiss, baby."

Vonda leaned across the seat and put her hand on his cheek. She pulled him in for a slow, deliberate kiss that was a missing for so long.

"I almost forgot what it was like to kiss you proper. We always steal a quick kiss here or there but never proper like. That was nice."

"Yes, it was baby. But we don't have much time. We have to talk."

"What's the matter, Chuck? Is it about what you told me last night? Is the Klan really commin' to Birmingham? I told who I could. I told my momma and papa then they told our pastor. I'm not sure what good it's gonna do…"

"That's exactly the point. No matter who we tell or what we do, they commin' baby. They commin' and there's gonna be a whole lotta trouble. Birmingham is gonna turn into a battleground and we ain't gonna survive. None of us. That's why I got this car today. I'm supposed to pick up some of them Klan from a train station outside of town and bring them here. There's somethin' big goin' on, Vonda. We can't stop it. It ain't no use to fight it. Our only choice is to run and get out of here. We got no need to be the martyrs. We just stay here in this car and drive as far away from here as we can and don't look back."

"But what about my family? Am I supposed to just leave them all to get slaughtered like sacrificial lambs?"

"Baby, I can't save everybody. I told you last night what I could so they can help themselves but now we gots to go. We have to just drive out of here and start a new life."

Vonda sat back in her seat and looked over at Chuck and just stared at him in shock. It took her a few moments to focus and the magnitude of the situation hit her all at once.

"Are you crazy? We got nowhere to run to. Sure, you got a car but how far is that gonna get us? We got no money. We got no place to go to. With your father in bed with the police they are surely gonna set the dogs on after us. We can't run. I know you want to save me and escape this mess but it don't make no sense. You didn't think this through, Chuck."

The tears appeared on Chuck's cheek as they began to flow like a leaky faucet. Slow at first and then a steady stream. He knew that she was right but he wanted to run away from this place to save them both.

"But Vonda…"

Grabbing his hand with hers, she used the backside of her other hand to wipe away his tears. She knew what he was feeling because she had the same thoughts.

"It's gonna be ok, Chuck. This world is crazy out there but in here…" Vonda pointed to his heart. "…in here we are one. There's nobody or nothin' that's ever gonna take away the love we got for each other. You hear me, Chuck?"

"I hear you baby but I don't know…"

"All you gotta do is believe in love. Believe in us."

Chuck lowered his head for a moment before looking up at her.

"Do you really think there is ever gonna be a day where we don't have to hide? Where we can even go off and start a family somewhere in peace? Do you really think this world is gonna let us do that? Ever?"

Vonda held his hands in hers and looked at him with her own tears flowing.

"I pray for that every day, Chuck. I pray that somewhere, somehow, God will show us the way. The way to be together and be happy."

"Maybe this car is His answer."

"This car ain't goin' nowhere except where you supposed to go, Chuck. You know that and I know that and no matter how much we wish it away, that's exactly what's gonna happen."

He nodded in silence. Pulling her against him, he held her tightly trying to get the whole world from crashing in on them. This was their only bubble and soon enough that protection would be gone.

"Vonda…you gotta promise me somethin' baby. If you won't run away with me, you gotta promise me somethin'. Can you do that?"

She was now crying too. They held each other tightly, afraid to look in each other's eyes to see the reality of the situation.

"Sure, Chuck. Anythin' you want. Just tell me what you want me to do."

Pulling back from her, he took a moment to wipe his eyes before saying anything. Once he regained composure, he took her hands in his and looked her in the eyes.

"Vonda, you gotta promise me to go home now. You and your family go home. Stay in your house. Don't go anywhere near that motel no matter what happens. Don't let them call you out. Stay in your house 'til it's all over. Can you do that for me, baby? Can you just be safe?"

With so many thoughts running through her head, she didn't know what to say. She needed to be there for her family so that part was easy. But what if her people needed her? What if her congregation needed her? What if her family all decided to go and pray at that hotel for Dr. King? What then?

"Sure, Chuck. I'll stay home with my family if that's what you need."

She wasn't sure if it was a lie or the truth. By the end of the day she did not know where she was going to be. All she knew was that deep in her heart, she knew there was no coming back.

10

Chuck drove the Cadillac slowly up to the train station in Gardendale. He was on time like his father had instructed, but the train had gotten in a few minutes earlier. The four men were standing outside the station with their small satchels. It was clear they packed light because they weren't planning on staying long. They had a job to do and when it was done, they were going to crawl back into whatever hole they crawled out of.

Seeing the sedan pull up, they slowly started towards it. They had never met Chuck but they were alerted, just like he was, what to expect. He had barely put the car in park before the ringleader approached his driver's door and knocked on the window. Rolling it down slightly, the connection was made.

"You Charles?"

"Yes sir, but you can call me Chuck."

"I don't need to call you anything, you hear me boy?"

"Yes, sir."

"Then get out and open the trunk, boy, so we can put these bags in there."

Chuck turned the car off and started to exit. He moved slowly to not alert the men who were seemingly on edge already.

"Move any slower boy and we're gonna stuff you in the trunk instead of these bags."

Chuck stopped dead in his tracks and looked the lead man in the eyes. For a moment, his teenage fire burned to the point where he was ready to attack him. He was suddenly filled with dread as he thought of Vonda and what these men might do to her and her family. Silently, he moved to the trunk and opened it. He turned away from the men as he returned humbly to the driver's seat and closed the door behind him. Moments later, the men filled the car and began their banter.

"Ready to go coon huntin' boys?"

The three men in the backseat came to life and started to hoot and holler like they were on a cattle drive on the prairie. As if someone flicked a switch, they all took out cigarettes and started to light up. When Chuck started to cough on the smoke, he rolled down the driver's window to get some fresh air.

"What's the matter, boy? Been too used to livin' in the city with them coons? Not used to real air no more?"

The four men shared a hearty laugh at the expense of their young driver. He instantly regretted not driving away by himself even though Vonda would not go with him. Was there something more he could do to stop the wheel that was now in motion and that he was now a cog in? He felt dread come over him.

"You lookin' a little green there, boy. You gonna blow chunks in your old man's car? I don't think you're up to any of this?"

"What's that supposed to mean?"

"Your old man thinks you're ready to be a man, to take on the cause but it doesn't look like that to me. Looks like you're nothin' but a street punk. Are you a commie, boy? You don't look like an American to me, boy. You remind me of a coon lover we just strung up the other day. Are you a coon lover boy?"

Chuck was filled with rage. He wanted to drive his father's Cadillac right off a cliff and kill the redneck Klan members he was transporting. He decided to fight instead of flee and wondered if he was throwing himself off the cliff alone.

"Who you callin' a commie you backwoods panty waste? You think you're a man because you smoke and beat up little black girls? You're nothin' but a bully and a coward at that…"

The fist connected with his chin so fast that Chuck barely had a chance to understand where the pain was coming from. His head became dizzy as he gripped tightly to the steering wheel. The car veered slightly as it became difficult for him to focus. The four men simply laughed at his reaction.

"Suck it up, boy. You want to be a man then be a man. It's easy to run your mouth but you got to be able to back it up with your pain. That's what bein' in the Klan will do for you. It'll make you a man."

Chuck struggled to get words out but he tried. "I…never…said…" The men ignored him as they were on a mission.

"As our Imperial Wizard said this mornin', we the men of the Klan are willing to give up our lives to protect segregation in Birmingham. Great men like your daddy are doin' the right things for Alabama. We gonna do his biddin' today and you'll see who is a coward and who is a commie. If you're lucky, we'll let you come along for the ride."

"I'm pretty sure I'm the one takin' you for a ride."

"See that boy. You might be a man after all. Takin' it on the chin like a man then comin' back with the words. Maybe your old man was right? Maybe you got it in you to kill some coons today."

"Killin'? No one said anythin' about no killin'. I'm just givin' you a ride. That's all I'm gonna do."

"Relax, boy. No one puttin' a bomb in your hand…"

The four men broke out in hysterical laughter. They laughed until they were all choking and gasping for air in their smoke filled lungs. The inside joke was not so hidden to Chuck in his perception of the situation. The leader sensed apprehension in the young man and let the laughter sibside.

"What's so funny?"

"Don't you worry boy. Ain't no killin' happening today. We just here to have a nice little talk to your father's friends down at the police station. That's all."

"You are just a bunch of friends, aren't you? My dad, the cops, the governor, the Klan...one big happy family."

"Just shut up and drive boy. You got your kin and we got ours. In the end, we gonna see who is left standin' and who will fall."

Chuck took the advice of the redneck Klansman and stopped talking. The faster he dropped them off to the police station, the sooner he would be able to warn Vonda. He now knew what the Klan was planning. They were going to bomb the Gaston Motel and the police were going to help them do it.

11

Chuck Connor rode the rest of the way to the Birmingham police station in silence. As he drove and the four Klansmen carried on, he thought of his every move. Once he dropped them off, he would return the Sedan to his father's office and leave the keys as he was instructed to do. Bull Connor must have been plotting his next move because he specifically instructed Chuck not to come inside when he got back. Most likely, he wanted plausible deniability in case anyone saw the boy dropping off the Klan at the police station.

During the drive, the men's conversation shifted to Reverend King and his brother. A.D. King was a strong target, especially if his famous brother was being guarded. Chuck quickly realized that the target was not only one brother but both of them. If they had a plan to take one out and failed, then their time in Birmingham would have been wasted. If they went after both brothers, odds were that they would be able to get one of them.

Chuck knew what he had to do. Once the car had been returned, he would run back to his house and get his motorbike. He had multiple stops to make with the first of which going back to the fray. If Vonda wasn't there, he would try to get to her alley again. If she wasn't there, he could always try her church. It was not safe nor wise to go there, but if that was his only option, he was prepared to cross the line and come into the light. There were lives at stake and he was the only one willing to stop it.

As they crossed into Birmingham city limits, the passengers began to get antsy. They were clearly whispering and making plans so that Chuck would not hear them. With the police station coming into visibility, the leader of the pack interjected.

"Change of plans there, driver boy."

"What? My dad is expecting me to go to the police station and drop you off first. Apparently you don't know how he can be when people don't do what they are told."

"Oh, we is gonna go. We just want to go see Bull first. Take us to his office and we will walk from there. Can't be more than a few blocks."

"He doesn't like it when people just drop in. Maybe I should just stick with the original plan and…"

"Listen, boy. Take us to Bull's office or we're gonna have a problem. You were goin' there after the cop shop anyway. Just doin' things our way. We got a little matter of a donation to collect first."

"Ok. Ok. I'll take you there first. But I'll wait for you and drive you over to the police station. I don't want my father mad because I didn't do what he said."

The four men broke out in laughter. "You are nothin' but a little man. I don't know what Bull was thinkin'…"

Moments later, the Cadillac pulled up to the Birmingham Municipal Offices. Once the car was parked and shut off, the four Klansmen got out of the sedan and stood on the sidewalk waiting for Chuck to get out.

"Let's go boy. We don't got all day. We need our bags from the trunk."

"Now? I thought I was takin' you to the police station after…"

"Just open the damn trunk, boy."

"Ok, ok. Hold on a hot minute."

Chuck Connor got out of the driver's seat and walked around to the back of the large sedan and put the key in to open the trunk. As soon as it began to open, two of the men stepped behind him and blocked his exit. He never saw the slapjack, but he saw stars once it hit him on the back of his head. A second later, his body fell into the vast trunk as he was knocked out cold. The four men grabbed their bags out of the trunk and removed them. Closing the trunk with Chuck inside, they were soon greeted by Bull Connor walking up on the sidewalk.

"Took you long enough. I was waitin' in my office window watchin' for you. I thought you were never gonna get here."

"Sorry, boss. Your kid drives like an old woman. We almost had to take him out on the way just to put some gas in his step."

"That's fine boys. That's fine. You know what to do now."

"We know where we goin' if that's what you mean. Cop shop first then the other stops later. We got this covered. Don't worry none. What we don't know is what you want us to do with your son. He's not gonna stay knocked out for long."

Bull Connor squinted his eyes in hatred as he looked at the trunk of his prize possession. He hated that his own flesh and blood was inside it polluting it as he spoke.

"Do what we do with any other coon lover. Take him down to the dark side of town and throw him in an alley with the rest of the trash. If he likes them coons so much, maybe they'll take care of him. I'm done with him. I don't want no coon lover in my family. If he gives you any trouble, find the nearest tree and string him up."

12

The elders of the congregation were now gathered at the same kitchen table in the Hart residence as Pastor Jake sat just hours before. There were five of them including Sampson Hart and Pastor Jake. The other three were comprised of two women and one very elderly "elder". Franklin Dodd was 85 years old and was barely able to climb the stairs to the meeting place but he was not about to miss it. With his pride intact, he sat at the head of the table even though Pastor Jake was the faith leader of the congregation.

On either side of Franklin sat two sisters. Mahalia Johnson and Bertha Johnson had been part of the Birmingham community and the congregation longer than anyone. They were born and raised in the city and attended church as school girls. In those days, Franklin had become the church administrator and for decades had controlled the finances of the church. Now in retirement, he was the oldest living member of the congregation and his opinions were good as gold. Mahalia and Bertha performed a more basic role in the emotional balance of things, holding both conservative and liberal values as many siblings do. The deciding votes always came down to either Sampson or Pastor Jake. In the matter of what to do with their newfound information, the conversation was more like a tilt-a-whirl.

"We gots to do something."

"Why do we have to, Franklin? Is it not enough for them to turn their fire hoses on us and have their dogs attack us? I say a more passive approach at this time is prudent."

"What my sister is trying to say in her long wind is that we are not activists. We are just good God-fearin' folks who come together and pray. Let the police take care of things. They will stop the Klan. We can just provide refuge for those who seek shelter from their persecution."

"Why is it that everythin' that comes out of your mouth sounds like you are a politician runnin' for office? The time is now to strike back. We have the momentum of the Truce Agreement. Let's use that to unify the congregation. I say we gather all the peoples up and go down to that motel and stand together. The Klan won't dare make a move on a whole mob of us."

Vonda had been listening from her room and gasped at the thought of her family going down to the motel. She had promised Chuck they wouldn't go.

"Sampson, please. Perhaps we need to pause and reflect for a moment. You are full of the fire and you want to let it out somehow. The sisters would rather sit passively and not enact any actions. Perhaps Franklin is right. We need to do something but quite possibly not everything."

The five elders nodded their heads. They often found the middle ground in such conversations as the best road to travel on. Getting there in the first place was the challenge. Once arrived, as they just had, the answers seemed much clearer than before.

"What do you have in mind Jake?"

The Pastor seemed to be in silent meditation and did not answer at first. He closed his eyes and swayed back and forth until the small light bulb went off in his thoughts. He sat forward and opened his eyes.

"Where is young Vonda?"

Sampson looked over at his wife who was standing against the kitchen counter in silence. She motioned towards the hallway and Sampson knew where she meant.

"I believe she is in her room. You want me to bring her out Jake?"

"With all due respect. I would like to speak to her alone. I think there is a missing piece to the tale that we just ain't got yet. Maybe she can shed some light. Can you send her out to the porch? Mayhap we can talk with open privacy there."

"Of course, Jake. Of course. Let me go get her."

Deidre Hart left the kitchen and walked down the hall to get her daughter. Meanwhile, Pastor Jake made his way out to the porch as the others refilled their coffee cups. Moments after sitting down on the porch, Vonda appeared with an uneasy look on her face.

"You wanted to see me Pastor Jake?"

"Yes, of course child. Please have a seat and let's have a little chat."

Vonda sat nervously across from the Pastor and collected her thoughts.

"It's been a long day now, hasn't it Vonda?"

"Yes, sir."

"Especially after that late night conversation you heard out your window. I'm sure you didn't sleep much after that."

"No, sir."

"I know if I heard people talkin' about such things like the Klan and such, I wouldn't sleep much neither."

"I'm sure you wouldn't Pastor."

"Now how many people you say you heard?"

Vonda started to become uneasy. She wondered where the conversation was headed.

"I think two."

"Are you sure there were two? Is it possible that there were three?"

Vonda became hopeful. Perhaps she was not in any trouble here.

"I guess it's possible. There might have been three."

Pastor Jake nodded slowly as if he was choosing his words very carefully before saying anything more.

"So, please Vonda. Tell me. You thought you heard two voices, now there might have been three. Is it also possible that there was just one voice coming from the alley last night?"

Tears started to flow down the teenage girl's cheeks. She could not lie any more to her Pastor. She was tired of living in lies and she just wanted to let the truth set her free. She nodded in silent response to the holy man.

"Who was it, dear child? Do you have a secret love that you do not wish your parents to know about?"

Vonda slowly lifted her head and looked at the Pastor with teary eyes.

"How did you know?"

"Vonda, I have known you all of your life. I have known you to be a good girl, a faithful girl to the church and an honest girl. Did you not think that I wouldn't know that you told a white lie this morning to your parents?"

"I'm sorry Pastor Jake. I didn't mean to lie. It's just...it's just that the message was so important I just had to find a way to tell people."

"So the message was true child?"

"Yes. Yes. I swear to you. That part was true."

The Pastor nodded silently once again, pausing for seemingly dramatic effect.

"...and did your *friend* tell you anything else?"

"Not then. I told you everythin' he said when I told you this mornin'."

The Pastor leaned forward to grasp her hidden meaning.

"So, I'm a gatherin' he done told you somethin' else. Have you seen him since this mornin'?"

More tears started to flow as Vonda wasn't sure how to proceed. She wanted to tell her Pastor everything but she was not sure the words could come out.

"Yes, sir."

"When did you see him Vonda?"

She was writhing her hands at this point and biting her bottom lip. Sensing she was troubled, the Pastor reached out and took her hand in his.

"The truth shall set you free. Remember, child. I am your Pastor. Everthin' we say will stay between us."

Vonda thought in a long pause on how to answer. In the end, she simply opened her mouth and let the truth walk out.

"I saw him over by the fray. That's where we usually find each other.

Sometimes we have other places to meet up but this time I was just hopin' to get more information on what he said last night."

"Ok did he?"

"Yes sir."

"This is gonna take all day if I have to pull all the words out of you, child."

"Yes sir. He told me more today. This time he had his daddy's car so we talked more in there. He told me everythin' he knows."

"So you were alone in a car with a boy, Vonda. Did he respect you?"

"Yes, sir. Of course he did. Chuck always respects me."

"So, his name is Chuck?"

"Yes sir."

"Ok. Go on then. What did Chuck tell you today that he didn't tell you last night?"

Vonda started to cry again. She was so afraid.

"He told me that the Klan is commin'. He told me his father had him pickin' some of them up at the train station with the car. He told me that the men were goin' to the police and then they were goin' to do somethin' at the Gaston Motel. He was so worried 'bout me and my kin. He just wanted me to stay clear."

"Wait, wait, wait a minute. How is it that one of us was sent to pick up members of the Klan? How could that be?"

Vonda did not want to take this final step across the bridge. She was afraid her whole life would crumble.

"He is not one of us, Pastor Jake. Chuck is a white boy."

The Pastor was momentarily stunned but simply patted Vonda's hand before continuing. "Love does not know color, Vonda. I understand why you chose not tell your parents of your secret love but do not be ashamed. If it is true love it will not matter the color of your skin or even his."

"Ohhh, Pastor Jake."

Vonda began to sob. She was so relieved to finally get it off her chest about her love for Chuck. She had been afraid for so long and to hear her Pastor say it was ok made her whole life in balance.

"I am confused about one thing, though, so please gather yourself. I understand how Chuck is white and how he might be allowed to be in the presence of the Klan without harm. But tell me how it is that he knows such things. He must know someone to get such information. Where is Chuck gettin' his information from??"

Vonda looked down at her hands. It was as if she was telling her Pastor that her boyfriend was the son of Satan himself.

"Chuck is not just any white boy, Pastor. He is the son of Bull Connor. The Commissioner of Public…"

"Oh. I know who Bull Connor is. I just didn't know your boyfriend was Chuck Connor. Now it all makes sense. You are sayin' that the son of Bull Connor told you that the Klan is commin' and there is gonna be trouble down at the Gaston Motel?"

"Yes sir."

Without a moment's hesitation, Jake got up from his chair and walked back into the kitchen where the elders and Deidre were waiting patiently.

"We have to go. We have to go now."

"Where? Where are we goin' Jake?"

Looking back to the porch where he left the crying Vonda, he turned back to the group. "We are going to the Gaston Motel. There is trouble brewing. Gather everyone you can and get down there now. It's gonna be dark soon enough. We have to face the Klan in force."

13

The blue Cadillac Sedan pulled up to the back of the Gaston Motel and parked. An officer from the Birmingham Police Department had already secured a room earlier in the day under the check in name of the Alabama Christian Movement and left it unlocked. In the darkness of the parking lot, no one noticed the four men enter the premises.

Inside the room, the Klansmen set up their supplies on one of the two beds. There were wires and detonation devices as well as the explosives in small separate piles. The men went to work quickly to assemble the units needed for the night's activities.

"Remember, we need three of them. Two small ones and then the big bang."

"We know. We got all that. You just didn't say which one goin' where."

"Once you finish, we gonna take the two little ones and bring them over to the hospital. The cops are gonna take those from us and take care of the first round. When they done, we gonna come back here and take care of the big one."

"Why we still taken out this place when that King fella' done left?"

"I reckon it's to send a message that we ain't standin' for their nonsense. They can get all the papers they want that say they can de-segregate, but the Klan ain't lettin' it. Besides, that's what the boss says. He says we still blow the places up, then we blow the places up. You gotta problem with that?"

"Nope. Not at all. Just hopin' we take a few of them out when they all blow. Hate to waste all this just to make a pile of rubble."

"Well, we know we gonna take out at least one of them now, don't we boys?"

The four men broke out in laughter as they finished up making their bombs. When they were finished, they set the bombs up on the bed ready to go.

"Why don't one of you go out and make sure we clear. Nobody needs to see us bringin' things out or in at this point."

One of the men exited the room and took longer than expected to return. When he did, he had a troubled look on his face.

"What's up?"

"I heard a bunch of noises around the front side so I took a walk around to see what was goin' on. There's a bunch of coons that showed up. They must think that King fella is still here. He ain't right?"

"Nope. He is back in Atlanta but that's good they here."

"Why?"

"Looks like you gonna get your wish after all. We gonna take some of them out when this place blows. We gotta move now though before one of them wanders back here. Take the bombs out to the car and bring him in."

The three Klansmen exited the motel room carefully with the bombs in their hands. They returned a short time later carrying Chuck Connor who was now bound and gagged.

"Is he awake?"

"Nah. He's still out cold. I told you not to hit him so hard."

"Well, he shouldn't have tried to get out at the police station. Good thing that cop had his baton handy. Besides, what difference does it make? Boss man said he don't want no coon lover in his family no mo'. Either way, he gonna get his wish. Now throw him on the bed and tie him to the frame. We gotta get out of here."

The men did as they were instructed and a few minutes later, they all headed out the motel room door. Before shutting it closed, the Klan leader looked back at the Connor boy tied to the bed.

"You shoulda listened to your old man, boy. If you woulda loved one of your own kind you wouldn't be about to meet your maker. Stupid kid."

Closing the door, the Klansman sealed the fate of Chuck Connor.

14

The crowd gathered around the front of the Gaston Motel was growing. The elders had spread the word and people were pouring in from all around the city to provide a united front. Vonda Hart stood with her family, right next to Pastor Jake, as they led the rally at the motel. She had no choice but to ignore what she had promised Chuck. There was no possible way her family was going to leave her at home alone. She took some comfort in knowing that if something bad did happen like Chuck had warned her about, she would be with her family at the end.

"Is your friend here?" Pastor Jake had leaned over and whispered to the young girl.

Vonda looked around the crowd but she couldn't see much beyond a few people in front of her. Had she been able to see past the crowd, she would have seen Bull Connor's car coming around the motel from the back of the building with the four Klansmen inside.

"No, sir. Can't see him anywhere but it's pretty dark and crowded here. Didn't expect to see him anywhere near here though. He was pretty clear on that."

The Pastor nodded. He had much to worry about as he tended to his flock but Vonda Hart was at the center of all of this. He was staying close to her as if she would give him a sign. If she recognized her young boyfriend, then trouble was at hand. He did not want to frighten her but the facts were there.

"That's fine, Vonda. But if you see him, please let me know. I don't want to put the boy in harm's way."

Little did they know that Chuck was already there and deep in harm's way. Had anyone known what was happening in the back of the motel, the situation may have turned out differently. Instead, they stood side by side in that parking lot and sang like it was a Sunday service. Spirits were high as they sang passages from Amazing Grace, and Onward Christian Soldiers. With no sign of the Klan, the crowd began to think that is was all a hoax. They hoped they would simply have their peaceful rally and return to their homes safe and sound. All was comforted until the first bomb exploded at 10:45 pm.

15

Martin Luther King's brother, A.D. King, lived in the Ensley neighborhood, a short distance from the Gaston Motel. While his brother had left earlier in the day, King and his wife Naomi were resting comfortably inside their house when several members of the Birmingham Police department rolled up to their house.

One of the uniformed officers got out of his patrol car and placed a small package on the front porch. After knocking on the front door, he walked briskly back to his car and sped off. The package was retrieved from its resting spot and brought inside the house. Moments later, sensing that it was a bomb, A. D. King threw the package out the front window where it exploded on the porch.

At 10:45pm, the group gathered outside the Gaston Motel heard the blast and started to move quickly in that direction. Their immediate thoughts were that the information they received was wrong. There was trouble; there was a bomb; it was just not happening at the Gaston Motel.

The second explosion occurred as King was escaping out the back door of his house with his wife and children. The larger bomb was placed in the front of the house by another policeman that had arrived in an unmarked car. The much larger blast than the first rocked the foundation and destroyed the front of the house.

By 11pm, all but a few of the people that had gathered at the Gaston Motel had left. They all travelled towards the sounds of the two explosions as they assumed that was where they would find the opposition from the Klan. They were wrong in their assumptions and when they arrived at the house, all they viewed was a pile of rubble surrounded by emergency vehicles.

The Hart family was the last to leave the Gaston Motel parking lot as they clung to the premise that their daughter had been correct. While it was possible that she had heard the conversation wrong, there was a clear indication that trouble would be centered at the Motel and not anywhere else. The Pastor, along with the Harts, thought the two events were unrelated.

"I really thought the trouble was commin' here. I'm so sorry."

Pastor Jake patted her on her shoulder. "Don't be sorry, child. There was trouble brewing as you said, it just don't seem to be here. It was the right pew in the wrong church. Mayhap we just have to go join everyone else and leave this Motel behind. If there is trouble here tomorrow, we can always come back."

As the Hart family exited the parking lot of the Gaston Motel, Vonda looked back with wondering eyes. Had she gotten it wrong? Did she not understand what Chuck had told her clearly? Were her emotions clouding her judgement and her recollection? She missed him dearly and was deeply concerned for his well-being. She had never been in love before and she did not know how to handle any part of their relationship, especially this worry. Walking after her family, she prayed for the man she loved. She prayed that they would someday find each other again. In the same moment, she knew deep in her heart that she would never cast her eyes or her lips upon his again.

16

Chuck Connor woke up in the motel room shortly after the second blast occurred. Finding himself bound and gagged, he struggled to no avail to get himself free. When all hope was lost, he was reduced to laying on that motel room bed, reminiscing about the love he had for Vonda. He prayed that the explosion that startled him awake had nothing to do with her or her family. If he only had the ability to cry out, she may have heard him on the other side of the building. His tears were rolling down his face as she was exiting the parking lot.

Like Vonda, Chuck had never experienced love before. Of course he had his share of school boy crushes on various members of the opposite sex, but nothing that he would classify as love. In her absence, he constantly cared for and missed his Vonda. Whenever they were together, he felt butterflies in his stomach and his heart seemed to skip a beat. He would have risked everything in life just to be with her and in the end he gave up the only thing he had for their love; his life.

At 11:58pm, the blue Cadillac Sedan returned to the parking lot of the Gaston Motel. At this point, there were no other bystanders looking for a fight. They had all moved on to the site of the last explosion. When the bomb was thrown out of the moving sedan, it detonated immediately upon impact and destroyed the motel. While the bombing was meant to be symbolic to those that had aided Reverend King when he stayed there, it ended up being so much more.

When the rubble was cleared, there was only one casualty from the bombing. Happening late at night after all the excitement had passed, only one body was found. A young man was crushed to death when the walls and ceiling of the motel collapsed on top of him. He was still bound and gagged when they found him and was immediately identified as the son of powerful Commissioner of Public Safety, Bull Connor. Chuck Connor was dead at the age of 17 and his death would soon fuel a division of hatred that would be felt across the country.

17

Just hours later, Bull Connor stood in front of the rubble at the Gaston Motel and addressed an angry mob. Armed with a battalion of state troopers at his side, he used the death of his son to fuel a war on the negro population.

"My dearest son, Charles Connor, was murdered here tonight. Not by a knife, or a gun, but by a cowardly explosion that took his life. These negroes were not happy enough just taking our liberties away in their worthless truce agreement. They came back for blood. They captured the boy, beat him, bound him and gagged him, then left him for death. They did this to get back at me for trying to do good for this city. They struck out because I use force to keep peace for the good people that live here. They took his life because I rained on their parade. Now the wrath of God is upon them. Go forth and take care of this disease. Go forth and eradicate those who took my son's life. Go forth and take back our city..."

Troops flooded the city and all manner of civil unrest followed. By morning, the number of injuries and death were many but none felt the pain more than Vonda Hart herself. She was with her family and her Pastor when she heard the news that Bull Connor's son had been killed. Overcome with grief and heartache, she collapsed in the street before them.

Days later, she accompanied her parents and her Pastor to the funeral of her dearly departed love. Standing in the back of the cemetery, they were the only people of color in attendance. Somehow, Vonda made eye contact with the devil himself as Chuck's father looked upon her knowing her secret. Through his eyes, he saw nothing but the color of her skin and the fire that burned in hatred. In hers, she saw nothing but the sadness of loss. She knew that Chuck Connor had died with love in his heart and she knew that she would hold that love in her heart for eternity.

Wednesday- Spaghetti Day

1

The calendar read Tuesday, October 9, 1945, but the colors told a whole different story. The RMS Queen Elizabeth had been painted battleship grey during the war years but the thousands of GIs coming back from the war still adorned their Army greens. The trees along the Hudson River were in full Autumn color explosion as the ship slowly made its way up the river towards Pier 90. Though Central Park was 4 blocks over and 10 blocks up from the dock at 50th and 12th, there was not a GI on deck that couldn't smell the crisp autumn air emanating from its trees.

Private "Paulie" Scarpacci was returning from the war with the droves of other GIs, happy to be alive and looking forward to life in the post-war era. At 18, he had joined up with his high school buddies looking to explore the world and give his all to good old Uncle Sam. After 3 years in the Pacific theater alone, he found out that his brothers in arms who had been battling the European theater, never made it back from the beaches of Normandy. He had made plenty of new buddies while overseas, but he would be alone on the train ride back to Bridgeport at the end of the week.

With the war officially over, MacArthur was sending them all home to their families in one piece. Paulie was looking forward to seeing his Italian clan after being away from them for so long, but he had a little steam to blow off before he saw his mama. Until he had to catch the train from Grand Central on Sunday, he planned to paint the Big Apple red with all the excitement he had built up for years.

The petite framed girls of the orient were nice and all but he was a red-blooded Italian. He desired a full bodied woman, complete with all the right curves in all the right places and New York City was full of them. He already had a plan as soon as he stepped foot on U.S. soil, to head 8 blocks south to 42nd and Times Square. It was the heart of the world and what better place would it be to find love.

Paulie was shaken out of his day dreaming on deck by the sound of the two smoke stacks blowing their horns. The ship was coming into port and the noise became deafening. The thousands of servicemen aboard the vessel erupted into cheers as they had finally made it back to the United States. They had seen foreign countries they had only read about in grade school, met foreigners they only dreamt about, then proceeded to kill them on sight without a word ever spoken. They had seen death, destruction and depravity of every kind in their time abroad, but now they were home. Whether they were just passing through NYC like the young Scarpacci to further destinations or not, the shores of Manhattan were welcoming them with open arms.

The roar of the servicemen was slowly drowned out by the cheers coming from the dock. Thousands of loved ones were waiting for their GIs with smiles as big as the New York skyline. Wives, girlfriends, lovers and friends were all packed against the fencing, trying to get a glimpse of their man returning from the war. For Paulie, he knew there was no one in the crowd.

The Scarpacci family would surely be waiting at the train station in Bridgeport but his brothers, sisters, and cousins would not bring the same love and desire that he saw in the faces of the crowd on the dock. He hoped that one day he would have a girl he could call his very own but not for today. He was a lonely Army Private, freshly home from the war, and he knew that he was going to be a commodity heading into the best city in the world. Perhaps in that sea of women he was looking out in was the next Mrs. Scarpacci. He smiled at the prospect of returning home to his family not only wearing his Army uniform proudly, but a beautiful woman adorning his arm. Life would be grand.

2

Similar to the rest of the soldiers getting off the boat, Paulie Scarpacci was tired, hungry and ready to start civilian life. After hours of disembarkation from the ship and his official farewell to Uncle Sam, Paulie headed out into Manhattan. He found himself a cheap room that catered to GIs and rented it out for the next 5 nights. He barely looked at the inside of the room before dropping his duffel bag on the bed and closing the door behind him. He rushed out the door still in uniform.

It may have been a Tuesday night in 1945 but he was in the most exciting city in the world. Like many of his fellow ex-soldiers, he followed the trail of excitement all the way down to Times Square and 42nd Street. Serving his aching stomach for something more than the Army chow line, he walked into the famous Automat to get some dinner. He marveled at all the food choices illuminated behind glass and wondered how anyone could choose just one. Gathering up his new found change from his pocket, he dropped the coins in the machines and began his selection. His first trip to the Automat yielded a ham dinner complete with veggies and roll, a side of mashed potatoes and two pieces of pie for dessert. He felt like a king as he sat down with his tray at a table by himself and removed the wax paper.

As he began to eat, Paulie felt the heat of eyes on the back of his head and heard the gaggle of a group of females behind him. Pausing only slightly, he turned his head to see where the laughter was coming from. The three girls could have been models on a Hallmark card as they were a picture of beauty with a blonde, redhead, and brunette in attendance. The young Army veteran blushed at the sight of them.

"What's the matter soldier? Never seen a redhead before?"

"None as pretty as you, ma'am."

His polite line sent the three women into another fit of laughter as they pretended to cool themselves down by flapping their bare hands.

"Ooh boy. We got a hot one here ladies. Tell us soldier, boy. You got a name honey?"

It was the blonde's turn to entice the young man and he was eating it all up, regardless of the food before him.

"Paulie, ma'am. My name's Paulie. Do you all have names or should I just call you the Andrew Sisters?"

Laughter once again filled the halls of the Automat as the other patrons went about eating their meals. The young man's flattery was cashing in dividends. The redhead was the spokeswoman for the group so she answered happily.

"Well, now Paulie. My name is Lenore. Blondie here is Suzy and the brunette Polack on the end is Marta. Too bad you didn't get here earlier. We got to get out of here. We're going to The Strand to watch a flick."

Paulie looked down at his first meal as a civilian as he was looking forward to eating it peacefully without a bunch of grunting men in the mess tent next to him.

"It was nice meeting you ladies. Maybe I'll see you round town. I'll be here all week."

The three women stood to exit while Lenore stepped forward. "Maybe you will, maybe you won't, but the pleasure was all ours."

The trio broke out in laughter once more as they exited the Automat. Looking after them, Paulie thought happily to himself with a broad smile.

It's gonna be a good week. I think I'm gonna love New York.

3

Stuffed to the gills, Paulie stepped out on the sidewalk. He looked at the choices before him in Times Square as the lights, sounds, and the sights engulfed his senses. Looking to his left, just a few doors down, the Strand Theater was calling out to him. He could be the lonely sad sack and go stand outside the theater until their movie got out but he knew he deserved more. Maybe before he went overseas and went through what he did in the war, he could justify waiting for some women that may or may not like him. But he wasn't a horny little teenager anymore and there were thousands of other women in the city just waiting for a man that just came home from the war. Dropping his gaze to the bar between the Automat and the theater, we saw a bar that showed him the way.

The White Way Bar and Grill reminded Paulie of a bar from the silver screen itself. The waiters and the Maître de wore white jackets and black bow ties. For a moment, the young soldier looked down at his dress uniform and thought he was underdressed. Sensing his reluctance, the man at the podium stepped forward.

"Come in, please. All men in uniform are welcome here. You defend our country and we welcome you. Come sit at the bar and have the first Rheingold on the house."

"I'm more of a Ballantine man if that's ok."

"Whatever you like, you have. Please come in."

Paulie didn't know what it was like to be treated as a war hero. During his time in the Pacific theater, the people of the orient had mixed feelings about American soldiers. The Chinese were an ally, fighting right beside the Brits and the Americans against the Japanese. Together, there were no individual heroes, just a group of men fighting for a cause. Now, back in the states, it seemed that every man in uniform held the hero trophy on his chest.

Making his way to the bar, he stood at the end while his beer was poured. As the bartender slid the glass in front of him, he gave him a smile and a nod as if he was honored to serve a man in uniform standing at his bar. Paulie had spent far too many hours and days laying in jungles and crawling through rice paddy fields. Standing on the deck of the ship, he felt as if he could stand for days and never get tired. Now, with a row of bar stools at his disposal, he was torn between comfort and keeping an eye on the door for romantic prospects.

The bar was a quieter environment than he expected stepping out of Times Square. One part of him wanted to be out carousing with the other GIs all over Manhattan while another part of him was thankful for the peace and quiet of the moment. He felt that the piano player in the white tux playing in the corner was a bit over the top and was catering to a much older crowd, but he took in the scene for what it was. He felt that he could endure one beer, especially since it was on the house.

When he was half way through his glass, the solace of his surroundings started to get to him. He was reminded of his nights out on patrol, when the silence starts to eat away at you and makes you uneasy. Like shadows in the night, Paulie started to see things that weren't there until the darkness of the bar cast shadows on three beauties at the front podium. Destiny brought him from half the world away to meet a match from the theater next door.

A moment earlier Paulie was ready to run away, but now he was staying for the challenge. The only question was which of the three beauties would become the next Mrs. Scarpacci. He waved the bartender over to order.

"I'll take another Ballantine."

"Yes, sir. Coming right up."

Paulie watched with wonder as the three women came in and sat at a table in front of the bar. Whether their eyes were adjusting to the interior light or they simply had not seen him at the end of the bar, the women gave no indication that they had focused on him. Once the waiter had come and greeted the three and taken their drink order, he wandered away and left them as prey to the nearby hunters.

Within moments of being alone, two gentlemen in suits approached the table and introduced themselves to the trio. Paulie watched on to see which woman would be left alone at the table. Lenore and Suzy seemed enamored by the two businessmen but that was the same scenario Paulie had encountered in the Automat. Marta laughed along with any of the group jokes but barely spoke a word otherwise. He wondered what the storyline was behind each of the three as he was trained to do in combat.

The scenario played out as the two businessmen excused themselves to go get drinks at the bar. Paulie took it as an opportunity to reveal himself as being in the bar as well. Walking up to the table it was Lenore who recognized him first.

"Look who is here, girls. Soldier boy followed us to the White Way."

The trio cried out with elation as the quiet bar turned their attention on the table.

"I don't think we can say that I followed you here since I was already here while you were at the movies. So how was it?"

Lenore and Suzy shared mixed emotions about the movie while Marta looked on with a smile. Paulie noticed for the first time that her brown doe eyes sparkled as she looked at him.

"What about you Marta? Are you casting the deciding vote? Was the movie good or bad?"

Marta was stunned that Paulie was addressing her directly. She was clearly not used to the attention. Looking to her friends for support, they laughed at the fact she was floundering. Giggling among themselves, they left Marta to fend for herself.

"Well, like Lenore said we went to see *Janie*. She kind of reminded me of myself. Just a small town girl that liked Army men in uniform. Since you came along at the same time of the movie, it made me think of you."

"Wait. The movie is actually about a girl that falls in love with an Army soldier like me? Doesn't that sound a little too coincidental?"

"Maybe it's destiny?" Suzy's comment sent her and Lenore into another fit of laughter. For Marta, it seemed to resonate too close to the truth to laugh about it.

"Well, destiny or not I'm glad you enjoyed the movie."

"Did you enjoy your meal from the Automat?"

"The Automat?"

Marta and Paulie turned to see the two businessmen who had returned with the drinks from the bar.

"Yes. It was a good meal."

"Come on, soldier boy. Looks like you are fresh off the boat. You couldn't get a better meal than the Automat?"

"I think we can do better than that for you ladies. Would you care to join us for a little supper?"

After the business man's comment about the Automat, the ladies were reluctant to admit they ate there earlier as well. Lenore was the quick thinker and brought out the charm.

"With all the popcorn at the movies, the only thing we can fit is something sweet. Do either one of you have something sweet for us?"

The foursome broke out into more laughter as Paulie and Marta felt like the extra wheels on the bus. They seemed happy to let the bus leave the station without them. Marta decided to pass on the invitation.

"Why don't the four of you go get a table and eat some dessert. Mr. Paulie and I can stay here and enjoy our drinks."

All were in agreement as Paulie patiently waited for the scene to play itself out. The two businessmen escorted Lenore and Suzy over to the maître de who quickly found them a table in the dining room. Alone together for the first time, Marta broke the awkwardness.

"Are you going to sit down or are you going to go join them?"

He didn't have to be asked twice. He grabbed a seat opposite hers at the bar table and placed his beer on the table. Marta touched her glass of wine delicately waiting for the gentleman to start the conversation.

"So Marta. Are you three lady's sisters or something? What brings you into the city?"

Smiling softly, she replied. "No, we're not sisters. Why do we look alike?"

"No. Nothing like that. It's just...well...before I left for the war women didn't travel much on their own. I was just curious."

"Are you really just curious if we are travelling with fellas or something?"

It was Paulie's turn to blush. "Naw...I mean yea...I mean...are you?"

"No fellas. At least not for me. Lenore and Suzy usually find a fella or two wherever we go. We all live in New Rochelle. We work at a department store there, Ware's Department Store. Have you heard of it?"

"Didn't that place burn down?"

"It did. Then they rebuilt it. There's a lot of talk about it becoming a Bloomingdales. That's why we are in the city; to look for other jobs."

"What kind of work do you want to do?"

"Well, I'm ok with staying in the department store business. Macy's would be nice. But Lenore and Suzy got their sights on something more glamorous like working on Broadway or something."

Paulie took a moment to drink some of his beer and look into the dining room where the two ladies were hanging on their new acquaintances.

"I guess I can see that."

"How 'bout you, Mr. Paulie? I guess we were never formally introduced."

"Oh. Sorry about that. I'm Private Scarpacci. I guess not anymore. Just used to saying that. Now I'm just plain old Paulie Scarpacci from Bridgeport."

"Bridgeport? No kidding. We're practically neighbors. Why aren't you on the way home already? I figure a guy like you, fresh off the boat, would be running back to home. When's the last time you were there?"

"Well, I was stationed over in Okinawa so I didn't get home at all while I was gone off to the war. I guess to answer your question; I haven't been home in a few years."

"Wow. A few years. I can't even imagine. Even more a reason to go running home. Why are you still here in the city?"

Paulie thought about the best way to answer so he didn't sound like such a heal. He decided a different approach.

"Marta. What's your last name?"

"Slowik. In Polish it means 'nightingale' or something like that. I'm not much of a singer but that's a horse of a different color. The Polish people aren't famous for their singing but we do love our music."

"Well, Marta Slowik. I can't speak to Polish families but Italian families can be a bit much. I miss my brothers and sisters and all the rest but I know they are going to smother me with attention and not let me take a breath. The way I figure it, before I get back to Bridgeport and start a new life working at the Sikorsky factory or something, I'm gonna live life a little. I've had the Army bossing me around for the last 3 years and I'm sure my family is gonna push me around when I get home. I might as well enjoy a week of freedom, real freedom, before getting boxed in again."

Marta smiled. "I think you know more about Polish families than you let on. My family is just like that. My mamushka is always telling me that I don't act like I should or dress like I should. When she was a girl in Poland she did this or that. I love my family but they are a bit much too. That's why I want to come to Manhattan. Put a little distance between the family. I think I will be happier with a little freedom too."

"See that. What a coincidence. The only difference is you're Polish and I'm a Wop."

Marta looked at him with her large doe-like eyes and smiled. She could feel the blushing on her cheeks as she lit up looking at him.

"I don't see a wop at all Mr. Scarpacci. I see a handsome man in uniform that I'd like to know more about."

Paulie looked at her in silence as he drank more of his beer. Picking up her wine glass, she drank demurely as the glass touched her lips leaving a noticeable lipstick mark on the edge. Paulie was smitten just looking at it. Calling over the waiter, he ordered another beer for himself.

"Would you like another glass of wine?"

"I think I would." Looking over at her friends in the dining room, she knew they were not leaving anytime soon.

As the waiter left with their drink order, Paulie took the opportunity to push the conversation further.

"Now, I know that you are beautiful. I can see that for myself. And I know you work at a department store. I guess I can picture that. But what else can you tell me? What does a looker like you do in a place like New Rochelle? I want to hear all about you."

Marta went on to tell her newfound acquaintance all about herself. She found the conversation easy and told Paulie more about herself than she usually told strangers. In return, he told her about life back in Connecticut and a few chosen war stories he wanted to share. Their conversation continued for a couple hours until the happy foursome from the dining room appeared. The two men broke off and headed to the door leaving Suzy and Lenore to stand over the table.

"Don't you two look chummy."

"Stifle it, Lenore."

"Well, I'm sorry to break up the party but we got to get going if we are going to make the last train home tonight. These fine gentlemen are going to hail us a cab so say your goodbye to your new beau and we'll see you outside."

Before Marta could protest, the two young women exited the bar and headed out into the Times Square scene.

"I guess I have to get going."

"I'm sorry you have to go. I was hoping we could go paint the town a little tonight."

Standing up, she smiled at him.

"Well, Mr. Scarpacci. That makes two of us, but tonight I have to go home with the girls. I can come back on the morning train if you like?"

Paulie was beaming. "Heck ya. That would be swell. Do you want me to meet you down at Grand Central?"

"That would be perfect. How about by the clock tower off of Park Avenue at 11am? Does that work for you soldier boy?"

Paulie was overcome with joy. He was hoping for just this type of meeting when he decided to spend the week in New York.

"Sounds like a date. Before you leave, can I get a kiss?"

Marta Slowik smiled from ear to ear but heard her friends calling by the door. Reaching down, she picked up a cocktail napkin, put it between her lips and left a kiss imprint.

"There you go Private. That should hold you until tomorrow."

Paulie picked up the napkin off the table and smiled. He knew that he would dream about his new Polish girlfriend all night long with her kiss laying on the pillow next to him. His Italian family would kill him for going on a date with a Polish girl but they were a state away in Connecticut. The might as well be back on the other side of the Pacific. He was free of the Army and temporarily free of his family. He was going to enjoy this week of freedom with love in his heart.

4

Paulie Scarpacci woke up the next morning to the sounds of the New York City traffic outside of his window. He had slept with it open to capture the cool crisp autumn air that was typical of the Northeast this time of year. Having spent so much time in the orient, he was used to the humidity of the tropics but he looked forward to being back in New England for the splendor of the fall once he left New York.

He was a civilian for the first time in years but he didn't feel much different yet. He woke up in his own room which was strange in itself not having his fellow grunts making all manner of noises next to him. His dress uniform was hanging on a hanger as he was trained to do after wearing it. The government issued clothing hung in the tiny room closet with the small amount of civilian wear he had with him. If not for the lipstick stained napkin next to his face on the pillow, he may have thought it was just a dream.

He had replayed the events from the night before many times in his head. The comment about destiny was not that far from the truth. He had no idea what the Automat was so why had he ventured in there for food? Was it fate that caused him to sit in front of the girls in the first place? When they left to go to the movies and the decision was made not to follow them, how did they wind up meeting once again in the bar? Serendipity was playing tricks on him or perhaps it was a woman named Marta that had gotten caught in the web of destiny.

Paulie had spent a great amount of time last night holding and staring at the napkin that was next to him. Reaching over, he picked it up like he had so many times since receiving it. He thought of the lips that made the mark and his stomach became a flutter of butterflies. Marta was not a bombshell like Lenore or sultry like Suzy. She was simply a girl with the kind of beauty that you take home to your mother. He could never imagine his mama meeting either of the other women but last night he dreamt of returning to his family house in Bridgeport with Marta on his arm. What would they say?

He knew the answer without hesitation because he had grown up in the

Scarpacci household. No matter how worldly he had become since leaving, he knew that time sat still in their outdated views. His family only saw the German occupied Poland in their dislike. They did not know as Paulie did, that the Polish soldiers in the concentration camps gave food to the Italians that were captured. In their ignorance, they simply had a dislike for the Polish people. They were both immigrants and both had their own neighborhoods in Bridgeport, but they rarely danced to the same music in the streets. In their mind, the Poles married the Poles and the Italians married no one but another Italian.

Trying to pass off Marta as an Italian was a stretch. She had light skin instead of the olive tone, and her features were more Eastern European than Southern European. Paulie wondered how a simple mountain range running through Austria could cause so much division in culture and looks. Her beautiful brown eyes were captivating but they were definitely not in the dream like state of most Italian women. He knew it would be insulting to her to even try and pass her off as anything other than her ancestry, but it was good to think it through anyway.

Looking at the clock hanging on the wall of his room, the former Army Private felt like he had slept in far too long. In the barracks, reveille was at 5am and the chow line in the mess hall was long by 530am. If you didn't wake up early, you missed the bacon and were forced to settle for the powdered eggs. Just thinking about the breakfast food made his stomach rumble. He knew he would have to grab a roll on the way to Grand Central but for now he needed to get ready.

Even though it was his first morning in a strange place, he went about his preparations with precision. The Army had taught him how to take care of the basics in the most remote of circumstances. Take care of the basic human functions such as bowel movements whenever you can. Check. Wash or bathe the essentials of the face, armpits and privates. Check. Once clean, apply some deodorant and some after shave if possible so that you can remain smelling clean. Check. The only difference came in the final steps. He no longer had to worry about keeping his Army green socks clean and dry every day. He no longer had to have a crisp uniform for inspection every day. From this day forward he could dress how he pleases. Looking to impress the girl, he put on a pair of slacks, a white tee and a button down shirt. Finishing it off for the cool fall air, he put on a suit jacket and slicked his hair back. He was ready to meet the girl that made his heart flutter. He hoped that she would be there as promised.

Heading out into the New York street, he had a spring in his step. Civilian clothes felt good to wear once again and he was very happy not to have a pair of Army Infantry boots weighing down his feet. In his youthful infatuation, he hoped that Marta had not been more impressed with the uniform instead of the man wearing it. He knew that whatever she was wearing would light him up like a GI Zippo lighter. He hoped he would have the same effect on her.

Paulie arrived at Grand Central Station at 10:45am, hoping that her train had not arrived early. Banking on the fact that trains were never early and most often late, he had stopped at a bakery and gotten a hard roll with some butter. Taking it with him, he ate the roll and drank his black coffee while strolling down Park Avenue. The colors seemed more vibrant today than they were yesterday but then again many things had happened since he stepped off that boat, He believed the main difference for the acuity in his senses was coming in on the 10:50 train from New Rochelle.

Standing underneath the centerpiece clock. Paulie began to get nervous. What if she didn't show? What if she stood him up? What if she changed her mind, or something came up, or she simply was...there? As he was daydreaming about all the reasons or possibilities why she would not come, his eyes suddenly focused on the fact that she was already there. Standing on the platform steps, she was dressed like an angel sent from heaven. She wore a white polka dot dress with bobby socks and her hair pinned up in a bow. Adorned with a string of pearls, Paulie thought he was looking at the most beautiful woman he had ever set eyes on. He was not sure why he didn't have the same effect when he first met her yesterday, but he was now viewing her with much different glasses. Walking up to him, she began to smile and his world melted away.

"Hey there soldier. Looking for someone?"

"Not just someone. I only have eyes for you."

"Well, aren't you the next Clark Gable."

"Does that make you Miss Scarlett?"

"Mr. Scarpacci. I'm a little too Polish to be a southern belle and you are too much of a city slicker to be on a plantation. Let's just be a cute Army Private and his love interest spending a day in the city."

"Is that what you are now? My love interest?"

"I don't know Mr. Scarpacci. Are you interested in love?"

Taking a step towards him, Marta turned her head slightly and kissed Paulie on the cheek. Without waiting for an answer, she walked off towards the Park Avenue exit with a young man frozen in her rear view mirror. He had travelled half way around the world just to fall in love with a girl who lived just over the state line in New Rochelle.

5

The couple stepped out onto the Park Avenue sidewalk like they were entering a new life together. The October air was crisp as the sun hit their faces and disoriented them for a moment. Seeking comfort, Marta reached out her hand to grasp Paulie's and the connection was made. Together they stepped forward to explore the greatest city in the world.

The conversation flowed as if they were long lost friends re-united in new circumstances. Paulie shared stories about his family and they shared light laughter as he described the different characters. In turn, she painted a different picture of deepened cultural routes and a family paved with good intentions. Somewhere in the middle, they shared that both families were packed full of tradition and values.

The clock approached midday and Paulie's Army's conditioning kicked in. It was time to head towards the mess hall and find something to eat. In civilian life, it was time to lighten the mood and find something to eat with his new girl. Crossing over to 5th Avenue and 49th, they found many street side cafés full of young couples in love. Stepping off the sidewalk, they entered one of the deli restaurants and found a table with a view.

"What does a Polish girl eat at a Jewish deli in Manhattan?"

"Does it matter if I am Polish or Jewish? The lunch meat is all good to me. How about you, Italian boy? I don't see any Italian food nearby. Are you ok with a sandwich?"

"I think it's funny that we refer back to our roots when we talk about food. In the Army, they didn't care what nationality you were. We all got the same grub for every meal. There was never French food or Italian food or Polish food. It was just food. Now that I am back eating like normal people, I want to eat a little bit of everything. How about you?"

Marta looked over the menu and gazed over the top at her date. They had known each other less than 24 hours and it was already comfortable. She felt safe with her Army Private protecting her. She could not put her finger on it but their connection was real and they reacted to each other as if they had known each other for years. Smiling, she put the menu on the table and waited for Paulie to decide. When the waiter approached, they each placed their order and relaxed in the moment.

"Why do I feel like I have known you for a long time Paulie Scarpacci?"

"Maybe we met in Okinawa. Were you there?"

The two broke out in laughter. "I'm pretty sure I have never left the country, Paulie. You are the world traveler, not me."

"If you could travel anywhere in the world, where would you go?"

"Are you asking me to travel with you?"

"Travel? I think I'm still traveling since I have not been home in years. I guess we are traveling together in New York."

"We both live less than an hour train ride from here, Paulie. I'm not sure that technically is traveling to anyone."

"So, if you could travel, where would you go?"

Marta thought quietly for a moment. Her life had been limited and had never traveled out of the tri-state area. Her family had traveled across the George Washington Bridge to New Jersey many times to visit relatives. Beyond a few day trips, she had never taken a true vacation and had never slept anywhere but her family's home in New Rochelle.

"My mamushka always talks about the old country in Poland. She talks about it in such a romantic way. I think if I could go anywhere, I would go to Europe and experience that romance for myself"

Paulie chose his next words carefully. He knew that he was entering a mine field and it could explode on him at any point.

"Don't you think you could find romance here in New York?"

Smiling, Marta reached across and took his hand on the linen covered café table. In the moment, they were the only ones in the city.

"I think I already have."

The two stared dreamily at each other and the moment was captured forever. The only thing breaking them out of their trance was the arrival of food. They each ate their sandwiches with vigor and enjoyed every last bite of their chips and pickle until their plates were cleaned. They washed it down with their fountain sodas and sat back, deliciously fulfilled.

"Oh, my. I haven't had an appetite like that in ages. You must bring out the hunger in me Mr. Scarpacci."

"I'm not sure when I've enjoyed a meal more. Definitely beats the chow in the Army."

"You haven't said much about your time there, Paulie. Was it as bad as they say?"

Paulie took a drink of his fountain soda before answering. He was a mix of emotions as he was clearly smitten with the girl before him, but his time in the war was not table conversation to be shared over dessert.

"I left Bridgeport with a few of my buddies. They went to Europe and I went to the Pacific. Here I am sitting here with a beautiful girl in New York City because I drew a different card from the deck than they did. They all got killed in the invasion of Normandy. I survived because I was off in Okinawa when all that happened. I'm not sure what I can say about the war except I'm going home and they won't."

Paulie fell silent as he moved his napkin around in awkwardness.

"Well, I for one am glad you came home, Mr. Scarpacci. If you didn't get off that boat, I would never have met you."

Reaching out, she squeezed his hand once again. This time he left his hand there and enjoyed the moment.

When lunch was finished, Paulie paid the tab and they resumed their tour of the city. They took a walk in Central Park and marveled at the color explosion before their eyes.

"I love this time of year. It is always so pretty."

"In Japan, it was a good time too. I mean, it wasn't a good time for the war, but the weather turned nice. The rains finally stopped in October and it was kind of a nice time, weather wise anyway."

They continued on in silence until they arrived at the edge of the lake. Sitting down on a bench, they each contemplated the moment at hand.

"Are you having a good day, Paulie?"

"I'm having a great day. Why do you ask?"

Marta blushed and placed her hands on her lap. Looking back at him she asked demurely. "Do you like me Paulie?"

"Well, sure doll. I'm falling for you by the minute. I just wasn't sure how you felt about me. For me, the day has been a slice of heaven."

Marta smiled and placed her hand on his. "Paulie Scarpacci. Maybe you were in the Army too long and don't realize when a woman is smitten for you. I came to the city just to see you. If you were a gentleman, you would have kissed me by now. Unless you don't want to."

The former Army Private had never felt so nervous. It was like he was raising his gun for the first time in battle. Slowly, he turned his face towards her and leaned in for a kiss. The actions that followed sealed their fate forever. Each was overcome with love in the moment. After a few seconds that felt like hours, they broke their kiss and exhaled. Looking down at her watch, Marta was suddenly aware that her time was limited.

"Oh, my. I completely lost track of the time. I need to be going soon or I will miss my train. I wish I could stay here with you the rest of the day."

Holding her in his embrace he never wanted the moment to end. "I feel the same way doll. Can't you take the late train home like you did last night?"

"I would but my family would be mad, It's my turn to cook dinner tonight so I have to get home."

"Beautiful and a good cook? Look out. I think I won the sweepstakes boys" Marta blushed. "You are a sweet talker Mr. Scarpacci, but family calls."

Taking her hand in his, he held her tenderly in his grasp. "You know I'll be here until Sunday, right? Do you think you could find your way back to see me tomorrow?"

Leaning in, she pressed her lips against his as they kissed. Releasing him, she leaned back and smiled. "Try and stop me Paulie. I am yours for the rest of the week and beyond."

6

The days that followed were magical even for New York standards. With three full days to go until he returned home, Paulie wanted to make sure he celebrated life with his new girl and love, Marta. Each day, he met her at the train station and each night, he brought her back. In between, they took in the city for all it had to offer.

On Thursday, she introduced Paulie to the Russian Tea Room which clearly was not the young man's cup of tea. After a hearty Italian dinner, they ventured to nearby Carnegie Hall. Side by side they listened to beautiful music while holding hands and dreaming of a new life. Kissing goodbye to her on the platform at Grand Central, they both marveled at how close they had become in such a short period of time.

On Friday, they attended mass together at St. Patrick's Cathedral. Both devout Catholics, they prayed together to ask forgiveness for their sins and to bless them in their journey together. When mass had ended, they walked out onto 5th Avenue and watched the very first Columbus Day parade since the holiday had just been named by FDR himself. There was joy, there was laughter and plenty of American Flags. Paulie Scarpacci thought he would never feel more American and wondered if he could ever be more in love.

In the evening they wandered back to Rockefeller Center where they took a Caleche ride through the park and finished off the night with a show at Radio City. The audience was filled with men in uniform and their dates. To the new found couple, they did not notice anyone else. Paulie and Marta started to wonder how they would ever live apart as his departure home was a little over a day away. Walking her to the train station that night, he stopped and bought her a rose from a street vendor. Their kiss was more than a farewell that night. It held the resonance of the future as it lingered on both their lips for long after.

Saturday was set to be their last day in the city together. After re-uniting again at the train station, Paulie asked her if they could just take a walk in the park before setting out to see more sights. Marta wondered if her new beau was planning to break it off as he set off for Connecticut by himself. To Paulie, he had something much different in mind.

"I've had a swell time this week, Marta. Really swell."

Clutching his arm at his elbow, she feared for the worst.

"I did too Paulie. Why does it seem like you are saying goodbye to me already?"

Paulie was shocked. "No, no. It's not like that, doll. It's not like that at all. Actually, it's quite the opposite."

Marta looked back at him confused. "The opposite? What is the opposite of goodbye? I don't understand you Paulie."

"What I mean is, I don't want to say goodbye to you at all. I think we got something special going on here. Don't you think so too?"

"Of course I do. But I still don't know what you are talking about."

"Ok. Ok. Let me explain it out some. Tonight, you are going back to New Rochelle and not coming back here with me. Tomorrow, I am getting on my own train and going home to my family in Bridgeport without you. What happens after that?"

"Oh…well…we talked about that Paulie. I'm your gal now and you're my guy. I'll come see you next week in Bridgeport and then you can come meet my family in New Rochelle. It will be fine. It's not too far."

"So you see us going in that direction? Maybe we'll have Thanksgiving together with one of our families and then Christmas? I sure would love to spend my first Christmas back in the states with you doll."

Marta blushed and squeezed his hand while they walked. "I like talking about these things with you Paulie. I like it a lot. I know it's only been a week but I see us together in the future, don't you think?"

Paulie smiled and became nervous all at once. "Well, that's what I was wondering. When the time comes…not that it's here now, that's not what I'm saying…but when it does come up…well, you always talk about your mom…in your culture…if I wanted…do I ask your father for your hand…when the time comes?"

Marta pulled him in for a big hug while she gushed in silent tears. Releasing him, she wiped her face and smiled back at him. "Paulie Scarpacci. I am very happy to hear you say that, even though it seemed hard to say. Not that we are there yet, but when we are, and you want to, yes, you will ask my father. That is how it is done."

To end the conversation, they put it away and sealed it with a kiss. Without another spoken word, they exited the park and resumed their tourist visits to the all the sights they could take in for the day. When evening came upon them, the inevitable goodbye was looming and Marta tried to be the sensible one.

"So, it is Saturday night and you are catching the morning train back to Bridgeport. Will your family meet you at the train station?"

"Yea, they'll be there like a bunch of mooks. They'll make a fuss and all because I'll be wearing my uniform. It's probably best that you don't see such a spectacle."

"I'm sure they will just shower you with the love you deserve. They haven't seen you in years, they'll have lots to talk to you about."

"...and I'll have lots to talk to them about. I can't wait to tell them all that I'm in love with a Polish girl named Marta."

"Do you think they'll like me, Paulie?"

"Of course they will. What's not to like? You're beautiful and smart and you come from a good family. Break some bread with them and drink some wine and they will love you forever, doll."

"Will you love me forever, Paulie?"

"Of course doll. I'll love you so much that someday I'll give you my name."

That was all that needed to be said. They ended the evening with a regular goodbye kiss and not one signifying a forever farewell like in the movies. They had plans to see each other in a couple of days and if destiny prevailed, they would spend the rest of their lives together. Or would they?

7

The train ride from Grand Central Station in Manhattan to the station in Bridgeport, Connecticut usually took a couple hours. On Sunday mornings, there were less stops along the way so Paulie would be home for breakfast. He had sent a telegram the day before that he would be arriving on the 830am train but did not receive a response. In the Italian neighborhood where his family resided, there was not much need for private telephones. All the families on the block shared one party line so in the interest of some privacy, he sent the telegram.

The Scarpacci family was like any other immigrant family that came over and landed on Ellis Island. They had planted their roots in one place and never left. Paulie was the first one to leave town in the military, even though he was not the oldest son. His older brother, Albert, was identified as 4F when he tried to enlist. Al had lost hearing in one ear at a young age and never recovered. It never dawned on him that it would prevent him from fighting for his country. The younger brother, Joseph or Joe, was the youngest of all the siblings and had just recently finished school. He had all intentions of enlisting like his other brother but the war came to an end before he could.

There were two daughters in the family and both spent most of their time in the kitchen with their mother. Ann Marie was the oldest sister with Nancy the younger. The girls were sandwiched between their brothers in a boy-girl descending order starting with Al and ending with Joe. The four had formed strong bonds with each other while their middle brother was away. They had all prayed for their brother's safe return but they all shared some concern how his re-entry into the family dynamic would send things off kilter.

Maria Scarpacci was the heart and soul of the family even though her husband, Lou Anthony, technically wore the crown. In the old world tradition, she took care of the house and the children and he managed the family business. Lou Anthony was a man of very few words and those that came out were not full of warmth. He had fought with the Italian Allies in WWI and hardened his heart when he watched one friend after another die in the trenches next to him. He was not happy when Paulie followed in his footsteps and went off to war, but as his father, he was concerned that Paulie's friends dying in Normandy would have the same affect.

In the Italian community, there were many so called "cousins" as well as "aunts" and "uncles" but none were properly related. It is said that it takes a village and in the small Italian neighborhood of Bridgeport, everyone was family. There was not a member of the family that was not aware Paulie Scarpacci was coming home from the war today. The festivities had all been planned out and after all the welcoming and church time had passed, they planned to eat, drink and dance in the streets.

Only the immediate family was going to the train station to meet Paulie. His brothers and sisters, Al, Ann Marie, Nancy and Joe were all in attendance along with their mother. Lou Anthony would not be waiting on any platform for his son to return home. He had been clear on his opinion of his son running away to war and he would not congratulate him for coming back alive. Many men didn't. In his opinion, the smartest ones were like Albert, who used his 4F status not to risk his life.

At 8:32 am, the train whistle could be heard as the train came into view on Water Street. Maria felt her heart flutter as her lost son was finally returning home. She was certain that she could not keep her family intact for long but she was determined to have all her children under her roof at least for a short while. She immediately rose when the train came into view so she would be ready to receive her Paulie when he stepped off onto the platform.

The train rolled to a stop and the doors to each car opened with a hiss. Since it was an early Sunday morning, there were not many passengers arriving from the city. The few that did got off the train quickly and went off with their waiting connections or hurried off to the nearby cab stand to catch a ride to their final destination. When the family had almost given up hope that the prodigal son was returning, a dashing young man appeared in the doorway of passenger car number 3. Standing at the top of the landing in his dress uniform, he held his Army issued duffel over his shoulder as he tried to focus his eyes in the daylight. Seeing his family on the nearby platform, he began to smile. Paulie Scarpacci was home.

8

"What do you mean you got back last week?"

The Scarpacci family was sitting down to a breakfast feast to welcome the war hero. The whole day was upside down due to the fact that Paulie came home on the 830am train. By the time they had finished all the hugging and kissing on the train platform, they didn't get back to the house until almost 930am. There was no way they were going to make the 10am mass down at St. Peter's Church. Their usual Sunday routine was delayed and they would need to go to the 12pm mass. The afternoon festivities would be put together while they were all there. Maria took the opportunity to whip up a big breakfast. She didn't want his first meal back at the table ruined by his father's grouchy state.

"Eat, eat. You look like they starved you while you were in the Army. Did you not get a good meal the whole time you were gone?"

"If he's not gonna eat more sausage, I'll take some mama." Joe reached out his hand to grab the serving fork and was instantly slapped away.

"Joey! Marone! Let your brother have first chance. You've been here eating your mama's cooking while this poor boy was withering away. He is all skin and bones. He looks like one of those oriental people that eat nothing but rice."

"They eat other things mama."

"I hear they eat their dogs. Is that right, Paulie? Do they eat their dogs?"

"Well, Nancy. When you are at war..."

"...you eat whatever you can to survive. Capice? If the boy was hungry, he probably ate a cat too. I know when we were in the trenches we would get the rats and cook them up."

"Papa! Now? We are eating."

"Yes, Ann Marie. We are eating late because your younger brother took his time coming home. I had to have late breakfast because he was doing whatever he was doing in New York. Again, I ask you. What do you mean you got back last week?"

This time Paulie would not be saved by the banter with his brothers and sisters. He had let the cat out of the bag that he had not just gotten back and now he would have to pay the piper for it.

"It's not a big deal Pop. I took a few days to myself. I've been listening to orders for years and I finally had some R and R time. You remember what it was like, don't you Pops? When you finally got out. I just needed a few days to get used to it."

"Yea. I remember what it was like. I remember carrying the coffins of my friends off the transport when I got back. They had us load them all into wagons. I remember walking with my bag on my shoulder just like you came into the house. The difference is I didn't need no few days to get used to it. My family was waiting for me so I came home."

"Well that was a while ago, Pops. This time, there were thousands of GI's getting off that ship. We all hit Manhattan and turned the place around. I saw all sorts of things while I was there. I ate food at a place called an Automat where you put your money in a..."

"So you got back from the war and the first thing you thought to do was waste your money on some food cooked by someone else. Didn't you think your mama would want to cook for you here?"

"Yes, Pops but..."

The other children sat silently as they ate their food. They had all been on the receiving end when their father got something under his collar and they had no desire to turn the tables on themselves.

"You think I'm a mook? I went off to war once. Saw some horrible things like I'm sure you did too. But I also know what happened when we all got home. Don't sit there at your mother's table and try to say you didn't come home for a few days because you wanted to take in the sights. I know better."

"What's he talking about Al?"

"Shush your face and eat your eggs, Joey. This don't concern you."

Paulie knew he should let his father get it out of his system but if the Army had taught him one thing it was to stand and fight.

"That's right Joey. It don't concern you and what I did in New York City when I got back is no concern to anyone either. I'm home now. That's what matters."

Paulie could see his father thinking about how to react. It was a big day in the Scarpacci family and he didn't want to wreck it by toeing the line with his son. They would have their day in the neighborhood and he would deal with his son later.

"That's fine, Paulie. You be the big man today and play the hero. But know things have changed since you've been gone."

Paulie looked around at his brothers and sisters and sized them up. They certainly had grown since he had gone off to war. Both his brothers were taller than he remembered and his sisters clung to their mother more than ever. Those changes were visible but he didn't think his father was referring to their growth spurt.

"Besides the family growing a bit, I don't see many changes. The house looks the same. You and mama look the same. In fact, the whole neighborhood looks the same. What has changed since I left?"

His mother sat in silence as well. She was worried about the tension between her son and her husband and was hoping it would find some resolution soon. They needed to get ready for church.

"Everything changed since you left, young man. Pearl Harbor put a fire in your belly so you ran off and signed up. You didn't ask me or your mama. You didn't even tell your older brother what you were doing. You just left. Well, with one less mouth to listen to and the war going on, we all got a little more in line. Now, your brothers and sisters don't walk on the other side of the street without checking with me first. You want to be home. Great. But you are going to fall in line like them. You are back in my unit now, son. You will listen or you will go right back out that door you came in from."

"Lou Anthony! My son just came home. Do not push him away again."

Paulie's father simply shook his head. "See that? Now you got your mother all worked up. Finish your food and go get washed up. We are going to St. Peter's together as a family. Whether you like it or not, you do what the family wants and not what Paulie wants."

With that, his father got up from the table and threw his napkin down on his plate. He walked out of the kitchen but his presence was still felt. For Paulie Scarpacci, all he could think about was Marta and the wall his father had just been placed between them.

9

"So the prodigal son retuns…"

Paulie turned to see the Priest standing behind him.

"Father Dominick. It is good to see you. I enjoyed the mass today."

Paulie stood with his family outside St. Peter's and greeted all the well-wishers as they passed by. While he was not a decorated war hero, he may well have been the way he was heralded in the church community.

"I see you have returned safe and sound like the prodigal son."

"Forgive me Father. Does the parable not refer to a son who took his family's inheritance and goes off to live a life of sin. I do not think that I did either Father."

The Priest simply nodded. "Perhaps the correlation to the parable can be discussed further in confession young man. I would imagine your sins are many having been off to war."

The young Scarpacci looked at his family with hopeful eyes. Would any of them save him from the persecution of the older Priest? They had all been scolded at some point in their lives and shuffled their feet in awkward discomfort to the situation.

"I met regularly with our Army Chaplain, Father. He absolved me of any wrong doings in the actions of war long ago."

"I see, I see. Well, that being said, please come visit me soon. I long to hear more about your journeys overseas and help you transition to civilian life."

"That would be swell Father. I'll come see you soon."

Father Dominick put a comforting hand on the shoulder of Lou Anthony as he walked away. There clearly had been conversations about his son before his return.

"I feel like a Christmas decoration down in Seaside Park. How long are we going to stand here and be gawked at?"

Lou Anthony gave his son a stern look. "I told you Paulie. If you want to be home with us, you will act like a Scarpacci. I will tell you when we are done here and until then you shut your mouth, capeesh?

Paulie simply stood there in his dress uniform and looked at his father in silence. He had spent years in the Army and knew when to shut his mouth. He may have been an adult by age but it was clear he would be treated like a child here in Bridgeport.

His parents were standing on either side of him as his brothers and sisters fanned out from there. At first glance, one would think they were a receiving line at a wedding or a funeral. All the well-wishers came down the line and made various comments.

"Look how big he has gotten..."

"Did they feed him over there? He looks so thin..."

"He looks so handsome..."

All of the people spoke about him like he wasn't even there. The conversations were had with his parents and not him. He was not even introduced to the people he did not recognize. They continued to speak about him like he was a war story and not the living flesh. All that changed when the family was approached by another family dressed to the nines and clearly out of place in the Bridgeport community.

"Lou Anthony. There you are. I thought we would have to wait until the festivities later to see you. I'm glad you are still here."

"Of course. It's a big day for your family and for mine. Let me introduce you to my son. Paulie Scarpacci. Meet Salvatore Francucci."

Paulie reached out and shook hands with the gentleman. "It's a pleasure to meet you, sir."

The man was dressed in a pin stripe suit with a cashmere coat draped on his arm. Standing next to him was a woman with more diamonds than teeth and her fur shawl draped her shoulders in the cool October air. On either side of the couple were clearly their children. Both the brother and sister exuded an air about them that indicated they were disgusted having to follow their parents to such a nasty place such as Bridgeport, Connecticut.

"We have heard much about you, Private."

"Well, sir. The uniform is no longer valid. I'm a civilian now."

"Of course, of course. If you were not out of the Army yet, we would not be here to discuss the business."

Paulie looked nervously to his father. He knew there was something up but he could not put his finger on it.

"The business, sir?"

"I see your father has not had a chance to discuss with you yet. Not to fret. We will discuss later at the festivities."

"You are coming to my homecoming party, sir?"

"Of course, of course. We would not miss it."

Paulie looked at his father and mother with no resolution. Looking back at Mr. Francucci, he grew even more nervous.

"I'm very confused. If you don't know me, why would you come to my homecoming party? Are you a friend of my parents?"

Salvatore came up to the young man and lightly tapped his cheek with the inside of his palm. Laughing, he added a pinch to the cheek to leave a sting.

"All will be clear soon, Mr. Scarpacci. Your father will let you know all about our business deal. For now, I want to smell your mother's sauce and dip some fresh baked bread into it. Where is there a bakery near here?"

Lou Anthony explained how to get to the nearby Louigi's bakery and the family bid their goodbyes for the moment as they walked off together. They climbed into a nearby Pullman limousine and the car drove off before a word could be spoken.

"What was that all about, Pops? You rubbing elbows with rich people now?"

"It's business...and family..."

"I don't understand. How is it both?"

Lou Anthony looked over to his wife who nodded in agreement. It was clearly time to let the cat out of the bag.

"It's part of the business agreement. We get to be part of Perri Sausages. Francucci is making me a partner."

"A partner? That's great, Pops. I didn't know you had that kind of pull. A lot has changed since I went away."

Lou Anthony grinned. It was rare for him to show any joy but the comment clearly did. "I don't have pull, Paulie. But I do have something Francucci wants."

"Oh yea? What's that?"

Lou Anthony took a step towards his son and looked down at him in a dead stare. "I got you, that's what I got. He wants a husband for his daughter, Carmen, and I gave him you. Congratulations, Paulie. You're betrothed to be married."

10

"What made you think this was ok?"

The family rode home in silence. The fact that Paulie clenched his fist and raised it in anger at his father while they stood in front of the church shattered all protocols. A son never raised his fists against his father. An Italian son never challenged his father in a decision. A Catholic son never disrespected his family at church. Paulie may have returned home from the war in the Pacific but his actions created a new war with his father.

"I am the head of this family and I decide what's best for us. You came home to this family, because you are part of the family. You are here so you will do what I tell you to do."

Paulie slammed his fist on the table. "I will not be treated like a child. I went to war and fought for my country. I went and fought so that my family could be safe. I did not go off and risk my life so that you could ruin it for me when I get home."

"Ruin it? I am not ruining it, you stunad. I am giving you a life. I got you a wife, I got you a job. You are going to be well off working at the sausage factory with your father-in-law. How did I ruin your life when you have nothing but your uniform?"

"I don't need a wife. I already have one."

Everything stopped as the air was sucked out of the kitchen. Maria stopped stirring her sauce and Lou Anthony froze in his tracks. The children who were listening behind closed doors collectively gasped when they heard the words uttered.

"What are you saying Paulie? Did you run off and get married while you were away without telling us?"

"No, mama. I wouldn't do that to my family so why would they do that to me? Of course I would not disrespect my mama or her papa without asking him for her hand but isn't that what pops did to me? Get me all hitched up without asking me?"

"So, who is this girl? Are you making up stories to get out of the marriage to Carmen Francucci?"

Paulie got up and walked across the kitchen to the window. Somewhere out there he knew she was with her family too. He prayed she was not going through the same pain he was just so that they could be together.

"No story. Her name is Marta. She lives in New Rochelle."

"New Rochelle? When did you go to New Rochelle, Paulie?"

"I haven't mama. I haven't been there yet."

Lou Anthony had a scowl on his face as he sought to put the pieces together.

"If you never went to New Rochelle, how did you meet this girl Marta? Was she in the USO or something?"

Paulie was not ready to discuss his relationship with Marta. It seemed that everything that happened since he stepped off the train this morning was happening too quickly. He didn't have time to even think about how to explain.

"No, Pops. I met her in Manhattan."

"So, let me get this straight. You met this girl a few days ago and now you want to marry her? Is she a floozy or something?"

Paulie stepped quickly in front of his father. "You want to disrespect me by promising me off like some goat at the market that's one thing. But you don't disrespect my future wife. Besides, what difference does it make if it's only a few days? I didn't even meet this Carmen girl until today and haven't even said a word to her but now you tell me you want me to marry her. For what? So you can have a sausage factory? I don't think so. Find your riches on someone else. I'm no carpet bagger."

The slap was quick. Having been out of the Army for less than a week, Paulie thought he should have seen it coming. Had his memories of battling the enemy been forgotten already? All he knew is that he stood in his parent's kitchen and his cheek stung from the palm of his father.

"You don't disrespect me either young man. I am your father and I will not be talked to that way. I don't care what war you fought in. You are in my house now."

Paulie rubbed at his cheek. Looking at his father he knew they were both troubled by the way the situation had deteriorated. His mother tried to be the mediator.

"You both disrespect each other. That is not the family way. We need to find a way to fix this mess."

Lou Anthony looked to his wife and he knew she was right. They needed to figure this out. The Francucci family would be arriving within the hour and they expected a husband for their daughter.

"This woman. This Marta. Does she know of your intentions to marry her? Does she know you want to talk to her father?"

Paulie looked his father without fear. "Yes, Papa. She knows of my intention."

"*Va fanool*" Lou Anthony swore as he slammed a dinner plate on the floor of the kitchen. Paulie recoiled from his father but Maria had a different reaction.

"Lou Anthony Scarpacci! Do not use that language in my kitchen, on a Holy day no less. Now you disrespect me on the day my son comes home from the war."

Her husband turned away in shame. He knew he had overstepped.

"Paulie? Will she be joining us today?"

"Maria! How dare..."

"Hold your tongue, Lou Anthony."

She was clearly in charge on this day. The men both knew they were defeated.

"Is she Paulie?"

He looked back and forth between his two parents and wished his answer was different.

"No. She wanted to come home with me today but she also wanted to give me time with my family. She went to work today and she is coming tomorrow to meet you."

Lou Anthony stood upright and squared his shoulders facing his wife.

"Can I speak now?"

Maria knew it was just a formality. At the end of the day he was the man of the house but she was pleased that he took a step back to realize something.

"What does this Marta do for work?"

"She works at a department store as a clerk."

Lou Anthony nodded while deep in thought. Looking over at his wife, it was clearly her turn to ask a question.

"Will she continue to work once you get married, Paulie? Does she not cook? Who will cook for you if she is at work?"

Paulie laughed lightly. He was happy to break the severity of the conversation. "She cooks mama. Her family is rich in tradition like ours so she cooks all of her family recipes."

The opening was not going to be lost on his father. "What is her family then? Sicilian? Sardinian? Tuscan?"

The answer would not be well received but Paulie had come too far to turn back now. In for a penny, in for a pound.

"Her family name is Slowik."

Lou Anthony acted as though he had heard his son wrong. "Slowik? That's not an Italian name. It sounds like..."

"Yes, Papa. She is Polish."

The gasp actually came from a collection of his mother along with his brothers and sisters who were still listening behind the closed door.

"Wait a minute. Wait a darn minute. You come home after years away and the news you have is that you are going to marry a Pole? Is that the present you bring home to me? It is not enough for you to not honor the arrangement I made for you but now you tell me you are marrying a Pole?"

Maria had a minute to digest the shock and soon she wanted to apply the salve to the sting. She wanted peace in her kitchen.

"I don't think it's that bad Lou Anthony."

"Maria? What are you saying? The boy is not true to our house!"

"I do not think this is true. Not at all. First, you say *the boy* but really he is a man. He went off to war just like his Papa. He honored his family, his name and his country by wearing a uniform. He comes home with love in his heart, for a girl who does not sit home but works for a living. He wants to marry this girl but honors us, his parents, by not asking her until he talks to her papa. I do not think he has not been true. I think he is a Scarpacci, true and true."

Lou Anthony listened to his wife finish and said nothing. He walked over to the kitchen table and sat down in a chair looking at the table. Paulie looked at his mother and wondered what they should do now. Should he push the issue or let his father sit and think? He opted for the latter and was happy he did. When Lou Anthony finally spoke he did not admit defeat or acknowledge that his wife was correct. He was a man of action and responded in the only way he knew how.

"You say this Marta woman is coming here tomorrow not today, right?"

Paulie was confused but went along with the conversation. "Yes, Papa. She is taking the morning train from New Rochelle. She will be here tomorrow to meet you and Mama."

Lou Anthony continued his silent thinking on the subject as he formulated a plan to get through it all.

"Then we let tomorrow be tomorrow and today be today. On this day, my son has come home from the war and we will gather with friends and family to celebrate his life and his health."

Maria walked over and hugged her husband from behind. Walking over to the kitchen counter, she poured a glass of wine for him and brought it over to him as a reward for good behavior. Paulie stood baffled by the conversation and did not see the resolution.

"I don't mean to look a gift horse in the mouth…"

"Oh, Paulie…don't…"

"It's ok, Mama. I just want to know what Papa wants me to say to the Francucci's today. They are coming here today because they think I will marry their daughter. I can't do that. I already told you…"

"No need to say more. Tomorrow we will meet your bride. Today you will be like the Army. Sometimes you have to stay in the foxhole and not move. You will not say anything of your new bride to anyone. I will take care of the business with the Francucci family. You will have plenty of others to take up your time without talking to them. Capisce?"

Paulie hesitantly put his faith in his father. "Yes, Papa. I will lay low in the grass while the enemy passes. Just like the Army taught me."

Like his time in the rice paddies of the orient, he would wait for the attack. He hoped that the battle would pass but he was ready to fight for the woman he loved.

11

An Italian family celebration is nothing short of a feast. While the specialty of the house is always celebrated, every well-wisher brings along their favorite dishes as a token of love. Like the three wise men bringing gold, frankincense and myrrh, the Italian community brought the bread, wine, and pasta dishes. The food tables kept expanding with each family's favorite and the end result was nothing short of extraordinary.

The house was packed with everyone from the neighborhood and beyond. There was a mix of young and old, of close friends and acquaintances, but all were there to celebrate life. Too many from their community went off to war and did not return. They were all happy not only that one of their own survived to tell tall tales, but also that the war itself was finally over. The celebration was not only for Paulie, but for the community to finally heal and move on.

The Scarpacci clan settled in to their given host mode. Maria controlled the flow of all the food in and out of the kitchen and the other Italian women followed her lead. Ann Marie and Nancy waited for instruction from their mother and the other women as they were eager to please. They brought out full dishes to the tables and returned with the empties.

Al and Joey manned the desserts table, entertaining as many of the ladies as possible. They poured on their charms and offered sweets to the sweet to every single lady that crossed their path. When the men walked by and snuck a cannoli or an anisette cookie, the pair simply turned away like they never saw anything happen. In the Italian household the cannoli took the priority.

Lou Anthony and Paulie played their roles perfectly. The proud father put aside the earlier drama to showcase his son. The war hero has come home to be placed on display in front of everyone. The familiar responses were all the same as they received at the church.

"You should be proud Lou Anthony."

"You raised a good man Lou Anthony."

The men had various replies without their wives around.

"Your son is bigger than you, Lou Anthony."

"Which one of you killed more enemies?"

"How were those women over in the orient?"

The women were all focused on one thing without the men around.

"Does he have a girlfriend?"

"Is he ready to settle down?"

"How will he support his wife?"

The Francucci family was late to the party and made a grand entrance. Their limousine pulled up to the curb while the children were outside playing. They all raced to the windows to see what celebrity was gracing them with their presence and were disappointed that it was just another old Italian couple with their son and daughter. Once they had cleared away from the doors, the family stepped out and came into the house for the celebration.

Upon seeing the family enter, Lou Anthony and Paulie split up. The father went to greet his new guests and future business partner while the son disappeared into a sea of people. Their plan was simple. Let Lou Anthony do all the talking and keep Paulie busy with everyone else. Before his subtle exit, the conquering hero got a good look at his promised bride and shuddered at the thought of marrying her. Carmen may have been the balance to be paid in the deal, but she surely wasn't a prize.

"Salvatore! How good it is to see you. I am so glad you could make it to the celebration. Come, come. We will break bread and drink some wine together."

"Lou Anthony. You remember my wife and children. They can go make nice with everyone while you show me to your family. Where is that son of yours?"

"Which one would you like? I have three strapping young men."

"But the party is for only one, is it not Paisano?"

"Ah, yes. The man of the hour. Young Paulie is around here somewhere making his rounds with everyone. Come, let us go see what we can find to eat."

The two men wandered off into the crowd as Paulie watched them go off in a different direction then he was in. He would have to be quick and alert to avoid Salvatore Francucci. He was clearly a man on a single mission and Paulie had no intention to be his prey. He was also acutely aware that Carmen may want some of his attention as well.

As the day progressed into the night, many guests came and went. Paulie became disoriented as to which people he had spoken to and which he had not. All the while, he watched his back to avoid an ambush from anyone in the Francucci family. He hid himself in the kitchen for a short time as his mother and sisters doted on him with the other ladies. When he sought out his two brothers, he put on the brakes when he saw who they were entertaining. Carmen was seated between them as the three became much too cozy for his comfort level. He would have to thank Al and Joe later for running interference for him.

The crowd diminished as the hours grew long and Paulie became concerned with the fact that the Francucci's were still there. When the chauffer appeared at the door at 9pm, the young Army veteran was overcome with a sense of relief. Sending someone to get his father, Paulie disappeared into the corners of his parent's house. He tensed up again once he saw all the Francucci's walk a path towards the front door across the living room.

"So then our business is done here, Salvatore."

"I guess it is but I cannot believe we were here all day long and did not see the conquering hero."

"You saw how many people were here, Salvatore. The audience time was very short. Perhaps another day and time."

"Perhaps, perhaps. For now, we must go. Many blessings Lou Anthony. Thank you for your hospitality. We will talk soon."

Mr. Scarpacci stood at his front door and watched as his future got in the chauffeured limousine and drove away. Soon, he was joined by his wife and his son behind him. Turning to see them, he looked serious.

"We need to talk. Right now."

12

The morning train from New Rochelle to Bridgeport was more crowded than expected on a Monday morning. Marta Slowik was surrounded by businessmen reading their morning newspapers. Although she was adorned in a blue and white polka dot dress complete with a set of pearls, she did not even get a second glance from the men. It was as if she already had hung her married shingle out and she didn't even get to enjoy the wedding.

She had left Paulie at Grand Central less than 36 hours earlier and it felt as if it had been ages. She went home that night and cried on her pillow, quite certain that she would never see the love of her life again. She was convinced something would happen; that the universe would somehow throw itself off kilter and she would lose her knight in Army armor.

On Sunday, she went to church with her family and wished Paulie was by her side. From there, she went to work and wished that her man was one of the many that shopped in the city on a Sunday afternoon. That night, as she sat down to supper with her mother and father, she wished that they were meeting Paulie for the first time. She longed for the moment when her man would ask her father for her hand in marriage. She dreamt like a school girl and wondered if she was simply living a fairy tale.

In their whirl wind relationship, they had failed to discuss the big questions. What was their timeline? When would they marry? Where would they live? With the holidays right around the corner, where would they feast on Thanksgiving and Christmas? Perhaps she was fooling herself. Was there really a middle ground for a blended family? Would they celebrate in Italian tradition or Polish? Would they eat pasta or kielbasa for Christmas breakfast? She was not entirely certain that Italians ate pasta at all meals but she knew that food was a big part of their culture.

She rode along the rails through Westport and Stamford and grew nervous by the mile. As the train stopped at the Fairfield station, her fear became palpable. She was afraid that he would not be there at the station. Every day last week Paulie was standing there at grand Central for her. Every night last week, he kissed her goodbye and said that he would be there the next day for her. He was there then and he would be there now. She should not worry that he would not be there. She knew he was, but the real question was if he had his family with him.

Paulie had virtually told her nothing about his family. She knew he had brothers and sisters and that he was one of five. She knew that he had a mother and father and that they were all Italians that lived in Bridgeport. That pretty much summed up her total knowledge of the Scarpacci family. She did not know what his father did for work or what his mother's favorite flower was. Was she really considering marrying someone she knew so little about?

"Bridgeport! Next stop, Bridgeport Station."

The conductor startled her out of nervousness and catapulted her off the cliff. She was here. The train ride felt so long yet so short. How was her hair? Did her lipstick last? Did she need to freshen up before seeing them? Was there any time? The answer was no. Looking out the window of the train she saw Paulie standing on the platform. Thankfully he was alone and standing with a bouquet of flowers in his hand. A smile instantly solved everything.

Walking out onto the train exit stand, she looked over at her man as his smile radiated as well. With each step down the stairs their excitement to see each other escalated. Walking to reach out and help her down the last step, Paulie held her hand in one of his own while the flowers were raised in the air. Enveloping herself into his arms, he hugged her back, bouquet and all.

"I'm so glad you made it. I was worried you would not come."

With tears in her eyes, Marta replied back. "You were worried? I was worried you wouldn't be here to greet me."

"Of course, I would be here doll."

She smiled back. "…and of course I would be on the train. We are like two silly school children."

"That we are, but hopefully we are more than schoolyard crushes for each other."

Marta leaned forward and kissed him softly. In return, he handed her the flowers as he blushed on the train platform, unaware that the people around him and the train had already departed.

"I guess that answers that question."

Marta looked around seeing if the Scarpacci family was waiting somewhere off on the sidelines.

"Did you come alone?"

Paulie laughed nervously. Her questions brought him back to reality and the challenges he had faced in the last 24 hours since he had arrived.

"Yes, just me doll."

"You did tell them I was coming didn't you Paulie? I don't want to just drop in on your family unannounced."

"Of course, doll. I just wanted a moment with you alone first. I missed you terribly."

Smiling, she gazed right back into his eyes. "I missed you too. I can't imagine those people in love whose men went off to war. I'm glad we did not find each other until you got back."

"I would have spent all my time in the Pacific more miserable than I already was."

"Is your family waiting at the house? Did you tell them all about me?"

"I did, doll. I did. I even told them that you are the girl I intend to marry and that after you meet them and get their blessing, I plan to ask your father."

"Oh, Paulie."

She lept back into his arms with tears of joy rolling down her face. Looking off into the distance behind her, he hoped he could shield her from everything else going on with his family. Releasing her from the hug, he held her free hand as they walked together out of the train station. Whatever lay ahead, they would face it together.

13

The reception that Paulie Scarpacci had received when he got off of his train was much different than the welcoming that he received when he walked through the doors of the Bridgeport home with his bride to be. Instead of all of his brothers and sisters embracing him along with his mother, his siblings were nowhere to be found. Maria and Lou Anthony were seated at the dining room table when Paulie walked through the door and announced their arrival.

"Mama? Papa? We are home."

Paulie looked around the living room until he caught site of his parents seated at the table. While it was not even noon yet, they sat with a bottle of chianti and four glasses precisely placed around the table. Since his mother and father were already seated at 12 and 6 on the dial, Paulie and Marta were expected to fill the 3 and 9 spots. Walking into the dining room, the young man introduced his love.

"Mama. Papa. I want to introduce to you Marta Slowik."

Maria Scarpacci rose to her feet immediately and walked to hug the young lady. With a kiss on both cheeks, she gave her a welcoming hug.

"Marta. How wonderful it is to meet you. Paulie has told us so much about you. Welcome to our home. Please come break bread with us."

As Marta continued around the table, she was surprised by the presence of Lou Anthony who had also rose to greet her.

"Good morning young lady. Buongiorno."

It was she that gave him a kiss on both cheeks this time as a symbol of her respect for him and to silently thank him for his greeting.

"Please sit, sit."

Lou Anthony gestured for Marta to sit in the remaining chair so the four of them could talk without interruption.

"Would you like some wine or would you prefer some coffee? The hour is late for the morning but early for the afternoon. You decide."

"Wine would be fine, Mrs. Scarpacci. Thank you."

"So formal, this girl. Please call me mama."

Marta blushed at the immediate welcoming of Paulie's mother by her intention to call her in such an informal manner.

"Thank you, Mama. Wine would be fine."

Lou Anthony grabbed the bottle of chianti before his wife could get to it and poured out four glasses for them all. When he was finished, they waited ceremoniously for the man of the house to make the toast. Without more in depth, he settled for the standard toast as he raised his glass.

"Salute!"

"Salute."

The three others had raised their glasses and toasted while finishing it off with a sip of their wine.

"The wine is delicious. Thank you Mr. Scarpacci."

Lou Anthony did not correct the young lady as his wife had done a few moments ago. With the lack of sentiment hanging in the air, the conversation went silent for a moment. Maria, always the social one, kept the conversation alive.

"Marta, dear. How was the train from New Rochelle? We have never ventured there ourselves."

"The train ride was fine. The train itself was filled with many businessmen on a Monday morning but I kept to myself. No one seemed to notice I was there."

"Wonderful, wonderful..."

"Tell us of your family."

Lou Anthony was never one for small talk. He often got right to the point.

"My family, sir?"

"Yes. Your family. I assume you have one. Tell us about them."

Marta looked to Paulie for assistance but she was on her own. He knew his father was all business and he wanted them to get to know each other.

"Yes, of course. My family is from Poland. Like many families, they came over to start a new life. We settled outside of New York City in New Rochelle."

"What does your father do?"

It was clear that this was some sort of interrogation and Paulie was just an observer in the process.

"My Papa works hard. He was at the Tierney Dining Car factory until they closed. He worked the assembly line, I think they call it. When they closed a while back, he went to work for the Madame Alexander Doll Company. Now he works the line for them. He works many hours and comes home still happy to be with us."

Lou Anthony seemed to savor this fact as he drank his wine. He would not show his hand of approval so early in the conversation.

Maria on the other hand was more than happy to rein in her new daughter-in law before Lou Anthony beat her too much.

"Did you learn the Polish cooking from your mother, dear child? They call her the mamushka, do they not?"

"Yes, Mrs..I mean Mama. I have cooked in my mother's kitchen since I was a small child. My mamushka taught me everything I need to know about cooking."

"Humph…"

Marta knew instantly that she had insulted the woman in some way. She quickly back-pedaled.

"That is to say she taught me everything there is to know about Polish cooking. I know very little about Italian cooking."

Maria was content with the young lady's response.

"I'm sure you could show her a lot, Mama. She knows a different way of cooking. I look forward to trying it."

"A woman must know how to satisfy her man's appetite in the kitchen. Do you think you will take care of that for him?"

"Of course, Mrs...of course, Mama."

Mrs. Scarpacci simply nodded and smiled. "I believe this to be true. I can tell by your hands that you are not a stranger to the kitchen. My son's appetite will do well in your hands."

This pleased Marta. She wanted so desperately to reach out and hold hands with Paulie but she knew this was why they were seated this way. Divide and conquer.

"Enough talk of food. It is making me hungry."

The others chuckled in light laughter at Lou Anthony's comment. Paulie knew that Marta appreciated the break in the conversation but he also knew that his father was just redirecting to the more pertinent matters at hand.

"Does your family have a dowry for you?"

The sheer mention of such a thing at this point in the conversation was shocking to all, but least of all Marta.

"Papa!!"

"What? Can a man not ask what the intentions of her family are? If they are offering something more to this family, I need to know about it."

Paulie simply shook his head. He looked at Marta with apologetic eyes and she knew what he meant. She was strong and resilient, though, and did not falter.

"My family is humble, Mr. Scarpacci. We are like you, a family of immigrants that work hard to put food on the table and a roof over our heads. We are not a wealthy family but my father would honor you with some kind of offering if Paulie asks him for my hand. Like you, my family is deep in culture and want to honor the old world traditions."

Lou Anthony seemed very pleased at this. He nodded in agreement as he drank more of his wine. His wife wanted a lighter approach.

"Do you love my son?"

Marta nearly choked on the wine as she sipped it. She was not expecting such a blunt response from the woman about her son. Looking across to Paulie who remained silent, she could see the love in his eyes that the two shared.

"Yes, Mama. I love your son. Is that enough?"

Maria reached across and held Marta's hand in comfort.

"Love is more than most people have." Looking across to her husband with disdain, she continued. "So many couples these days are a product of a business arrangement. They are put together because one family can provide something for another. Marriage is not about business. It is about love. If you love my son and he loves you back, that should be enough. There should be no business to be had, no dowry to be collected. You love each other and make each other happy. What more could a mama want?"

Maria Scarpacci wiped her eyes with a napkin and silenced herself before her husband could tell her to. She had overstepped and she knew it. The reaction from Lou Anthony would dictate how she would feel about it later.

"Your family is Polish, correct?"

Again, Lou Anthony had startled them all with his bluntness. For the second time, Marta remained un-phased by the patriarch's comment.

"Yes, Mr. Scarpacci. My family is Polish. Does that matter?"

Lou Anthony seemed to ponder this question carefully before answering. Suffice as to his own answer, he replied to Marta confidently.

"I do not believe it does. The fault is not Poland's that they were invaded by the Nazi's. They were our Allies and stood by us to the end. I think the Poles are welcome in this house."

Paulie beamed with happiness at this remark. He never thought his father would welcome a Polish woman into his house let alone his family.

"Thank you, Papa."

Instead of reassurance, Lou Anthony answered the resolve with more challenges.

"Marta Slowik. I am happy you love my son. I am also happy that your family plans to respect me in some way with some token of dowry, even if it is a bottle of wine. With that being said, we must make peace. Before we can break bread to go with our wine, we must have resolution on a matter."

Paulie looked at his mother fearfully then back to his father. He did not want the business of the family to destroy everything he had built with Marta since he returned from the war. Surprisingly, it was Marta herself who threw the gauntlet on the ground.

"Speak your peace, then, Mr. Scarpacci. I want to marry your son. If there is a barrier to the promised land, let us speak of it and find a solution together."

Lou Anthony smiled and took another drink of wine. He admired the spunk of this young woman and rose to the challenge to face her.

"So be it, Marta. We have a problem."

Paulie's father continued on to describe the predicament of the family. They were now partners in crime, set out to do the bidding in the war of the roses.

191

14

Christmas in an Italian household was sacred ground. Every part of the holiday had deep rooted family traditions and the Scarpacci family was no different. Through the month of December there were various rituals such as the family trip to cut down a tree, but all things led to the two days of Christmas Eve and Christmas Day.

On the day of Christmas Eve, all manner of baking and food preparations happened in the kitchen. Maria and her daughters busied themselves with preparing anisette cookies, lemon bars, freshly poured chocolate treats and of course the cannoli's. Lou Anthony and sons often left the house so their hunger pains in smelling the delicacies were not taking over.

When evening came, the traditional feast of the seven fishes was prepared and eaten before the family departed for midnight mass. Linguine with clams, oysters Rockefeller, baked white fish and calamari were house favorites and the immediate family along with invited guests were anxious to get started. The knock at the front door might as well been the sound of the dinner bell ringing as they all knew it meant that they would soon be eating.

"Bonjourno. My son is finally here with his wife to be no less."

"Sorry we are late, Mama. Had to pick up a few things along the way."

"Come, come. We have much to talk about and even more food and drink to consume before mass on this, your first Christmas together."

As they crossed into the dining room, they were greeted by everyone who was already seated at the table, anxiously waiting to start eating. Lou Anthony had a fork in his hand just in case food should magically appear on his plate. Ann Marie and Nancy were busy bringing out the dishes and bowls of the feast while Joe busied himself with a dinner roll that he already had begun buttering. He knew not to take even one bite until the blessing was made by his father but he wanted to be prepared when it happened.

At the far end of the table were the invited guests. Salvatore Francucci and his wife, along with their son, sat together at the other end of the long dining table

192

that had been decorated for the occasion. To Salvatore's right sat Albert and his new fiancé as well, Carmen Francucci.

"It's about time."

"Merry Christmas to you too, Papa. Our apologies to everyone. The train was late coming in with the holiday."

"Well, if you would hurry up and have this wedding, you wouldn't have to commute back and forth to the city and to each other's houses."

Maria once again was the voice of reason.

"Don't pay any attention to the Grinch, Marta. Please sit down and get comfortable. The sooner he gets food in his stomach the sooner he will stop being so grouchy."

Paulie and his bride to be sat down at the table and poured glasses of wine to get things started. Looking around the table, he took in the sights and the smells. He had missed the gathering for the years he was off at war and it felt good to be home for the holidays. The last two months seemed to have flown by as he ventured to build a new life for himself and his fiancé.

The trip to New Rochelle to meet Marta's family was very smooth and welcoming. When he took the courage to sit with her father and ask for her hand in marriage, they both had tears in their eyes. Paulie looked forward to having a father-in-law that treated him already like one of his own sons. He was not as comfortable with Marta's mother who doted on him hand and foot when he saw her but he was getting used to the attention slowly. He looked forward to spending Christmas day with her family.

The job at the sausage factory was part of the package deal he had turned down, so Paulie had to find other employment. He and Marta both fulfilled their dreams of working in Manhattan and were both busy building their lives in the suburbs while commuting into the city.

It was Lou Anthony that had the revelation that he had more than one son to offer up as a sacrificial lamb. Paulie thought that it had stemmed from the Priest's comment about the prodigal son returning to remind his father that Paulie had not one but two other brothers. To Salvatore Francucci it mattered not which son married his daughter, he just wanted her to be set with a family. The deal was amended to secure Albert with a good job at the factory, give Lou Anthony part ownership in the sausage company and Carmen became a bride to be.

"Now that everyone is here, can we finally get this meal started?"

"Yes, Lou Anthony, yes. Give me one minute. I need to get something from the kitchen."

The patriarch shook his head as he waited impatiently for his wife's return. Moments later, she appeared with two bombonieres which she placed in front of Marta and Carmen.

"These are for my future daughter-in-laws. They are the first presents of

Christmas for the bride-to-be's to enjoy. I made them for you. The sugared almonds represent health, wealth, happiness, fertility and a long life."

"Oh Mama, thank you."

Marta was already tearing up at the sentiment. As for Carmen, her reaction was more subdued but still grateful. Her life of luxury will take a few turns going forward to get used to the common family practices.

"Thank you Mama Scarpacci. That was very nice of you."

"Can I say the blessing now, Maria? The fish want to swim away already."

Maria sat down quickly. "Yes, yes. Say your blessing quickly, you old goat, so we can eat this wonderful meal."

Everyone made the sign of the cross and joined hands while they waited for Lou Anthony to say the blessing. Clearing his throat, he kicked off the holiday officially.

"Blessed Father, our Lord. Bless this house and all the bounties you have bestowed on us. Welcome home my son from the war. Welcome our guests who will soon be family. Welcome my two daughter-in-laws as they will soon take the Scarpacci name. Bless the food and the wine as we begin this feast of the seven fishes. Seven blessings for seven fishes. May God bless us all. Amen."

Paulie Scarpacci looked around the table and took it all in before digging in to the food. He was home with his family, he was healthy and he had the love of his life at his side. He could not have asked for more. Reaching out and squeezing Marta's hand, he grabbed a roll and broke bread on his new life.

Thursday Walks
in the Garden

1

The sun was barely over the horizon as the dew stuck to the grass on the cool morning in Northwest Massachusetts. A nearby rooster could be heard with his natural morning call as the bucolic setting was awakened by the interruption of solace. Spring was on the calendar but the temperature had not yet responded to the call. The chill in the air would burn off with the sun on the rise, but the gardeners would be working for hours by that point.

Rounding the corner of the New England road, the battered pick-up truck rambled along with caution in case the stray deer crossed in front of its path. The truck never carried many items in the back, usually some mulch or composting, but the most precious cargo existed inside the cab of the truck. The driver was the head gardener of the Green Mountain Farm.

Founded in the early 1900s, the farm was a family owned business that no longer had any family members in its lineage to take care of daily operations. For the past 20 years, the task of keeping up with the gardens year-round was given to Michelle Walters. There were others that took care of various departments such as the groundskeeper and the retail store, but Michelle held the most prolific role of bringing beauty to the farm through all seasons.

She had taken the job at Green Mountain farm after serving many years at a public garden in Connecticut. Now at the age of 50, she worked seven days a week at times, lived by herself, and tended to her three cats who often were more difficult than the semi-annuals that adorned the property. For most of the year, she was a staff of one but took on seasonal help as needed. It was a simple life that provided her an outlet to her love and passion; her gardens.

Michelle took care and pride in her many gardens located on the farm property. People came from all over New England just to revel in the moon garden, the rose garden and of course the long border garden. The begonia house was a local media favorite and had been featured in many trade magazines across the country. A humble woman, Michelle never put stock in any of the articles or awards about her flowers. Her joy came from the visitors that came to the farm as they wandered about for hours taking in the wonders.

Since the farm could not survive on simple esoteric commodities, it relied on the sales of its flowers in the nursery, its catalogue, and of course the retail shop itself. To disregard the dollar signs attached to the work that Michelle endured daily, it was difficult to put a value on her efforts. Without the beauty of the gardens, there would be no visitors. Without visitors, there would be no sales. If there were no sales, there would be no need for gardens and essentially a gardener. It was a chicken and egg dilemma so the different departments existed in harmony, giving no greater value to any one part of the whole of Green Mountain Farm.

The early sunrise hour was not for the faint of heart but for the gardener it was the little slice of heaven that God gave them to plant the seeds of life. Any farmer or gardener can speak of this moment in daily time, where there is no chaos, there are no shoppers or commercialism, it is just pure. The crow of the rooster, the song of the birds in the trees and the hum of the beehive are the only things hustling and bustling. It is their time to breathe in the air, to feel the temperature on their noses and lips, and to touch the soil in order to determine the rich quality ripe for planting. Michelle captured that moment daily.

Parking the truck outside of her small office, she exited the door with a creak and placed her L.L. Bean boots upon the driveway gravel. The crunch that ensued cut through the silence of the morning as a pre-cursor of the day ahead. Each step created a momentum to build upon as she entered the small building and trudged up the stairs. Placing her coffee thermos on her desk, she looked at the most critical factors before engaging her work day. The temperature was still in the 40s but the barometer was high. There was no rain in the forecast so it would be a productive day in her gardens. With the weather in check, she could proceed to the negative aspects of her job; paperwork.

Michelle Walters did not go to school for business. She went to school all those years ago to learn about agricultural sciences. She learned about the various plant hardiness or "grow" zones so she could see what subtle differences there were in growth patterns. She learned which plants and flowers would do best in New England as opposed to Florida or Arizona. She learned all about annuals, semi-annuals and perennials but at no point did she learn how to be a business manager.

She did not mind being a manager to others but she was happy it was only for a couple months during planting season. As she grew closer to that time, she knew she would have to start interviewing and her trepidation with the process was growing. Michelle sat down at the computer on her desk, keyed in her magical password and the business end of the plant world came flooding in at a keystroke. Emails, budgets, spreadsheets and reports were all things foreign to the gardener and she did not enjoy any of them. The blessing came with the fact that although she was head gardener, she was not expected to be a business analyst or auditor.

She had a budget for her gardens and knew where to get the best prices on all the garden essentials. As long as she stayed within her budget parameters, much like a bowling alley lane, she would not have to worry about throwing a gutter ball.

The budget for Green Mountain Farm had three seasonal gardeners on their payroll. With a weekly budget of 100 hours for six weeks, Michelle could hire 2 full-timers, each with 40 hours a week and then a part-timer for 20 hours a week. Of course there were many other scenarios she could make for the three of them to be more balanced but she liked to view her predicament within those terms as it made it easier to regard the applications as potential part-time or full-time gardeners.

Clicking on the file folder marked "applicants" in her email, pages of applications had already been filtered through the Human Resources department and sent to her. She need only read them, call them, interview them and see if she liked them. If the applicants had passed the pre-screening, someone out there thought they were qualified for an interview. The only questions that remained would be if she could tolerate them enough as she drank her morning coffee. Rising from her desk, she walked over to her instant pod coffee machine, placed a pod inside and pressed the button. Through the convenient magic of modern technology, her coffee immediately began brewing and soon her coffee cup was filled. Turning back to her desk, she returned with cup in tow and began her first sip when she heard footsteps coming down the hall.

"I thought I heard you come in."

Tim Bidwell was the head groundskeeper at Green Mountain Farm and was one of the few soles that would beat Michelle to the time clock every morning.

"...and here I thought you might have slept in."

The older gentleman cackled with laughter. "Maybe if I ever retire I'll sleep in but that's not very likely, young lady."

At the age of 50, it was a rare occasion that anyone called her young but she could always count on Tim to make her feel that way. They had known each other almost as long as she had been employed at the farm. They worked well within the confines of their own individual departments and often collaborated on projects. Michelle respected him for all of his talents and marveled at the beauty of the farm outside of her gardens. A finely cared for lawn was just as important as the flowers that adorned it. The two departments worked hand in hand, a yin and a yang, to complete the picture.

"I recall your age being closer to 70 than my 50, Mr. Bidwell, so maybe retirement is not that far out of the equation."

"If I retired, who would be here in the morning to greet you and smell your coffee when you get started."

"Would you like a cup?"

"No, I'm good. I'm actually on my second pot of coffee already. Been brewing long before the sunrise out in barn #2. Say, are we going to walk the new tree project later? I just want to plan out my day."

Michelle laughed. They had the same meetings every Thursday for the last 10 years but Tim always acted like he didn't know anything about them. She often thought that it was his excuse in case he missed one. He could say that his old age made him forget.

"We always have our garden walks at 830am on Thursdays. We can meet at the oak right after that and talk about the re-planting. Did he give you the ok to add that for the budget this year?"

The "he" that Michelle was referring to was Jackson Hartley, the surviving member of the Hartley family that had owned the farm for over a century. There were a couple of grandchildren that were growing older by the minute but they were still years away from taking part in the farm. Jackson still had the final approval on major farm expenditures even though each of the departments controlled their individual budgets.

"He said he would approve it but he had some thoughts on the matter. I think he wants to bring in some new trees to line the driveway. There were some that got destroyed over the winter, as you know, but it's not going to happen overnight. You know Jackson. If it wasn't done already, it's too late. The man has no patience."

"Oh, I know that. But we also know that he writes the checks. So if we want the money to get this project done this season and not wait for another winter to wreck the branches, we need to take his feedback."

"You are much too kind-hearted Michelle. There is a reason why we are head of our departments. If he keeps having us answer to him, how are we ever to get things done? I would think progress would be more important. The man is almost 80 and he thinks we have all the time in the world."

"No, he has all the time in the world. He just got back from his snow bird time in Vero Beach. He does this type of thing every year. He sits down in Vero Beach all winter long and dreams of new things he wants done. Remember when he wanted a flower bed outside his house? We dropped everything to do it for him. He owns the property so I guess we just have to answer to him."

"Yes, but nothing says we have to enjoy it."

The two shared a good chuckle as Tim began to exit her office.

"I guess I'll let you get back to your coffee and whatever else you are working on. I hate those things."

Tim was referring to the computer screen that Michelle was now back to looking at. She often thought that he hated technology more than she did.

"Watcha working on now?"

Michelle shook her head. "Same as you. Looking at applications so I can hire my seasonal help."

"Not me."

"What do you mean, not you? Who is going to do all that mowing when the warmer temps kick in if you don't hire people?"

"Oh, I didn't mean that I'm not hiring this year, Michelle. I meant that I'm already done. I found a couple of college boys that want to make some money while staying in shape this summer. The way I figure, I'm doing society justice since I am fine tuning a couple of young bucks so they are ready for their coeds."

Laughing, Michelle went back to looking at her screen. "I don't know how you are done already. I'm just getting started."

Exiting the door, Tim turned back to give her some fatherly type advice. "Well, young lady. You are the last department to do so. Everyone else got their summer hires done already. If you hadn't procrastinated so much..."

"Yeah, yeah, yeah. It's like taking your car in for service. You put it off as long as you can because you know it's going to be a painful process."

"Well, you know what happens if you let that check engine light stay on too long, don't you? If you wait much longer to hire, you'll have the same problem."

Tim left without another word but Michelle knew he was right. If she didn't get people hired soon, there would be no time for garden walks or any other administrative duties for that matter. She would have to do all the planting herself. She would enjoy doing it but the little bit of life she had outside work would cease to exist. Letting out a big sigh, she returned to the screen in front of her.

2

The whistler on the spout of the tea kettle began its slow steam response. The pitch on the whistle gradually changed as the water reached its full potential at 212 degrees. Crossing the small kitchen, the gentle man lifted the kettle off the burner and poured the boiling water over his tea bag into the mug. He left it on the counter as he turned back to the stove top and put the water on the cold burner.

Moments later, the egg timer went off after 3 minutes and he shut off the water on that burner as well. Using a small strainer, he removed the single egg and placed it onto the slotted poached egg holder. Moving slightly across the tiny counter, he placed the egg and the mug on a breakfast tray. Synchronized to perfection, the toaster popped up and the rye toast was placed on the empty plate that lay on the tray.

The breakfast set up ritual was complete. The same process existed seven days a week. The half glass of orange juice already had been placed on the small dining table after drinking the first half with his medicine. The steps were complete. As Randall Simms sat down, he opened his tablet with a tap and pulled up the morning news from the Times.

This part of the daily process had changed a few years back when the newspaper was no longer delivered to his doorstep. He could have paid for the premium service to have this luxury but the local paper boy no longer delivered it and he thought it was time to take the leap to digital. There weren't many amenities in the Northwest hills of Massachusetts and his timid nature convinced him to roll with the changes.

Skimming the headlines on his tablet, he absentmindedly steeped his teabag into the water. After precisely five dunks into the water, the bag was removed and placed against the spoon as he wrapped the tea string and squeezed the tea into the water below. Once drained, the spoon was placed on the side of the mug and the used teabag on a small paper napkin so it would not leave a ring on the tray.

There was no music playing in the background and the television was not on either. There was a time for each of those indulgences and breakfast was not one of them. Randall did not participate in social media and his cell phone was strictly for purpose instead of entertainment. He understood the need to maintain a cell phone in today's world, but his comfort zone was not in technology. His passions lay in the world of nature itself.

His tiny one-bedroom apartment was selected not simply because of its functionality. Randall had chosen it because of its proximity to the town park. He loved to wake up to the sounds of birds singing outside his window. His gentle alarm clock was often not necessary as many birds nested on the window sill depending on the time of the year. With spring in the air, many robins, swallows and warblers had returned to the park choir. The birds he longed to hear were from another continent altogether but he still hoped to have a lovebird in his heart soon.

Randall lived a lonely life. His work as a medical researcher meant that he spent long hours by himself with only his microscope to set eyes on. He kept odd hours as it did not matter what time his research had to be done. While the world around him slept, he often migrated himself to the lab where he could conduct experiments without the constant droning of office gossip by his fellow researchers. He was content in his solace so that he could concentrate on the work at hand. However, he knew very well that being a recluse at work and at home meant that his chances were very few to pursue a love interest.

At the age of 52, Randall had never married and in fact only dated one woman with any seriousness. She was a graduate student at the university he had attended and she was also in the medical profession. Their relationship had simply fizzled out when she became more interested in a rugby player than spending time in the lab with Randall. They parted ways and although she never married into the rugby world, he later found out that she married a doctor with more character than he could ever dream of having.

Through his long and lonely life, he dated only a handful of times and it was usually at the prompting from the female. He found his sanctuary in art, nature, literature and all things intellectual that were centered more to individual tastes than the greater collective. Through a blend of his science background and his love of nature, he had a great interest in gardening. He conducted much research into the different types of soils and nutrients that could provide the greatest yields. He wondered greatly at the healing power of plants and thought that one day his medical research and his love for gardening would find a happy marriage in the scientific world.

Springtime in New England brought love to the hearts of many but to Randall Simms it simply designated a time to venture out. Like most people his age, he tapered off his hikes in the wooded paths sometime around Thanksgiving and the first snowfall and did not resume until after the Easter eggs had all been collected. He had started to explore more in recent weeks but he had yet to resume his seasonal residence at the local gardens. He looked forward to seeing what new flora and fauna would greet his senses.

In the previous year Randall had travelled to some different New England gardens on day trips. He visited Elizabeth Park Rose Garden in Hartford and even the Coastal Botanical Garden up in Maine. While the more travelled public gardens gave him insight into various growth patterns and soil differentiation, he preferred a simpler approach much like his life. Tapping into his poached egg, he thought fondly of his favorite local garden; Green Mountain Farm.

He had discovered the gardens at Green Mountain Farm a couple years previous when he ventured to the retail store there to pick up a window box for his small apartment window. While there he also viewed a small bird feeder that was hanging outside on a faux display tree. Looking up at it in the sunlight, he spotted the long border garden directing his sight to the full gardens beyond. From that day forward, he was enamored with the beauty of it all.

From that day on, he began to visit the gardens whenever he could. In the remote areas of the moon garden and beyond the greenhouses, he would sit for hours on the walkway benches. He would read and take in the sights completely indifferent to the people around him. What first was a place of research later became a comfort zone. There was never interference from any of the workers there and he seemingly went completely unnoticed.

The dynamic of his being a silent observer at the Green Mountain Farm changed right before the gardens closed up for last season. Signing up for one of their free garden instructional lectures, Randall was interested in finding out about how the various flowers and plants were cared for during the cold, harsh New England winters. When he arrived that Saturday morning, his interest in the process took a back seat to a much more interesting subject; the head gardener herself, Michelle Walters.

Michelle was giving the lecture and garden tour that morning and Randall barely heard a word. Her quiet, subtle demeanor evoked feelings he had not felt for anyone since his college days. By the time the lecture broke for the day, he longed to see more of her. He lingered for hours after just to catch a glimpse of her but he did not see her again that day. He had returned to the garden two more times before they closed for the season and both times he was disappointed by not seeing his new interest even for a moment. Now, as he finished up the last bite of his toast and washed it down with the remnants of his tea, he could think of nothing else. He was headed to the garden early this morning before going to the lab and with any luck at all, he would see the woman who had captured his interest away from anything else.

3

"What are the plans for the rose garden?"

The small group of department heads walked the garden grounds. Each had a topic to be discussed and the rose garden was on the current docket.

"The new trellis archways will be delivered at the end of the month. There was an issue with the wrought iron so delivery was delayed."

Michelle was never comfortable being on the receiving end of such questions but she always had an answer to each and every challenge.

"How long will it take for the installation? Will we be ready for Memorial Day?"

"I can answer that."

Tim Bidwell interjected, saving Michelle from the scrutiny of Jackson for the moment. He had been in her shoes many times and it was never very comfortable.

"So answer then. How long will it take for your crew to install?"

"They sent over the plans from the architect. We are going to dig the trenches early in preparation for their arrival. When the arches arrive at the warehouse, we will come up with the small pay loader and drop them in. The whole process should be done in a weekend. From there, Michelle and her team can work their magic with the roses. As long as the arches aren't delayed beyond the 14 days that they promised, we see no reason that the garden will be delayed. Do you Michelle?"

"No. We will be ready. Like the landscaping team, the gardening team will do the prep work to make sure the installation will be seamless."

"Fine. Let's move on to the moon garden."

As the group moved across the vast lawn towards the moon garden, Michelle turned to her old friend and mouthed the words...*thank you.* Even though no thanks were necessary, Tim smiled back because he knew the conversation would turn against his ground keeping crew before the walk was over, but it felt good to go toe to toe with the old man every once in a while.

"I have an idea for the summer. It's similar to the fall events with the hayrides but it is for the summer months."

The Event Manager for the farm, James Henley, spoke up. He had the look and charm of a political contender but chose to put his charismatic personality to use booking all manner of events for the farm. His big "hay day" was in the fall when the Green Mountain Farm sponsored hayrides through the many fields which attracted guests from all over New England. The spring time was always filled with weddings that wanted the backdrop of either the beautiful gardens or the rustic nature of the farm for the backdrop on their magical day. The summer always seemed to be a miss.

"Explain James."

"So hear me out...what if we use the same concept in the fall of the hayride but we give it a summer twist. On select summer nights, especially when the moon is full, we promote a romantic moonlight ride. We highlight the moon garden as the flowers glow, but we can also do some creative things in the big barn. We can set up some overhead lighting in the loft and take the ride through there. We can call it *Moonlight under the Stars* or something along those lines. What do you think?"

Jackson nodded silently as the small group waited for his reply. In his typical skeptical form, he reserved comment until he had more information.

"What type of price-point would we have on the tickets?"

James was quick to answer.

"The same as the hayrides but I figure we would have less child tickets and more adult tickets due to the nature of the event."

"Is that something your flowers would be willing to do? Would they like to be the stars of the show for a while?"

Michelle smiled at his old world charm. "Of course. They love to be appreciated in the moonlight. However, we just have to limit any other lighting in the area in the evening. Any artificial lighting will diminish their effects."

"Very good. Very good. Although this is technically new business I am glad you brought it up here and now, James. Can you put a full proposal together and get it to me? Work on the name though. I'm not sold on that. I know I am not part of the daily operations anymore but I would like to have some input on this new endeavor. Can you do that James?"

The head of the event department smiled broadly. He knew he had hit a home run with this idea.

"Of course, Jackson. I'll put something together."

The old man seemed to be stuck on something while he was ruminating about an idea in his head. It was Michelle who brought him out of it.

"Is everything ok Jackson?"

"Yes, sorry everyone. I got lost in the finances of it all. As you all know the summer months are lean for us. After the planting season, the wholesale orders drop off tremendously. The small amounts that come in from the retail shop do not offset the loss before the fall catalogue comes out. Perhaps this will be a nice bridge over troubled waters. I look forward to hearing more about it. Now, Michelle. What can you tell us about the flower changes in this wonderful garden?"

Michelle Walters ran through the gamut of the planned changes to the garden bed and all were pleased with the direction they were headed in. When that discussion had ended, Jackson was anxious to move on to the smaller group.

"Very well, then. If there is nothing else, I would like to meet with Tim and Michelle about the tree project for the driveway. Can we adjourn?"

The larger group disbanded with everyone going off to their various directions on the farm. Some walked while others jumped into their various carts and drove away. When all the excitement had ended, the trio started to walk slowly down towards the driveway entrance where the trees needed to be planted. At the early hour, the gardens had just opened for the day and a single car was driving up the dirt driveway. Out of curiosity, the three leaders looked to the solitary visitor and saw a Prius come to a rolling stop and park. Moments later, a small man stepped out with books in his hand. Michelle thought the visitor looked familiar but could not be certain. With so many visitors coming and going from the farm and gardens, it was difficult to know specifics. Though she returned her gaze to the driveway at hand, the lone visitor looked back after them. He was pleased to know that his visit to the Green Mountain Farm that day would be productive. The reason he had come had just walked across his path.

4

Randall walked in silence from the parking area. Even though his was the only car there, he chose not to park up at the top of the walkway. He enjoyed the scenery along the walk and regardless of how many cars were in the lot, he always chose to park farther away. The walk up the gravel road was easy enough but he still stopped at the welcome center to get refreshed.

The white cottage building was set up like an old carriage house. The old bay doors were not operable to the public as they entered on the upper level. In the center was a reception desk with maps of the vast property. There were also various photographs of the farm in different stages over the past century as well as accompanying descriptors painting the history of Green Mountain in the most interesting light. Randall Simms had seen them all before and had done his own research at the town library. What medical researcher worth a dime would ever take propaganda as the given truth? In the case of the Green Mountain Farm, Randall was able to ascertain that all the information was true.

Bookended on either side of the reception desk were the men's and women's bathrooms. Wishing to relieve himself before sitting on a bench for hours, Randall set his books down on the sink and approached the urinal. He always made it a point to stop in this restroom because he was fascinated by the ornamentation details they went to in order for the visitors to feel like they were in a real carriage house. Directly above the urinal was a barn light housed within a cage. The scene always brought a smile to Randall's face even though it was nothing more than a decoration. Since the gardens were never open in the evening, he would not know if the light even was operable.

Continuing his short journey, Randall turned and walked towards the retail shop that was located in front of the gardens. He had no desire to purchase anything today but was inspired by a few of the outdoor decorations. One in particular, was a small ceramic garden statue of two love birds. He dreamed of that statue all through the winter months and wondered if they were a pre-cursor to his destiny. Would he find his love bird toiling away in her gardens today? Only time would tell.

Randall continued through the retail area until he came to the bird feeders that adorned the pathway towards the gardens. He smiled as they too were an indicator that all roads led to the object of his affection. Passing them and leaving all the retail workers in peace without any conversation, he climbed the stone steps up to the next level behind the retail shop. There he took in the spring fragrances as the flowers of the long border were starting to bloom. They produced all manner of lilac, yarrow, and a hint of upcoming honeysuckle, so the bouquet of odor was like lightning to the senses. As he walked along the path at the early spring developments he could not help but think of an old poem by Tennyson.

If I had a flower for every time I thought of you, I could walk though my garden forever.

Randall had the thought that he should stop and write that down before he forgot but he knew that he could not forget such a feeling. It would dwell in his heart and mind for the duration of his visit and he would not be able to contain himself from writing it down many times in his journal.

Continuing down the path, he was amused by the presence of the tall hedge that separated the retail area from the hillside and garden beyond. The hedge itself had to be at least ten feet tall and he wondered if the head gardener herself balanced on a ladder to clip the top branches of the hedge. Even at this early spring date, the hedge had been manicured and ready for guests to enjoy. He thought that it was clearly done before Thursday morning which he was now enjoying. Perhaps if he tried visiting on other days of the week he would find out when she trimmed them. He waxed poetically thinking that he could be her hero if she fell off a ladder and caught her. His common sense knew better as his physique would be challenged catching a bouquet of roses rather than a woman falling off of a ladder.

At the end of the path he was currently on, Randall was faced with a few choices. He could walk across the field and peruse the greenhouses where he thought he might catch another glimpse of the head gardener. Logic would dictate that after her walk along the driveway, she would retreat back to the greenhouses to get work done. That is what he would do. Return to the lab to see life through a microscope; but he wasn't a gardener and had not done enough research to logically decide she would end up there.

He could cross the long field and sit on the bench in the moon garden. While it was a wooded area, it would provide shade as the sun rose. On the side of logic, it would also tend to be colder as the temperatures were still somewhat in the chilly range this morning. The other disadvantage would be that the bench in that area to sit on would force him to turn his back on more than half of the acreage of the garden. That would not suffice at all since he was not here to research the moon garden plants but rather the person who did the planting.

His third and most logical choice were the two benches that were in the center of the main garden. Both gave excellent views of the whole garden area as he had tried both of them out on previous visits last year. One was along the main pathway that ran through the center of the gardens and would most certainly put him in the path of the gardener had she travelled east or west along the pathway. The second bench was nestled in a more picturesque location, directly next to a three tier birdfeeder. Since it was a bird feeder that initially directed him to the gardens beyond the retail store, he chose that bench in hopes of feeding destiny a little morsel.

Parking himself on the bench, Randall got comfortable. He had with him a book on bee pollination and another on medicinal plants. The third book was actually his journal which as soon as he sat down he removed and wrote down the poem by Tennyson that he remembered. Placing the journal aside for the moment, he sat back and took in his surroundings. From his vantage point he had a pretty good view of the retail shop and the parking area. If he turned his view to the back right side, he had a good vantage point of some of the greenhouses, especially the begonia house. In his research of the farm, he found out that the head gardener had been heralded in many magazines for her work with begonias so he thought that she might be going there at some point.

Randall knew that the farm offices were somewhere over the horizon but regular guests were not allowed back that far. It was possible that she had retreated back there but on such a beautiful spring morning he thought it was a reasonable bet that she would be out in her gardens somewhere, tending to the flowers that craved her attention. His perch on the rustic garden bench would be perfect. His scientific mind was reasonably certain.

Eyeing a few bees fresh out of hibernation, Randall picked up his bee pollination book and started to read. He thought it would enrich his mind and lend to the conversation if he ever had the opportunity to engage the head gardener. He had motive, purpose and opportunity. He felt that if he was conducting one of his medical experiments he would already have the outcome. He hoped that his deductive reasoning and slight planning efforts would pay off. He had nowhere to go and all day long to get there. His flexible work schedule meant that he could arrive at any point and still get his work done. If the head gardener crossed his path of destiny on this Thursday, he would be ready for her.

5

Michelle Walters happily loaded her supplies into her John Deere Gator. She actually had two different size utility vehicles that she used on a daily basis but at this early stage in the planting season the smaller of the two was suffice. She loaded her tool box with pruning shears, gloves and a hand trowel. She had the longer handle tools such as her hoe and rake sticking over the tail gate since she was in the small gator but that was fine since she didn't plan on traveling far across the farm this morning.

She was relieved to get her meetings out of the way and looked forward to literally digging in and cleaning some of the flower beds. The administrative part of her role was not something she really enjoyed. As the head gardener, she reveled in planning out her gardens and could envision their creations long before they started to bloom. Unlike others in a managerial position, she loved to get her hands dirty and toil away in her gardens for hours.

The basic gardening tools mirrored her personality and approach to gardening. She did not need all the glitz and bling of state of the art tools. She was not concerned about keeping her gator new and shiny and often liked it better when it was a little messy and full of dirt. Simple tools for a simple job in a simple life. Who could ask for more?

As she backed the gator out of her equipment shed, the morning sun caught her eyes and made her smile. She was a true New Englander through and through and enjoyed every season. Unlike those who complained about the cold winter months, she enjoyed snuggling up with her cats in front of the wood stove at the end of a cold day. She enjoyed the summer time activities filled with agricultural fairs and the friendly barbeques. In the fall, she marveled at the foliage as the colors set her heart afire. Springtime, however, remained her favorite season.

Hope springs eternal and for a gardener springtime is nothing but hope and faith. You dig a hole and fill it with flower bulbs. You cultivate it, fertilize it and water it constantly. In the end, your springtime efforts bloom summertime beauty and you wonder at the growth cycle as an act of God in all creation.

Michelle's faith was based around this continual act of creation. She viewed all that she did as a gardener as a simple conduit. She was put on this Earth for a reason and she was certain that she was there to create life in gardening. Her faith and her beliefs went deep as she was a practicing Catholic in all of her days.

Thursdays were special for Michelle not only because she had to endure the administrative garden walks, but she had something to look forward to at the end of her day. Thursday evenings were a time for her bible study class and also a time for social reflection with her friend Alice Germain. Many years previous, the two had been co-workers at Green Mountain Farm and struck up a friendship. Alice worked in the production greenhouses while Michelle created her gardens but they found commonality in many things outside of the farm as well.

As devout Catholics, the two shared many secular conversations about the meaning of life and where the world was heading. On lighter notes, they liked to peruse the thrift shops together and grab an ice cream in addition to their Thursday night bible study class. While Michelle did not have much of a social life to share with her friend, they often spoke about Alice's marriage and family and Michelle lived vicariously through their escapades. Of course the conversation often drifted back to two main subjects as they discussed the life of a cat mom and the continuing tales of gardening.

They often took in additional training by attending plant seminars or visiting various gardens in neighboring states. Their escapades were not limited to their imaginations but simply by their lack of time. As Michelle entered her planting season, she knew that she would not be able to get out as much as she would like to as her free time would be limited.

With a night of bible study and conversation ahead, Michelle happily engaged the clutch on the John Deere and set out into her gardens. Her thoughts quickly came back into focus as the plans for her rose garden and moon garden replayed in her mind. Could the moon garden actually become a centerpiece to a nighttime event at the farm? Would the new trellises add to the beauty of her gardens or would they detract from it? Perhaps her time this morning would be best spent pruning back many of the roses that surrounded the projected path.

Driving slowly down the path, she approached cautiously noting that a few visitors were already milling around in the garden. She often worked with an audience in attendance so thought nothing of continuing her plan in the rose garden. Pulling out onto the main path, she slowly came to a stop before driving through the center. Along the main path an older woman was taking photographs and she did not want to disturb her. When the woman moved a little further, Michelle noticed that there was also a man seated on the bench in the center of the rose garden.

As she removed her tools from the gator, Michelle looked casually towards the man at the bench. Although there was not anything memorable about his face or features, she thought that she had seen him here before. He was a thin man with glasses and sat with his legs crossed over one knee as he concentrated on the book he was reading. Thinking nothing more of it, she put on her gloves and took out her pruning shears. As she approached the bench where he was seated, they both shared a momentary acknowledgement. For Michelle, it was nothing more than a common courtesy to smile and say hello but to Randall it meant the world. Moving past the man, she took a couple steps off the path and knelt down in the dirt next to the first rose bush.

Placing her ear buds in her ears, Michelle turned on the music and tuned out the world around her. She began to make her 45 degree cuts in the stems, removing dead, damaged and crossing stems. She went along the vines and removed any dead bark with her wire brush leaving the rose bushes fresh, vibrant and ready to bloom once again. When one plant was done, she started a small pile of debris next to her and went about pruning the next one.

This process continued for some time until she paused to wipe her brow. The springtime air was getting warmer and she thought she might need to remove her sweatshirt for comfort. Standing, she retreated out of the garden acutely aware that the man on the bench was staring back at her. Smiling at him, she retreated back to the John Deere where she took the ear buds out of her ears and removed her sweatshirt. Now dressed in a long sleeve gardening shirt, she took a drink from her water bottle and placed it back on the front seat of the gator. Turning, she walked slowly back up the path but did not put her ear buds back in yet.

"Getting warm, isn't it?"

The man's comment caught her off guard. She knew he was still there and he didn't startle her but she did not expect to talk with him.

"Excuse me?"

"I'm sorry. I didn't mean to disturb you. I just noticed you took off your sweatshirt. I was saying it was getting warm."

"Oh, yes. Indeed it is. You are not disturbing me. Are you enjoying your visit to the gardens today?"

This time it was Randall who was taken aback. He did not expect the woman to answer him with a question.

"Yes, thank you. I like it here. It is very peaceful."

Michelle started to turn away but paused for a moment. Looking back at the man, she found him staring back at her.

"You have been here before haven't you?"

Randall blushed. It would seem that his crush did recognize him.

"Yes, I have been here a few times. I also attended your seminar in the fall."

"My seminar?"

"I'm sorry. I guess you called it a garden walk. It was on preparing for the winter months. I'm just used to things like that being called seminars in my profession."

"Oh. That's probably where I remember you from. That walk is usually well attended but it was kind of cold that day."

"Just a blistery fall day. Not that bad for true New Englanders."

"Have you always lived here in Massachusetts?"

"Yes. Tried and true. I grew up over in Worcester the spent some time in Gloucester before settling here in Western Mass."

"I thought you might be from Worcester. Your accent gives you away."

"I get that a lot."

An awkward silence settled between them and Michelle took the opportunity to get back to the tasks at hand.

"It was nice meeting you. Or I guess, seeing you again. I need to get back to my pruning. Enjoy the peace and quiet."

Lifting up his book he motioned to it. "I have plenty of reading to take care of as well. I'll let you get back to your garden."

The two shared a polite smile as Michelle turned and re-entered her rose garden. Placing the ear buds back in place, she once again turned up the music and tuned out the world. She was not aware that the man behind her was beaming happily. As she continued her pruning over the next two hours, the man remained in place. Every once in a while she glanced back over to him and noticed he was still reading in solitude. She saw no indication that he was listening to music as he was simply content to be surrounded by the beauty of the garden, lost in his world of literature.

When her internal clock told her it was time to break for lunch, she rose from her position on her knees and cracked her back. Wiping the sweat from her forehead, she left behind a small trace of dirt where there once was perspiration. Turning, she was once again greeted by Randall staring back at her from his bench. Feeling obliged to say something to him on her departure, it was she who engaged the conversation this time.

"Time for lunch."

Randall looked back at her hoping there was an invitation or at the very least an opportunity for one ahead.

"Do you leave the farm to eat or do you stay here?"

Michelle was taken aback by the question. She found it to be a little too personal from a guest in the garden.

"Oh, I always eat in my office. It lets me catch up on computer work at the same time."

Randall was deflated. "Oh..."

Again, the awkwardness returned and again Michelle turned from it.

"Well, enjoy your afternoon here."

Randall looked down at his book and then back at her.

"Will you be returning to the garden this afternoon?"

Feeling strangely preyed upon, Michelle politely replied.

"No, but feel free to stay and enjoy."

"Thank you, I will."

Michelle walked back to her gator acutely aware that he was staring after her. She was both flattered and concerned at his obvious flirtation but she let the situation abate. Sitting on the bench, Randall was disheartened that he did not get more time with her but was romantically hopeful at the possibilities that lie in the future.

6

Michelle and Alice sat in a corner booth at Panera's. Their bible study was still an hour away so they had some time to relax and catch up on their activities from the last week. Michelle had just enough time to run home, shower and feed her cats before meeting her friend. They were both enjoying a small meal of soup and salad before heading out to the church.

"What did Dwight say?"

"Oh, you know Dwight. He just laughed it off. Those kids have him wrapped around their little fingers."

"He is such a good father."

"Don't be fooled. He has his moments, Michelle."

They both laughed lightly as they continued to eat.

"Doesn't everyone?"

"I guess they do."

"No, really. I am asking a real question here. Do all men have their moments? Am I too picky about things?"

"What are you getting at girl?"

"Well, look at you, Alice. You have been married to Dwight for a long time and continue to be happy. Everyone around me has someone to love. I have my cats. I think I love them the most because they don't talk back. They are predictable. I know what they want to eat and where they want to sleep. For men, they seem to say the wrong word and I lose interest."

Alice put down her fork, wiped her mouth and looked her friend with intent. She was trying to read her cues but was not figuring it out.

"Ok, girl. Tell me what's going on? Did you turn down another man?"

Michelle picked at the bread that came with her soup. Tearing off a small piece, she put it in her mouth and let it melt before answering.

"Maybe…"

"Maybe? What does that mean? Did someone ask you out?"

"No, not really."

Michelle continued to be coy but her friend was not letting the conversation go.

"Ok. That's it. Tell me what happened. We don't have all night before we have to get to bible study."

"There's not much to tell. I just met a man today. I guess I met him last year but I don't really remember."

"You met him today? I thought you were working in the rose garden?"

"I was. He was visiting the farm."

"Does he visit often?"

The two women chuckled. They both heard the subtle innuendo in the statement at the same time.

"Apparently he enjoys the garden. He sat on a bench for hours just reading and taking it all in. We had a brief discussion, that was all."

"Ok. So that seems pretty harmless. How did it spark this sudden interest in the meaning of men and the universe?"

"He was...well, I guess he was just a little flirtatious."

Alice laughed as she took a spoonful of her soup and blew it off. Before she put the spoon in her mouth she delved deeper.

"What, pray tell, did that entail?"

"Well, first it was just the weather and stuff like that. Just regular conversations you have with people. Then he was asking me where I ate lunch and if I was coming back to the garden. I was like, *why does this man want to know where I eat lunch*?"

Alice burst out laughing. If she had any soup or salad in her mouth at the time she would have spit it out unexpectedly.

"What's so funny?"

"Are you really that much out of practice to realize when a man is going to ask you out on a date?"

"No, he wasn't. he was asking a personal question. Why did he care where I ate lunch? Then asking me if I was coming back to the garden after lunch. It was just weird."

"Michelle, you are ridiculous. He was obviously asking if you were coming back because he enjoyed your company. He probably just wanted to know if you were worth waiting around for after you ate."

Michelle seemed to ponder this thought for a moment while eating more of her salad. Putting aside her apprehension, it was possible her friend was right.

"Ok, maybe that's what happened but what about the whole lunch thing? Why did he care where I ate lunch? I half expected him to ask me what I packed for lunch as well."

Alice went back to her soup and shook her head. "Oh, you poor girl. He was looking for an opening to ask you out. If you said you always brought your lunch, he would probably brown bag it himself so he could join you next time. If you told him you go out for lunch, he would most likely ask to take you somewhere."

"You think?"

"I definitely think. If you see him again, you should take the first step and ask him. He sounds shy."

"I could never do that."

"Of course you can, Michelle. Just strike up a conversation with the man. You never know. Maybe your prince charming is hiding in your garden as a frog in disguise."

Michelle silently nodded as she took in the advice of her friend. She had never asked out a man before. At her age, what did she have to lose? They returned to finish their light dinner as the conversation segued to cats, plants and the universe beyond.

7

Springtime days fly by in the gardening world. With all of the preparations, pruning, planting, watering, and of course nurturing, the days are long and the dates on the calendar flip over without hesitation. That first weekend the gardens were open at the Green Mountain Farm were no exception. Friday, Saturday and Sunday saw a constant flow of visitors to the gardens, the farm itself and the retail shop. By the time the new work week was upon her, Michelle was already knee deep in her gardening.

Thankfully, the new week started with a little bit of help as one of her seasonal gardening helpers was hired on. Taking a short while to acclimate them to their new role, she proceeded to delegate some of her weeding and pruning task so that she could concentrate on planting, fertilizing and watering. Soon, the gardens were hopping with Michelle and her first assistant digging away.

By mid-week, the rose trellises had arrived at the warehouse and more assistance was needed. The calls were made and a second assistant was quickly added on Thursday morning. With the administrative garden walk at hand, Michelle placed the second seasonal gardener in the hands of the first as they went off to work on the long border. Freed up at the moment, she was able to concentrate on the meeting at hand.

"Tim, I understand the trellises have been delivered."

"Yes, Jackson. That is true. They came in ahead of schedule instead of being delayed. There is one more section that is still in transit but it was never part of the initial installation. That section will be installed along the garden entrance by the tree line."

"So, we will be fully installed by the weekend?"

"Well, Jackson. It is Thursday. Seeing that it came in ahead of schedule we will have to move some people, projects and priorities around. I think this weekend is not feasible. We can deliver the trellis installation by next weekend at best."

"Tim. Last week on our walk you indicated that you could put them together in a couple days. Now you are telling us it will take ten? Is that what you are saying?"

"Jackson. Yes. That is what I said and while I understand you are not part of the daily operations anymore, you have to understand the challenges on a daily basis. We have our work schedules with our people already in place. As soon as we found out the trellises were delivered, Michelle went out and hired another person. I need to change the tree project timeline because of the early arrival. So, yes. In a perfect world that we could have stuck with the plan, it would have been completed in a couple days. Now, this is the best we can do."

"Ok, ok. Let's move on. Does that timeline work for you Michelle?"

"Yes, Jackson. But I'm not the one under the gun. By the time Tim and his team get everything installed, my team will be ready to move forward with the roses."

"Fine. Let's move past this then and talk about the new moon garden experience. Is that what we decided to call it James?"

"Yes, Jackson. On the tag line. The main billing will be *Moonlight Serenade, the Moon Garden Experience.*"

"So you decided to showcase my garden after all? Did anyone want to include me on your side conversation?"

Jackson stopped dead in his tracks. He had never heard the Head Gardener speak out so strongly before.

"Michelle? You are normally soft spoken. I wasn't aware you felt so strongly."

"I'm sorry Jackson. To you as well, James. It's just that you want to have this whole big summer event centered around the garden. Did you once think to ask me if this will be a peak year? Maybe I had some changes planned that I wouldn't want showcased so much. It's not a problem. I can put those off. It just would have been nice to be included in the conversation."

Silence fell over the group. Michelle opening up so honestly in the group dynamic was a change none of them were ready for. The conversation was derailed and Jackson was at a loss for words for a change. Tim decided to move things along to get past the moment.

"If we can get past the roses and the moon garden, I'd like to show everyone our tree installation project along the driveway."

The group was more than happy to get walking towards the driveway area. Michelle, however, had heard enough. She needed to get her tools, get in her gator and dig in the dirt. The week had flown too fast and left her with a certain degree of anxiety. She had two new people working for her and it seemed that her peaceful garden world had been turned upside down. She needed to find some degree of control and the one thing she could control was her gardening.

Michelle walked to her office and changed into her garden boots. Walking out to her equipment shed, she once again loaded up her tools but wanted to get away from the conversations of the day. Her newly hired help were working on the long border and she had heard enough about the rose and moon gardens for one day. The time had come for her to retreat into the Begonia house.

One of the highlights of Green Mountain Farm was the cultivation of tuberous begonias. The Head Gardner was the sculptor behind the masterpieces that were showcased in media outlets worldwide. She meticulously cared for them throughout the year and only opened the Begonia House for viewing when they were near perfection.

Michelle drove her John Deere up the back path to the greenhouse and approached using the back door. By going this way, she was not subjected to any of the visitors in the gardens at this hour and could definitely avoid the administrative team that could still be walking and conversing on their Thursday walk. Taking out her tools and placing them on her workbench, she went about caring for and cultivating the flowers that had brought her notoriety. Placing her ear buds in and activating the music, she was transported to a much more peaceful existence among her begonias.

The world outside the greenhouse was starting to buzz with springtime activity but Michelle remained immune to it all as she toiled away. Before she knew it, she had spent several hours in the begonia world and realized that she had two employees she needed to check in on. Wrapping up her current projects, she set her tools aside, took off her gloves and exited the greenhouse out the front door.

There were many visitors walking along the garden paths as she took off on foot towards the long border where she had instructed her new people to weed and clean. Turning the corner from the row of greenhouses, she had a clear view of much of the garden area. She could see her people working along the long border and she also eyed a familiar face by the rose garden. Randall was seated once again on a bench reading his books.

Although it had been a week since she last saw him, Michelle felt that it was just yesterday that the man had asked her about her lunch habits. She took the extended way around to get to the long border because she was not sure what she would say to him. The day had not started well and she let her emotions get the best of her. The time in the begonia house had set her back in balance but she did not feel balanced now. The sight of the flirtatious man in the garden was like a gentle wind on the high wire. She wasn't ready to fall but had to take the next step with caution.

Michelle walked slowly to her workers that were digging weeds in the long garden. She joined the pair and talked with them for a while as she helped them pull weeds together. When the two felt comfortable with the fact that their boss would join them in such efforts, Michelle decided to leave them to their own accord. They had plenty of work to keep them busy for the rest of the day and they didn't need supervision to get it done. Brushing herself from the garden dirt, Michelle set off in the direction of the rose garden.

Later on that day, she would wonder why she didn't avoid the area Randall was seated in and just go back to her gator, but the answer was obvious. Her interest was piqued. She wasn't sure what exactly that entailed but she was brave enough to venture further. Perhaps her run in with Jackson that morning gave her the courage to take on new possibilities. On the other hand, maybe she was just looking for something other than cat conversations.

Walking up the path, Michelle and Randall looked up at each other and gave an awkward wave. She was uncertain how long he had been there that day but it was evident that he was pleased to see her.

"Hello. Are you enjoying the gardens today?"

"Yes, yes I am. Definitely more now than a moment ago."

Definite flirtation.

"I don't think we were formally introduced the other day. My name is..."

"Michelle Walters. The Head Gardner here at Green Mountain Farm. I remember from taking your...garden walk, as you called it."

She chuckled awkwardly. Again, it felt as though he was a little intrusive.

"Then you have me at a disadvantage. I don't recall your name, I'm sorry."

"No need for apologies. I am certain you meet many people here at the farm. My name is Randall Simms."

He put out his hand in an odd business-like fashion and they shook hands. Not exactly the greeting to spark a romantic encounter.

"It is very nice to meet you Randall." Looking down at his books, she tried to keep the conversation going. "What are we reading today?"

He looked down at the book in his hand and almost forgot what he was reading before she walked up. He seemed a little flustered.

"Oh...well...nothing too exciting. It's a book on bee pollination."

"Really? I took a class on bee pollination. It has many medicinal purposes."

"That is precisely why I am reading it. I am in medical research. I am seeking new uses of supporting the body's immune system with infusions of the vitamins, minerals and antioxidants that are in the bee pollen."

Michelle radiated with the connection. "That is absolutely fascinating. Did you know we have a collection of bee boxes here at the farm?"

"You do? Where? I don't think I have ever seen them."

"They are a little off the beaten path. If you follow the rock wall that lines the right side of the driveway, it will take you to the boxes. The beekeeper Rich is usually there through the morning hours. I am sure he would have all sorts of useful information for you."

"Oh my goodness. That is fantastic. I will definitely venture over there and check them out. Thank you so much for letting me know that."

"My pleasure. I hope you enjoy your bee exploration."

There was an awkward pause as the conversation seemed to have run its course. This time, it was timid Randall who breached the unknown.

"How can I repay you for the information. That will help considerably."

Michelle knew what he was fishing for a decided to be brave enough to take the bait.

"Well…I'll tell you what Randall. Maybe you can buy me a cup of coffee one day. How does that sound?"

Randall fumbled with his words as he was truly pleased with the invitation.

"I…um…sure. That would be wonderful." Pausing to take the next step. "Would one day have specifics or are you just being polite to a stranger."

Michelle answered with little hesitation. "Well, you are a stranger but I would like to know more about you and your medical research. How about tomorrow? Can we meet for coffee in the afternoon? Around 4pm?"

"That…that would work perfectly. I will make it an early morning in my lab."

The two agreed on a place nearby and said their goodbyes. Michelle would have much to tell Alice that evening at bible study while Randall would be floating on cloud nine for hours. He had no idea how the connection was finally made but he was happy to bring it to fruition. He would no longer have to be a secret admirer of Michelle and her gardens. He looked forward to telling her all about his appreciation for all that she did. Springtime love was alive in his heart and he wanted to watch it bloom.

8

Meeting for coffee is an interesting concept in the dating world. If there were a more cautious approach it would be hard to find. Asking someone out for a cocktail implies there might be a meal following or some other sort of activity. The coffee meeting is in its definition more of a meeting than a date. Corporate deals are made over coffee. Job applications are reviewed over coffee. You meet your relatives for coffee. The coffee date in itself has many forms but few of them equate to romance.

The coffee meeting can occur in the morning, afternoon or early evening. The coffee dates late at night are usually reserved for the young at heart since older coffee drinkers switch to decaf after some magical hour. For Michelle, living the early morning farm life meant that a 4pm cup of joe would definitely be in the decaf family, regardless of the company she keeps. If she didn't, her three cats would be asleep far earlier than she could ever approach dream world.

Randall was the opposite. Even though he kept a regimented schedule in the morning, he drank full throttle coffee at any point in the day. Since his research in the lab often went through the wee hours of twilight, the caffeine would keep him looking through his mystical microscope without falter.

Marty's Café was a small town staple that resembled something from the turn of the century rather than the modern day equivalent of the fast paced barista parade of artistic coffee creations. Marty's had old battered hard wood floors and ground their coffee in an antique coffee mill, complete with a hand crank and whole coffee beans. You would not find any neon lights or fancy ornamentation on the walls of the coffee shop, but rather nostalgia. Marty's was a true New England tradition. It had photos and maps on the wall dating back to the early 1800's and captured the historical base of Massachusetts. Even though Western Mass was a good distance from Boston and the creation of democracy, that old world charm emanated from the walls once you entered the humble surroundings of Marty's Café.

Randall was the first to arrive and agonized for some time over what would be the best table. There were not that many choices but some gave a good view of the exterior of the shop while others were more secluded in their positioning. In the end, he chose a small table in the corner that had full view of the windows and the outside world so neither one of them would feel boxed in as the drank their coffee.

Michelle arrived a few minutes after 4pm and looked nervously around until she found the familiar face in the corner. He welcomed her to sit down and took her decaf coffee order as he departed for the counter to get their drinks. Leaving her at the table, she took in the situation. Randall had brought along not one book, but two and both brought a smile to her face. The first of course, was the book on bee pollination and the second was a book on the healing traits of plants. Michelle was fascinated by the world of homeopathic medicine and was curious to see what the opinions of a medical researcher would be in such a non-commercial arena.

After a few minutes, Randall returned with the coffees and the conversation began about his books.

"I see you are reading a couple different books. Both topics interest me."

"I would have hoped that you had some things to say about the healing power of plants. Most people just think about aloe but in the world of medicine, the implications of plants and flowers as healing powers are limitless."

Michelle smiled as she took her first sip of coffee. "It is refreshing to see others realize that there are other applications for botanicals besides beauty and food. Aroma and fragrances for example, came as secondary outgrowth of the flower industry. As more people adopt old world teachings of plant medicine, we can stop our dependency on pharmaceuticals."

"You seem to have given this much thought."

Michelle paused before continuing. She did not want to scare him away. "I am very passionate about what I do, Randall. I look at my daily chores in the garden as God's work and I am just a vessel or conduit from which He wields His magic."

Randall burst out laughing. "You sound like some kind of evangelical preacher."

Michelle was not amused. "Do you find my religious beliefs comical Randall?"

"Of course I do. The whole concept of religion is a farce to people in the scientific community. While you view your work in the gardens as a miracle, I view them as basic science. You have control groups, the soil, the plant bulbs, the tubers, and you manipulate them through various scientific methods. You add water, nutrients, and fertilizer and monitor growth. Gardening is scientific not divinity or theology. An atheist can grow a flower just as well as a person of faith."

Michelle was shocked at his blatant disregard for her beliefs. "So, science just discounts any divine intervention into the growth of gardens?"

"I'm afraid so. Let me ask you this. If you had an infestation in one of your gardens and aphids were eating away at your prize begonias, would you pray for resolution or would you spray with a chemical compound that was safe for your flower but deadly for the bugs?"

Her blank stare was all the answer he needed.

"You don't need to reply. We both know it would be the latter. While I do not discount your belief system, I don't find its relevance to the amazing work you do in your gardens.

Strike One.

Michelle drank her coffee in silence for a moment before breeching a new topic of conversation. The first one did not fare exactly well.

"I guess we have to agree to disagree on that subject."

"I'm sorry. I didn't mean to offend. Since we are both scientists I assumed we had the same approach to our work."

"Scientist? Why would you think I am a scientist? I am a gardener. If anything, I am a laborer not a scientist. The science of my job is just a necessary evil. I need to understand what chemicals are good for my plants and flowers as well as those that are not."

"Ok. I see your point. But can you see mine? I assume in your position you had some secondary education?"

"I did. I received a degree in Botany from UMASS."

"That degree... was it a Bachelor of Science?"

Michelle smiled. "You made your case. Can we move on?"

"Of course." Randall smirked smugly as he thought he had the upper hand in the conversation and wielded it to his advantage.

"So, Mr. Science. Tell me about your interest in bee pollination. Did you go visit the bee boxes as I suggested?"

"Indeed I did. I spoke to the beekeeper and he was quite informative."

"Very good. I'm glad to hear that. A lot of visitors to the farm do not make it over to that area so Rich doesn't get to talk to many people. He is a very nice man though."

Randall shrugged and took a sip of his coffee. "He seemed nice enough. It's a good thing he tends to the bees though. I have a feeling that if he wasn't in charge of the bee boxes his job at the farm wouldn't be so nice."

Michelle was about to take another drink of her decaf but stopped in mid approach and put the coffee cup down.

"I don't understand your meaning."

Randall chuckled.

"I'm sure you do. Look, he seemed like a nice guy and he had lots to say about caring for the bees in the boxes. He didn't have many answers besides bees and honey, though. He had no idea bees were used for medicinal purposes. He is just a task man. He goes to the boxes, takes care of the bees, and collects their honey. Any idiot could do it. It's not like he is educated like you or I. He's just a dolt. If he wasn't tending to the bees, they probably would have him cutting the grass or digging some ditches somewhere. There's nothing wrong with people like that, we all need them. Someone has to cut the grass and pick up the trash. The rest of us are educated and serve a greater purpose."

Strike Two.

"Wow."

Randall looked back at the object of his desire with a little less luster in his eyes.

"Don't you agree?"

Michelle stiffened her back and sat up in her seat. She was tired of being challenged by people with small minds and she was growing tired of this conversation by the minute.

"No, I do not agree. I do not measure people by their degree of intelligence or rather the degrees that hang on their walls. Yes, you and I have attended college and we use our knowledge for practical applications. However, I have met amazing people that did not attend college. As for your antiquated viewpoint about people's station in life defining their purpose in society, I whole heartedly disagree. I have the same amount, if not more respect for the dishwasher at a restaurant as I do the chef. Both have a purpose and without each other, the food could not be produced and served."

"Wow. I wouldn't have taken you for a Marxist."

"A Marxist?"

"You seem to view utilitarianism as a more purposeful approach. I guess that works best in a farm environment. No offense intended."

Foul Ball

Michelle took another drink of her coffee in an attempt to wash away the bad taste in her mouth. She was glad that they had met for coffee and not drinks or dinner. If she had to endure this man much longer, she was not sure she would survive.

"Ok. Let's change the subject. Tell me about your life Randall."

"There's not a lot to tell. I live alone. I have an apartment by the park so I can take in the nature and the wildlife there."

"That's really neat. How long have you been doing medical research?"

"Hmm. I guess about 20 years now. I find working in the lab, behind the scenes, as a better use of my intellect and talents. I grow tired of making the "big pharma" even bigger so that is why I am so interested in plants, bee pollination and other non-chemical methods of medicinal healing. They can keep their billions. I just want to know that I helped one person get better. I know it's not a grand idea but it's what drives me."

Michelle thought for a moment that he may still have a chance. He might have some redeeming qualities even though he has so many bad ones.

"Do you have plants and flowers at home?"

"I love tulips, hyacinths and lilies. I try to keep them alive but I don't have a green thumb like you do."

"Are you aware that those are three of the most toxic plants to animals? Specifically cats? They can kill them."

Once again, Randall burst out with laughter.

"Is that funny to you?"

"Well. Kind of. You know what they say, there is no cat like a dead cat. If those plants are deadly to cats, I need to get more of them."

"Don't you like cats?"

"Heavens no. They are just overgrown rodents. I never met a cat I didn't want to see killed and stuffed."

Strike Three. You're out!!

9

"Oh my goodness. What did you say to that?"

Alice and Michelle were having an ice cream cone before heading to their bible study class the following Thursday. The rainy day that preceded their outing was a blessing in disguise. Michelle's gardens needed watering and it was also pretty much a guarantee that Randall would not be seated in the middle of the garden reading a book.

"What could I say? I told him I had three cats and they were my life. That basically ended the date right then and there."

"Wow. Talk about your basic nightmare."

"Yes, I have been on some bad dates before but none as bad as that one. Why do you think I got it so wrong with him?"

"You never know, Michelle. You meet someone and they seem interesting. You invite them out for coffee and the next thing you know, they are psychotic. It's just a crap shoot. Like that movie saying. *You never know what you gonna get.*"

"I know. I know. But he seemed so quiet and nice. Who knew he was going to be that way when we actually started talking."

"There are plenty of other fish out there, Michelle."

"Why do I take dating advice from you?"

"What do you mean?"

"I mean I take dating advice from a person that does not date. You have not dated in years. Do I even want to know who was President when you started to date your husband? I'm not saying you give me bad advice, just that maybe I should get a second opinion."

The two women broke out in laughter. There was something special about eating ice cream with your friend and bashing the opposite sex.

"So where do you go from here?"

"To bible study I guess. There's not much time to go anywhere else."

"That's not what I meant and you know it."

"Ok. But it's better than getting a lecture on my dating life, or lack thereof."

"I know you. This was a bad date so you are ready to retreat to your garden or your begonia house. We won't see you try again for months."

Michelle took a bite of her ice cream and savored the flavor. After giving herself time to digest Alice's comment, she had her own take on the situation.

"Let me ask you this. When is the best time to transplant a tuber?"

"What? How did we get from talking about your love life to transplanting a begonia? That doesn't seem like a logical pattern."

"Just bear with me. When do you take the tuber out of your small kitchen container and plant it in the garden?"

"Well, when you see the roots I guess."

"…and what happens if you move it too soon into the pot? If you move it too soon without enough roots?"

Alice smiled and nodded. She knew where the conversation was going.

"The flower dies. It needs enough of a start, enough roots to take hold, for the flower to bloom."

"Precisely. My love life is like a begonia. If I try to push it along before it's time, before it has the right roots, it will just die off. I want to find the right tuber with the right roots and plant it at the right time. Only then will my love life bloom."

Alice just laughed. "I guess that's true of any gardener. *To plant a garden is to dream of tomorrow.* Let's hope you never stop dreaming my friend."

The two women clinked their ice cream cones together like champagne glasses and laughed. Life in the garden was eternal.

Friday Night
Musical Revue

4 PM

The Continental Trailways tour bus passed the main gate of Ocean Beach Park with the equipment truck following close behind. Normally the roadies would get to the venue first and get things rolling long before the talent arrived but they were on a tight schedule. The *express set up*, as the Road Manager named it, was made especially for circumstances such as these and the roadies would get everything ready long before the opening act started at 8pm. The gig at the Pensacola Fair on the other side of the state wrapped up late last night around midnight. The road crew worked quickly to get them packed up but it was almost 3am before their tires hit the road.

The six-week summer tour of the 1970 Rock n Roll Musical Revue had skirted along the Southern half of the United States. With the country still buzzing over the far-out tales from Woodstock the summer before, every live music venue was flooded with screaming fans trying to replicate the experience. The six performance acts that traveled together on the bus tour were from all over the south so every now and then, the hometown crowd was cheering one or more of their names as they arrived.

The tour bus had taken them from Pensacola to the Florida Keys and they all had seen more of the great state of Florida than they had bargained for. They were all hot, tired, and achy. They had 4 hours until the first act hit the stage and they all intended to take that time to unwind the best they could. Greg McDonald, the promoter for the tour, had arranged for accommodations at a boarding house across the street from the park and they would all have access to the beds and showers there. They had slept in worse places in the last 5 weeks but the end of the tour was still a week away and they all were anxious for their own home comforts.

The two vehicles parked outside of the concert hall and the roadies jumped out. They knew they were under the gun and set about to unload the equipment truck while the Road Manager went to check in. By the time he appeared with assistance from the concert hall personnel, the roadies had a good jump on unloading the equipment.

The talent was a little slow on their exit but some screaming fans were there none the less to greet them. The Florida Keys were the home of one of the star performers, Micah Read. A soloist with gospel roots, he had found some notoriety by appearing on The Lawrence Welk Show some years previous but had never been picked up by a major label. He floated from one road show to the next and was a crowd favorite. Being back in the Keys, the local fans turned out to see one of their own perform on the big stage at the park.

Following Micah off the bus was a newcomer to the circuit by the name of Landon Noland. The young man heralded himself from upstate and was just in the upswing of gathering a following. The youngest member of the musical revue, Landon possessed an uncanny resemblance to the King himself, and played it up to the young ladies. The classic Elvis mutton chops were a draw and the promoter made certain that Landon was featured on many of the tour posters. A one-man band, Landon was a fast-strumming guitar player while using a base drum to rock the beat. He occasionally pulled out the harmonica and the tambourine and drove the young girls wild as he moved to the groove. His welcome by the female crowd at hand was loud and piercing as their screams could be heard across the park.

With Landon and Micah already in motion to exit the park and hit the boarding house, the first female performer found the Trailway stairs and exited the tour bus. Fo'i Meleah was from the Islands and sang with soul. Her warm smile and outward greeting made her popular on the tour. Strumming her folk guitar, many were amazed by her tone and delivery and while she was not a headliner, she certainly brightened up the stage and warmed the crowd throughout the night. Fo'i had been on the tour before and Greg saved a spot for her on the lineup before the rest of acts were booked.

The rocker of the group was a man named Marcus Gullen. The young man didn't let his Celtic name get in the way of establishing himself as a rock headliner. Having appeared all over the south, Marcus called the Carolinas his home but was well known as a multi-talented musician. During the revue, he took the stage at different times playing piano, switching up to guitar and belting out the lyrics on everything from the British Invasion to Creedence and beyond. Marcus brought down the house as he rallied the crowd to their feet. The promoter knew that he was bank-rolling talent and someday would find a venue large enough to showcase the man's talents. For today, he was happy billing Marcus as the headliner.

If Marcus represented the new age rocker of the 70s, then the next performer to get off the tour bus was certainly the face of the 60s. The original flower child, Nicole Equerme stepped off the bus completely decked out already in her go-go boots and short skirt. The sash that wrapped her head went well with the rose colored glasses that sat upon her nose. She was the walking picture of peace, love, and rock movement and was often asked about her experiences at Woodstock the year prior.

Somewhere along the path of the fringe, Nicole picked up a partner.

Accompanying her down the tour bus stairs was her flower power mirror image, Nicole Wren. Decked out in a long flowy white blouse and brown leather vest, this Nicole had a ring of flowers sitting atop her golden mane. Together they were the Bobbsey twins and the audiences ate them up like hot apple pie and ice cream a la mode. They were the face of Americana. Sweet, pretty and full of folk music that the crowds had grown accustomed to in the last decade. When the strumming started, the people closed their eyes and swayed. Nicole and Nicole brought the smiles and so they were book-ended with their fellow musicians in the middle of every poster for the musical tour.

The final act on the 1970 Rock n Roll Revue tour was a man named Paul Buttery. The Italian with the million-dollar smile, roman nose and hard Bronx accent was the only performer on the tour that was not from the south. The fact that he was a brown eyed piano singer belting out songs by old blue eyes, brought a different sort of crowd to the revue. He was the cool cat wearing the sunglasses while he played his piano for the audience. If the tour had allowed him to have a drink on stage with him, he would have resembled Sinatra's sidekick, Dino, in a New York minute.

Where Landon and Marcus attracted the younger audience, Micah and Paul had the older women swooning. Since men of all ages brought dates to the concert venues, the promoter thought it was best to balance out the offering with youth and maturity, male performers mostly with some females added for flavoring. Together the group had sold out venues all over the south in their five-week summer run. There was already talk of another tour but contracts had not been presented yet and all the performers were anxious for a break after the final week ahead.

With all of the talent off of the tour bus, they all followed directions at their own pace to the boarding house across the street. Paul was not happy that he would be the last to get to the showers after such a long drive but he was also too cool to move any faster. Each act was a musical entity among themselves and each one had a story and a life to go with it. Sometimes the music was a showplace for their talents while other times it was a window to their souls. As they all approached their home base for the evening, the music was already pulsing through their veins.

5 PM

"I need a cheeseburger."

Landon was standing on the deck patio of the boarding house with Marcus and Paul. The latter two were smoking cigarettes as they leaned on the railing facing the ocean.

"A cheeseburger? We are in the keys, man. Go get yourself some fish."

"Listen, man. I'm a red blooded brother. I need meat, not fish. Bring me a cheeseburger or bring me death."

"Landon, you are no Shakespeare. You're an Elvis wanna be. Now you are eating just like him. Are you going to get fat like him too?"

"Hold on, hold on. You can say I look like Elvis, act like Elvis and even eat like Elvis. But you can't call the King fat."

"Relax, bro. I saw it on the Mike Douglas Show. He's out in Vegas now doing his thing and all he eats is cheeseburgers."

"Is that true, Paul?"

"Dammit, man. How the hell do I know? I just got out of the shower. A cold shower at that thanks to all of you."

"You need a cold shower after last night. Did you see that chic was there again for you? Right in the front row. What's that? The third or fourth show she has travelled to?"

"Actually the fifth. She's been traveling behind us ever since New Orleans."

"Damn, Paul. I think you have yourself a certified groupie."

"They are not all that they are cracked up to be, man."

Landon and Paul looked at each other. They knew there had to be more to the story so they pressed on it.

"Ok, Marcus. There has to be a story there. Spill the beans."

Marcus took a drag off his cigarette before turning around to see his fellow performers. They had not become the best of friends in the past five weeks but they had shared a lot. Like most performers in the business, they had a mutual respect for each other and shared the same commonality of music.

236

SEVEN DAYS OF DESTINY

"Man, I've just had my share of crazies that's all. You know what it's like. Chicks always throwing themselves at you. Heck, I've had a few throw their bloomers up on stage while I play. What the heck is that about? Anyway, I'm just saying. Sometimes those groupies go a little far. It's nice to get the attention and all but I got a girl back in Carolina. I don't need anyone disrespecting her by hanging all over her man."

"Marcus, you are such a southerner. Trust me. None of my boys up in New York talk that way. A good lookin' babe throws you their bloomers, you gotta do somethin' about it."

"That's what my buddy, Marshall says. He's another southern rocker in South Carolina but I think he is too much like you northern boys. He's trying to put together a group but his old lady doesn't want him on the road. I'll convince him one of these days."

"So that's your big advice for someone like me just starting out? Watch out for crazy groupies? Sounds like a fun Saturday night if you ask me."

The three men shared a good laugh before Landon broke it up.

"Well, you boys can sit around chewing the fat if you want but I'm going to go find some real meat. I'm sure they sell cheeseburgers down on the boardwalk."

"You better watch your six there Landon. You know McDonald doesn't like us mingling with the locals before the shows."

"Aw, he don't scare me. He'll show up right before the show and put on his blazer. He puts out these rules like he's really going to kick us off the tour. He's not and you know it. We got a week left and all our shows are sold out. Besides, I'm just getting a cheeseburger. I'll be back shortly to eat it with of you old people."

Landon walked off the deck and down the front steps. His features led no one to believe he was impersonating Elvis in any way. Paul and Marcus chuckled though, as the young man tried to replicate the King's gate.

"Do you think he has a chance?"

"Who the kid? Sure why not. He has to stop trying to be someone else though and just work on his music. He's got one hell of a good strum on the strings and his voice ain't too shabby either. Put him in the right place at the right time, I'm sure someone will cut a record with him in the future."

"You know as well as I do, Paul. It's not just about the talent. Heck, if that was the case, you and I would be rich as kings and we wouldn't have to play in no two-bit musical revue to make a living."

"Hey, man. It's not so bad. I've played in some dives in the city, let me tell you. There are nights when I can't tell if I'm playing for street bums or paying customers. They all look the same after a while. I've enjoyed this tour. The south has been good to me."

"Not to mention your little groupie."

Paul took a drag off his cigarette. "So about that…"

Marcus looked back at him casually. "What? She's not good looking enough for you?"

"Nah. That's not it. She's a certified babe. I just don't know."

"What's there to know? She's hot. She's into you. You're a single guy. What's the hesitation all about?"

"Let me ask you this, Marcus. I've seen what you were talkin' about. You get up on stage playin' that rock shit and all those chickies want a piece of you. How do you do it? You seem to stay true to your woman back home. How is it you can be in our business and be a one-woman guy?"

Marcus threw his cigarette butt off the deck into the sand. He pulled another out of his pack and lit it. Drawing in a deep breath, he answered the question.

"It ain't easy, man. Some of those girls are…you know…a real smoke show. But I keep sayin' to myself it ain't worth it. Sure I might get my jollies for a few minutes after a show but at some point the show's gotta end, you know? In another week, you gonna head back up north and I gotta go home and see my girl. How am I supposed to look her in the eyes if I'm out scatchin' my itch every time I got the urge. Nope. Not me. When the shows over and those roadies pack everythin' up, I get in my truck and drive on home to my girl. The longer we go, the greater the homecoming, if you catch my drift."

"That's a great way to look at it Marcus."

"Why do you ask?"

"Excuse me?"

"Why are you asking about my relationship? Are you thinking of making something more with this groupie chick?"

Paul Buttery flicked his cigarette butt out into the sand like Marcus had. The discussion had given him food for thought.

"Who knows. Right now, I gotta walk around. Let's go see if the others are inside."

"Sure, Paul. But one more thing before we go. What are you gonna do if your pretty lady is sitting in that front row again tonight? That will make six shows in a row. Let me tell you. My old lady likes to come hear me play but there ain't no way she crossin' three states just to hear me play the same shit in a different town. Especially when it's not just me playin'. If she's out there tonight, what are you gonna do, Paul?"

The piano playing Italian had no idea. He patted his fellow musician on the shoulder and gestured for them to go inside.

"I have no idea, man. No idea at all."

The fact was that Paul had many thoughts about the woman running through his head and the cold shower did nothing to dispel them.

5:30 PM

Paul and Marcus walked in the community living room of the boarding house. Two unknown tenants were off to the side of the room playing a game of chess while Fo'i, Nicole and Nicole were rehearsing a number. The pair walked quietly into the room as the two guitar players were strumming with all three of them singing. When they saw their fellow performers come in, they stopped playing abruptly.

"How's it sound?"

"I like it. It has a nice harmony to it."

"Three-part harmony always makes a nice triad chord."

"Is that the new song by CSNY? I heard it the other day on the radio."

"Yes, that's the one. We thought we might get some good response since they are playing it all over the airwaves."

"Good thinking. What's Greg say about it?"

The three women laughed. They seemed to have the same opinion as Landon about their promoter.

"What's he going to say? He doesn't know one song from the back of his elbow. We'll just slip it into the third act. He won't even know the difference."

Paul simply shrugged. Apparently the politics of the music business in the south did not have the same punch as those in the north. If you crossed the promoter up in the city, you might as well pack your bags. You would be lucky if you didn't get tossed out with the garbage in the alley before your second set was finished.

Marcus was the experienced one in the group to add his two cents about the promoter.

"Listen. Greg is a cool cat. He just like's his people to be groovy with the audience, that's all. I've been on many tours with him. He'll keep bringing you back as long as you float in his boat. You want to rock the boat; you end up swimming with the fishes."

"Well, the water looked pretty nice out there, Marcus."

The three women laughed lightly as the long haired rocker shrugged his shoulders. "I get it. I know when to mind my own biz. Stay cool."

Marcus threw up a peace sign and walked out. His mustard colored bell bottoms swayed in the wind as he walked back out to the patio for a smoke.

"Is he ok?"

Nicole was asking Paul out of true concern not because of the passing comment.

"Yea. I think he's just a little on edge. We have one week to go and everyone is a little homesick. I think he misses his girl."

Nicole and Nicole looked at each other and smiled. Fo'i and Paul seemed to be left out of the hidden message between them.

"Ok, what?"

"We think the opposite is going to happen."

"The opposite? I don't understand. What gives?"

The two women looked at each and nodded, both agreeing to let the cat out of the bag and tell them.

"We are not going home when the tour ends. We are heading to California."

"Holy cow."

"That's groovy, chicks. What made you decide that?"

"Listen Paul. You know. The big city is where it's at. The music scene, the night life, and of course Hollywood. We're going to split Florida and head to L.A."

"Los Angeles is a cooky place. Do you think you're ready for the west coast?"

The two women looked at each other and held hands. It was clear they wanted to explore a totally new life together.

"The question is whether or not California is ready for us? Look at these beauties. We are flower power on a box of cereal. We belong to be in the happening music scene in L.A. That's where we are going to get our big break."

"Well I for one am very happy for you. I'm sure you're going to be great. You are both very talented. You just need to be heard by the right person so you can jump up. I can see you now plastered all over Tower Records."

"Thanks Fo'i. Coming from a talent like you that means a lot. I know you are a Florida girl and you will keep playing in the beach world. What about you, Paul. Have you decided what's next on the Paul Buttery tour?"

Paul seemed to get antsy at the question. He wasn't trying to avoid it but he also didn't have a clear vision of what was coming next.

"You know? I'm not sure. The way I look at it I got 88 keys to play all day every day. Sometimes I spend my time hanging with the 52 white keys. Every so often, I dig the 36 black keys. But most of the time, I play them all and see where the music takes me. That's kind of how I'm digging on my life right now. I'm just going to keep on playing until the keys tell me where to go."

The three women smiled at his answer. While they were all performers, Paul had the music flowing through his veins. They were all certain that if they watched him sleep, they would see musical notes coming out of his mouth as he snored.

"Does your decision have anything to do with that hottie that keeps coming to our concerts looking for you?"

Paul blushed. He wasn't aware that his number one fan was a topic of conversation with all members of the musical revue.

"She is…well…so I'll let you get back to playing. Have you seen Micah around?"

"Nice way to avoid the question. Anyway, he's in the kitchen."

"Is he cooking something?"

"If you were hungry, you should have gone with Landon."

"I don't want a greasy burger from the boardwalk. Is Micah cooking?"

"No. He's not cooking. We just got here an hour and a half ago. Where would he get the food? He is just sitting in there working on something."

"On his guitar? I only heard you gals playing."

"No, something else. He's got his sketch pad with him. If you want to know more, go ask him. I'm sure he'll show you."

"Far out. I'll let you get back to your harmonizing."

Paul walked out of the common area towards the kitchen. He hadn't reached the doorway before the music started to play behind him. Smiling, he thought to himself that he loved being around other musicians all the time. You never knew when a random song would begin.

Entering to kitchen, he found Micah sitting at the kitchen table with his sketch pad. He was always doodling something and his art was very good. While riding on the tour bus, Paul would watch Micah for miles recreating all manner of landscapes that they passed. He often envied the guitar player's talent as he was well rounded. Sure Paul could play piano and sing but Micah was so much more. Besides playing his guitar and belting out music, he also had amazing artistic abilities. Paul regarded Micah as the real McCoy.

"Hey, Micah."

The singer looked up from the sketch pad he was doodling on to see his new visitor. He thought he had found some solace in the kitchen and was surprised at the interruption.

"Hey Paul. Heard you got the last shower. Pretty chilly was it?"

"Yeah, yeah. That's what I get for being nice and letting all you mooks go first."

Micah laughed. "No, that's what you get for walking so slow. Being cool has a price attached to it."

"Everything has a price, man. You ever hear of this inflation thing? The 70s are killing me and we just got here."

"That's why you have to expand your horizons, brother."

"I don't take that LSD shit, man."

241

"Not that kind of horizons Paul. I'm talking about your money horizons. You are like every one of us. We live from gig to gig. What we make we spend on food and travelling. It all gets eaten up. The only way to get ahead is to branch out. Find another source of income, man."

"Is that what you are working on?"

"Yes, man. Have a seat."

Paul pulled up a chair next to his fellow performer. Looking at the sketch pad he eyed what looked like a kid's book.

"Is that what you were working on in the bus? I saw you drawing some landscape."

"Yea. The landscape was the background. I needed to draw a scene for my characters."

"Characters?"

"Characters for my children's book. It's kind of groovy. I figured it was a good way to make some side dough. I wrote the story, now I'm adding the pictures."

"Far out, man. Like Dr. Seuss and Highlights and stuff like that?"

"Exactly like that. I got the idea from a cool cat that I met on The Lawrence Welk show. He was doing some doodling in the green room and I asked him what he was doing. You know what he told me? He was planning for his retirement. So I got to thinking, what about me? What am I gonna collect when I stop touring someday? The green has to flow from somewhere. The way I figure, if I can get this children's book published, I'll collect royalties the rest of my life. Some cool shit, right?"

"Definitely man. That's cool."

Micah went back to his drawing while Paul sat and watched him for a few minutes. Without looking up from his work, Micah reacted to his viewer.

"Was there something else, Paul, or did you just come in here to watch me draw?"

Paul sat at the table and didn't respond at first. After a few moments, he was soft spoken to his fellow performer.

"How many shows do you do a year, Micah?"

The artist put down his drawing pencil and looked over at Paul.

"Why do you want to know? You seem just as busy as I am with bookings."

"That's true, but I don't have a family at home."

"Is that what this is all about? Do you want to know how I can do both? Have a family and still perform so much?"

"Something like that."

"Look, man. It's not easy. Set aside the part that you are missing them like crazy, you also got no way of knowing what's going on. When I'm on the road, I got to call from a pay phone when we stop for gas just to see how my son did on his Math Test. If something bad happens, you find out the next time you check in. It's some rough shit."

Paul just nodded thoughtfully.

"So tell me. Why the sudden interest in the family life? I thought you were happy being the confirmed bachelor."

"Yea. It's all good. I just get to wondering if I'm missing something, you dig? I love playing and I could do gigs every night of the year if I could. But at the end of the night, it sucks coming home to an empty hotel room."

Micah looked up at him. "Listen, man. On the flip side of the album, there ain't nothing like coming home to the family. Someone there that actually missed you. Heck, even the dog comes running if you know what I mean. You want my advice? Go find a girl and settle down. Create a life together. Make some memories together. There's a lot more love songs out there than single guy jams. You fall in love, that music is going to pour out your piano."

Paul nodded his head in agreement. "I think you are right on in that department brother. I'll let you get back to your sketching. I got some things to do before the sound checks."

"What time we doing that?"

"Greg wants us there at 630pm. Before the crowd gets let in."

"Sounds good."

Paul got up to leave the kitchen and Micah stopped him.

"Hey, man. Good luck with finding the right chick. You never know, she might be sitting right in the front row waiting for you."

Paul shook his head. They all knew about his number one fan.

6:15 PM

The 1960 Volkswagen Beetle was parked in one of the first parking spaces at the Ocean Beach Park concert hall. The woman driving it had gotten there a half hour previous and was already out on the boardwalk looking at the scenery. She had her Kodak camera hanging on her wrist strap and was already half way through her film roll. She had another package back in the bug but she was saving that for the actual concert. She had already gotten the photos back from the first two concerts she attended and could not wait to see how the rest came out.

Sandy Taylor was simply a woman that loved music. She was on a journey of exploration of mind, body and soul that had started out from her home in Houston, Texas and had taken her all the way to the Florida Keys. She supposed it was poetic that she found herself at the outskirts of the United States. Just a little further south from the boardwalk she currently stood on was mile marker 0. Her life was starting over and the trip she embarked on had no destination and no visible end. She was alone on the road of life seeking some kind of direction.

When her former husband, an advertising executive, left her for his secretary, she was devastated. She milled about their house looking for answers and getting none. Why did this happen to her? Would she still be attractive to men after being married for so long? She tired of all the public appearances with him; playing second fiddle to the adman with the winning smile. In the end, he won a new life with his secretary and Sandy won her freedom.

The VW had been a gift from his client when he worked on their ad campaign. He felt it did not fit his public image so he had given it to his wife while he retained their Cadillac. Like the Beetle itself, he wanted her contained in her little cage. The symbolism between his massive sedan and her small bug was not lost among their so-called friends in the advertising agency. They often chuckled when she came by the office to visit him and she became the butt of many office jokes. The *little* woman driving the *little* car in her *little* life. He left their marriage without notice and with no conversation about her car. In the end, it became her ticket to freedom.

When the divorce papers were delivered to her door two weeks prior, she took it as a sign. He left her their house and her car and agreed to pay her some alimony but she was not holding her breath for the checks in the mail. Her husband had always been cheap when it came to her and she never expected the fool to part with his money in her absence. Quickly signing the paperwork, she dropped them in the mailbox and packed a bag. She had a ticket to ride and she didn't care anymore. Pressing in the clutch, she put the beetle in gear and set off for her new life.

Coming to the end of her driveway, she had two choices. If she took a left, she was heading to all points west. She would cross Austin and San Antonio and eventually reach the dust bowl called New Mexico. Sure, there was the call of California and the glitz and glamour of Hollywood but she had had enough of the fake smiles with her Ad-man ex-husband and had no desire to keep shaking hands with people that would not even notice she was gone.

Taking a right turn, she was now headed East. The shoreline always intrigued her and although she sat at home while her ex-husband often ventured out on fishing trips, the allure was always there to join him. Thinking back, he never returned with any fish so it was altogether possible that his trips were simply excuses for him to get away with his secretary. Caring not for him nor his excuses, the shore line was calling out to her.

In the days that followed, Sandy found herself approaching New Orleans. The city had a reputation of civil unrest in the 60s but it was now a new decade. She had heard conversations at cocktail parties that the city was filled with all manner of tasty cuisine and that she would adore the architecture and nightlife. All of that sounded wonderful but she was most interested in their musical offerings.

Sandy always loved music. It filled her house with joy whenever she was allowed to play her records and not just the ones that her husband thought were proper for occasions. When they entertained, it was always Montovani or segments from The Lawrence Welk Show that he wanted for their guests. She was bored just moments in and could not wait until they left. When she was alone, she grooved to the Beetles and Telstar. She danced while doing her house chores, listening to Herb Alpert and the Tijuana Brass and simply adored any piano rock she could pick up at the record store.

First arriving at The Big Easy, there was such an eclectic mix of music she didn't know what to listen to first. She hit Bourbon Street and listened to jazz, blues and something called zydeco music. She longed for some rock, some folk music and her favorite piano rock. Soon enough, she was pleasantly surprised. On a telephone pole advertisement, she learned of a traveling Musical revue coming to New Orleans that had all of those things wrapped up in one show. With six musical acts, she was certain to find something she was looking for.

The first surprise at arriving at the 1970 Rock n Roll Musical Revue was her acceptance. She was always regarded as beautiful but she often felt like an ornament for her former husband. He would take her out in public, parade her around as his trophy wife, and place her back in her display case when he was done showing her off. Being out on her own, she received a different sort of greeting and she was happy to receive it.

"Where's a doll like you sitting?"

The usher checking tickets to the New Orleans show was told by the producer to put the more attractive looking people up front. It played well for the tour when the local papers ran photographs of the performances with picture perfect people in the front row. With an eye for beauty, the usher honed in on Sandy.

"I think my ticket is towards the back."

"Not anymore doll. Let me bump you to a front row seat. How would you like that?"

"Seriously? Is there a catch? I'm no floozy."

"No catch, honey. The musicians just like to see a pretty face in the front row when they are playing."

She had been called out of the crowd not because of her husband or the current ad campaign he was working on. She was called out for her looks and was given a front row seat. Her evening was off to a great start.

Sitting there, waiting for the revue to start, she read through the playbill. The acts were a nice mix but the one that intrigued her the most was a piano player named Paul Buttery. According to his bio, the man had three things going for him that made Sandy smile. The first was that he was a piano player. Nothing like a fine piano player to get her to swoon. The second was that he was Italian. His good looks and cool demeanor set her heart afire. Finally, the fact that he was from New York City completed the whole package for her. Her ex had taken many business trips to The Big Apple but had never taken her along. While he was sitting in meetings on Madison Avenue, she could have been walking down 5th Avenue near Rockefeller Center, or taking in a Broadway show. Instead she was stuck at home, never seeing the city that never sleeps. She had slept her life away but would do it no longer.

When the house lights dimmed and the music started to play, Sandy Taylor was hooked. She had spent too many years of her life cooped up in her cage and she was so happy she made the choice to hit the road. With each act that came out and played, she questioned every choice she had ever made in life. Why did she settle? Why was she not seizing the day like all these musicians were singing about? There was life, there was love, there was a whole world out there around her that came alive in every song they played. They were no longer notes and words to be heard. They were messages being told to her to play out her destiny, wherever it may lead.

The piano playing interest did not disappoint her and she quickly labeled him her favorite. She had never experienced love at first site so she wasn't sure she would exactly label her experience that. She was certain, however, that she could sit and listen to him all night long and was disappointed that each of the performers only got to play a few tunes in the show. She longed for more and when the encore was played and the house lights came back on, she felt lost with nowhere to go. The show had given her life and love and everything she was looking for. With the revue all done, where would she get her fix? Where could she go to replicate the feelings she had encountered during the show? The answer was to follow them to the next show.

On the back of the playbill was a tour date listing of all the shows the group was performing. They were a few weeks into a six-week tour and they were headed East as well. Having no place to go and nothing but time in her life, she put gas in her VW Beetle and headed East, following the production. Each show, the usher placed her in the front row and each show she was treated to more music she could ever hope for. By the third show, they seemed to recognize her in the audience and she felt like the performers were singing just to her. Paul was still her favorite and she even blew him a kiss after one of the shows was done. She had heard the term "groupie" before and she gathered she technically fit the bill now. She was not a crazed fan like some of the young girls around her, but she had a fondness for the Italian piano player that was growing with every show.

Now, standing on the boardwalk at Ocean Beach Park, Sandy began to question it all. She was so far from the home that she knew that she wondered if she would ever return. She had found freedom and music and a free spirit that she had no idea she was capable of. She was no longer the wife of an advertising executive or a stay at home housewife. Sandy Taylor was on the edge of a cliff and knew she had to spread her wings and fly or forever fall into the abyss.

Turning towards the concert hall, destiny was about to cross her path. Just footsteps away, Paul Buttery was walking along the boardwalk heading towards his performance. Knowing the time had come to take her first steps, Sandy started walking towards him to intercept him before he went in. It was time for her to fly and her wings were ready to unfurl.

6:30 PM

Paul knew he was already late as the sound checks were due to start at 630pm. He also knew that if he wasn't there on time, they would just continue with the other acts, checking their instrument and mic levels before getting to him. Taking his leisurely stroll down the boardwalk, he came to abrupt stop when he saw her. The woman that had adorned the front row for the last 5 shows was standing before him. She was not blocking his path but rather looked as if she was sight-seeing. Noticing him at the same time, she turned to greet him.

"Hello."

"Hey, there. I was wondering if we were ever going to get a chance to meet or I would just continue singing to you every concert."

Sandy looked down as she blushed. "I'm so sorry. I must seem like some sort of groupie or something."

"Well, I would be lying if the thought hadn't crossed my mind. In any case, my name is Paul as I'm sure you know."

Though it felt strangely like meeting her ex-husband's clients, she smiled as she put out her hand to shake his.

"Hi Paul. My name is Sandy."

The two shook hands and smiled at each other awkwardly.

"It is nice to finally have a name to match the face in the front row. I would ask you if you are coming to the concert tonight but that seems like a silly question seeing that you are out here."

"Yes, I got here a little early so I could take in the sights. It's really beautiful here. I've never been this far south before."

"Do you live here in Florida?"

"No, I actually live in Texas. I guess *lived* is a more appropriate term. Not sure where I call my home now. I'm kind of in limbo as they say."

Paul looked at her inquisitively but did not want to press the question too much as time was the issue.

"It sounds like there's quite a story there."

248

Sandy looked down once again and folded her hands with the camera dangling to the side. She felt awkward talking about her situation; especially to a total stranger.

"There is. Maybe I'll tell you some time."

Paul smiled. "Well maybe I would like that. For now, though, I am late for sound checks and I'm sure I'm in some hot water already."

"Oh, I am so sorry. Go...go...don't worry about me. I'll just keep checking out the beautiful sights before the concert."

"It was very nice talking to you Sandy. Maybe we can talk some more after my sound checks. The concert doesn't start until 8pm. Are you going to be around here in a little while?"

Sandy was beaming from ear to ear. "I'll be here. Go take care of your things. When you're done, I'll be walking the boardwalk nearby."

Paul turned to go and stopped after a few steps.

"Hey Sandy."

"Yes, Paul?"

"The boardwalk might be a pretty sight to see but you're the most beautiful thing I've seen all day."

Sandy stood in shock as this wonderful man actually paid her a compliment.

"Anyway, I'll see you in a bit."

Waving, Paul turned and quickened his usually slow step. If he could have seen behind him, he would have seen a woman that was now in love.

6:45 PM

"Where the hell have you been, Paul?"

The Road Manager was not happy with the fact that one of the acts was not on time. Paul knew better than to engage him but he did it anyway.

"Did you already get through everyone else?"

"No, wise ass but you know we are on quick set tonight. I want to make sure your piano is all set for your highness."

"Well, Marcus plays as well. He could have checked it for you."

"Marcus was busy setting up his guitar and microphone. Is this really a problem Paul? With a week left you got to bust my balls?"

Paul decided to let it go. He knew he was in the wrong and he needed to drop the attitude.

"Man, it's all good. Sorry you had to wait. You ready for me now or should I just chill until you are good?"

"Just take five. We'll be with you in a minute. I just wanted you to be here when we were ready."

The two men retreated to their corners like fighters in the ring. The invisible bell had been rung and the round was over. There were always challenges between the techs and the talent but at the end of the day, it was talent who held the upper hand. If push came to shove, everyone knew the silent hierarchy and if the diva performers wanted to keep them waiting all night, they would have to wait. Some took advantage of this balance but not Paul. He respected the balance of power knowing that someone had to push that piano around and he knew it wasn't going to be him.

"Who went already?"

Paul was sitting down next to the Nicole's, Fo'i and Landon. The latter was still eating some fries to keep the furnace burning. Paul thought as he always did that it must be nice being at that age and touring. Your body still had endless energy when you were in your 20s and the concert road tour was often a young man's game.

"Just Micah and Marcus. Don't let him get under your collar. He still has the rest of us to do sound checks on so you could have been later. You know how he gets on these quick sets."

"I know. I should have just let it go but Greg lets him treat us like one of his techies. We are not road crew. We are talent and should be respected that way."

"Speaking of Greg, he's backstage."

"Already? Why is he here for the sound checks, Nicole?"

"Not sure. Landon says he is here to sign on talent for the next tour."

Landon seemed lost in a world of his own. Paul didn't want to get in his fog if he was running music in his head but he pressed on.

"Is that true, man?"

Landon continued to bob his head up and down without paying any attention to Paul or his question.

"Dude? You there? Earth to Landon."

"Oh, sorry Paul. I was running lyrics. What's up?"

"Hey man. No big thing. Just heard Greg was around early. You know anything about him signing on talent?"

"Yea. He's talking about a fall tour. This time up north. None of that cold shit for me, man. You know what I mean? I don't know how you do it being in New York and all."

"He's doing a Northern tour?"

"Yea. Some New England gig. I'm sure he will catch up to you. He was asking about you when we got here."

"Thanks man."

Landon walked off hearing the music in his head and mouthing the lyrics. Before Paul could get settled the Road Manager called him up to the stage. The process was easy enough, just tedious. Since every performer had their own volume level and every venue had their own individual acoustics, the tech guys had to mark off and balance things out before you hit your first note.

"Where do you want me?"

"Let's put you on Mic 3. The one in center stage for a minute. Fo'i can you hop on Mic 1. I want to check things for that duet number."

"But I'm sitting down at the piano for that number. Why check this one?"

"How the hell should I know Mack. Greg wants to test the sound this way and I said sure. He pays the bills. If you want to know why, ask him."

"Fine, that's cool man. Just didn't want to screw you up brother."

Fo'i and Paul took their places and the background track started to play. They sang their parts for the first half of the song into the chorus. When they arrived at the second verse, the track stopped playing.

"That's good enough. We got what we needed. Let's get you alone on the piano. Fo'i, I'll get to you next after I finish with Liberace here."

Paul shrugged it off. He had been called worse in his professional career and he thought positively of that performer. Taking a seat at his piano, he started a blues rift to limber up. He was cut short abruptly by the sound techs who told him to test the mic there.

"Test one, test two..."

"Sing something. How about that opening number?"

Paul sat back for a moment before starting. In some ways, he hated sound checks because they wanted him to not only produce sound but also to perform. It was often difficult to flick that switch on a dime.

The song began and the rest of the performers sat and listened. Paul had become a favorite on the tour and they enjoyed his personality as well as his music. Individually, they all hoped to work with him again in the future but that was up to the booking gurus. Part of life on the road meant you never knew who you were going to get teamed up with or play as an opening act for. In some ways, it was difficult to form bonds with other musicians that may be passing in the night.

When he got half way through the song, the techs once again stopped him and told him he was all set. When they Called Fo'i to the stage, Paul knew it was his cue to depart. He was looking forward to finding out more about Sandy but he had another conversation to seek out first. With a week to go on this tour and nothing but a few solo gigs on the horizon, he wanted to talk to the tour promoter, Greg McDonald.

Paul exited the stage and walked past the two Nicole's and Landon who were patiently waiting for their turn at the sound checks. Coming around the back of the stage area, he almost walked into a wall of amp cases, lighting and piles of cables. He half expected the roadies to tell him he was in an area that he didn't belong but after five weeks together, they were used to his face being around.

In the back of the concert hall stage, Paul found Greg talking to a woman with a clipboard. She obviously was part of the Ocean Beach Park staff and he seemed to be giving her last minute instructions about his group. Seeing Paul approach, he cut the conversation short and the woman walked away.

Greg McDonald was tall but had a calm demeanor to him. Even with his facial hair, he was well received and that was most likely why he did so well in his job. He was quick to smile and shake hands and his happy face never faded until he was behind the scenes where others could not see him.

"Well, look what we have here. The Italian Stallion himself."

"Is that my new billing, Greg?"

"We'll see how that new movie plays out. It's pretty low-budget but I hear the star has some potential. I like the name though. Any thoughts?"

"Not bad, man. Kind of paints a picture if you know what I mean."

"That's what it's all about my friend. Painting the right picture on the concert posters and playbills and drawing in those crowds."

"Speaking of that, Greg. Are there any other concert posters, playbills or any other type of advertisements for upcoming tours that I will be a part of?"

The tall man laughed heartily. He appreciated the candor coming from Paul.

"I do love the way you show biz folks always put it out there. Just cut to the chase. No bullshit. I like that. Too much bullshit in my line of work."

"So are you stalling or was there an answer in there somewhere?"

"You New Yorkers are always in a hurry to get somewhere. Well, this time I hope you are in a hurry to get back up North."

Paul decided to play it off like he was not aware.

"Why? Is there are another tour starting somewhere?"

Greg laughed again. "I'm sure you heard about it already but I'll play along. Once this summer tour wraps up, I am pulling a new road show together. This time up North. We are calling it the *Fall Foliage Musical Revue*. How's that sound? Got a nice ring to it don't it?"

"It does. How long you thinking on this one?"

"Well, I got the first few dates locked in. They'll start in a few weeks, or a couple weeks after Labor Day. I'd like it to run for 8 weeks this time. That will take us right up to a week or two before Thanksgiving. From there, I'll do a Holiday show for everybody."

Paul was smiling. He was pretty sure where this was leading but wanted to hear it from the promoter's mouth.

"Does this mean you are officially inviting me to attend?"

Greg laughed again. "Attend? Hell, no boy. I want you to headline it. We'll kick off the tour in New York, your home town and let the crowd go wild with you as the main event. What do you think?"

"That sounds great, Greg. It really does but I will need more than the base pay if you are going to headline me."

"Look at you, boy. Playing hardline with me. What type of bump you looking for?"

Paul was not used to moving up to the front of the line. He was not sure what to ask for to be the headlining act.

"How does base plus 20% sound?"

"I think you are out of your league, boy. This is your big chance."

"Ok, how about base plus 10% and you sign me on that Christmas show as well."

"Look at you. A man that thinks ahead. I like that. I'll give you the base plus 10% for the fall tour and guarantee you a spot in the holiday show. If you pull in the crowds on the fall tour, we can headline you again and match the offer. So, we got a deal?"

Paul smiled. This deal meant that he had solid bookings for the next four months. In the music world on the road, that was a pot of gold. Putting out his hand to shake on it, the deal was sealed.

"I'll get the papers together and have them to you before the Miami show tomorrow night. You're a good man Charlie Brown."

Paul turned to walk away. He knew his show tonight was going to be on fire. He was on top of the world with good fortune coming his way. He was hoping there was a woman out on the boardwalk that would help him celebrate his good news.

7:15 PM

Sandy Taylor was not on the boardwalk when Paul came out of the concert hall. He was still beaming about the news and was bursting at the seams wanting to tell someone. He looked around in the area he had left his biggest fan when he went inside and she was not there. It was possible she had migrated into the concert hall as the time was edging towards curtain call. Paul was about to give up when he noticed her out on the beach towards the water. Her hands were on her hips and she was clearly lost in thought. Taking the three steps down into the sand, Paul approached her quietly. Coming up beside her, he stood silently until she noticed he was there.

"Oh, hi Paul. I didn't hear you come up."

"I didn't want to startle you. I actually thought you might have gone inside already."

Looking down at her watch, she was surprised at the time.

"I guess I don't have much time. I should head back soon so I can get my customary seat in the front row."

Paul blushed slightly. "I may have already spoken to the usher and he assured me that you have a reserved seat right by center stage."

Sandy turned to him slightly and smiled. "Are you getting used to me being in the front row for your shows Mr. Buttery?"

"Maybe something like that. What about you? It looks like you were deep in thought. What goes through your mind when you are watching such a beautiful sunset?"

Sandy took a couple steps back as if she were going to get sucked up into the waves. When she regained her footing in the sand, she resumed the conversation.

"I've really never seen anything so beautiful. Sure, we get some nice sunsets in Texas but this...wow...just amazing. The water, the sand...it's just perfect."

"I would agree on the perfect evening. It's been quite a day already."

Sandy tried to play coy. "Is there anything or *anyone* specific that made your day great?"

"We'll get to my news in a minute. Back to your question. You seemed pretty deep in thought when I walked up. Is everything cool?"

Sandy had nothing left to lose in life and everything to gain. She could play off her thoughts but she had come all the way to the Florida Keys. Maybe it was time to try new things.

'Well, I was thinking about life. Been kind of crazy lately. The two-minute tour on my life is that my husband left me for his secretary a while back. I know. Cliché right? He left me my little car and my house along with divorce papers. I signed them a few weeks ago, got in my car and started driving. The road brought me to your show in New Orleans. I'm not really sure why, but I latched onto your magical carpet ride and held on. Now I'm standing in the Florida Keys with no reason why and I'm just taking it all in. How's that for an answer?"

Paul stood there in silent shock for a moment before he realized he was being rude by not responding. Smiling, he thought he would lighten the moment.

"I thought you were going to tell me you like the hot dogs in New York City. They have always been a favorite of mine and I think about them often."

The couple burst out laughing and the moment felt right. Sandy walked over to a nearby bench between the beach and the boardwalk and took a seat. Following her, Paul sat down right next to her.

"Well it sounds like you have had quite the journey. Here I thought you were just the most beautiful groupie I had ever laid eyes on. You actually have quite the backstory. I don't know whether to hug you or call the men in white."

"Oh, don't call the men in white. It's almost Labor Day and they will be out of style."

The two shared another moment of laughter. They both felt relieved by letting it out into the universe.

"Well, it's not quite Labor Day yet. We have a few more shows on this summer tour. It won't end for another week."

"Then what? Where does the great Paul Buttery go from here? I think in the playbill it said you were from New York. Are you going back there after the tour ends?"

"It's funny you should ask that doll…"

"Why is that funny?"

"Well, as luck would have it, I just got offered two more tours. One after Labor Day and the other through the holidays."

"That's fantastic Paul. I'm so happy for you. Where is the tour? Does it continue from Florida?"

"You haven't heard the best part yet. They want me to headline the next tour. It is kicking off in New York City, my home town and going all over the Northeast."

"Wow. That sounds great, Paul. I'm assuming that's a big deal for someone in the music business. To be booked up for the next four months already?"

"You are darn tootin' it is. I've played plenty of gigs, both solo and part of a group, but I've never headlined before. The fact that it is kicking off in New York just makes me happier than a June bug."

"I think you spent too much time in the south Mr. Buttery."

"I think you're right." Looking at his watch, he knew he had to go. "Speaking of time, I think you better get inside to the concert hall and I better go back and get ready. Time's a ticking doll."

Sandy looked down at her watch and was surprised at the time as well.

"I guess so…it's just…well…I was really enjoying talking to you."

Paul stood and thought for a moment before moving on. He nodded as though he had worked out the answer in his mind.

"I tell you what, Sandy. I always have downtime between my sets. Since you have seen the show 5 times already, maybe we can talk some more later? I can have the usher come and get you."

"That sounds like a great idea, Paul. Now go get yourself ready for the show. I'm going to find my way to my seat."

Paul took that as his cue to leave and waved goodbye as he got back on the boardwalk and headed towards the boarding house where his clothes were. It wouldn't take him long to put on his show apparel and he couldn't wait to get back and play. He felt like a million bucks tonight and he planned on putting on quite the show.

For Sandy, she watched as Paul walked smoothly down the pier. She made her way across the vast boardwalk and followed in with the crowd that was heading towards the Ocean Beach Concert Hall. Later, she could not recall how long she waited in line to get in. Her thoughts were elsewhere as she wondered how beautiful New England would be in the fall. She couldn't wait to find out.

7:55 PM

"Look who it is. Mr. Headliner."

"Wow. Word travels fast. I haven't even signed the contract yet."

"Greg's been telling everyone. Trying to get them to hop on board the Paul Buttery train through New England."

"Any takers, Marcus?"

"Hell no. None that I know of anyway. He might have had a chance doing the Northern tour in the summer but none of us southerners want to freeze."

"The temps are not so bad in the fall. Plus, it will be beautiful. I know the Nicole's are heading out west but I figured someone would bite."

"Well, Landon might jump on board. I saw Greg taking to him a few minutes ago. As for Micah, Fo'i and I, we will stay in the south. There's nothing like turkey day when you can go swimming afterwards."

The two shared a good laugh. While they were waiting for the show to start Marcus asked something a little deeper.

"You ever headline before, Paul?"

"No, I've always played second to talent like you, brother."

"Man, that's horse shit and you know it."

"Dude, I have no problem sharing the spotlight with others and I do fine when I'm playing solo gigs. It'll just be different being the main attraction in a room full of talent."

"Man, you are already the headliner you just don't know it."

"What's that mean?"

"I mean look at the rest of us. We are all great guitar players and singers. You stand out tickling the ivory, brother."

"You play the keys too, Marcus."

"Yea, but it's second fiddle if you get what I mean. Can you dig?"

"I dig, I dig."

"TWO Minutes"

The cry came from the Road Manager which meant it was time for everyone to get set up for the opening number. They would all come out and welcome the crowd to the 1970 Rock n Roll Musical Revue.

"Is your chick going to be out there tonight?"

"She's not my chick man."

"Ok sure. Whatever you say. We all know she's here for you."

Paul smiled.

"Yes, she's here. But she's not here just for me."

"Well, you're the one that makes her light up like a Christmas tree. She's got the hots for you whether you know it or not."

Paul nodded as he stood behind Marcus ready to take enter from stage left. The other performers were waiting behind the curtain on stage right. As soon as the house music was cued, they would make their entrance.

"You're probably right about that, Marcus. But maybe she's here for herself too."

The house music blared on cue and the lights started flickering everywhere. It was show time at the Ocean Beach Park Concert Hall.

8 PM

(cue music)

 Ladies and Gentlemen...welcome to the Ocean Beach Concert Hall...for one night only...we welcome the fantastic talent of the 1970 Rock n Roll Musical Revue...six musical acts....hours of music...all under one roof....are you ready?...I SAID ARE YOU READY?...because here they are...the members of the tour...we give you...

 Fo'i Meleah...
 Landon Noland...
 Nicole Equerme...
 Paul Buttery...
 Micah Read...
 And Marcus Gullen...

 The crowd erupted in applause as all the performers took the stage for their opening number. The selection was actually a compellation of songs from classic 60s bands that Greg had picked out and each artist had a say in the transition towards their act. It showcased all the individual talents with each of them taking a soloist break during the montage. The sixteen-minute opening number ended with Marcus who immediately started on his segment of the show.

 Each member of the revue exited the stage quietly as Marcus made the girls swoon. Some of the performers were in the second set which included Micah and Nicole along with the man currently playing on stage. Micah was on to bait the audience to continue listening until he sang the final set. They did not travel far because they knew they would take the stage in 20 minutes. After they performed their smaller group number, Nicole would take the stage for her set.

 With a minimum of 20 minutes to relax, they all went their separate ways. Micah parked himself on top of an amp case to do his drawing. Nicole found Nicole who would not join the stage until Nicole's segment and they just sat down to wait. Fo'i and Landon headed over towards the hospitality table where they would make plates of snacks and pour themselves a beverage. They were part of

260

the third act so they had time to relax. They were 40 minutes from their transition number and they would make the best of it.

"Hey Paul. Do you want to grab some chow with us? Didn't look like you had time to eat between the sound checks and now."

"No, man. I'm chill. Just gonna take some time to figure things out."

"You planning out that fall tour already?"

"Does everyone know about this?"

Landon and Fo'i looked at each other and smiled.

"Yes, Paul. I think we all do and since Fo'i and I decided to sign on too, we figured we would chill together."

"Well, that's great. I'm glad you guys signed on. I really am. Looking forward to sharing New England with you, and New York for that matter. Anyway, we'll have plenty of time to chill together on the tour. For now, I have to find someone."

"Would that someone be a sexy lady sitting in the front row?"

"Really Fo'i? You too? Is nothing private around here?"

Landon and Fo'i laughed.

"You know better than that Paul. There is no privacy on tour. We are lucky to take a crap by ourselves. Your love life is our love life."

Walking away, Paul called back. "Sorry guys. I'm not sharing my love life with anyone. You want a hot looking groupie, you'll have to get your own."

On that note, Paul set out to find an usher to escort Sandy backstage. He had found his own groupie and he wanted to find out more about her.

8:20 PM

The usher went out to the front row and retrieved Sandy who followed him blindly backstage. When she got there, she was amazed at all the activity that was going on while Marcus was singing on stage. She made certain not to trip over the miles of cable and wires that lay on the ground, connecting speaker to speaker and creating the magic of music.

Each of the talent acts set eyes on her as she walked around back stage. They smiled because they knew she was not here for them. While she admired and applauded each one of their performances, her eyes and heart were reserved for only one member of their traveling show. She smiled and waved to each of them as she followed the usher but she was seeking a piano player that night and none of the guitar players. They were clear on the correspondence and waved back politely.

Rounding the corner of the back of the stage, Sandy came across the hospitality table where Fo'i and Landon were filling plates. They both smiled back at her but Landon pointed in the direction of the green room where Paul was sitting down on a couch. The usher brought her to the doorway and stepped back to let her enter. In a few moments, she was in the presence of her favorite piano player, Paul Buttery.

"Hey there doll. Glad you could make it back. I'm sorry to take you away from the show after the opening number. Come have a seat on the couch with me."

"You know I actually buy the tickets to the show. I'm not sure I'm getting my money's worth this way."

"I'm sorry. If you would rather see Marcus perform for the 6th time, I can arrange for the usher to take you back out."

The pair shared a light laugh together.

"I'm just messing with you. I'm happy to be back here with you. Kind of neat to see the wizard that's behind the curtain."

"Would you like something to drink? They have all sorts of sodas and alcohol if you want something stronger."

Sandy just laughed.

262

"What's funny about soda?"

Sandy kept laughing.

"Was it something I said?"

When the laughter subsided, Sandy was able to explain.

"It's just funny to me that people from the North call it soda. In the south, they call it pop. Over in Texas, we just call it coke."

"What if you want a Sprite instead of a coke. What do you call it then?"

"We just call all of it a coke."

"Doesn't it get a little confusing? When you want a Sprite and ask for a coke?"

"There's a lot of pointing to the menus in Texas."

Again, they shared a nice laugh before Sandy sat down next to Paul.

"I'm actually ok for the moment. I drank some *coke* out on the boardwalk earlier while I was watching the surf."

"About that...you kind of spilled a big story in a few minutes. Care to fill in some of the gaps with a stranger you just met?"

"How much time do you have?"

"Honestly, about 45 minutes give or take five. Depends on how much my fellow performers interact with the crowd."

"I notice there's a big difference in the crowds between locations. I never knew that before. I have been to many concerts before and didn't realize the crowd makes the show."

Paul got up to pour himself a whiskey on ice. Turning back to the couch, he tried to be a gracious host.

"Are you sure I can't get you anything?"

"Not right now. Maybe after I tell you my story."

"Cool."

Sitting back down, Paul took a drink of his whiskey and followed up on the conversation after the slight delay.

"It's not very often a fan realizes that secret about performances. I have to tell you, with all else the same, the audience makes all the difference in the world. When you are on a tour like this one, you play the same songs every night. Sometimes, you don't even know what town you are playing in until the announcer says it. You come out, play the notes, sing the words and wait for the response. I have nights when I have played like crap and the crowd brings down the house with applause. Other times, I am on fire and everything is jamming and all I get is polite clapping. Makes no sense but it is interesting you see that."

"I guess there is some advantage to becoming a groupie."

Paul took another drink of his whiskey before moving the conversation forward. He was anxious to fill in the gaps in her story but he knew they would be crossing some invisible bridge towards something closer than strangers in the night.

"About that...you were going to tell me the whole story not just the abridged version that you gave me out on the beach."

Sandy looked down at her hands as she rubbed them together. She also knew she was venturing into uncharted territory with Paul and was not sure where they were going with the conversation.

"I'm not sure where to start."

"You know...as a songwriter...there is a simple formula. All good songs start with an intro or a prelude. Maybe it's a few notes, maybe a whole refrain. Then the song moves into the first verse and then a break into the chorus. That sequence repeats itself several times until the song tells its story. That being said, tell me your intro. Where are you from Sandy Taylor?"

Sandy smiled. Talking to a musician about anything always goes back to the music. She loved the way their conversations flowed.

"Well, I grew up in Minnesota of all places so I am not a stranger to the cold. When I met my ex-husband, we moved to Texas for his work."

"What did he do?"

"He was an advertising executive. I should have known from day one that a person who spends their lives manipulating people to buy different things would try to manipulate me."

Paul smiled. "See, and just like that you went from your intro into your first verse. Carry on, just like the song says."

"Ah, the 'B' side reference. I like it. Do you live and breathe music Paul?"

"It's all that I know and all that I want to be. So, let it be..."

"I should have known better. Will there always be music in our discussions Mr. Buttery?"

"As long as blood flows through my instrument and a song is my soul..."

"I don't know that one."

"Just some lyrics flowing through my head along with a million others. So, back to your first verse..."

"Ok. yea...so we started living in Texas..."

Sandy went on telling her whole story from the beginning of her relationship with her husband to the ugly ending. Paul thought in his musical prose that when the husband ran off with the secretary it was probably the third verse of her song but he let her continue. The story kind of faded out without a real ending so he gathered it was musical destiny that way.

"Five minutes Paul."

The stage hand gave him his warning to get into place for the segue act. It was still not time for his full act but he was in the next group coincidentally with Landon and Fo'i.

"I'm sorry to cut this short. I've got to go do my thing now. Do you want to wait for me here or go back out there?"

"Did I not bore you enough? You must be a glutton for punishment."

"Well, I found your story intriguing but it was definitely one sided. You don't know anything about me yet."

"I know I like to hear you sing."

"Well, then, come on. I'll have the usher bring you back out. You can come on back after the segue piece. I won't have as long next time but we can still chat. How's that sound?"

Sandy smiled. "Like everything else you play; it sounds perfect to me."

The pair exited the green room and went their separate ways. Paul went to take his place to go back onstage and Sandy followed the usher back to her seat. They had each gone into the discussion with unknown expectations and crossed the bridge together. On the other side, they both realized they were now something more than strangers in the night.

9 PM

Ladies and gentlemen...welcome back to the stage...Landon Noland, Fo'i Meleah and Paul Buttery...

Sandy was already in her seat as the trio took the stage from the two Nicole's. Apart from the previous segments with Marcus and Nicole, Act 2 was all about the three performers. Paul could not help but wonder the road that lay ahead. He would not be sandwiched in the middle of the show any longer. Marcus kicked things off and Micah drove them all home. In the middle, the other four kept the crowd wanting more. Even though Paul was the last act before Micah, he understood the hierarchy of things. If you are not first and not last, you are just a filler.

The trio kicked in their number as the audience responded well. Even while Paul was singing, he could not help but think back to his conversation with Sandy about the audience making the show. The joint was rocking and more than half of the crowd was on their feet dancing and clapping along. While there was never a meter that measured audience participation, this was a great sign. Marcus and Nicole had rocked the house and they were hungry for more. Even though Landon and Fo'i had their solo acts ahead, there was hope that the audience would still be on their feet by the time Paul took the stage.

Sandy was smiling on the exterior but she was thinking deeply about her conversation with Paul. Had she revealed too much? In reality, she had known the man for one day. They had seen each other as she went from performance to performance sitting in the front row, but they had not officially met until earlier in the day. Could she really be having feelings for this man that was just passing through like Brigadoon? At the end of the evening would they have anything to hold on to besides memories of the day? Would she have to wait another 100 years to experience the warmth and compassion that the two had shared? With all that she had gone through with her ex-husband, she remained skeptical of love.

In her flow with the universe, she fully intended to follow the tour for the next week. According to the playbill, they were moving up the Florida coast through Miami, Ft. Lauderdale and Daytona Beach. When they played their final show in

St. Augustine, she would be lined up with Interstate 10 and choices would have to be made. Where would she go from there? I-10 would take her 'home' to Texas and the bad memories that awaited her there. She could continue going north on Interstate 95 to all points North or she could park herself in Florida and create a new life. So many choices, so many questions and just a week to figure it all out.

From the stage view, Paul looked out into the audience and could only see one fan smiling and cheering him on. Sure, there were a chattering of chicks in the audience all screaming and giving him their bedroom eyes. Before the night was through, he was certain that more than one of them would be throwing their panties up on stage and screaming out their love and devotion until the end of time. He could take any one of them back to the boarding house or simply to the beach beyond the boardwalk and have a passing fling. They would be nameless, faceless and he would leave nothing behind but a memory to some lucky young lady of bedding a rock star. It was enough for some, but he yearned for more.

Paul's career was definitely heading in the right direction. The fall tour with him headlining had changed everything. The fact that the holiday tour on top of that would give him a little bit of security added whipped cream and a cherry to an otherwise great tasting day. Was he dancing with the devil by entertaining Sandy? Could there be any type of future with a woman he had just had a couple of casual conversations with? She had been in his sights for the past couple weeks but the connection was made just today.

They had a handful of shows left in Florida before they had their finale in St. Augustine. From there he would fly solo back to New York while the rest of his fellow performers went their separate ways. The two Nicole's were heading out west while the rest of them would return to their nearby homes in the south. Landon and Fo'i would be meeting him up in New York in a few weeks but what about the time in between? Was there a possibility that he didn't have to take that flight back to New York alone? As he danced around the stage and waited for his turn to sing, he wondered if there was a VW Beetle waiting to take him on a road trip up the coast. He could think of worse ways to get back to New York but he could not imagine a better way to travel there than to be with Sandy at his side.

9:20 PM

The trio wrapped up as Landon took over the stage and started driving the young girls wild. He kicked off his set with an Elvis tune and gyrated his hips until the old were filled with envy and the young were weak in the knees. Fo'i and Paul exited stage left and right respectively and they could feel the roar of the crowd behind them as he brought down the house. The audience in the Florida Keys was electric and they were all super-charged towards a fabulous performance.

Fo'i resolved to wait in the wings. She would take over the stage in 15 or 20 minutes depending on how much Landon milked the crowd. In some ways, she was the calm between the storms. Like the Nicole's, she was sandwiched between two power house performances yet remained true to her brand. She was a highly talented guitar player and her smiling presence brought warmth and comfort to the stage after Landon tore the audience apart. She brought them all together and the feeling was akin to a Christmas Homecoming.

Paul, on the other hand, had a little spring in his step. His usual calm, cool and collected stride had a little momentum to it. Heading towards the green room, he looked forward to conversing with Sandy again gaining more clarity. It was odd to say the least but love stories were written on less. Since they were in each other's presence for weeks, he would not clarify it as love at first sight but could there be love blossoming in the green room? He looked forward to finding out the answer to that question as he arrived at the same time Sandy was being ushered back.

"Hey there stranger, did you miss me?"

"How could I miss you when you were dancing and singing right in front of me?"

"So tell me. Was I the best one on the stage?"

Sandy laughed. "Let's just say you were my favorite on the stage. Is that enough to stroke your ego, Paul?"

Paul laughed in return. "Fair enough fair maiden. Shall we have a seat?"

Sandy came in and took a seat while Paul walked over to the mini bar set up. Pouring himself another glass of whiskey, he turned to his guest.

"Have you reconsidered your drink selection?"

The smile melted away the ice in his glass.

"Do you have the ability to make me a martini?"

Paul raised his eyebrows. He liked a woman that could handle a stiff drink.

"Shaken or stirred?"

"Shaken *not* stirred…and make it a vodka martini please."

Paul chuckled. "Why, yes, Mrs. Bond. Coming right up."

"That's Ms. Bond to you, sir."

"I stand corrected."

Paul went about making the martini, shaking it and pouring it out to a glass. Adding an olive for good measure, he presented the drink to the lady sitting on the couch.

"Do I need to ask where you acquired an affinity to martini's ma'am?"

"You don't stay married to an advertising executive without attending an endless parade of cocktail parties. The fruity drinks with the umbrellas were fine for the women passing through, but for those of us that had to endure the life day in and day out it was martinis that eased the pain."

"Well that makes total sense. I suppose a toast is in order."

The pair raised their glasses and clinked in mid-air.

"To possibilities…"

"I'll drink to that."

The couple each drank a sip of their drinks and savored the taste before moving forward with the conversation.

"How long do you have this time?"

"Depending on the crowd, somewhere around half hour. Landon and Fo'i will keep them going but I have to take over after that."

"Then you have a full set before Micah joins you on set?"

"Wow. You ought to be the new Stage Manager. You have this sequence down pat. Do you remember what happens after Micah's set?"

"Then you all get on stage for the finale."

Paul put down his drink and clapped. "Very impressive."

"I pay attention. I'm not just a pretty face."

"Damn, doll. You are a *beautiful* face. Don't sell yourself short."

Sandy blushed. "Flattery will get you everywhere, Mr. Buttery. But this time, the conversation is about you."

"What would you like to talk about?"

"Well, start with your intro and let the song write itself…"

"Ah, the student becomes the teacher…teach the children well…"

"Are you going to hide behind song lyrics or are you going to tell your story?"

Paul laughed. He enjoyed being challenged. "Ok, Ok. It's really not that exciting. I am just a New Yorker, tried and true."

"So, you were born there?"

Paul explained how he was born in the Bronx and detailed his life from there. He told her about his piano lessons as a child, his vocal lessons as a teen, and his launch to become a performer along the way. He spoke to the dives he played in to get to where he finally got a break and then segued to his current tour.

"This Greg McDonald? He seems to think highly of you."

"I guess, doll. He signed me for this tour and two more to come."

Sandy took a drink of her martini before venturing further.

"So tell me about this new tour. What's that going to be like?"

Paul smiled. "I can't tell you much besides the fact that he asked me to headline it. I will be the top billing. Apparently he is signing Landon and Fo'i as well but that's it from the current group."

"Where does the tour go this time?"

"To me, that's the best part. We kick it off in New York City and then travel New England for two months."

"I hear New England is gorgeous in the fall."

"Have you never been?"

"No. I've seen pictures in Life magazine but that's as close as I've gotten to it."

"Well, you are definitely missing a slice of life, doll."

"Maybe I will see it soon."

They both came to an abrupt halt at the sound of the statement in the air. Was Sandy seriously considering following Paul on his fall tour? Would she be welcome? How would Paul feel if that was the path of her course?

"Is that something you would consider? What is waiting for you back in Texas?"

Sandy looked down at her glass and twisted it in circles in her hand. "That is the million-dollar question."

"Which one?"

"What is waiting for me in Texas. The answer is nothing. I came on this road trip to get away from Texas. I have no plans on going back any time soon. There's nothing back there but my ugly past. I prefer to look in other directions for a brighter future."

"Five minutes, Paul."

Once again the stage hand gave him the warning to get ready to take the stage. It was finally his turn to take the show to a new level. His set was going to have new meaning as he wanted to set the tone for his new tour.

"I guess it's time again, doll."

"I guess so."

Sandy finished her drink and put it on the table with the other used glasses. As she turned back towards Paul, she was surprised by how close he was behind her. She froze looking up to his eyes as he pulled her to him and kissed her by surprise. Backing her head away for the moment, she didn't know whether to slap him or embrace him. In a split second, she made the decision to the latter. Leaning forward, she kissed him warmly. Although it lasted for a few seconds, they both felt the clock ticking over them.

"Can you come back after my set?"

"I...sure...I guess...won't your time be limited?"

"I'll have around 20 minutes before the finale. Micah's set goes a little longer. Would you come back?"

Before she could answer, the stage hand reappeared with the urgent warning.

"Two minutes, Paul. You have to get out there."

Paul stood there in silence waiting for Sandy to answer.

"Yes, yes. I'll come back. Now go before you keep the crowd waiting."

Paul hustled out the door smiling broadly. The stage hand followed him quickly to make sure that he was going to make his entry on time. The techs all knew how the talent seemed to stray when they were supposed to be on stage.

The usher waited patiently for Sandy to come out of her frozen state before escorting her back out to her seat. When she finally came out of her trance, Fo'i was taking her bows and Paul was already entering the stage. In more ways than one, she needed to make a move before the Paul Buttery train left the station.

10 PM

Welcome back to the stage...the Italian Stallion himself...Mr. Paul Buttery...

The crowd went wild as Fo'i took her leave of the stage and Paul entered. Walking to the center of the stage, he grabbed the main microphone and started singing a Tom Jones song. With the women screaming he looked down just in time to see Sandy take her place in the front row. Her face was still flush from the kiss they shared before he took the stage and she glowed radiantly.

Paul was on fire. It had been a night to remember and it was not over yet. With his career taking off in the right direction, he belted out the song with confidence and euphoria. There is an old adage in show business that if you are smiling enough, people will never hear the wrong notes. Not a soul in the audience at the Ocean Beach Concert Hall would hear a stray note from the Italian singer as he was beaming from ear to ear.

When the entrance song ended, the crowd erupted with applause. Not a single soul was sitting as they paid Paul the highest compliment of a standing ovation. He was truly bringing down the house. In the control room Greg McDonald was already counting the money he was going to make off the singer on the upcoming tours. His smile was just as large as Paul's but for different reasons. He knew he was making the right business decision to headline him.

"How's everyone doing out there?"

The audience screamed all manner of cheers and accolades in response to the performers question.

"Are you having a great time?"

"*Yes!*" The answer was a resounding yes.

"All of us here on the tour are having a great time too." Looking down at Sandy in the front row he winked at her and she smiled back. Of course every female in the audience thought that he was winking at them and once again the screams erupted. As they continued to hit new decibel levels in the concert hall, Paul crossed over to his piano and sat down. He started playing intro music and the crowd settled down.

"Now all night long you've been listening to some groovy tunes from the cool cats I'm touring with, but now it's time to tickle the ivories. If you thought rock and roll was limited to those guitar playing riffs, you ain't seen nothing yet."

Popping out of the intro and letting his fingers fly across the piano keys, Paul entered into a three song montage from Jerry Lee Lewis. Looking down, he saw that Sandy had joined the rest of the women and was dancing along by her seat as he belted out the song. There was something magical about the moment and he felt as though he was playing just for her. In the flick of an instant, all the other people in the audience were reduced to background noise and he could only see and hear Sandy cheering him on.

The montage ended and Paul stood up from his piano bench and waved as once again the audience rose to their feet for a standing ovation. Waiting for the applause to die down he took the seat once again and addressed the crowd.

"This next tune…"

"*We love you Paul…*" Someone from the audience cried out and the women resumed their screams towards the man.

"Thank you. I love you all too…but there is a special someone sitting in the audience tonight…she knows who she is…has put a little twinkle in my eye and an extra beat in my heart. For this lovely lady…this one's for you…"

Paul started playing an Elvis ballad and the noise in the crowd died down. Looking out, he could see women crying as they imagined him singing just for them. He often wondered why that was but the answer was simple. For many, music was a drug and they became intoxicated with it. In that state, anything is possible and their wildest imaginations run wild.

Looking down at Sandy, he saw real tears of joy rolling down her cheeks as she looked back at him with love in her eyes. They were clearly connected not simply by chance or happenstance. The conversations they had, the kiss, and now the ballad were stepping stones towards something bigger than they each thought was possible at the start of their day.

When the love song ended, Paul remained seated and so did the audience. The challenge with slowing things down with a ballad meant that the performer cooled down the excitement in the room. Heading into his last number, he would need to end with a show stomper that would get them all riled up again before Micah took the stage.

"Now before I kick off my last number, I want to say thank you for being such cool cats tonight. You have rocked this house and we are all loving you for it, can you dig?"

In one line he flicked the switch back on and the audience once again energized the concert hall with their applause. Before the noise level could die down, Paul kicked in to his final song, a Beatles tune that would surely send them all to their feet. In the middle of the song, the crowd was dancing and clapping their hands and Paul knew he had reached nirvana. They were all not only listening to the music but experiencing it, letting the notes flow through their bodies like electric current.

Finishing up his final note, Paul jumped to his feet as the crowd went wild. He took a bow at center stage and looked down at his new love interest with a broad smile. In response, she was beaming right back at him and the pair couldn't wait to both get back stage for more conversation. Paul was high on adrenaline from the performance and with a little bit of summer romance fever. The look on Sandy's face indicated she had the same ailment.

As Paul took his final bows, the announcer kicked in with signaled his departure from the stage.

Ladies and Gentlemen, let's hear it one more time for Paul Buttery. (as the crowd screamed their love for him, the next performer stood on the wings)

Now welcome back to the stage, the man from the Florida Keys himself... Micah Read.

The audience continued their frenzied applause as Paul exited off to the side and Micah entered the stage. The traveling show was often like a carousel ride with a seamless parade of talent going round and round. With 20 minutes left until the finale when all the performers would come back out, Paul hurried off to the green room to share his euphoric glow.

10:25 PM

"That was some performance Mr. Buttery."

Paul and Sandy were back in the green room. The performer was drinking some seltzer water to try and rehydrate after the set. Sandy was happy just to be back in his presence.

"You seem to be on top of your game tonight. Not that you weren't great at the other shows, but tonight was amazing."

"Thanks doll."

"Was it because of the upcoming tour or because this one is almost done?"

Paul stopped to ponder the question. "I guess a little of both...plus some other things I would guess."

Sandy smiled coyly. "Would I be one of those other things?"

"I guess you would Miss Taylor."

The two fell silent for a moment. They knew they didn't have much time but they were hesitant to push the conversation forward.

"That was some kiss before you took the stage, Paul. So, was it just to shake off performance jitters or was there something more behind it?"

"I never get performance jitters so you can rule that right out. I could perform in a stadium of people and not get nervous."

Sandy turned towards him on the couch.

"Do you get more nervous in a one on one setting?"

To answer her question, Paul leaned in and kissed her softly. Settling back, he gazed into her eyes and reached out for her hand.

"I'm not nervous. Are you?"

Sandy looked away for a moment before turning back to meet his gaze.

"I would be lying if I said I wasn't. I haven't kissed a man besides my ex-husband in a very long time."

Smiling, Paul broke the tension. "So, was it worth the wait?"

In response to his question, Sandy leaned forward and returned the kiss. Holding her hand, Paul pulled her closer before they both released.

"Definitely worth the wait."

Breaking away, he walked over to the wet bar and poured himself another glass of whiskey. He knew the clock was ticking and they only had a few more minutes before they would come for him.

"I have a question for you."

"Why do you sound serious all of a sudden?"

"Well, I have to go play a finale in a few minutes so I was just cutting to the chase."

"Ok. What's the question?"

Paul hesitated for a moment and then took a side road.

"Are you coming to the Miami show tomorrow?"

"Is that what you really wanted to ask me?"

Paul looked at her with a cautious response.

"That is part of it, yes."

Sandy smiled. She thought his shyness was endearing given his stage presence. Take away the crowd and he was just a young boy at heart.

"Yes, I plan on following the tour to Miami. Why stop now?"

Paul smiled and nodded. "That's good. That's really good."

"Five minutes to finale."

The stage hand returned as expected and time was short.

"Was that all you wanted to ask me?"

Paul turned and took a step towards her.

"Do you think we got something cool going on here, doll? I'm kind of digging on us and I just wanted to know if you were feeling anything like that at all."

Sandy rose and stepped towards him. Reaching out for him, they kissed long and passionately. When they broke apart, she took a step towards the door of the green room.

"Does that give you your answer, Mr. Buttery?"

"It does. It sure does."

"Two minutes."

"I have to go. Will I see you after the show?"

Smiling, Sandy grabbed his hand. "You can count on it. Now go give us a final number to remember."

Paul put a spring in his step and headed out to the stage to join the others. It was time to wrap up this concert but he had a feeling that is was just the beginning of a much bigger event of the heart.

11 PM

Ladies and Gentlemen...from all of us here at the 1970 Rock n Roll Musical Revue we want to thank you all for coming and listening to our talented performers. For one final bow...Landon Noland...Nicole Equerme...Marcus Gullen...Fo'i Meleah...Paul Buttery...and Micah Read...Goodnight Florida Keys...we love you...

All the performers left the stage while the audience was still giving them a standing ovation. The stage lights dimmed as the house lights came up and the applause diminished. The show was over and many would say it was the best one yet on summer tour. With only four more shows in the next week, it would be difficult to top this one.

The audience started to thin out as Sandy remained seated, not entirely certain where to go. Paul had asked if he would see her after the show but no concrete plans were made. She was certain that even if she could get backstage again she would be met with chaos. All the talent would be winding down from their show and packing up their instruments. The road crew would start tearing apart the set and loading out the equipment truck so that they could get a jump on the road to Miami. With no place to venture to yet, she stayed in her seat and watched the world revolve around her.

After fifteen minutes, the crowd was down to a few stragglers and an usher approached her from the backstage area.

"Ma'am? Is your name Sandy?"

Sandy answered cautiously.

"Yes it is."

"Paul Buttery sent me out. He told me to tell you to stay here for a few more minutes and he would be out shortly."

Sandy smiled. She would not be abandoned after all.

"Tell him I'll wait right here."

The usher ran off never to be seen from again. Sandy remained in her seat as she watched the stage hands work their elf magic and make the set slowly disappear. Ten minutes after the usher had come and gone, Paul came out from backstage.

"I'm sorry doll. Lots going on back there."

"I figured as such, I was going to give you five more minutes and then I would just see you in Miami tomorrow night."

"Well then I guess I came out just in time."

"The finale was great. I really think this was the best show that I've seen so far on the tour. Of course there are four more to try and top it."

"Will you be at all four?"

Sandy looked at him with a coy smile. "Sure, why not? In for a penny in for a pound. Isn't that what they say?"

"I'm glad to hear you are going to finish the tour with us."

Holding his hand, she looked up into his eyes. "The question remains, though. Will I see more of the show tomorrow night or less of it?"

"Do you regret missing parts of the show tonight?"

"Not for a New York minute."

Paul chuckled. "That's right. I heard that Texans had a phrase for us city folk in New York. I forgot for a moment that you are from there."

"We have a much better phrase for Italian piano players from New York."

Smiling, he replied. "Oh yeah? What's that?"

"Come over here and kiss me Stallion."

"I like that phrase much better."

Closing the gap between them, Paul pulled her close and kissed her warmly. Coming up for air, they separated slightly.

"So tell me Miss Taylor. What are your plans for tonight?"

Looking at her watch, she sighed.

"Tonight is coming to a close Mr. Buttery. I'm not in show business. I can't keep the late hours like you can. It's been a long night after a long day driving. I just want to get to my hotel and crash."

"Can I at least walk you to your car?"

"That would be wonderful. But don't you have to get on the tour bus?"

"Not tonight. They put us up at a boarding house across the street from here. After I walk you to your car I'm just going to walk over."

Taking his hand, she prompted the exit.

"Well, I've sat here long enough. Shall we get walking?"

The two left the concert hall hand in hand, exiting up the main aisle towards the back of the concert hall. In ironic coincidence, there was a small crowd of fans waiting by the stage door to get autographs of some of the talent as they exited but no one expected Paul to just walk right out the front door. When they got into the parking area, the lights were dim and none of the people near their cars could make him out in the moonlight. As fewer cars were left at this hour, the VW Beetle stood out in its parking spot.

"So this is the famous Bug from your story."

Sandy rubbed her hand along the roof and smiled. "So it is. My pride and joy. Besides the house that I intend to sell, it is my only possession."

"Well, I think your ex-husband is a total fool. I think it's a great car. The VW Beetle has a lot of character to it."

"Is that the only reason you think he is a fool?"

Paul pulled Sandy in for a kiss. He held her passionately under the moonlight as the two of them became lost in the moment.

"I think he is a fool for letting you go. Can I ask you something, Sandy?"

"Again with the questions? Make it quick. It's almost midnight and I might turn back into a pumpkin."

Laughing, Paul continued.

"Do you believe in destiny Sandy?"

Settling back on her heals, she answered quickly without hesitation.

"How could I not? I had no idea where I would end up when I left Texas. I just got in my car and drove. This Beetle brought me to your doorstep. I think that is the definition of destiny."

"That's what I was thinking too. I think that everything in life happens for a reason. There was a reason our paths met and connected. I'm not sure where tomorrow will bring us besides a gig in Miami, but I am glad that you will be there to share it with me."

Leaning forward, they shared another kiss.

"On that note, I really should be going. We can pick this back up in Miami tomorrow. How does that sound?"

Paul was smiling from ear to ear.

"I think that sounds great."

As Sandy reached for her car door, Paul pulled her back for one last hug and a kiss. Releasing her he held on to her hand.

"Can I ask you one more thing Sandy?"

She smiled even though the exhaustion of the day was taking over.

"One more Paul and that's all you get. I don't care how cute you are this gal has got to get to bed."

Paul hesitated only for a moment and then acted instinctively from the heart.

"I was just wondering...would you like to see New England in the fall?"

<u>New Year's Eve Gala</u>

You are cordially invited to the wedding of

Sandy Debra Taylor
To
Paul Michael Buttery

Where: Four Season Hotel, NY, NY
When: December 31, 1970 8PM
Dinner and Reception to follow featuring musical performances by...
Fo'i Meleah...
Landon Noland...
Nicole Equerme...
Micah Read...
Marcus Gullen...
And the groom... Paul Buttery...

Saturday

AT THE SHADOWLAND RANCH

1

"Today, we gather on this crisp October morning, to pay respects to our friend, our brother, and our gilded cowboy, Hank Peterson. Like the cattle that roam this ranch, Hank was a driving force in all of our lives, determined to take life by the horns. He was confident. He was direct. But he also had a tender side that was brought out by his wife and children. Evelyn Peterson stood by Hank's side, through thick and thin for the greater part of her life. While Hank built this ranch up over the years, Evelyn gave him a homestead to raise his three children and give him comfort until his passing day..."

The small crowd was seated on the edge of the East pasture where Hank would have his final resting place. Staying with Montana tradition, the rancher would be buried with his ranch. In the great cycle of life, once the grass grew back over the gravesite, the cattle would graze on it until they would move to the slaughterhouse. Since this herd of cattle was just a month away from their big day, the cycle would have to wait until next year.

Seated on one side of the casket was the immediate family. Evelyn his widow, along with Wesley, Fred, and Anastasia, the surviving children, were all in the front row. Various ranch hands and other employees of Shadowland Ranch were seated in the chairs behind them. There were not many relatives to fill the other seats on this side of the make-shift aisle but the few that were there blended into the background.

On the other side of the casket were people from the Cattlemen's Association and folks from around Fergus County. Some had traveled out from Lewistown or Denton and others came from the cattle ranches that were spread throughout the county. Seated in the front row on that side was a who's who in the county.

Jack Hampton was the Mayor of Fergus County and he had the rightful place nearest to the casket across the aisle from the widow. Besides his political stature in the county, Hank and Jack had been best friends. One always warned the other when political currents and opinions were shifting and action was needed to please the masses. In return, Jack always had an open ear to what the other ranchers were doing and how it would affect things over at Shadowland Ranch. Jack was a regular at Sunday dinners and other social gatherings over at the ranch. He would be the first to speak after the Pastor had his say.

Sitting in the chair next to Jack Hampton was the head of the Cattlemen's Association, Bill Foster. "Old Iron Shoes" had been given the nickname years earlier when he would throw horseshoes at his ranch hands when he was displeased with their work. When one too many of them ended up in the hospital with bleeding heads and concussions, Bill received a visit from the county Sherriff, Jay Monsky. There was no paperwork drawn up and no man ever was brave enough to bring charges against Foster, but the message was clear. If Bill continued to bean his men off the head with iron horse shoes, there would be hell to pay and he would find himself in the back of Jay's patrol car with a set of matching handcuffs. While the method of his rage changed after that, he kept the nickname. Now, he simply ruled with fear across the whole county by his ruthless tactics.

Seated next to Foster for the next three seats were his muscle. They had no business paying respects to Hank Peterson since they had many a run in with the man over the years. The fact remained that their boss never went anywhere without them. All three men were packing side arms in concealed gun holsters under their jackets. The irony that they were attending the funeral for a man they had all three pointed their shotguns at was not lost on any of them.

The second row began a host of secondary characters from around the county starting with the Sherriff. Sitting behind the Mayor, he was there for silent protection but also had a great amount of respect for the deceased. Hank never stepped out of line and was generally a man of even temperament when it came to disputes among the ranchers. Jay knew far too well that the death of the head of Shadowland meant a distinct shift on power. Hank Peterson was truly the only strong opposition Bill Foster ever faced on a myriad of issues. If the other ranchers rose up against an issue, it was generally because that was the opinion of Hank and they were falling in line behind him. Now, without any bull to lead the charge, Foster would plow over any man that would get in his way.

Sitting next to the Sherriff were the heads of three of the nearby ranches. Mitch Hagland was a relative newcomer to the county, having bought his ranch ten years' prior from a bankrupt drunk who had driven the ranch into the trenches while he soaked his liver. Politically, he sat on the fence on many of the issues brought up through the county and the Cattlemen's Association. It was a common opinion that Mitch's vote could be bought for a price and bargaining chip on any matter at hand.

To his left was Roy Benally, the modern day equivalent of tribal heritage. The Navajo reservation was disbanded years prior but Roy's ancestry with the tribe put him in line to run the ranch as an active business. No longer receiving government subsidies, he had to turn a profit like the other ranchers around him. The main difference was that the ranch hands he commanded were formerly of the Navajo Nation and lived on the land for free in return for their daily labor. Compared to the other ranches in the county, Roy's ranch had the lowest amount of turnover and the most seasoned employees around.

At the end of the row was Dylan Shepard. The rancher was the closest in proximity to Shadowland Ranch and probably second in friendly relations to the Peterson family behind the Mayor. Dylan ran Dolomite Crystal Ranch. His father was a miner back in the day before he got into the cattle business and gave the ranch it's unique name. Dylan had never married and was thought to be the most eligible bachelor of the county, even though his age was far from that of the average young buck in competition. Like Hank, he was always level headed in relations with others and became close with the deceased over the years due to their peaceful business practices. If there was going to be any opposition to Foster going forward, it would most likely be Dylan. A quiet man, the general opinion was that he would not be leading any brigades against Iron Shoes any time soon.

The Pastor continued. "As you all know, Hank's love for horses and well-intentioned nature is what led to his untimely demise. He didn't want any of his ranch hands to get harmed taming that mustang and took it upon himself to climb in that corral with it. The call of the west took his spirit that day but his legend will last forever..."

One of the three musclemen sitting next to Bill Foster chuckled. The talk of the local saloon was that Hank was a fool to get in that corral with that mustang. As the owner of the ranch, he could have sent any of his paid hands in there to do the work. The fact that he took it upon himself to do it was not bravery but stupidity in the eyes of lesser men. As the chuckle was heard throughout the small crowd, the tension grew. Evelyn saw that Wesley's hand clenched into a fist and she placed a calming hand over his. She did not want her oldest son to get into a brawl at her husband's funeral for any reason.

"...Before I give the final blessing, I understand Mayor Hampton would like to say a few words."

Jack Hampton rose from his chair and approached the podium. Reaching out his hand, he thanked the Pastor for his kind words about his friend. Behind him, members in the crowd silently hoped that Jack would not launch into some kind of half-baked political rant. Give a politician a soap box and you never knew what was going to come out of their mouth.

"Thank you Pastor. I am certain Hank would have appreciated your blessing in the wake of this tragedy. Dear friends of Fergus County, I am truly humbled to speak to you today about my friend and yours, Hank Peterson..."

At the very sound of the words, Jack and Evelyn both turned to view the reaction from Bill Foster. They were clearly not friends and his attendance at Hank's funeral was more insulting than an honor. Foster kept a face of stone as Jack continued.

"Over the years, I had the honor and privilege to become close friends with

Hank and the Peterson family. So many evenings I was treated to a fine meal here at the Shadowland Ranch while we talked about everything under the sun. Hank was a devout man to his land, to his family, to his community and to his church. There was never an ask that was too great as the man was benevolent with his time and attention to all. The people that worked here at the ranch were never thought of as his employees but rather friends. As it was in the end, he often put their needs before his own in the daily operation of the ranch..."

This time it was Foster himself who broke a smile. He often criticized Hank publicly for being a *soft ruler* of his ranch by letting everyone and everything get in his way of success. Time and time again, Foster had made offers to buy the land and turn it into *real profit* but Hank always turned him away. The departed man's philosophy was that it was much better to be a proper human being than make a few dollars by cutting wages and expecting more from his employees. Foster would have and could have crushed them all if the ranch was part of his domain. He despised the fact that he could never get his hands on it.

"In the community, Hank was a friend to all. During tough times when we all encountered the drought, it was Hank and Evelyn giving of themselves to help other. He led the charge to irrigate the flow of the river to allow access to all and not simply to keep his cattle fulfilled. His own herd may have weighed a few pounds less at the end of that season but he was content knowing he had helped others save their livelihood..."

Mitch Hagland nodded in deep appreciation. He was just a few years in when that drought occurred and he knew well that if the river irrigation had not occurred, he would have ended up like his predecessor and gone bankrupt before his herd ever saw the slaughterhouse. Men like Foster would have jumped at the opportunity to capitalize on his misfortune and he was forever grateful to Hank and the other ranchers for getting him through the tough time.

"To his Native American friends, Hank was a gentleman to all. He helped Roy Benally and his ranch by helping them navigate through our extensive and diverse system of ranches. Lending his business expertise, he never saw Roy or any of the other ranchers as competition. They were all friends to him working towards a simple goal to all work peacefully in life. In Hank's mind, there was enough land and cattle in Montana to make everyone happy. There was no reason to squabble over petty difference..."

This time, it was the Mayor's turn to give petty glances. He hated having someone like Foster in their community. The endless greed and despiteful tactics that the man used were no way to do business in this county or any other for that matter. Jack Hampton considered Bill Foster to be a stain on their otherwise beautiful county. He longed for the day to be rid of him and wished that it was Foster and not his friend that was being buried today.

"In conclusion..."

The Mayor, like any other public speaker, knew when it was time to wrap things up. He saw the pain on Evelyn's face and did not wish to prolong the inevitable. The rest of the crowd were itching to get on with their lives but Jack wanted one final reminder before they departed.

"...I would like to call on the community of Fergus County this morning to be a family. We have lost one of our best friends and citizens and in doing so have left the Peterson family without their patriarch. Let us come together and wrap our loving arms around them and give them the love and support they need and deserve in the days, weeks and months ahead. Getting through a day like today is hard enough. Resuming operations of the Shadowland Ranch is a more daunting task than any of us can imagine. Evelyn, Wesley, Fred and Annie need all of us to be their family, to assist them in getting past any obstacles that come upon them on the horizon. God Bless one and all."

Stepping away from the podium, Jack walked up to Evelyn who stood, along with the children, to greet him. With tears rolling down her cheeks, she hugged him warmly.

"Thank you so much, Jack. That was beautiful. Hank would have loved it."

"No he wouldn't. He would have said we were spending too much time on nonsense and you know it."

The widow chuckled lightly. She knew it was true. Taking a moment before the Pastor reclaimed the podium, Jack paid his respects to the children. Putting out his hand, Wesley shook it stiffly.

"You're the man of the ranch now, Wes. It's up to you to take care of things. Are you up to the challenge?"

Wesley stiffened his back to stand up straighter.

"Yes, sir."

"...and you Fred? Are you ready to work with your brother? I've seen younger men than both of you take over ranches. As men in your 20s, you have more stamina that most of the men here. Don't get pushed around. I'll come around in a few days so we can all sit and discuss things."

Fred was just as polite as his older brother.

"Yes, sir."

"...and Annie. Dear Anastasia. Be there for your mother. She will need you more than ever in the days ahead."

"Yes, Mr. Hampton."

Pausing for Jack to get back to his seat, the Pastor resumed.

"If we could all bow our heads for the final blessing..."

The Pastor took out all the stops and most people in attendance wiped away their wet eyes before all was said and done. The exception was the cold hearted man and his hired muscle sitting in the front row. For them, they couldn't wait for the ceremony to be over so they could throw some dirt and walk away.

With the final blessing given, those in attendance filed by the grave site one by one and took part in the ancient ritual of throwing dirt on the coffin. The Pastor kicked things off by stating the phrase from Genesis...

"...for dust you are and to dust you shall return."

Jack watched as Foster and his men smirked tossing the dirt. They were happy to be rid of their opposition and even happier that they didn't have to be the ones to do it. Walking in the direction of the main house, they would appear cordial yet brief at the reception that followed before taking their leave. When the crowd had dwindled down and all were in route to the reception, Jack and Dylan Shepard stood to the side as Evelyn and the children wept in their final goodbyes. They would accompany the family back to the house when it was over and provide a blanket of protection against the wolves that were already circling the wagons.

2

Gatherings on a cattle ranch were always a large production. Whether it be a wedding, a funeral, or any other celebration of life, there was always plenty of food to go around for all. By midday, the barbeque was in full swing with a seemingly endless supply of fresh meat sizzling over the hot coals. A large event tent was erected next to the main house and all of the guest's tables had been set up under it. Much like the seating arrangement at the funeral service itself, everyone had separated off into their own comfort zones.

The ranch hands along with the rest of the staff from Shadowland Ranch were taking care of all the accommodations and cooking, leaving the family members to sit back and be taken care of by others. This enabled them to grieve in their own ways while in the public eye. Hank Peterson's life would be celebrated for hours and the family would not be able to recoil to the privacy of the house until the evening.

Evelyn was the center of attention and was closely being protected by Jack and Dylan. People would come by, pay their respects and move along to the food area with limited conversation due to the men that flanked her. This was all fine by Evelyn as she was simply trying to get through the day. The men were on high alert as Bill Foster and his bodyguards approached.

"Evelyn. I wanted to come by and offer my deepest condolences. Hank was a good man and he passed far too soon."

The widow tensed as she knew they were false praises for her dead husband. She was well aware of Foster and the bad blood between him and Hank. She also knew that he would present her with the greatest challenges as she tried to hold the ranch together in the coming months.

"Thank you, Bill. It was nice of you to attend the service. Hank would have been pleased that the Cattlemen's Association was well represented."

"He was a valued member, ma'am. His absence will be deeply felt in the organization as we move past harvesting."

"I am certain your meetings will be much quieter without my husband raising his concerns about the agenda."

Bill Foster felt the slight sting from the widow and thought it best to let the words pass without opposition.

"Hank was a very passionate man about the cattle business. Please let me know if the Association can be of any assistance getting the herd to auction."

Dylan Shepard and the Mayor both responded at the mention of business.

"Today is a day to celebrate Hank's life. Let's not cloud it with any talk of business. Besides, Jack and I will make sure that the family is taken care of."

"Of course, of course. I also know you both have your own responsibilities. If I can be of service in any way, please let me know."

With that, Foster and his goons tipped their hats towards the widow and moved along. They would not be staying for any of the food or further discussions. There was plenty of both back on their ranch and there was no use in mingling where they knew they were not welcome.

"So nice of him to slither by,"

"Be nice Dylan."

"That man's a snake, Evelyn and you know it. It would be best if you steer clear of him and his people."

"He is the head of the Cattlemen's Association. I'm not sure how much I can steer clear of him moving forward. As long as he holds the power in our business, we all have to deal with him."

"Well, you just leave that up to Dylan and I. We'll make sure the boys have some good direction and backing when they have to deal with him."

"My boys are going to get eaten alive by him at the first chance he gets."

Patting her hand, Jack tried to re-assure her before the next well-wisher approached.

"Don't you fret Evelyn. We will be there sitting right next to the boys when they attend their first meeting. Until then, all they have to do is worry about getting the herd to auction."

"So, there's not a meeting before then?"

"Well, the slaughter cattle auction is six weeks away so there will be one more before then. That's where they determine the order at the sale barn."

"What do they have to do there?"

"Evelyn. Don't you worry about that. Like I told Foster, today is not the day to talk business. Jack and I will make sure the boys are ready. Besides, it's a silent raffle when it comes to that. They have to pick a number out of a hat."

The widow nodded. She was reasonably certain her boys could do that but looking over at them at the moment, she had her doubts. Across the other side of the event tent, the two boys were sitting with a small group of ranch hands. They were all drinking beer and given the number of empties that were already on the table, there was certain to be trouble later in the day.

"How old are you now, Wes?"

"I'm 29. I'll be 30 come spring. Fred's 25 but he'll turn 26 in January."

The cowboy simply shook his head.

"You got a problem with that?"

"Nope. Not a problem exactly. I just never had a boss that was so young before. Your daddy was a good man and treated us right. Long as you and your brother carry on your father's legacy, there ain't gonna be a problem with any of us."

The other men nodded their heads in agreement.

"Well, our father always groomed us for this day. We've been driving cattle since we both were old enough to sit on a horse. That parts easy. Long as we got a horse and a saddle, we'll be alright."

"We know. We've been riding alongside you boys ever since I can remember. You're right. That parts easy and there's not a man here on the ranch that doubt you can rope a stray calf when the time comes. But there's more to running a cattle ranch than just wrangling cattle. You got to have the smarts to deal with the business end. All of us men like to get paid regularly."

It was Fred's turn to jump in. "We got that covered. We'll make sure of it. Our mother has been savvy enough to keep money flowing for years. With help from the Mayor and the other ranchers, we'll make sure we keep getting top dollar for the herd."

The ranch hands seemed happy with that response but a couple remained skeptical and it was evident on their face.

"What's eating you now, Lucas. My brother told you we'll take care of things."

The two men looked at each other until one gave the nod, approving to proceed.

"With all due respect, Wes. It's not just the cattle or the price per hundredweight we gonna get at auction that you boys got to worry about. There's more than a stray bear or bobcat out there that are gonna bite you in the ass."

Wes put his beer on the table and looked at the man with seriousness.

"Meaning?"

"Listen, Wes. Your old man was the best. He really was. Never had to think about the other ranchers when he was around. Everyone kept in their own lane and did their own thing. Old Foster was gunning for him, though. With Hank barely gone, you seen him circling the drain. He was only here today to show his strength. He was just pissing on his cactus so the other coyotes know that he intends to mark his territory. You boys gonna be able to keep him at bay?"

"I reckon so. Fred and I will do whatever it takes to look after the ranch. You hear that straight from my mouth. No one is going to take any part of what our father built and protected."

"Does that include your mother and your sister?"

Looking around the tent, the men eyed Evelyn sitting with the Mayor and the head of Dolomite Crystal Ranch. She looked like a wounded animal protected by two wolves.

"I think our mother will be just fine for now. Plenty of people like her and respect her. With those two men around, I'm sure nothing is going to harm her."

"So what about Annie?"

The men looked at the young woman with a mix of emotions. Having been the only Peterson family member to attend college, she had returned to the ranch just months previous. Annie was a beautiful blonde that used her looks to get what she wanted from men. Currently, she was getting two boys to fetch her some food as she sat there with a few of her female friends. Her brothers looked at each other and simply shook their heads.

"Anastasia is a Palomino. She is a horse of a different color and if we have one weak section of our herd, it would be her. For a college girl, she is as gullible as they come."

"So what's that mean?"

Both picking up their beers and taking a drink, it was Fred that finished first and answered.

"That means if someone is going to get to this family, it's not from Wes or I and definitely not by my mother. If you boys want to protect something around here, keep a watchful eye out for her. If a wolf is going to attack our cattle, they are coming for her first."

3

Anastasia Peterson was the all-American dream. She was blonde haired and blue eyed and when she donned a cowboy hat on top of head, she could be photographed and put on a poster with the best of them. The four years she attended the local high school were a blur to her brothers and father as they turned away every suitor that came to call. In classic form, she wore a cheerleader outfit for every Friday night game and in her senior year even had the captain nametag to sit on top of her cheerleading pyramid. Be it football star or rodeo winner, there was not a boy that was worthy enough to date their sister and daughter. She had the protection of the family and if anyone thought differently, they were run off the ranch faster than a wandering coyote.

All of that changed when Annie was offered a cheerleading scholarship to UCLA. The wandering scout that had come to their small town to look at a running back set eyes on a remarkable sideline sight. Forgetting about the running back altogether, the scout returned to UCLA and made the recommendation to the cheerleading squad that there was a star waiting to be captured out in the sticks of Montana. Two weeks later, the college representatives were sitting at the butcher block table in the kitchen of Shadowland Ranch with Evelyn and Hank Peterson along with their daughter Annie.

"A cheerleading scholarship? What the heck is that? I never heard such a thing."

The two reps smiled. It was something they heard often in response to their inquiries on the road.

"Well, Mr. Peterson, I can assure you that the scholarship is very much a real thing and many of the top universities offer them."

"Please explain, then. Do you want our daughter to be a professional cheerleader?"

The representative laughed.

"While we have had our share of girls go on to careers in cheerleading, that is not our sole intention. We would like your daughter to come cheer for the UCLA Bruins. It's as simple as that."

"You are going to pay our Annie to go stand on the sidelines and cheer for your football team? Is that what you are saying?"

"Yes and no. We don't pay Annie directly, Sir. We pay her tuition along with her room and board to the university. In return, she will be on the cheerleading squad for all the sports, not just football. While that program gets the most exposure, she will also cheer for the basketball team and others."

Annie sat quietly with nervous excitement. She wanted to jump at the offer but she knew her parents had to get all the questions and information out of their system, before she would be allowed to go.

"What about her schooling? What classes would she take?"

"That would be entirely up to your daughter, Mrs. Peterson. We have reviewed her GPA along with her transcripts and any of our schools housed at the university would be happy to have her. She can basically choose whatever major she is interested in and we will take care of the rest. She will be assigned a faculty advisor to guide her through course selection and her coach will take care of her cheerleading scholarship requirements."

Evelyn and Hank looked at each other in shock. They always figured their daughter would go to college but they never imagined it would be out of state, especially in California. Their sons were happy being ranchers but Anastasia was destined for so much more.

"What you are asking is a lot to take in. Our Annie is a simple country girl. Look around you. You are in the middle of Montana and did you see much around here?"

The two reps kept their best smiles on and simply shook their heads.

"Now you want this sweet girl to pick up and go to one of the biggest universities there is and live in a place like Los Angeles? Is that really what you are suggesting?"

Without hesitation, the rep replied.

"Absolutely. We want Annie enrolled for the fall term next year. This is her senior year. It's time to make choices. If you decide to send her, we can sign the paperwork right now."

Hank looked over at Evelyn and the two of them looked on to their daughter. Annie was sitting there like a wild bronco ready to come out of the rodeo chute.

"What do you think, kiddo? Do you want to be a big city girl and move to Los Angeles?"

The answer did not need to be vocalized. Annie jumped out of her seat and ran over to hug her parents. At the end of the night, Anastasia Peterson officially signed on to be a UCLA cheerleader.

The rest of the school year, Annie was dubbed 'the California Girl". In a graduating class of less than 100 students, she stood out in all categories. The

Captain of the cheerleader squad, straight A student and finally the Queen of the Prom. What she was not able to capture was the title of girlfriend. With an overprotective father and two brothers for chaperones, the boys were too afraid of what would happen if they dared to ask her out. Even the King of the Prom was nervous of being photographed with her. If her family saw the photo, what would be the punishment?

All of that changed the day Annie Peterson left for Los Angeles. Her whole family came to the airport to see her off and under their watchful eyes, she said goodbye to the life she once had. With every mile behind her, she felt liberated. She could talk to boys without worrying if one of her brothers would beat them up. She would meet people that had never even seen a horse let alone ride one. She looked forward to going out and eating a burger like other girls her age and never having to worry about which ranch the beef came from. She would become the California girl and leave the cattle world behind.

Los Angeles was everything she had read about and so much more. The lethal combination of her beauty, a cheerleader outfit and her new found freedom, Annie became a magnet to the opposite sex. Every day she received a myriad of offers and every night a different date. She quickly realized what she was missing all those years in high school and decided not to limit her experiences with just one man. In the back of her head, she knew she could never bring home a boyfriend so why would she set herself up for failure?

Each year she would come home for the Christmas break and that was enough country to remind her of why Los Angeles was so special. She skipped summer break by taking summer classes because she knew she would be forced to be out on the ranch herding cattle. By her sophomore year, she limited her holiday return home to barely a week and was home in L.A. in time for a New Year's Eve kiss with a new boy.

By her Junior year, she had all but forgotten about her family back in Montana. That year, she flew home for a 3-day holiday weekend and before the Christmas roast had barely cooled, she was on a return flight to the city. A few hours after she wiped the last bit of cow patty from her designer boot, she was back in the lap of luxury.

The senior year at UCLA proved to be a major disappointment for Anastasia. The final installment of her scholarship was paid to the bursar's office and she began to see the end of the road. With no more money coming in for food, housing and classes, she would be forced to find employment if she planned to stay in Los Angeles. Unfortunately, when you are a senior in college before you decide to grow up and look for a job, you are miles behind the competition. Since she had no intentions of becoming a professional cheerleader, she had not attended any auditions. Her degree had become nothing more than a piece of paper for her parents to hang in the living room at the ranch and she had no interest in pursuing any kind of work that would require her to punch a time clock.

On graduation day, Annie's parents flew in to LAX to share her big day with her. She had no idea that day that her father's life would be ended tragically just months later. If she had any foreshadowing, she would not have cried through the ceremony. Hank and Evelyn held hands with each other in the stands and cried with her. For them, the tears were full of pride and joy. For the princess at the ball, the fairy tale was over. Her wings had been clipped and she was being transported back to a world of horses, cows, and the Shadowland Ranch. It was the only job she would not have to interview for and the only one guaranteed not to have a time clock. Perhaps in the family business she would find a way to use the degree she had spent four years ignoring; a Bachelor of Arts Degree in Business Management.

4

Three days after the funeral, the reception tent had been taken down and the tables were all stored back in the barn. All the visitors had spent the weekend nursing their celebration of life hangovers and the cows in the herd were three days closer to the slaughterhouse. The Peterson family had begun their long, slow process of mourning and recovery.

Although Annie had been away for the last four years, she still pained for the loss of her father. Her brothers were distant and busy hiding their emotions among the cattle that roamed the ranch. In the absence of any comfort from a boyfriend, she went about her day simply going through the motions.

Evelyn was hiding her emotions well. Besides the tears shed at gravesite, she had put on a solid face whenever anyone was around. Privately, she rode her horse by Hank's grave countless times in the last few days. In every pass, she kept a firm upper lip and just gazed at the ground with the fresh dirt above it.

The ranch had resumed regular operations. Wesley and Fred were taking care of the herd along with a team of ranch hands while Evelyn and Annie directed the small staff at the homestead. The gardens were cared for without a hitch and from a crow's eye, all was back to normal. The exception, of course, were the constant gifts to remind the family of their loss.

Some sent flowers but it was well known that the gardens at Shadowland Ranch supplied the family with enough beauty year-round. Still others sent unique offerings as a token of remembrance to the great Hank Peterson. There were a few painted horse-shoes from men that had been on countless cattle drives with the former head of the ranch. A couple of carved hitch posts arrived at the property to memorialize the cowboy and his ranch. The greatest offering was of course, the food.

Evelyn and Annie had never seen nor even heard of so many varieties of casseroles in all their days. Baked goods providing comfort were dropped off by the tray full and the symbolic bottles of whiskey were lined up on the kitchen counter, enough to supply the local saloon for months. As each well-wisher dropped by to offer their condolences and food item, the female Petersons were already plotting avenues for distribution. All the ranch hands and other workers at the ranch had quietly taken home items for their families. There was no sense in the food going to waste and the intention was that the benevolence that Hank had given to his team over the years would be carried on in tradition.

By late afternoon of the third day, most of the visitors had come and gone which signaled the green light for Mayor Hampton to return. He was planning on arriving for dinner but came by a little early to discuss business with the family.

"Thank you so much for coming by Jack."

"Of course, Evelyn. I'll be by just as much as before, probably even more. Besides, I can never turn down one of your home cooked meals."

Evelyn looked around the dining room to see an ocean of prepared dishes still staring back at her.

"Well, I'm afraid to disappoint you Jack. With all of these dishes people keep dropping off I won't have to cook for quite a while. You will have your pick of things though. The boys have eaten well this week."

"Where are Wesley and Fred, by the way? I came by early to talk some business with them. With the cattle auction less than six weeks away I want to make sure they plan accordingly."

Evelyn looked out the window and did not see their trucks or their horses nearby. She was not concerned, however, since she knew they would come running once the dinner bell was rung.

"They will be around soon. I told them when they came in for lunch that you were coming by today to see them. I'm sure they won't be late."

Jack Hampton simply gave the ladies his best political smile in return. "That is quite alright, Evelyn. We are in no hurry whatsoever. Besides, it will give us time to chat on some things while we wait for them."

Annie thought it was her cue to leave the room but was stopped by the distinguished Mayor in her tracks.

"Not so fast, young lady. I have some business for you as well. Shall we all sit and talk for a bit?"

Looking over at the dining room table covered with desserts and such, Evelyn thought it best for them to move to the living room.

"Why don't you two have a seat while I get some coffee. Would you like some Jack? It's getting a little crisp out in that October air."

"That would be wonderful. Thank you,"

"I'll take a cup too mom."

Evelyn stopped in her tracks for a moment and simply looked at her daughter. "You know I keep forgetting. You left four years ago a young girl and you returned a grown woman. I'm sorry to discount you, Annie. I'll get you a cup as well."

The widow wandered off into the kitchen as Jack and Anne took a seat in the living room. The Mayor seized the opportunity to take a temperature in the room. Lowering his voice, he leaned in to talk softly.

"How is she holding up? Really?"

Anastasia looked back over her shoulder towards the kitchen to make sure her mother was still not within listening distance.

"She's a tough bird, my mother. She has just been going through her paces every day and taking charge of things. At night though…well, I hear her crying down the hallway in her bedroom. I'm sure it's toughest when she goes to bed without daddy."

Placing a warm hand on top of hers, Jack offered comfort.

"Well, it is best that you are here with her all day, Annie. She needs you now more than ever. Your brothers are out on the ranch all day and I think she would not be as strong if she had to walk around this big house all day with no one around. It's good that you came home when you did."

Annie was uncertain how to answer the statement with honesty. She would have rather stayed in L.A. but she was happy to spend some time with her father before…

"Here we are…"

Evelyn came out of the kitchen with a coffee service tray along with three cups. Setting the tray on the table, she poured the Mayor a cup and placed 3 sugar cubes on his saucer.

"Just the way you like it Jack. Strong and sweet."

"That's very kind of you. Thank you."

As the three of them prepared their coffees, it became evident that Jack had something he wanted to discuss with them. With too much hesitation on his part, Evelyn prodded.

"Ok Jack Hampton. Out with it. I've known you long enough to know when something's eating at you. Don't beat around the bush. Get it out of your system."

The Mayor put his cup and saucer down on the coffee table and rubbed his hands. He had been in politics most of his life and knew how to prepare a room for news.

"Let me first tell you this. Hank had planned for this day for quite some time and made sure that you and the children would be well cared for if…well, when the time came."

Evelyn remained stoic through the conversation. Even if it were just her daughter and the closest friend to the family, she would not show emotion.

"I'm aware. We spoke of the life insurance policy for both of us. While we are not hurting for money in any way now, I am sure it will help the children establish themselves and give me a nest egg when I retire."

"Retire? Dear woman you are barely 50 years old. You won't retire for 20 years or more if I know you."

The widow put on a polite smile. "Thank you Jack. That's very kind of you to say but in any case, there is nothing to worry about in that department."

"Well…"

The mother and daughter looked at each other with concern. It was actually the young college grad who spoke up for clarity.

"What are you getting at Jack? I thought you just said…"

"What I said was that your mother and your brothers are all cared for and provided for in your father's will. He had me keep a copy in my office but I also did some checking. There is a young man that work's in the Mayor's office that also works part-time over at the courthouse. It's always good to have someone with an ear open to things over there. Anyway, I had him check to make certain that Hank never filed an update to his will. He confirmed that he did not."

"So, I'm confused, Jack. If he didn't change the will what are you worried about."

The man took a sip of his coffee before continuing. They all knew it was a political stall tactic and he knew how to use it to his advantage better than anyone.

"To be clear, Hank did not make any changes to his will. His *personal* finances were all in order and there is enough in your family's personal accounts along with the life insurance policy to give you peace of mind, Evelyn, along with the children."

"I may have spent too much time in a city that has made me skeptical but I think you are inferring that there may be an issue with the ranch."

The man simply looked back at Annie without commenting.

"Is that true, Jack?"

"Maybe…"

"What does that mean, maybe? Is there a problem with the ranch or isn't there?"

"It means there is a grey area that we want to make sure becomes black and white. When someone in the cattle business passes, there are certain people out there that might try to capitalize on it."

"You mean Bill Foster?"

"Among others. Let me try to explain. Many years ago, Hank thought it best to incorporate the Shadowland Ranch as a separate entity from Peterson family holdings. It was a great idea and that time and I helped in but through the red tape. By incorporating, the family had limited liability in case someone got sick eating some of your branded meat or some ranch hand got hurt on the land."

Evelyn looked down at her hands squeezing them tightly. "I know. That is why he always took risks. He thought it best if one of his men didn't get hurt if there was no one to blame. In the end…"

Jack cut her off politely. "…in the end, Hank did what he had to do to protect his family. There are definite advantages to the ranch being a corporation but there are disadvantages as well."

"You are referring to ownership and control?"

"That's right Annie. See? I always knew your business degree would come in handy around here."

Evelyn seemed confused.

"I don't understand Jack. We own the ranch so we control it. Why would that become an issue?"

"Again, it is a grey area. Technically, the Shadowland Corporation owns Shadowland Ranch. It was set up as an LLC to limit the financial responsibility to the family. While Hank was the manager of the corporation, that is no longer the case."

"Won't the management of the corporation pass to me automatically?"

"Yes and no. It is not like flipping a switch. The answer is that it will eventually. In the duration, the ranch is basically tied up in probate."

"But that also means that it is protected by probate right?"

"Again, I have to admire that college mindset. Yes, it is like the ranch is in a protected bubble where no one can buy it or sell it or basically do anything with it."

"So that's good I would imagine."

Jack took one more sip of his coffee before continuing.

"Yes, that part is great. The ranch will be protected."

Evelyn smiled at her daughter but she could see the concern on the young girl's face.

"But that's not all of it, is it?"

"The grey area is this. Because the ranch is now basically stuck in probate, an argument *can* be made that there is no acting management of the ranch. Without someone official calling the shots, a voice could be raised indicating there is no one official to sign over the sale of the herd at auction."

Evelyn looked shocked. It was if the ground just gave out under her footing.

"You can't be serious, Jack. If we can't sell the herd..."

"I'm well aware of the consequences and that is why we are having this discussion. I will get the boys all set to have a great day at the auction but we have to be certain no one will throw the cautionary flag."

"He wouldn't..."

"He would and you know it. But Foster is not the only wolf out there to worry about. You never know. Your husband and your father was well known across most of Montana. Word of his passing will bring people like Foster out of the woodwork. I just want you to be armed with knowledge should the situation arise."

The room fell silent for a moment until Evelyn put up her chin and looked the Mayor straight on to do battle.

"What do you suggest we do, Jack?"

"Well, for starters. Keep doing what you are doing. Get up each morning and keep living the way Hank would have wanted you to. The boys can take care of things with the cattle and you, Evelyn can take care of the house as you always did."

"Was there something you wanted me to do, Jack?"

"You, dear child, are the Trojan horse. I want you to quietly arm your family with knowledge in case you go to battle."

"How do I do that? I didn't get a degree in Business Law. I know very little of it. I can help with general business questions but that's about it."

"Annie. That is why I want you to work with the young man from my office that I was telling you about. His name is Sam Walden. He's right around your age and he did his internship in a law office that specializes in business cases like this. He still has some contacts there along with the ones at the courthouse. I asked him to spend some time researching the possibilities with you. The whole thing may be nothing but I would like to err on the side of caution just to be sure. I always told your father I would look out for all of you if anything ever happened."

"We can't thank you enough for that, Jack."

With a light laugh, the man continued. "Don't thank me yet. Annie here will need to spend some time researching things over at the county library. I can point you in the right direction with Sam but the rest is up to you. As for you, Evelyn, it is going to cost you another cup of coffee and maybe a small piece of that lemon cake over there. There will be plenty more when the boys get in so dinner may have to wait."

Evelyn rose to get the man a plate while Anastasia was left to her own thoughts. Perhaps she did have a reason for not staying in Los Angeles when she did. Perhaps destiny was pushing her back to the Shadowland Ranch for a reason. Taking a sip of her coffee she pondered what that reason might be as she heard the mud room door open and her brothers came bounding in.

5

The University of Montana was a well-known university that prided itself on academia and research. While it was not full of the glitz and glamour of some of the more well-known universities, the student body there were *grizzly* about research. After four years there as a political science major, Sam Walden could find a crumb in any legal textbook better than most lawyers in the state.

During his time as an undergrad, Sam worked in the law library helping graduate students prepare for the bar exam at the only law school in the state. The twilight hours spent in the hallowed halls of Missoula gave him a broadened understanding of the intricacies of the law without actually working towards a law degree.

For Sam, the legal world served as a gateway to his higher aspirations of being in public office. He dreamt of being in politics someday and he knew that the climb to success in that field was built upon the shoulders of others. Even as an undergrad, he networked himself with every given opportunity. Being a summer intern at a prestigious business law firm allowed him access to the wealthiest and most powerful men and women in Montana. Gathering research in the law library he made contacts with the lawyers of tomorrow that would shape the Montana landscape. It was a tried and proven fact in politics that it was not about what you know but rather who you know. Sam Walden was armed in both categories.

With a Bachelor of Science Degree in Political science, he left Missoula and secured a position in the Fergus County Mayor's office. Moonlighting at the county's courthouse as a part-time clerk, he was able to see multiple branches of government at work concurrently. He was also able to further network himself in real-life settings. He had the drive, he had the ambition and with the right political connections, he was on the fast track to success. When the Mayor himself came to him and asked for his assistance on a personal matter, Sam jumped at the chance.

Sam Walden had little or no social life due to hours he spent on his career. In college, he burned the midnight oil sorting through law books while his fellow undergrads were out partying with their fraternities. He never attended a school sporting event or hung out at the local college bars and knew of the school's mascot only because of the grizzly bear adorned on school apparel. Upon graduation, he frequented the gym to stay in shape but because there was rarely anyone of his age pressing weights at 5am, his social life remained stifled. He worked two jobs which occupied seven days a week but yet he enthusiastically volunteered to help the Mayor out with his dilemma.

The research that Jack Hampton asked him to look into involved a blend of corporate law, family probate law, and good old Montana cattle ranching. For Sam, the situation hit on all cylinders and he could not wait to get started. The fact that the Mayor wanted him to work with a member of the family in question simply was appealing in the fact that it meant more networking. It never crossed his young mind that the family member in question would be a former cheerleading prom queen named Anastasia Peterson.

Filing papers in the Mayor's office late in the evening, Sam's private cell phone rang out disturbing the silence of the room. He was never permitted to use the official phone line of the Mayor to make calls nor would he ever think to answer it when it rang. Only office personnel at both jobs had his private cell phone line and his natural assumption was that the call was work related when he answered it.

"Hi Sam. It's Jack Hampton."

Dropping the papers that he had in his hand, the young man was instantly flustered at the top ranking official calling him on his personal line.

"Oh, hello Mr. Mayor. What can I do for you?"

The laughter on the other end of the line lightened up the situation.

"Sam, you can call me Jack when we talk outside of the office. What are you up to at the moment?"

"I was actually just filing papers in your office, Mr. Mayor...I mean Jack."

"Very good. Very good. I like a man that's not afraid to put in the hours. Sam, do you remember what we spoke about earlier today? The family I would like you to do research for?"

"Of course, sir. How could I forget. I look forward to it. The situation you described intrigues me on many levels."

"Excellent. I'm glad you still feel that way. I am here with the family in question and I would like to connect the dots so to speak. Instead of worrying about one of you contacting the other, we can get right down to it. I would like to put them on the phone so you can trade numbers and set up a time to meet. How does that sound?"

He always speaks like a politician. Sam thought that was a trait he looked forward to learning from the man.

"Yes, sir...I mean Jack, of course. Do you want to put them on now? I'll grab something to write with and take down the information."

"Atta boy. Hold on one moment."

Sam heard the phone get placed down on a table of some sort while there were background conversations going on. It sounded like more than just a couple of people talking and he wondered what prompted the Mayor to step away and call him now. What sounded at first to be a casual inquiry may have some urgency attached to it. When the voice finally came on the phone, Sam was not expecting it.

"Hello, this is Annie."

"Oh, I'm sorry. I was on hold with the Mayor. He was putting someone on the line."

Her light sweet chuckle made him melt.

"That would be me, silly. My name is Anastasia Peterson but you can call me Annie. I understand we will be working together on some research. Do you go Sam or Samuel? I just want to know what to call you."

The young clerk with high political aspirations was flustered once again. He hoped that someday he would be able to control his emotions like the Mayor does at every turn but not for now. At the moment he was derailed by the most beautiful voice he had ever heard.

6

The Fergus County Cattlemen's Association was not located anywhere near a cow or even a horse. When the Association was first founded more than a century ago, there were many equines lined up along their post but fast forward to modern day and all that could be seen were pick-up trucks and Jeeps. The downtown area where the building was located was neutral territory to the different ranchers. The office itself was a different story.

There were close to 25,000 ranch's located in the state of Montana and Fergus County had its fair share of them. With so many ranchers to govern, the leadership was less about politics and more about fear. It was the way of the west that the strongest would rule with iron whichever century they were in. That message was loud and clear as you stepped into the office of Bill Foster.

Subtleness was not something Foster practiced and he generally spoke with loud purpose whenever he opened his mouth. His desk was adorned with horseshoes as a blatant reminder that he could toss one at your head and kill you in the blink of an eye. In business, he had the same venomous attack as a rattlesnake and every rancher knew to stay clear of him.

"Where are we with Shadowland?"

The four men seated in the office were going over their weekly business agendas as they planned their attack.

"Boss, the man hasn't been in the ground a week yet. What do you expect us to do?"

"Graham is right. We make a move on any of the cattle or the ranch itself it's not going to look good for any of us. Hank was well liked."

The large rancher slammed his hand on his desk startling the men in the room. They were used to his outbursts but usually not so early in the morning.

"I don't pay you for your opinion or to think. I pay you to take action and all you are giving me are excuses. So what are you going to do about it Sollars?"

The man and his twin brother had been with Foster for years and neither one of them would ever get used to the man's temper. It kept them both on their toes.

"Rich and I were going to go pay a visit to our friend's down at the auction barn. We want to remind them who they work for."

Foster rubbed his hand on his chin. He was happy with the suggestion.

"Good. What about you Graham?"

"I'm gonna meet up with one of the old ranch hands at Shadowland. He's a drunk and will do anything for a pint. Rumor has it he's not happy taking orders from the two kids and is looking for a new home once the herd goes to slaughter. We don't have to poach him but I'm pretty sure he'll keep us on the line if we keep feeding him a bottle every week."

"That's great. It can't hurt to have an inside ear to what's going on there."

The three men sat on the other side of the big desk and looked at each other with curiosity. It was no secret that their boss couldn't stand the deceased but they were uncertain what the strategy now was.

"So, boss. Are you going to let us in on the plan? What's our end game here? With Peterson silenced permanently, you have no more opposition. Why are we going after the ranch? I'm pretty sure we could control those boys easier than any other rancher who would take the land. So why the big push?"

Foster picked up the nearest horseshoe and threw it across the room. One of the heels stuck into the drywall and the shoe was temporarily suspended in the wall. He made certain not to aim it towards his men but was clearly sending a message.

"Why did you jump Graham?"

"Um...well I kind of thought the shoe was coming at me."

"Exactly. Do you feel like asking any more stupid questions?"

"No, sir."

"That's my point boys. Let me explain power to you. If we want to stay in power, the other ranchers need to fear us. Right now, they might be afraid to get in the corral with that mustang but they are not afraid of us. Hank had a voice and now he doesn't. Somewhere out there, some rancher is going to start speaking his peace too. Maybe it will be Dylan Shepard or Roy Benally. If we don't send a clear message someone else is going to take up Peterson's soap box now that he is gone."

"What kind of message are we sending boss?"

"We strike like a rattler. Not so much that Monsky can come after us but we strike where the rest of them will understand. In their bank accounts. If we stop Shadowland from selling their herd, the rest of us will get top dollar for our cattle. Less cattle available makes each pound more valuable. He who dies with the most cows not sold kills his ranch right along with him. The ranch will have to go under. Then we can buy up the land for pennies on the dollar from the bankruptcy court."

"What about the Mayor? He's got his nose all over that family and their business. It won't be easy shifting things with him around."

Foster laughed an ugly, hearty laugh. The men that worked for him hated hearing that laughter as it came from somewhere dark.

"That is the beauty of it, boys. The Mayor is a law abiding citizen. He is above reproach. We have tried to buy him off time and time again and we have gotten shot down. As the Mayor of Fergus County, he will have no choice but upholding the law right next to Monsky. We are not going to stop Shadowland from selling their herd; the Great State of Montana is going to do it for us."

The man started laughing and a murder of crows took flight outside of the Cattlemen's Association window. The dark laughter could most likely be heard all the way across town to the Mayor's office himself. Old Iron Shoes was about to start throwing.

7

The Fergus County Library system had a limited amount of books on Montana State Law but it was a good place to begin the research. Sam Walden had arranged to meet Annie in the Reference Department on late Friday afternoon. The courthouse wrapped things up by 3pm and it was just a short walk over to the library building. A few hours spent digging through legal research before the library closed for the day would kick things off in the right direction.

Since court was adjourned early for the day, Sam arrived at the library thirty minutes before he was expected. Entering the reference section, he found the first two law journals he was looking for and took a seat by the window for no particular reason. He did not crack open the books but instead gazed out into the fall scenery and was taken aback by the sight of the fall foliage.

With temps only peaking around 50, he saw plenty of people walking the sidewalk with sweatshirts and sweaters and a few donning a jacket. For not the first time, he took a moment to reflect upon the world around him. In some ways, he was letting life slip by without a second thought. He rarely noticed scenes like the one he was watching because he was always inside a building looking at a file or a book. He had no one in his life to share such things with so he was content to continue looking at words on a page rather that the color of the leaves in Montana.

As he was gazing out at the scenery, Sam thought he was looking at a mirage. A pick-up truck had pulled to the curb with Shadowland Ranch emblazoned on the door panel. Stepping out into the street was a beautiful woman who was definitely out of place for the downtown backdrop. Blonde hair was blowing in the wind on top of a flannel shirt that was tucked into a tight pair of blue jeans. With brown boots that matched the brown leather vest she had on, she could have been stepping right out of the pages of a country fashion magazine. Turning her face up to climb the front steps, Sam caught a view of her smile that took his breath away. When she reached the top of the stairs, she disappeared from his view but young Walden knew she was coming to meet him.

Quickly looking down at his appearance, he realized he was dressed as he always did. As was his political attire for the courthouse, he had on a pair of dark slacks that rose above his penny loafers. His dress down shirt was nothing fashionable but he was happy that he had taken off his tie and left it in his briefcase when he sat down. Since he had no girlfriend to tell him otherwise, he viewed himself as being average. He was described by his fellow college classmates as being *politically handsome* and never fully understood their meaning. With a crisp haircut and a dimpled chin, he could smile and make the poor forget about their plight. Wearing the political attire was part of the process for him but the women that looked upon him knew that the outfit made the man.

At 3pm on a Friday afternoon, the library was scarcely visited. The local students had yet to venture from their classrooms to hang out and do their homework and the older day crew had already taken their reading materials and left. When Anastasia searched around the small reference section only to see a good looking guy sitting by the window, she felt very relieved. In her eyes, he was not Los Angeles hot looking but he also wasn't the boring cowboy type either. He was definitely someone she could work with.

"You must be Sam Walden."

Jumping to his feet, he nearly knocked his chair over backwards.

"Yes. I am Sam..."

Imitating the famous children's book, she responded.

"Sam I am..."

They both chuckled lightly. It was a welcome cut to the instant chemistry between them.

"You must be Anastasia. Please have a seat."

"Please call me Annie." Sitting down across from him, she looked down at the books on the table and frowned. She was never much of a library girl or a book enthusiast for that matter. Her grades had always done well without the need of senselessly torturing oneself over the printed word. "I see you have had a head start without me."

"No, not really. I literally just got here and found a couple journals for us to review. It might give us some ideas on how to proceed."

Looking back at the beauty in front of him, he caught her staring back at him and wearing her gorgeous smile.

"What?"

"I'm sorry to stare but are you related to Jack Hampton in some way?"

"No, I just work for him over at the Mayor's office. Why do you ask?"

"You could definitely be a politician's son. You have that look."

Sam felt a soft blush rising in his cheeks. "You are not first one to tell me that. People tell me I have a *political* look." He purposely left out the handsome part.

"Well, they are not wrong. You could pass for the Mayor's son."

"I'll take that as a compliment. I think Jack Hampton is a great man."

"That he is. He has been…I guess he *was* a friend of my dad's for many years. Jack is very close to my family."

"I'm sorry to hear about your dad. I didn't know him but Jack always spoke highly of the man. That's not something you hear often coming from a politician."

"Thank you. I would rather not talk about it if that's ok. Can we get started?"

"Absolutely. Just a couple things before we start digging in. First, can you tell me about the big picture? Jack didn't fill in many details and I am curious as to what the details are to make certain that we are on the right path."

"Sure, thing. It's pretty basic. My mom and dad own the Shadowland Ranch. At some point, my dad incorporated the ranch to limit his liability. Since he did not make it a sole proprietorship, it does not pass directly to my mom now… well, now that he has passed. The corporation is now tied up in probate with his estate. Like any other item of value in an estate, it is recommended that nothing be bought or sold that would change the value of the estate prior to probate being settled. The challenge lies in the fact that we have over 200 head of cattle going to auction next month. Jack is worried that someone might say we can't sell them because the corporation is tied up in probate."

"At roughly $100 per hundredweight and most cattle coming in over 1000 pounds, that's a big chunk of change that would be tied up if you can't sell them."

"I guess you know your cattle."

"Oh I know nothing about the cattle business but I do know research. There is plenty of public information on the sale of cattle in Montana."

"So do you think you can help us?"

Sam smiled. "I'm going to do my best, ma'am."

"Spoken like a true politician. Is Jack Hampton your idol Sam?"

The young man bobbed his head. "Something like that. Let's just say I would like to emulate the man."

"From what I can see, he is a good role model to follow."

Sam cracked open the first journal and was ready to begin. "Shall we get started?"

Annie nodded her head in agreement and then held up her hand like she wanted to ask a question. Sam chuckled.

"I don't think we need to be so formal Annie. What did you want to ask?"

"I was just thinking. Before you said that you wanted to ask me a couple questions. The facts of the case were just one of them. What else were you going to ask me?"

Sam Walden's face grew apple red as he choked on his reply.

"Well, I haven't seen anyone get that choked up since one of my roommates in L.A. went on an acting audition."

"I heard you went to UCLA. How was that?"

Annie put on a million-dollar smile as the sound of her alma mater lit her up like a Christmas tree.

"It was amazing. Best time of my life. Made me a little sad to come home if you know what I mean."

"I understand that fully. I haven't been back home in years. No sense going backwards."

Annie continued smiling. "That is exactly how I feel. Anyway, was that your question? About UCLA?"

Sam continued to blush and hesitated on his reply.

"Listen junior Mayor or whatever your title is. If we are going to work together, we need to talk openly. So spill it."

"I like a woman that gets right to the point."

"A trait passed on from my father. So...?"

Sam swallowed hard. He knew he had to just get it out of the way so they could get started.

"It's really nothing. When I saw you coming up the stairs, it looked like you were stepping right out of a fashion magazine. I was just wondering if you were a model or something along those lines?"

To Sam Walden, the comment may have meant nothing but to the young woman sitting across from him, his question meant everything in the world.

8

"What's your head count at?"

Dylan Shepard was sitting at a table with Fred and Wesley Peterson. The local saloon had been around for more than a 100 years and still had the original wooden planks that had been stained many times by bloodshed. *One Eyed Jack's* was a favorite haunt of local ranchers but it was also not the kind of place they would have brought Annie or any other self-respecting woman to. It was a saloon with an attitude and it was always best to be on your guard.

"I'm not certain we should be talking about that in here Dylan. The walls have ears."

Dylan chuckled. "I like your cautiousness Wes. Your father taught you well. He was always looking over his shoulder to see who was listening."

"Daddy always said only a fool goes around sharing his business with others. He never understood the internet and social media. He thought people were fools."

Dylan started to laugh. He took a draw from his beer before answering.

"Yes, he did. Your father had the heart of a lion but he thought most people were sheep. If they minded their own flocks instead of wandering off in other people's pastures they wouldn't get eaten so much." Pausing to reflect, he continued. "I think Hank told me that line at this very table over a couple of beers."

The three men were silent until Dylan raised his beer for a toast. "To Hank."

Fred and Wesley raised their beers to meet the man's and toasted to their father in remembrance.

"So, really... the number of heads you are bringing to the auction house isn't that big of a secret. Most ranchers could drive by your pastures and take a reasonable guess at the total without being too far off."

"We had 212 this morning."

"Shut your mouth, Fred."

"You heard the man. It's not a big secret."

Dylan was nodding in approval.

"That's a good herd of cattle, boys. Are they all up to weight?"

"There's a couple lighter ones but most of them are over 1000 pounds. Nothing less than 800 though."

The boys were clear on the minimum weight load for cattle to go to auction. They had sized up the smaller ones earlier in the week.

"That's great. With the current block rate, you should get around $100 per hundredweight. That is a great haul compared to mine. I only have 80 going this time around."

"Well, Dylan. Your ranch is a lot smaller. Less mouths to feed. You'll probably still yield a greater profit when all is said and done."

Shepard shook his head in jest and took another drink of his beer.

"There are times when you open your mouth Wes and your father comes walking out. He used to say that same thing to me every year at slaughter time."

"Then I guess we are in good company."

Wesley raised his glass in a half-toast gesture and drank it down. Gesturing to the waitress, he raised his empty glass for a refill. The conversation was on hold as she brought over a new glass of beer and set it down. When she was out of earshot, the men continued.

"So what is Annie up to these days?"

Fred looked at the man seriously.

"Really, Dylan? She's old enough to be your daughter. Aren't you mom's age?"

Dylan put his beer down and pretended to swing at the younger Peterson.

"I would smack you for disrespecting your sister if I thought you were serious. I'm not asking to date her, you idiot." Leaning in he lowered his voice. "Jack Hampton told me about her research project. How's that coming along?"

Wes just looked at his brother and shook his head. "It's coming. She thinks she has a lead on it. She is spending a lot of time with the guy from Jack's office doing research. They haven't told us much besides it's coming along."

"What's his name again?"

"Sam something or other. Seems like a nice guy. He came by the house the other night so they could read some books together. Better them than me. I would get a headache if I tried to read something like that."

"It's because your brain is full of rocks Fred. Shut up and drink your beer."

"I see the two of you are getting along as usual. You know your mother is counting on you two to hold things together over there. You can't be fighting like you used to when you were kids."

"Sure Dylan. Now who sounds like our old man?"

The mention of Hank silenced them once again as the three men drank down their beers and ordered another round.

"Put that on my tab Shirley."

The three men turned towards the door to see Bill Foster standing there with his hired hyenas. As usual, they looked like they were out roaming for trouble.

"That's kind of you Mr. Foster but we got it."

"I'm sure you do, boys. I'm sure you do. But where I come from if a man turns down an offer for a drink from another man, he's picking his battle."

The younger brother spoke out of turn. "No, sir. No battles here. Just didn't want to impose on your good nature."

Dylan almost choked on his beer with laughter.

"Is there a problem Shepard?"

Looking the man straight on, he did not back down.

"No problem at all, Foster. If you want to drop a few bucks on a round for us, you are more than welcome to."

The tension eased for a moment as Old Iron Shoes and his men crossed over to the bar and ordered their own drinks. Leaving his goons behind, Foster returned with a whiskey in his hand. Standing next to the table he raised his glass.

"Allow me to toast your father boys. He was a good rancher and knew how to drive cattle. His presence will be missed at the auction."

The three men seated at the table looked at each other in silent conversation before raising their glasses for the toast. They knew there was hidden meaning in the phrase coming out of the man's mouth.

"To Hank."

Wes and Fred clinked glasses with Dylan and raised a little higher in respect to the man buying the round. They each drank down half their glass before setting them down.

"Looks like you boys are getting mighty thirsty driving that cattle all day. I hope it's all worth it come next month."

Dylan kicked back his chair and stood up quickly. Facing the man in the saloon, the others seemed on edge for a fight.

"What's that supposed to mean, Foster?"

The man released his dark laughter while his three goons clenched their fists. They could smell trouble brewing.

"My, my. Aren't you all wound up today, Dylan. I was just making conversation with these boys."

"Sounds to me like you were picking off the herd like some hungry wolf, Foster."

"Not at all. It's all peaceful today boys. I just wish you luck in your first time at the auction barn. You never know what's going to trip you up. I hope you get top dollar for every head."

With that, Bill turned to walk towards the bar and join his crew. Behind him, Wes, Fred and Dylan dropped some bills on the table and walk towards the door. Before they exited, Foster got the last word in.

"I told you boys I had your tab. You might want to save your pennies for a rainy day. You never know when the well is going to dry up on you."

Turning back, he let out a laugh that ran up the spines of the three men exiting. The two Peterson boys walked ahead of Dylan but they all could smell trouble. Mayor Hampton had the notion that there may be a storm brewing and Old Iron Shoes just confirmed it.

9

After spending four years as a political science major, an internship at a prestigious business law firm, working at the courthouse and inside the Mayor's office, Samuel Walden had learned how to bluff. Every lawyer he saw in court and class had learned the same secret trait to successful negotiations. Never let the other side know what cards you are holding.

The lawyers each held back their secret cards as if they were waiting to throw the spade and collect the points. Playing the odds, they knew right when to throw it out on the table so they came out smelling like roses. For Sam, it was not only about impressing the Mayor and gathering some political edge, he wanted the girl.

The research had not taken long to figure out the key solution. If the director of a corporation passed away and there were no shareholders, the deceased's executor of his personal will could take on the deceased's corporate responsibilities until probate was settled. If there was no will, the directors nearest living relative would take on the director responsibilities. In the case of Hank Peterson and the Shadowland Ranch, there was clearly a Last Will and Testament and someone was named as the executor of the estate. That executor was Jack Hampton.

With a simple Limited Proxy Vote form, Jack would take over the general powers of the Shadowland Ranch and would be able to approve the sale of the herd. It was possible and even probable that Hank had trusted his closest friend to take care of his ranch and family in the untimely passing of his death. There was no question of the man's integrity and the deal was as good as done. Sam had already drawn up the form and all that was needed was for the Mayor to sign it in front of a notary and the deal would be sealed. Easy peasy Montana Grizzly strikes again.

Sam was not sure exactly why he had played the silent card but he had let his emotions get the better of him. Politically, he should march himself into the Mayor's office, present him with the paperwork and declare victory in their minor skirmish with Foster. The challenge was that he wanted to keep spending time with Annie on a more personal level. Each time they met and labored next to each other looking through law books, it felt like dating. They would accidentally reach for the same book at the same time and their hands would touch, sending electricity through each of their bodies. Other times they sat close to each other, their knees touching under the table and he could smell her sweet fragrance intoxicating him. He needed to find out if there was something more or if it was just busy work for the family business.

This evening, they were wrapping things up at the library as they were closing up at 6pm and Sam saw his opening. Whether she was dropping subtle hints or simply not aware of his intentions, he did not know. What he did know was that she was eating a cracker as they were packing up looking ravenous.

"You seem hungry Annie."

"I am famished. I'm not looking forward to the long drive home to the ranch without food. I'll probably stop and pick something up."

Sam had become comfortable enough being around the beautiful woman but he was still hesitant to ask the question.

"Um…I know it's not much but I was going to stop and get a pizza. Do you want to share one with me?"

"You mean like go out for pizza at a restaurant with you?"

"Well…yea. I mean we don't have to eat it there if you don't want to. I guess we can pick it up and eat it somewhere else."

Annie smiled. "You are so adorable. Of course I'll go on a pizza date with you. Will there be beer too?"

"Wait…I didn't…I mean it can be a date but I didn't…"

Annie took his hand in her own. "Relax, Sam. It's about time. I was wondering if you were ever going to pick up on my hints. I would love to go out with you."

"Oh. Ok then. I usually go to Pizza City but we can go wherever you like. Do you want to meet me there?"

"You haven't dated much have you Sam?"

"Well…I mean…sometimes…"

"It's ok. Let's take your car. We can leave my truck here and come back for it if that's ok with you."

"Yea. That sounds great. Let me just pack up all my notes."

A few minutes later, the pair was walking down the stairs in the cold October night. They had already gotten a snow flurry a few days earlier and the night air smelled like more was coming.

"I hope you have good heat in that little car of yours. I'm freezing already. This is going to be my first winter back home in four years after being in California. I have a feeling I'm going to freeze."

"I'll keep you warm."

The reaction just slipped out and although it was not what he intended to say, Annie still thought it was cute.

"I'm sure you will, Mr. Politics."

"No, I meant my car. I've got good heat…that's what I meant to say…"

Annie laughed. "It's all good. Let's just go before I freeze out here."

The couple got into Sam's Toyota as they drove the short distance to the pizza restaurant. They didn't have a chance to warm up much in the car and the heat inside the dining area felt good and comforting.

"Aah, finally some heat. I'm going to run to the ladies' room. Why don't you order us a couple of beers?"

Sam took the opportunity to get a corner booth away from the door and took off his jacket. He was optimistic in how things were going and looked forward to progressing past work friends. He was not sure how he would fit a relationship in his busy schedule but he was willing to try. When the server came over with the menus, he ordered two beers and sat back. He did not have to wait long as Annie returned shortly with her jacket in hand. Hanging it next to his on the coat hook alongside the booth, their coats were getting cozy.

"So, tell me, Sam Walden, what's your problem?"

He was stunned by the question and was not sure how to answer.

"Excuse me?"

"You heard me right. What's your problem? You are a great looking guy and incredibly smart. I'm sure you are going to be Senator or Congressman someday so where is the punchline? I can't seem to find fault in you. Believe me, I've tried."

"You've tried?"

Annie's response was placed on hold as the server brought the two beers and put them on the table.

"Are you two ready to order?"

"How does Pepperoni sound?"

"I love pepperoni pizza."

"Ok. I guess the lady has chosen. Can we get a large pepperoni pizza and a smile to go with it?"

The server smiled broadly as she turned to take the order to the kitchen.

"See? That's what I mean. You have this political way with everyone. Well, almost everyone. You pull that shy card around me but I know better."

Sam could not look her in the eyes as his heart was fluttering. He did not want her to see him shaking like a leaf on an autumn tree.

"Like that. Why can't you look me in the eyes?"

"Well, the answer is the same. I don't give you my *political* smile as you call it, because the smile I have for you is real. You drive me a little crazy Annie. Not going to lie."

"Aw. That's sweet." Reaching out across the table she held his hand. "But you are not getting away that easy. Back to my first question? What's wrong with you? Why don't you have some beautiful girlfriend somewhere that wants to go to some political function with you?"

"Would you want to go to a political function?"

"Are you really asking me?"

"Well, I haven't been invited to any yet but the holidays are coming. If there is a Christmas party at the courthouse, you'll be the first one I call."

"So...again...?"

Sam took a sip of his beer and looked across the table at her. He had the courage to start looking her in the eyes and he could feel himself melting.

"That is an easy question. I am a workaholic, Annie. I work two jobs, seven days a week. I go to the gym at 5am just to squeeze in some down time. Otherwise, I work all day and read all night. It's not an exciting life."

"What if you took a night or two off from reading? Would that set you back on your aspirations?"

Sam took a moment before responding.

"No, I think that would be fine. Actually, if I had the right person to spend time with, I think I could even manage a few nights off from reading each week."

Reaching back across the table, he held her hand in his and wondered how he got so lucky. Before the answer could come to him, the pizza arrived at the table.

The couple sat and ate their pizza and enjoyed a couple more beers before calling it a night. Sam went out to the car and started it so that it could warm up before they got in. Once inside the car, they traveled the short distance back to the library where Annie performed the same ritual and started her truck. Returning to the warmth of Sam's car, she closed the door while she waited for her cab to heat up.

"I had a great time tonight Sam. We should have done this sooner."

"Well, we have been a little busy."

"Do you think we are close to finding an answer?"

"Definitely. I am confident all will be taken care of."

Annie smiled happily and leaned forward to kiss him. He was more than willing to return the kiss and it lasted longer than expected. Later that night, he would wonder if the kiss was out of appreciation for finding an answer or if she just wanted to kiss him. In the end, he decided it did not matter either way.

"Like I said. We should have done this sooner. Goodnight Mr. Walden."

"Goodnight Miss Peterson."

Giving his hand one last squeeze, she got out of the Toyota and climbed into her truck. Moments later she drove off down the road into the darkness of the night. Sam sat there in his car for some time as he gazed at the library next to him. He was happy where research had brought him and could not wait to throw out his spade card and win the game of hearts.

10

The weeks that followed were like sands through an hour glass. The closer the date came to the cattle auction the more time Sam and Annie spent together. The family grew fearful of what might happen on auction day and resentment was building as they watched the couple grow happier in the wake of their research together.

There were many more pizza nights and a few movie nights but most of the time they spent just talking. Sam thought he had never talked so much in his life. For Annie, the dismal existence of living on a ranch in Montana became much brighter. Each day she spent with her mother managing the business and each evening she ventured out with Sam. Jack Hampton saw more of his office assistant than he imagined as he always seemed to be at the ranch when Jack came over. Even watching Evelyn cook dinner while he drank his coffee, the conversation was about Sam.

"Thanks for that, by the way."

"Thanks for what?"

"You know what. If he doesn't come up with a solution soon I'm going to lose the ranch and my daughter in one stampede."

"Has it become that serious?"

"Well the auction is next week. What do you think, Jack?"

"I meant between them. I thought they were just casually dating."

"They are never apart besides when they are working. When she is here, he is with you or at the courthouse. As soon as they get out of work, he comes here for dinner or they go out somewhere. It's been nonstop."

"It's just young love, Evelyn."

"Now you sound just like Hank, except he never stood for it. When that young lady was in high school..."

"I am well aware of the torment he and the boys put that girl through. It's a wonder she grew up at all."

"I am reasonably certain that California taught her a thing or two about men. She seemed very comfortable slipping into the relationship with him."

"Well they do look like they belong on the top of a wedding cake together. My campaign publicist couldn't have picked a more perfect pair."

"Is that what really happened, Jack? Did someone from your office decide that your assistant and my daughter would look great together?"

Jack drank down some of his coffee as he waited for the others to arrive home for dinner. Evelyn picked up on the hesitation from her friend.

"Were you going to answer that Jack or do I have to take away your coffee."

The Mayor pulled back on his coffee cup in jest. "Ok, ok. I may have had ulterior motives when I paired the two together. It was a win-win scenario. They did the research we needed and I kept my promise to Hank."

Evelyn stopped preparing dinner and looked over at him.

"What promise?"

"It was just a gentleman's promise, that's all. We were having a cigar out on the porch one night…"

"I hated when he smoked those things…"

"Anyway, we were drinking some bourbon one night and *enjoying* a cigar when he asked me to promise him something. He asked that if anything should ever happen to him, that I would keep a watch out for you all."

"Oh, is that all? He said that all the time."

"Well…"

"Well, what? Was there more to it?"

"He never worried about the boys. He figured they would argue and fight like they always did but they would get along. Sooner or later they would find some young fillies and they would give you grandchildren one day. They were never an issue. Anastasia? Well, that was another story. He worried that she had run off and become some big city girl. He was worried about her not having core family values and wasting her life in California. He was so happy when she came home to the ranch. It was then that he asked me to make sure she ended up with someone good. He wanted someone that would take care of her and not simply let her run off with some rodeo cowboy."

"Have you done that, Jack? Have you fulfilled your promise?"

"I think so. Sam's got a good head on his shoulders and he will go far in politics. I'll take him under my wing of course and show him the ropes but I think he knows enough now to build a good future. You could do much worse in finding a son-in-law Evelyn."

Just then, the kitchen door opened from the mud room and the cold air filled the room. Annie ran over and gave her mother a hug while Sam closed the door.

"Hi Jack. Hi Mom. How long before dinner?"

"Hello to you too, young lady. Hi Sam."

The young man smiled back at Evelyn, still nervous to be entertaining outside of the office with his boss nearby.

"Probably not for an hour. We have to wait for your brothers. They had some things to put in order before the auction next week."

"How's the research coming, Sam? Cutting it kind of close are we?"

Sam moved his briefcase from one hand to the other. He knew the answer was just sitting on top of some other files and all he had to do was take it out and give it to the Mayor. He decided he would do it tomorrow. Better to talk to him in the office rather than here at the ranch.

"I'm hoping to have something for you tomorrow, sir. I just want to check a few things first. That's why Annie was asking how long until dinner. We wanted to read a few case notes."

"Tomorrow? That's terrific. Go check your case notes. Cross your t's and dot your I's. We don't want to leave any stone unturned with Foster around."

The two young lovers scampered off to the den to have some privacy. With his briefcase in one hand, Sam held Annie's hand as they meandered through the house.

"They are so young."

Jack laughed.

"She is 21 and he is 22. If memory serves that's the age you and Hank got married."

"No, Hank was 23."

Still laughing, Jack had some of his coffee. "Now there's a big difference. I'm pretty sure if things keep going in this direction, Sam will turn 23 before the wedding."

Evelyn through a dish towel at the Mayor and returned to the cooking. Jack made himself useful and set the table for dinner, putting an extra setting next to Annie for Sam along with two for her brothers. Just as Evelyn was starting to put the food on the table, Wes and Fred came in stomping their feet.

"You do understand what the mud room is for, right boys?"

"Sure mom. It's just that the snow is really coming down out there. We didn't want to drag any of it into the kitchen."

"It's snowing?"

"Pretty hard, too. Radio says it's going to be a big one tonight."

"Let's eat first and worry about the snow later. You boys go get washed up for dinner. Tell your sister and Sam that supper is ready."

"Her boyfriend is here again? That's becoming a regular thing these days."

Evelyn and Jack looked at each other and chuckled. "Never mind that. Go get washed up and tell them to come on. If we don't eat soon we are all going to get snowed in."

The meal went as planned as all the Peterson family and their two guests sat around the large farmhouse table and enjoyed the evening. Several bottles of wine were consumed and by the time pie and coffee were served, everyone had a touch of the sleep crawling into their eyes. Looking out the living room window, Mayor Hampton made the declaration.

"Well, it looks like Sam and I are going to bunk here tonight. I can't even see the cars. Even with the pick-ups, it would be a tough trek back to town."

Annie perked up at the thought of Sam sleeping over. Evelyn picked up on the reaction and threw up the road block immediately.

"Sure Jack. You AND Sam can use the spare bedroom on the boy's side of the house. There are bunk beds in there. I'm sure Annie and I will feel much safer knowing you are over there with the boys."

Wes and Fred laughed as they knew what their mother was up to. Grabbing the last bottle of wine off the table, they headed towards their part of the house.

"Goodnight everyone. You too, Sam. Enjoy bunking with your boss tonight."

Sam was speechless as Wesley's comment resonated with him in dismay. He was actually going to share a room with the Mayor tonight like they were two teenage boys in a camping trip.

"Well come on, Sam. I'll show you the way."

Sam looked to Annie for help but she just shrugged.

"You go along. I'm going to help my mother clean up. I'll see you in the morning before you leave for work."

"That has a nice ring to it."

Sam leaned in to kiss Annie and Evelyn put up a hand.

"Ok you two love birds. Say goodnight."

"Goodnight Annie."

Kissing her goodnight, Sam turned and followed the Mayor down the hallway to the other side of the house.

"He's a nice young man."

"Yes he is mama." Annie paused as she looked down the hallway after him. Satisfied that he was not in earshot, she asked her mother the question.

"Do you think Daddy would have liked him?"

Evelyn looked at her daughter as she picked up the dinner plates from the table. Thinking back to the conversation she had with Jack earlier she chuckled.

"At least he's not a rodeo cowboy."

Annie laughed along with her mother as she helped clear the dinner table at the inside joke she knew nothing about.

By morning, the snow had stopped coming down. The boys had been out in the driveway with the plow hitched to one of the pick-ups and the way was cleared out to the main road. Jack Hampton was enjoying a cup of morning coffee with Evelyn when Sam came bounding in.

"Mayor...I mean, Jack. Why did you let me sleep so late? We have to get into the office. You have an early meeting with the Billings Mayor."

"Is that today? Surely he will cancel due to the weather."

"I wouldn't be so sure. I called Erna in the office and she said there were no cancellations yet."

"Ok, Sam. You win. But let's go right now. Your car is still buried in snow. We can take mine and come back for yours later."

"Will that be ok? I mean me coming in to work with you?"

"Of course, its ok Sam. I'm the Mayor. You worry too much. Now let's go."

"Is Annie up yet, ma'am?"

"No, she is still sleeping. But I'll tell her you said goodbye. Now you and Jack get on the road. You will have to take things a little slower this morning."

Sam nodded and looked down the other hallway towards Annie's room. He felt bad for leaving and not saying goodbye but he would be back later. Grabbing his jacket off the coat rack in the mudroom, he followed Jack out into the snow filled morning. Minutes later, the large sedan pulled out onto the driveway and exited the Shadowland Ranch.

Later that morning, Annie finally got out of bed and came in the kitchen to pour herself a cup of coffee.

"Looks like I missed everyone this morning. Why did you let me sleep so late?"

"There is nothing much going on. Jack and Sam left for the office together and the boys are out in the field tending to the herd already. I gave the house staff the morning off so I figured I would let you sleep."

Annie shrugged as she went over to the coffee pot and poured herself a cup. Her mother was working on some paperwork and Annie felt guilty. She should be doing something productive as well.

"I think I'm going to head back to the den. Sam and I were going over some case files last night and I'll see what I can find out without him looking at me with those big brown eyes."

Evelyn chuckled. "I think the term is love sick and he's got a bad case of it, young lady. If you don't watch out it may be contagious."

Walking over with her coffee cup in hand, she kissed her mother on the forehead. "I think I may have caught it already, mama. I'm afraid it might be terminal."

Evelyn looked after her daughter who had become a woman in the blink of an eye. She watched her as she walked down the hallway to the den. She thought for a brief moment that she might have to help her daughter pick out a wedding gown come spring time.

As Annie walked into the den, she reminisced about her father. She had spent countless moments watching her father work at his desk. It made her feel close to him to sit in his swivel chair and place her coffee in the same place he had kept so many before her. Looking around to see where they had left off before dinner, Annie saw that Sam had left his briefcase behind.

He must have been in some hurry this morning. He never goes anywhere without his briefcase.

Annie continued her search for the case file they were reviewing and could not find it. She supposed it was possible that Sam had placed it back inside his briefcase when she left to go get washed up for dinner. Taking one more look around the desk, she came up empty and decided to open Sam's briefcase. As she flicked the lock mechanism on both sides, the briefcase opened. Pushing back on the leather handle, the case opened with a stack of paperwork sitting in its main compartment. Placed on top of the pile was a document that caught her eye. Picking it up, she read it with shock and surprise.

Limited Proxy Vote Form

Effective _____ (date) I, Jack Hampton, surviving executor of the estate of Hank Peterson, do hereby take responsibility for The Shadowland Ranch Corporation, and all of its holdings until the matter of probate can be settled for the estate.

IN ABSENCE of directorship due to death, I, Jack Hampton, will take over the general powers of the Shadowland Ranch and maintain final voting decision on all business matters involving said corporation.

_____

(Signature)

_____

(sworn on this day)

_____

(Notary Public, State of Montana)

Sam had found the answer to saving the ranch and it was in the form of a Limited Proxy Vote form. How long did he have this in his briefcase? The form looked like it was all filled out and was just waiting for a signature. Did Sam really keep this from her? Did he keep this from her family that was on edge waiting to find out if they would lose the ranch or not? Picking up the phone, she was no longer in control of her emotions. At that moment, she no longer loved Sam Walden. She was full of anger and rage and she wanted answers to the questions that she knew would change her life.

11

"Why didn't you come to me first, Sam?"

Mayor Hampton was sitting behind his desk with his hand on his forehead. His assistant was sitting across from him still reeling in shock. The phone call was rough. He did not know that Annie was capable of that much anger.

"I was just waiting for the right moment. I was actually going to give you the paper today to sign. With a week to go, you could sign it and establish your voting power in the corporation. Foster and his goons would be silenced immediately."

"So you wanted to be the hero, is that what I am hearing?"

Sam Walden looked down at the hands that were folded in his lap. How did everything go so wrong? He had a plan and it should have worked. Shadowland would have its day at the auction and Annie would love him forever for saving the day. How did he let this happen?

"It was a political move Mayor. I did what I was trained to do. I did what every lawyer in town does every day. I did what you would have done. I held my card close to the vest until it was time to play it."

"The Shadowland Ranch is not yours to play with, son. You should have come to me when you found it right away. Why didn't you?"

Sam was quiet for a moment. He was searching for the right words but in the end there were none that could fix the situation.

"Annie..."

"What about her?"

"If I told her about the paper I would have never had a shot. I found it after the first day of research. It wasn't hard to find. I spent more time making sure she didn't read the right books until..."

"...until you started dating?"

Sam nodded. "It was not my intention to deceive her. It really wasn't. And it's not like I am a player that was manipulating her to go out with me. She basically made the first move. I...well...I just love her Mayor."

Jack Hampton smiled as he looked across to the young assistant.

"Why are you smiling Mr. Mayor? I've made a mess of things. I don't know how it came to this, I really don't."

Jack continued to smile as he reached for his key ring. Putting the small key in the locked drawer of his desk, he turned the tumbler and pulled on it. Removing a folder, he opened it and placed it in front of Sam.

"What is this?"

Looking down at the paper, the young researcher immediately recognized what it was. As he turned his view back to the Mayor, he was smiling back at him.

"I don't understand. This proxy form was signed by you over a month ago. If you knew all this time, why the ruse? Why have me look for it in the first place? Were you playing me Mr. Mayor?"

"Such a harsh accusation my young friend. I was just holding my cards close to the vest, just like you."

"But why? I don't understand."

"It's really very simple, Sam. The Shadowland Ranch was never in any peril. Hank Peterson was my best friend and I would never let his family be in any danger. I signed the paper the same day I met with his lawyer about the estate. I have been in control of Shadowland pretty much since the funeral."

"What about Foster? How did he get the idea that he could make a move if there was never an opportunity?"

"As the Mayor of Fergus County, I have a large voice and a great many listeners. Whispering a few misguided facts to the right person sent a little misinformation around. It's a nice tactic which I will show you how to use in the future. Foster found out that there might be a chance to take Shadowland away from the Petersons and the idiot acted on it. Now, with a little help from Sherriff Monsky, we have a chance to take Old Iron Shoes out of office."

Sam looked away in thought for a moment and turned back to the Mayor with a pained expression on his face.

"So let me understand this. The Shadowland Ranch is fine. The cattle will go to auction and the Petersons will all make money. On the flip side, you have a chance to take out your nemesis and clean up a stain on the county. In the end, the only person who loses is me. Is that it? Why would you do that to Annie and I?"

"Let me explain something to you, Sam. I love Anastasia like she was my own daughter. I helped raise her and when she went off to college, I helped Hank keep an eye on her."

"Sir?"

"Well, let's just say when one Mayor calls another Mayor, favors are exchanged regardless of what city that Mayor controls."

"So you had Annie watched or protected or what in L.A.?"

"A little bit of both. Just enough to make sure she was safe."

"Ok. So what does that have to do with me?"

"When Annie came home from California I made a promise to Hank. In some odd way he knew he didn't have long to live. He asked me to keep an eye out for Annie like I had while she was in Los Angeles. The only addition was that I was to make sure she did not end up with some rodeo cowboy. Hank wanted to be certain she would be loved and cared for by someone responsible; someone with a future."

"That's why you introduced her to me."

"That is correct, Sam. I figured with your background in research and her degree in business the two of you would solve the riddle right out of the gate. When you didn't come forward with it, I had to wonder if you had the right stuff. I played along to basically test you. As both of you fell in love with each other, I wasn't sure what to think."

"So you were testing me?"

Jack shrugged it off. "We all get tested, Sam. In politics and in life every day is a test. You proved a few things to me today."

"What? That I can royally screw up a good thing?"

The Mayor laughed. "Not exactly Sam. First and foremost, you proved that you are a good researcher."

"It was pretty low hanging fruit, Mr. Mayor. An intern could probably have found it."

"Ok. Maybe. But that brings me to the second point. You proved yourself worthy of a career in politics. You were absolutely right. Bluffing is a basic trait of all lawyers and every politician. You have to know when to hold back an ace up your sleeve to be used later. The trick is not to get caught with it."

"Like I said. I royally screwed up."

"Maybe. But it's not hopeless."

Sam perked up at the thought that there might be hope.

"I don't understand."

"If you look at the third revelation of the day it really is the most important. That girl loves you and you love her. If you didn't you would not have kept it from her in fear of losing her. You also wouldn't be so upset over it. The way she was screaming at you on that phone proved she loves you right back and that is all Hank would have wanted for his baby girl."

"It didn't sound like love on the phone. It didn't even sound human. She was screaming at me like a mountain lion or grizzly bear on attack."

Jack Hampton laughed heartily. "Welcome to the world of adult relationships my boy. When a woman chews you apart she is just showing you how much she cares about you. Isn't that great?"

Sam didn't feel great at all. He felt like he was going to throw up.

"Sure, Mr. Mayor. But the question still remains. How am I going to fix this with Annie? I don't know how she is going to get past this. I can't bear the thought of seeing her later when I pick up my car and briefcase."

"You just leave that to me, Sam. I got you into this mess and I sure am going to help you out of it. I'll have someone from the ranch bring your car to us later. Right now this is what we are going to do."

Sam Walden sat back and listened to the Mayor's plan to put everything back on track. Hampton was going for the triple play and everything was centered on how Sam was willing to play ball.

12

The day had finally come for the Fergus County Cattle Auction. Ranchers from all around the county had been transporting their herd for the last week and keeping them in the stockyard. The cattle had spent the last 15 months of their lives being fed grains, roughage and renewable feed in order to fatten them up by the weigh in. Most would come in around the goal weight of 1200 pounds but there was much variance. The fact that the auction was held in a Cattle Barn outside the meat packing plant was just the epitome of the cycle of life.

Bill Foster and his men had been at the auction barn all week long. As the head of the Cattlemen's Association he was there under the guise of protecting the rancher's rights. The reality was that he was there to rule his kingdom and if there was any rancher that didn't want to play ball with him and his men, they would be dealt with. As the governing body over the auction process, the Association set the protocols. The state department of agriculture kept a close eye on the back end and ensured that conditions were correct when the cattle entered the packing plant, but the auction itself was a different matter.

Foster and his boys had been greasing palms and intimidating people all week long. Even though the order of each cattle ranch coming to the auction block was done by "blind lottery", everyone knew that the system was fixed by Old Iron Shoes himself. The advantage of where each ranch went to the auction block was in the market price per hundredweight. The opening price today was $100 per hundred pounds of cattle weight. The challenge lay in the fact that no one really knew how much cattle the other ranches were bringing to the auction. Each of the early auctions received the set market price rate but if there was an overabundance of cattle, the market price dropped later in the day. If for some reason there was a draught and the number of cattle heads was low that year, the market price would increase throughout the day. Supply and demand economics at its best.

The ranchers in Foster's pockets always seemed to get the opening spots in the auction. It was just funny how things worked out that way in a blind lottery system. On this specific auction day, Mitch Hagland ended up in the premier slot and all the other ranchers wondered if the rancher with less than 10 years' experience had to sell his soul to the devil to get on the block right out of the gate. The last three ranches in the order of the day happened to be the ones that had given Bill Foster any opposition during the year. Roy Benally and his Navajo Ranch was third to last followed by Dylan Shepard and the Dolomite Crystal Ranch. Dead last to get to the auction block would be the Shadowland Ranch.

The day progressed smoothly while all the players were standing by watching events unfold. Jack Hampton gave a speech at opening bell and then proceeded to make his political rounds throughout the day. He made certain to shake every rancher's hand and give them his famous smile as he wished them good fortune in the auction day.

Evelyn and Annie sat in the stands while Wesley and Fred kept a watchful eye on their stockyard of cattle. Standing on the sidelines was a confused young man named Sam. He had never been to a cattle auction but the Mayor insisted that he attend. He had spent most of the day catching glimpses from across the way at Annie and he could not measure her temperature. At times, she looked like she was missing him and others she seemed to send daggers through her eyes at him across the cattle barn.

Before the last three ranches came up for their weigh in, there was movement on the podium. Graham, one of Foster's men approached the small table of men and whispered something into the caller's ear. Without a secondary glance, he exited off the stage and walked over to Bill Foster and the other men who were waiting off to the side.

There was a slight delay as the men on the podium had a brief discussion. One of them started typing into the laptop in front of them and all eyes moved to the digital projection board. The current price for cattle had dropped from the market price of $100 per hundredweight to $95. There was a moan through the cattle barn stands as the remaining ranchers could feel the pain in their wallet.

For Roy Benally, his small ranch was only bringing 65 head to the auction. The drop in price meant that he just lost somewhere around $5000 in market revenue. While that was a drop in the pan for the larger ranches, it would take a bite for the Navajo ranch. He proceeded with the sale of his cattle as more movement was viewed by the keen eye of Evelyn on the sidelines.

Jack Hampton had moved himself over to stand with Sherriff Jay Monsky and Sam Walden. The three of them were in a discussion which made the Sherriff look sternly over at Foster. There was trouble brewing in their little town and Evelyn Peterson was on high alert. With just one more ranch to sell their cattle before hers, she was a nervous wreck.

Next on the block was Dylan Shepard and the Dolomite Crystal Ranch. He moved quickly to the sale podium to get things started before the price could drop again. With the current price of $95 per hundredweight, he was set to lose almost $10000 from the rate an hour ago and he was not happy at all. He knew that because of his friendship with Hank and the fact that they had joined forces in the past in opposition to Foster in the Association he was paying the price. The lottery was rigged, the pricing was rigged and Dylan was angry. The loss would not be devastating but he would have to adjust his plans for the coming year.

As the final ranch for the day came up on the screen, the caller announced that there would be a brief intermission. The collective sigh of the crowd meant that everyone was ready for the day to be done. Another delay could only mean one thing; there was about to be a showdown. Meeting at center stage, Bill Foster approached with his three bodyguards in tow. From the other side of the stage. Jack Hampton and the Sheriff led the team of Evelyn, Fred, Wes, and Sam bringing up the rear. Annie sat riveted to her seat in the stands watching in earnest to see what would happen.

"Glad to see you are present Sherriff. Looks like we have a little problem. My reports show that the Shadowland Ranch has no right to sell their cattle at auction."

"Is that so?"

"Yes, sir, it is. Since Hank Peterson is no longer with us, there is no one on record for the corporation to sign the sale of the herd over to the packing plant. Unfortunately, as the head of the Cattlemen's Association I can't allow the sale."

"Well now. That does seem like a problem. Do you have a solution Jack or are we all ready to go home?"

The Sheriff was smiling because he knew Jack Hampton had the ace up his sleeve. He couldn't wait for the Mayor to throw it on the table.

"I do, I do. It's always best to come armed to a gunfight and my second in the duel, Sam here, has the paperwork you need."

Sam stepped forward and handed copies of the proxy vote to both the Sheriff and Foster. The former already had a copy sitting on his desk at the Sheriff office but the latter was in a state of shock.

"What the hell is this?"

"Oh, that. Well Bill, that is a paper I filed with the court taking control over general operations of the Shadowland Ranch Corporation."

"This is bullshit!"

"No, I can assure you it is not. As Mayor I made certain that all the laws were followed to a "T" and my assistant here, Sam Walden, witnessed them. That being said, I give my full authorization as representative for the Ranch for the sale of the stock."

The fumes were coming out of Foster's ears as he looked like a raging bull. Throwing the paperwork down on the caller's table, he stormed off the stage with his men following close behind. Evelyn and the boys exited the stage with the Sheriff as Jack and Sam trailed behind them.

"That's *one* my boy."

Sam immediately knew that his boss was referring to the triple play that he was working to achieve by the end of the day.

Once Evelyn had returned to her place besides Annie, Jack Hampton came up and sat on the other side of the girl. Leaning over, he smiled at her.

"Looks like your boyfriend saved the day, Annie."

She looked at him with a scowl on her face.

"He's not my boyfriend anymore."

Looking down at her hands, she began to tear up. Placing his hand on top of hers, the Mayor passed along his comfort.

"Well, maybe you will feel differently before the end of the day. It was just a minor error in judgement Annie. He's still quite the catch."

Before she could respond, there was another groan from the crowd still in attendance. The digital projection board had been changed again. Walking away from the stage, Foster himself had delivered the message this time and the crowd was not happy. The market price had dropped again. This time to $93 per hundredweight. With 212 heads of cattle going to the slaughterhouse, the Shadowland Ranch had just lost almost $25000 from what they would have made earlier in the day.

On the sidelines, Foster grinned as he knew he had just delivered a sharp blow to the Peterson family. He might not be able to stop the sale of the herd but he made sure it hit them in the wallet. Standing back, he let the auction proceed.

Jack turned to Annie with Evelyn looking on and changed to a more serious, softer tone in his voice.

"I have some pressing business to attend to as we wrap things up here but before I go, I want to give you something."

From the inside of his coat pocket, Jack removed a sealed envelope. The handwriting on the outside was very familiar to Annie as she read her name written on the outside. *To My Anastasia.*

"What's this Jack?"

"It's a letter from your father. Before he died, he asked me to give it to you when the time was right."

"...and the time for this is now? Here at the cattle sale?"

"I think it is. I'll let you read it while I attend to some business."

Kissing her on the forehead, Jack Hampton walked away from the young girl with tears in her eyes. He was halfway back to meet the Sherriff before Annie opened the envelope.

13

My dearest Anastasia,

If you are reading this, a few events have occurred.

The first is that I am gone. I'm sorry if I did not get a chance to say goodbye but life is like that sometimes. We all have a journey and like everyone else who has come before me, mine has come to an end. Your grandfather always told me that there is only one guarantee in life and that is that we all end up here. I hope my passing wasn't too painful for you, your brothers or your mother but if you have this letter in your hand, other things have occurred as well.

Secondly, if you are reading this, Jack Hampton has fulfilled all my wishes. As my best friend, I asked him to look after you and the family when I am gone. Don't be too hard on him as he is only doing my bidding. When you were in college, Jack helped me keep an eye out for you in the big city. Oh, it didn't amount to much more than having some people check in on you but if gave me great comfort to know that you were protected. Now, as I am no longer there to stand over you, I know that he is continuing to do that even as you read my words.

Finally, you are reading this on your wedding day because Jack helped find your Prince Charming. He was out there somewhere and while your brothers and I shooed away our share of crows that came knocking at our door for you, Jack has found the one you were meant to be with. Like everything with the ranch and our business, Jack has my vote. If he approves of the man you are about to marry, please know that I give my approval as well. Although I never set eyes on him, I know that this man will care for you all of your days and I can rest peacefully knowing that you are safe.

Enjoy your wedding day, Annie. Know that the hand that Jack gives freely of approval is blessed by me and your mother. I love you. Congratulations on your big day.

Love,
Dad.

14

The tears were still running down her face as the Cattle Auction came to an end. The viewers in the stand had begun to stand and exit but Evelyn stayed by her side. Placing her hand over her daughters, the two of them cried together. The widow Peterson was crying because the sale of the herd meant the last of the business from her late husband. All cattle grown from this day forward would be new business, in the hands of Wes and Fred.

For Annie, she cried for different reasons. She mourned for the loss of her father and felt him wrapping his arms around her through the letter. It was not her wedding day but it was a sign of her destiny. Her father had sent Sam into her life using Jack Hampton as his messenger. The answer to her dilemma was now clear to her and as she folded up the letter to put it back in the envelope, she looked around to see if Sam was still there. Up near the stage, Sam was following the Sherriff and the Mayor as they approached Old Iron Shoes.

"Bill Foster?"

The man turned to face the Sherriff with surprise.

"Sure, Jay. Why are we being so formal?"

"Bill Foster, you are under arrest for multiple counts of bribery to pubic officials, tampering with government operations and extortion."

The three men took a step back to distance themselves. From behind them, two deputies approached and stood behind them.

"Don't worry. The three of you are going for a ride as well."

"This has got to be a joke. Do you know who I am Monsky? I am the law around here, not you."

"No Foster, I am the law and you just crossed the last line. We have you on video all week long, bribing and threatening the men from the Montana Department of Agriculture. Don't worry about them, though. They are all forgiven in return for their witness testimony. The four of you are going away for a long time."

"You can't do this."

"Oh yes I can. I think the Mayor has something to say as well."

"Just wanted to give you a farewell present, Bill. Since you tampered with the market price at the auction today, all ranches are being paid full market price for their cattle. They will all get the $100 per hundredweight. Just thought you would like to know your whole day was a total waste."

Jack Hampton laughed as the Sherriff and his deputies took Foster away with his goons. Standing on the stage next to Sam, he turned to him and put up a peace sign.

"That's *two*. Now, let's go make it a hat trick."

The two men exited the stage and walked towards the parking area where Evelyn and Annie were standing next to one of the Shadowland Ranch trucks.

"What the heck was that all about? Did that really happen?"

"Come on Evelyn. Ride in my car and I'll tell you all about it. Let's leave these two to chat."

Evelyn handed the keys to the truck to her daughter and offered Sam a slight smile. It was not one of happiness but a gesture of hope on her part. Turning around behind Annie's back, Jack held up three fingers as Sam nodded nervously.

"Do you think you are a hero now? You saved the day for the ranch and helped get rid of Foster too? You must be pretty happy with yourself right now."

"I am not happy, Annie. I miss you,"

Annie looked around them to see if her brothers were going to interrupt them. With the letter from her father in her pocket, she knew Hank was already there with her.

"I miss you too, Sam."

He took her hand in his and looked at her with his doe eyes. "Can we get past this, Annie? I really am sorry for not telling you about the..."

With her other hand, she put a finger to his lips to silence him.

"That doesn't matter anymore. It all worked out in the end."

"Does this mean we are ok?"

Stepping forward, she kissed him in the cold November air. For a moment, their lips were frozen together in time.

"Is that a good answer?"

Giving her his best political smile, he answered her back.

"The best answer I have heard all day."

Stepping towards the truck, Annie jiggled her keys.

"I'm starving."

"I know this great pizza place that has the best pepperoni pizza. Maybe you've been there before."

Smiling back at him, Annie suggested he leave his car here and they would come back later to get it. This time she was in the driver's seat and she was not about to let her relationship get cold again.

15

"Thank you Lord for all of our bountiful blessings. Thank you for this wonderful meal and all the love that surrounds the table."

The whole Peterson family was gathered around the Thanksgiving table with Jack Hampton and Sam Walden seated among them. Jack was giving the blessing as it was the role of his best friend's in years past.

"Can we go around the table and give our thanks, each of us?"

The request from Jack was heartfelt and they all nodded.

"Why don't you go first Fred?"

"I'm just thankful it's time to eat. I'm hungry."

The group all laughed.

"How about you Wes?"

"I'm thankful the herd is all gone. We get to sleep a little now before we start on the next group."

"Amen to that."

Fred agreed with his older brother as they looked forward to growing the next group of cattle together.

"Sam?"

"I'm thankful to be here today with such a wonderful family. I am thankful for so many things, especially to Hank and Evelyn for giving me their Angel to love."

Reaching out his hand, he held Annie's on the table. She smiled back with love in her eyes.

"We are thankful to you, young man. You saved the day and made this Thanksgiving all the more thankful."

Jack added a wink for good measure and Sam knew that their secret was safe for all the time to come.

"Annie?"

Looking around the table, she smiled with tears of joy.

"I am thankful to be home. I haven't enjoyed Thanksgiving in our house for many years. I am thankful for all the love that was waiting for me when I got here."

Leaning over, she kissed Sam as the family looked on.

"Evelyn?"

The widow grew silent for a moment. Wiping a tear from her eye, she raised her glass of wine.

"I am thankful for Hank, the love of my life who continues to give to this family every day. Your love will never be forgotten and your gifts will never end."

The table was silent as they all raised their glasses to toast.

"To Hank."

Jack Hampton pushed out the final words as he choked back his own tears. Hank Peterson had left them all with his memories, his love and his land. They would each yield his direction for the future to carve out their own destinies.

Author's Note

This summer, I was in the middle of writing what will be my next book, *Terror Kingdom*, when I had a revelation. To better understand the light bulb that went off in my head, you have to understand a little about me, Peter A. LaPorta. For those of you that have been my constant fans, who have read my books for the past twenty plus years, I have given you a lot of choices. The reason for that is that I am an overachiever.

It all started out when I was a young musician. Simply playing the trombone was not enough. I had to go out and keep learning to play different musical instruments until I achieved the ability to play the 40 or so instruments I now know how to play. When I had worked my way through the whole family of brass, I went on to learn piano and now guitar and ukulele. In that department, my love for music combined with my drive for achievement and I am happy I can still make music at the age of 60.

Attending the University of Connecticut on a music scholarship, I again wanted to push myself to know more. Music was not enough and I yearned to soak in more knowledge in other subjects. Soon thereafter, I split my degree and graduated with a double degree in Business Management and Music. From that point on, I spent years going back and forth between Music and Business, trying to achieve greatness in both categories.

Somewhere along the way, I still needed more. Life is short and I knew I could offer more to the world than just managing businesses, leading people and playing music. I wanted to share my experience with anyone who would read and listen. One day, while being a leader for Walt Disney World, I sat down and started to write stories of all my adventures in those categories. Soon thereafter, my first book was published and I became an author.

Due to my overachievement nature, I could not settle on writing one book and soon thereafter the next one was written and published. For years, I pumped out non-fiction titles and segued into a public speaker career talking about those books. At that point in my life, I had achievements in business, leadership, music, writing and speaking that adorned my office walls. It was still not enough. To date, I had only written non-fiction and I had the desire to challenge myself once again. It was then that I entered into the world of writing fiction.

When my first work of fiction, *Normandy Nights*, became a best-selling success, I once again craved more. I had proven I could write historical fiction, but what about a thriller? *The Card* was born. What about horror? *Turtlemaster* was born. As I wanted to seek out new genres and attract different audiences, I launched into the creativity of *The Widow's Box* and the pain of redemption in *Sanctuary*. With every new book, I reached to push myself towards new heights and bring you, the constant reader, along for the ride.

As I was in the middle of *Terror Kingdom*, I realized I was back in the world of thriller fiction. I am certain you will all enjoy that work when it is finished next year, but in some ways I thought I was leaving other mountains un-challenged. The revelation I had was that although I have enjoyed reading collections of short stories over the years, I had never written one. The concept of being able to tell multiple stories under the umbrella of one theme fascinated me. I set aside *Terror Kingdom* and set my sights on writing a collection of short stories. The connecting life line would be a work of love.

There are many faces and aspects of love. You only need to walk into the greeting card section of your local retailer to realize that. Love comes in all shapes and sizes, young and old, in every variety imaginable. Love is love. Too many people put labels on that umbrella and limit the mind, the heart and the beauty that comes with it. Like life, love can be messy. Sometimes we make it that way and sometimes it is the product of outside influences. In the end, we can't all achieve the fairy tale ending and far too often, things do not work out. Love still endures and when complications rise, we can either overcome them or move on.

The seven stories you have just read encompass all of that and more. Born out of my need to achieve something new and climb a new mountain, I hope that I delivered new viewpoints for you to see something timeless. Each one of the stories expanded my heart and my understanding of human behavior and I learned a lot about the characters that walked through each of the stories. Sometimes, they acted and re-acted exactly as I imagined. Other times, like love in real life, the characters shocked and surprised me with their outcome.

As always, I thank you, my constant reader for coming along on yet another unforgettable journey. This time, there were seven different destinations set in different times and places. I hope you enjoyed every one of them. Through every era we traveled, in every setting, we found the possibility of love. It was our destiny to travel together and I thank you for coming along on my magic carpet ride.

Peter A. LaPorta
November, 2024